I'm not a coward.

It took a lot of courage to be the first black female prosecutor in Harris County. White people didn't trust me, most blacks resented me. I had to devise a ready response when they asked me how I could work for "the Man." *You better be glad I'm there. I can't vouch for these white people, but I know I can be fair.*

They hadn't thought about it that way. . . .

SHADES
OF
JUSTICE

Linda McKeever Bullard

AN ONYX BOOK

ONYX
Published by New American Library, a division of
Penguin Putnam Inc., 375 Hudson Street,
New York, New York 10014, U.S.A.
Penguin Books Ltd, 27 Wrights Lane,
London W8 5TZ, England
Penguin Books Australia Ltd,
Ringwood, Victoria, Australia
Penguin Books Canada Ltd, 10 Alcorn Avenue,
Toronto, Ontario, Canada M4V 3B2
Penguin Books (N.Z.) Ltd, 182–190 Wairau Road,
Auckland 10, New Zealand

Penguin Books Ltd, Registered Offices:
Harmondsworth, Middlesex, England

Published by Onyx, an imprint of New American Library,
a division of Penguin Putnam Inc.
Previously published in a Dutton edition.

First Onyx Printing, July 1999
10 9 8 7 6 5 4 3 2 1

To Bob, Kai, and Rob.
It just gets better and better.

Acknowledgments

I couldn't have come this far without the support and encouragement of my family and friends. Thank you, Leon and Margaret McKeever, for being my parents. Thanks, Ronnie and Bobbie, for being my sisters. Thanks to my in-laws, Betty, Paul, Jimmy, and Leon.

To Docia, Janey, Ava, April, Karen, Cathy, Suzette, Ruth, and Nathan—thanks for believing in me.

To Ronda Gomez-Quinones, thanks for making me go deep.

To Elaine Markson, thanks for everything.

Thanks to Jennifer Sawyer Fisher for all the help.

Every writer needs a good editor. I think I have a great one. Thanks, Michaela.

BOOK 1

—∞∞∞—

Who Dealt This Mess?

1

I keep trying to think of things to say to Michael to make him leave me alone. Nothing works. I always give it up. He says he's in my blood.

I told him I wasn't going to see him anymore after tonight. He laughed and rolled over and went to sleep. Wake me up at four, he said. He never stays out all night. Out of respect for Willette. Besides, if he's not home by five-thirty, she'll start beeping him. Incessantly.

I'm glad he doesn't sleep over. It cuts down on a lot of confusion. Especially with Ashleigh Lee upstairs. Though disapproval would be a welcome change from the total blankness I've been seeing in her eyes lately. I swear I don't understand her. She's her father's child, all right. I keep praying there's enough of me somewhere inside her that'll make her come around.

I snap on the radio and listen to another sad song by some sister who hasn't been hurt enough by some man. Michael calls them "open up a vein" songs. Naturally, he can't stand them. I kind of like this one. The singer's got a good voice, and she's saying something I can relate to. About a piece of a black man being better than no man at all. That's what I have, and it's not even my piece.

I look down at Michael sleeping, and I'm reminded why I fell for him in the first place. Smooth milk chocolate–colored skin, jet black, naturally wavy hair, wide mouth, thick lips you can really sink into. He's snoring softly and

looks like the spoiled-rotten, selfish dog-ass nigger he is.
Candy dick or not, he's got to go.

I nudge him. Gently at first. "Michael, wake up." One
beautifully thick-lashed eye cracks into a slit. I shake him
again.

"Michael, we need to talk."

"Okay," he says, "talk." He slides his hand under my
T-shirt and squeezes my breast. I catch my breath and sit up.
"Not now, Michael," I say.

He's fully awake now, watching me. Now that sleep no
longer distorts his features, he looks only slightly older than
the man I met fifteen years ago in law school. He smiles that
heartbreaker smile and reaches across me for his Rolex,
which he checks for the time and straps on. It's four-ten.

"Yeah, baby, what's up?"

"Michael, I'm not going to see you anymore."

He sighs, bored. "There you go with that shit again." He
slides from under the covers and reaches for his pants, laid
out neatly on the floor beside the bed. Lined up next to them
are his shoes. It's been three weeks, and he still lays his
clothes out as if he might have to grab them on the run. The
first night we slept together, he said an old man told him always to keep his pants and shoes within reaching distance
when he's with a woman. You never know when her old
man might show up.

He zips up his pants and looks at me, his eyes hooded and
worldly. I look away. He sits down and pulls on his socks.

"I mean it, Michael."

"And I mean this: you're not going anywhere, baby.
Otherwise, I tell Willette. She'll forgive me, but you won't
even be eligible for full-time ass kisser when she gets
through with you."

I stare at him. "You can't be serious. You're blackmailing
me for sex? You're that hard up?"

He smirks at the idea, simultaneously easing into his shirt
and vest, knotting his tie.

"You know better than that. You give your heart and soul

when we do it. I like that. There're still some things I want
to do to you."

A powerful invisible force is pressing down on me, suf-
focating me. I feel encrusted with dirt and shame. I look
down at my hands, surprised at how moist my palms are.

"Please, Michael—let me go. I can't do this anymore—"

"Yes, you can."

He pulls up my T-shirt and sucks one of my nipples. My
body slides down the headboard all by itself and sinks onto
the pillow. My eyes close, and I can feel him watching while
his mouth pulls on me. I'm willing myself not to respond,
but my soft panting gives me away. His hand slides between
my thighs. He lifts his head and grins triumphantly.

"I don't believe it, baby. I've been at this all night and
you're still wet."

He pats me. "I'll let you know when I don't want to share
this anymore."

He stands up to leave.

"Fuck you," I say.

"I don't have time, baby. I'll call you."

I want to be a judge. I've never told anybody this, but I've
already ordered my robe, which I go to the closet and look at
when Michael's gone. I slip it on even though I'm still
naked. The heavy cloth feels luxurious next to my skin. I zip
it up and stand in front of the mirror. I ignore my bare feet
sticking out underneath. I look good. I vow for the thou-
sandth time not to let anything—or anyone—keep me from
what I want. If sleeping with Michael keeps him quiet long
enough to get Willette to get her father to give me his blessing, so be it. If I could, I'd put my own foot up my behind
for letting him get next to me in the first place. If I were a
deck of cards, I couldn't even be the joker in a no-trump.

"All rise for the Honorable Gwenlyn Parrish," I intone. I
try to make my face look judicial, but I just look mad to me.
I'm just going to practice until I get that look of poker-faced

omniscience just right. Otherwise, how will I ever strike people with awe?

I'm practicing various facial poses when I feel a presence. Embarrassment engulfs me like a hot flash. I whip around. "What are you doing up this early, Ashleigh Lee?"

My fifteen-year-old daughter stands in the doorway, staring at me, looking just like her father—same slender build, same dark "bedroom eyes," same look of amused contempt. Maybe I could be more patient with her if everything about her didn't constantly remind me of Kwame.

"I heard a man."

"I . . . had company." I turn back to the mirror, feeling totally stupid. "You must've heard him leaving."

She smirks. "What, were you playing the judge and the criminal?"

"Of course not." I can't stand seeing myself in the robe now. I start to unzip it, remember I'm naked. Her eyes look around pointedly. "What?"

"I was just trying to see how he tied you to the bed."

Very funny. "Nobody tied anybody to anything. Go back to sleep." I close the door in her face. If I didn't know all teenage girls despise their mothers, I'd think there was something seriously wrong with our relationship. Yet as I take the robe off, a little voice whispers, "What if something is wrong?" I put the thought away along with my robe.

The only bright spot in my morning so far is the drive to the office. Spring has sprung in Houston as far as I'm concerned. I've been on the lookout for the first signs of buds or new green shoots poking through thatch lawns or sudden bursts of color since the middle of February. It's a game I play with Nature every year. Winters are so mild down here that people—the transplanted Yankees—claim we don't have a change of seasons "like they do up North." It's not true. You just have to pay attention. Otherwise, it'll just seem like one day it's nice, and the next four months it's just plain hot.

It heats up around here along about May. Ninety-five-degree heat and ninety-nine-percent humidity will make you slow down, if not sit down. People new to Houston learn that lesson real quick. I know I did. I moved here in 1971 in the middle of the summer, driving a car with no air, black "pleather" interior, and rear windows that did not roll down. I didn't get out of the car, I melted out. And I got dark. All the black people do in the summer.

Newly arrived carpetbaggers think we're lazy and slow-thinking because we move slow and talk slow. They think they're better than everyone because they don't. You see them by the end of the summer, and the almighty Houston heat has made a believer out of them: they're talking and walking slow too.

Arriving at my office, I pull my Jag right up to the entrance to the New Orleans–style two-story building. An Aryan-type white boy pulls into the stall perpendicular to me. We glance at each other as we get out. He makes a point of cutting in front of me as we enter the building. I let him go. We're both in a hurry. I left Clarence Anderson's file on Pat's desk, and I need it to plead him out this morning.

I never fail to glimpse the building directory on my way in. Seeing our names, Harris & Parrish, Attorneys and Counselors at Law, is reassuring, though I don't feel much like a lawyer this morning. My law partner, Eddy Harris, always kids me that I don't look like one either. He says I should go back to teaching school. I tell him to kiss my school-teaching ass. That always gets a laugh.

We originally met when he and his wife, Marsha, got run off playing bid whist at a Black Lawyers Association's picnic a few years ago, trounced after only one hand, humiliating even for rise 'n' fly. No one was waiting to play, so Eddy sat back down. Marsha, though, had had enough abuse from Mitchell Spence and Clark Goree, notorious bid-whist bullies who'd dominated the card table all afternoon. Though selling wolf tickets and talking trash are to bid what a football is to football, Mitchell and Clark were being downright vicious. Eddy really wanted to shut them up. I did too. They were sucking all the fun out of the game. I violated my cardinal rule against playing with strangers and offered to be his partner. We beat them like they stole something.

I curse softly when I notice the P in my name has fallen off our entry door again. We need to move out of this joint. When I open the door, Pat's at her desk, typing. She's wearing a gorgeous purple silk dress which complements her raisin black skin. It's something when your secretary dresses better than you.

"Judge Littson's coordinator just called," she says, not looking away from the screen. "They need you in the 73rd. Clarence Anderson called."

I grab the Anderson file and head for my office as the phone rings. Pat answers, then presses the hold button. "Gwen, it's Dirk."

I pause for a split second, go into my office, the larger of two cubicles off the cracker-sized reception room, inevitably banging my knee against the corner of the credenza getting to my chair, popping a slender run in my panty hose that trickles all the way down to my third toe. "Goddammit—" I remember the voice-activated recorder I had installed mainly on a whim. Pull open the credenza drawer out of curiosity, push Replay, and hear myself, "Goddammit—"

I change my mind about talking to Dirk, a.k.a. Mundane Man. He's sweet, but he's going to want to know everything that's happened to me up until now, and then he's going to want to tell me all about himself. I don't have time for him now. "Tell him I left already."

I leave before Pat can chastise me and head for the stairs, running into the same white boy I met on the way in, coming out of another office. He looks at me like I couldn't possibly have any business in the same building as he does. I deliberately cut in front of him going down the steps. He has no choice but to follow me, which I know he hates. He's that kind of white boy.

I get in my car and back up. The white boy apparently does the same thing—at the same time. Fortunately, we see each other at the last second and slam on our brakes. I'm ready to laugh about our near collision until he gets out of his car, sees how close we came, and bangs my hood like he wants it to be my head, startling me. "You nigger!"

I've been called a nigger before by somebody white, so I'm not offended or insulted or humiliated, or whatever he thought he was doing by calling me that. So I think, hold on, Gwen. You're the one in the car. He thinks you're going to get out and mix it up with him. Instead, I mash the Jag's accelerator and aim for his feet. White boy jumps back, stunned by my audacity. He's calling me all kinds of niggers now. I cruise up to him, which throws him off a moment.

"Your mama's a nigger," I say with a smile and jet off. I check the rearview mirror. He's jumping up and down like a monkey, pounding the air with his fist. I know how he feels. That's how I felt the first time too. Until I realized that being a nigger is a state of mind and anybody can qualify.

"Mr. Anderson, are you pleading guilty because you are guilty?"

This is the hard part in doing a plea. Criminals never like to admit they're guilty of anything, let alone what they're charged with. Clarence Anderson's beady eyes slide from Judge Bivens to me. I look down and hold my breath, playing my part. It's not supposed to look like I've put words in his mouth. His street-tough body jerks involuntarily.

"Yeah."

I breathe a sigh of relief and look at Judge Bivens. She stone-faces me, but I know she's pleased. No judge likes it when the defendant blows a plea. It's a waste of everybody's time, especially the court's, whose time is more valuable than anyone else's. They hold it against the attorney if anything goes wrong. I intend to be on the other side of this bench one day, so I'm particularly sensitive to staying in all judges' good graces. I'd rather sleep naked in a blizzard than get one mad at me, which is one reason why they appoint me to so many cases. Another is all the money I spend at their fund-raisers for reelection. So few people pay attention to the judicial races, even my money goes a long way.

Bivens was appointed to complete Judge Lloyd's term when he was kicked up to the Criminal Court of Appeals. Bivens has three challengers so far, so she's going to need every vote she can get. She already made it clear by courting the Black Lawyers Association, she's not squeamish about where she gets them from. I'm on the executive board. Our recommendation in the judicial races carries a lot of weight in the black community.

"Mr. Anderson," she asks, "you haven't been promised anything by the D.A. or by me in exchange for your guilty plea, have you?"

The answer's so obvious that the judge and the assistant D.A. are stunned when my client says, "Yeah."

"What have you been promised?" Bivens looks at me, totally pissed.

I grab Anderson's arm before he can say anything else. "If Your Honor please, may I have a moment with my client?"

"You most certainly may, Counselor," she says, gritting cigarette yellow teeth.

I practically yank Anderson into the hall. "What the hell are you trying to do? You're about to blow your goddamn plea."

"But—"

"But nothing. I've been over this with you ten times already and I told you: nobody's making any promises, just a recommendation. The judge can ignore the recommendation, but they usually go along with whatever the D.A. recommends. If you don't plead today, you're going to trial, in which case the deal's off. The jury can give you less time, but they could give you more. The judge'll damn sure give you more for showing your ass. You're a two-time loser, Mr. Anderson, and your defense is that you don't remember what happened after you threw the brick in the liquor store window. Now, you're going to go back in there and answer the judge's questions like you have some goddamn sense. Do you understand me?"

"Yes, ma'am."

He looks genuinely contrite. Most criminals come from abusive backgrounds, so they mistake any kindness for weakness. You can't be nice, which is what I was with this fool in the beginning. Which is why he's been jerking me around for the past six weeks, one day wanting a trial, a deal the next. Now that I've come out the box on his ass, he's cool. It's crazy. Which is why the first chance I get, I'm getting the hell out of the private practice of law.

I pull the Jag into the Groovey Grill's parking lot and park next to C.C.'s Lincoln. It's been a long day and I'm tired, but it's not over yet. When I get out, I see Willette's forest green Mercedes across the way. My heart skips a beat. My heels click noisily against the concrete as I head to the door, reminding me I need new tips. Walking around downtown really tears up your shoes, especially the back of the heel when you step in a crack and sink into that spongy black gunk holding the sidewalk panels together. You just know a man came up with it, since no thought was given to what it does to women's high-heel shoes.

The Groovey Grill is the oldest black restaurant in Houston. I'm told in its heyday, this big plantation-style mansion in the heart of Third Ward really jumped. Anyone who was someone made sure to be seen at the Groovey. I used to beg Kwame to bring me here when we were first married, just to see the niggers style and profile. Naturally, he refused, calling it "boogie bullshit." I treated myself once and came anyway. I had the whole fried trout. The crunchy cornmeal-coated fish melted in your mouth, and the fresh-made lemonade came with seeds in a tall, frosty glass. I sat in the corner and ate and watched all the pretty black people. It was great.

Icy cold air blasts me as soon as I step into the empty lobby. Miss Mert, the proprietor, is behind the counter as usual, wearing owl-like glasses and reading the paper. She nods at me, and per usual I inquire about her health. "Fairly middlin'," she replies, per usual. It's unnecessary, but she directs me to the sun porch, where the Black Female Lawyers Association is meeting.

I feel guilty as I cross the empty dining room. You can feel the abandonment. We want to eat with white folks now. I accidentally bump into the waitress, just coming from the sun porch with a tray of glasses. I smile when I see all the empties and place my order. The men can't hold a candle to us when it comes to drinking and pushing our titties in their chest, as my partner Eddy would say. I enter the glass-enclosed room, and I'm greeted enthusiastically by my female colleagues, which gives me a good feeling. I like being liked. C.C. sits next to Willette. They both wave me over.

"How's it going, Judge?" I ask. C.C. takes a swallow of her drink and trains bloodshot eyes on me. "Fine, now that my drinking buddy's here. No offense, Willette."

"None taken." Willette smiles at me. I can't help but wonder what she knows. "How's it going, Gwen? Still hanging in there?"

"Till somebody cuts me down," I say. "Which I hope is soon." We laugh. She doesn't know a thing.

The waitress arrives with C.C.'s Jack Black, water back, and my Wild Turkey. It's still early, and the sisters trickle in slowly. The meeting begins officially at six-thirty, but we rarely get under way before seven.

I glance around the table and count a dozen attendees. The group has grown considerably from the original founders, who include myself, C.C., Willette, and Sharon Lester, who's chairing the meeting tonight. The liquor melts something inside me, and I feel myself relax for the first time all day. I quickly polish off my drink and order another. C.C. joins me. Willette will nurse her glass of white wine all night.

As usual, the three of us are impeccably dressed and compliment each other on our respective outfits. I'm wearing my red suede and leather suit and feeling particularly fashionable. C.C. is a good twenty pounds overweight, and her excess pounds emphasize her basically homely looks. But she's a true friend. When I left Kwame, she insisted Ashleigh Lee and I move in with her. We had nothing but the clothes on our backs. She bought food and diapers for Ashleigh Lee, lent me money and her car. Later, I tried to repay her for the year we stayed with her practically rent-free. She wouldn't let me. "Save it for my godchild's college fund," she said.

Tiny lines radiate from the corners of her hooded eyes, and her mud-colored skin has a gray cast under the thick nutmeg-colored makeup she wears. I tell her she looks tired. She laughs with a smile so beautiful it makes you forget she's barely average-looking. She gets over with that smile of hers. "Being a judge is more than a notion, child. Everybody wants something from you."

"Yeah," I say. "That's what makes it so great. They all have to come to you to get it." She knows I'd give anything to trade places with her. I think she secretly enjoys being the only black female judge in Harris County. Some of us are like that. If another black comes along, they won't be special anymore.

C.C's natural charm contrasts sharply with Willette's innate cool. I always associate the color green with Willette. Probably because her eyes are green and green's her favorite color. She and I are about the same fair complexion and same size seven, but I always feel mammy-made next to her. I want to believe it's because she comes from money and my old man's still pushing a broom at Chrysler after thirty years, but in my heart I know it's because she's a natural strawberry blonde and I've just got your run-of-the-mill "good hair." When we were first-year law students, she told me how she and Michael would get stopped periodically by the police because they thought he had a white girl in the car. She'd sound annoyed, but I think she enjoyed being mistaken for white. People like her are born sophisticated. The rest—like me—just pretend.

I wonder how cool she'd be if she knew about me and Michael. Not that she doesn't know he plays around. She has to. He's been that way ever since I've known him. Only back then I wouldn't give him the time of day. I still wouldn't have, except that I got weak one night three weeks ago when I ran into him at a club and took him up on what he'd been offering me behind her back since the first day of law school. I didn't consider it cheating on Dirk because Michael's black. I didn't consider it cheating on Willette because it had nothing to do with his commitment to her. I just wanted—needed—an expert's touch. Little did I know I'd wind up in his trick bag.

Sharon calls the meeting to order and hurries through the agenda to the main order of business—the election of new officers. I'm first vice-president, so I'll automatically assume the presidency. As founding members, C.C.'s and Willette's elections to the executive board are a formality. The office I'm vacating is hotly contested. It seems that some of the younger sisters want to take the organization off into a new—C.C., Willette, Sharon, and I think, radical—direction. As a precaution I had my secretary call all the "old heads" and remind them to attend tonight. I'm pleased by the larger than usual turnout. After all, this wasn't meant to be some Mau Mau group. We're the highly educated, responsible niggers. Indeed, I personally plan to ascend to my judgeship from my presidency by proving just that to the white folks. I'm a good black.

Despite our numbers, the young bitches succeed in electing Geesala Brown first vice-president. Geesala's a "Hahrvard" graduate, coming to Houston by way of Wells & MacIntire, the only big white firm that employs blacks. Thurgood Marshall graduates don't get hired downtown—or barely anywhere else, for that matter. Which hasn't changed since I went there and it was called Texas Southern University for Negroes Law School.

That's the "South" part of being in the Southwest, and there's nothing "new" about it. That's why so many of us wind up in private practice, struggling or stealing or both. We don't get the corporate retainers, the billable hours, the government contracts. We're lucky just to get paid what we ask for. Most of us would get out in a heartbeat for a chance at the power, prestige, and a regular salary of a judgeship.

I congratulate Geesala on her victory, then vow to C.C. and Willette to undermine her every chance I get. No bunch of militants is going to stand in my way.

2

Who said life is like a card game? If it is, I'm playing bid whist: you can't be weak-minded and you better be lucky. For the moment, I've got no aces, no jokers, and no face cards, and the bid's on me. Whenever I got cards like these in college, I'd always throw them down and ask, Who dealt this mess? Twenty years later, I'm asking the same thing.

I sip my Wild Turkey, trying not to brood over the hand life's dealt me so far (you think long, you think wrong in whist), and trying to concentrate on Willette and C.C.'s conversation. They're discussing the upcoming county commissioner races. Willette's father, the right honorable Willie C. Shalandar, is running. He's one of the first blacks in Harris County to do so for a seat that was created especially for a "minority" to get the Justice Department off the county's back. He was handpicked, so his election's a sure thing. Still, he has opposition, and it always pays to take any challenge seriously.

I'm the campaign field coordinator. I make sure everything goes right whenever Willie's out pressing the flesh. Willette's his campaign manager, naturally. As a judge, C.C. can only be a loyal supporter, at least officially anyway.

Willie's been councilman for as long as anyone can remember. He was the first black to win citywide, and for years he was the only black elected official holding a municipal office. A single-member district lawsuit changed all that a few years ago, but he's still the only black with a citywide constituency. We're taking the night off from the campaign because our candidate's been called to Washington to consult with the president on his latest initiative for dealing with the drug problem, i.e., how to lock up more black folks without black folks noticing.

We're sitting in the gloom of the Chandelier Club, a small neighborhood bar in the heart of Third Ward, one of the oldest and economically diverse black neighborhoods in Houston. It has everything from shanties—they call them shotgun houses down here—to baronial estates, the latter thanks primarily to the affluent Jews who picked up and left when blacks began to move in. The Chandelier's nearly empty, since it's a weeknight and it's late.

"I hear Charles Garrett is planning to cut up at the Mayor's Youth Breakfast," C.C. says. "Somebody better make sure he takes his Thorazine." Charles Garrett is a professional community activist. That is to say, his full-time job is raising hell with white folks. He's suicidally running against Willie, along with a ragtag bunch of other opportunists and ne'er-do-wells who always surface whenever a new slot opens up for blacks.

The serious opposition knows better than to buck Willie. He can make life pretty miserable for any black man or woman who wants to get ahead in Houston. He has all the important white folks' ears. They do what he says when it comes to black issues. Willie says that's the only way to get things done for poor, ignorant people who can't articulate, let alone define, what it is they want from a white man. I admire him. He's paid his dues, and he's earned the right to be our leader. I just want him to come through with my judgeship.

I've never told C.C. this, but I was sick for three days when she got appointed to be the first black female judge in Harris County. Willette recommended her to Willie over me, and I guess I can understand why. She's closer to Willette than I am. They went to TSU undergrad together, plus they're "sand sisters," that is, they both pledged Delta as freshmen. I met them when I came down for law school. Even though I pledged the grad chapter and the three of us have been tight from day one, I'm always playing catch-up as far as our friendship goes. Crossing the burning sands together really does make a difference.

Still, I haven't been kissing Willette's ass all these years for nothing. Everyone does when they find out who her father is. C.C. says Michael chose her as soon as she set foot on TSU's campus. He was a year ahead of them and already had a reputation for being a Three "F" man—"find 'em, fool 'em, and forget 'em." According to C.C., it was like a young Hannibal meeting Cleopatra, since they both came from money and influence. "You should've seen 'em preening for each other, both smelling their piss."

Michael's father was the only black state senator in Mississippi at the time. The youngest of three sons, Michael was too wild and headstrong to stay there safely, so with a steady supply of cash from his family, he decided to make Houston his adopted home. Willie approved of him the moment they met, seeing him as a younger, handsome version of himself, minus the doggishness, which Willie doesn't see to this day.

I drain my glass even though the liquor tastes nasty from being mostly watered down. Willette's just going to have to come through for me as she did for C.C. I've dreamed of being a judge before I even went to law school. Everybody else watched Perry Mason to see him beat the mess out of Hamilton Burger one more time. I watched to see the judge. There was a new one each week, and he ruled the courtroom. I went to law school only when I found out you had to be a lawyer first.

After school, I sweated out five hard years in the D.A.'s office under Nazi Brad Yarrow, thinking it would be my stepping-stone as it was for the white boys. Boy, did I learn the hard way that what works for them doesn't work for us. They kept getting appointment after appointment to the bench. I wasn't even considered. Willie kept assuring me my time would come, and when I thought it had, he blessed C.C. because Willette recommended her over me. Which brings me full circle—

"There she goes. Daydreaming again." C.C. nudges me playfully. "Wake up."

I apologize. C.C. just shakes her head. "Girl, you have not changed from law school. Everybody else was trying to get the lesson, you'd be staring out the window."

"Or at a man." Willette's pert little mouth smiles mischievously. I wish I had lips like hers instead of the soup coolers I've got. A high yellow woman with big lips is like a high yellow woman with nappy hair. "Remember Bill Johnson? You used to stare at him like he was a Greek god."

How can I forget? Willette is sure to bring him up at least semi-annually. She enjoys needling me about men. You can afford to when you've got the Top Dog. I'd like to tell her just how much of a dog he is. "You stared at him so much he asked Professor Carter to move him to the other side of the room."

I laugh, but I'm really tired of hearing this story. It just reminds me how lousy I am at choosing men. I lift my glass in a toast. "To Bill Johnson, wherever you are with your fine self. Whereas it usually takes a year to flunk out of law school, you managed to do it in one semester."

Willette smiles impishly. Here it comes. "And don't forget the wedding of the century of Miss Gwenlyn Washington to Mr. Phillip Parrish or—as he's commonly known now—our illustrious state representative Kwame Nkrumah El'Kasid, the Great Black Liberator."

C.C. waves her glass for emphasis. "Who, even as we speak, is somewhere in Harris County defending the defenseless against the mean ol' racist white people."

I correct her. "Devils."

"Pardon me—mean ol' racist white devils. You'd think being a public official, he'd slow his role with all that 'Hate whitey' shit," C.C. says. "He should be more responsible now."

I scoff. "He thinks he is being responsible—to 'the peoples.' " I down the rest of my drink. "He'll never change."

Willette winks at C.C. and leans toward me, her voice confidential. "So tell us, Gwen, whatever enticed you to marry that crumbum in the first place? You've never said in all these years."

"Crumbum" is Willie Shalandar's favorite expression for someone who isn't shit. My first reaction is to take exception to her using it to describe Kwame. He's a lot of things—arrogant, hardheaded, totally idealistic—crumbum isn't one of them. "Let me put it this way," I say. "A prostitute told me one time men either look good or dick good. I deferred to her expert opinion." Willette asks which one was Kwame.

"Both."

Dirk catches up with me leaving out of the Chandelier. Willette and C.C. snicker about him tracking me down. To save face, I jump all over him, demanding to know how he found me.

"A little bird told me," he says, smiling like a happy puppy. At least he had the good sense not to come in.

"Little, my ass." I climb into his Honda. My secretary thinks I dog him too much. C.C. and Willette think he's a fool. That's one of the advantages of interracial dating. White people think taking abuse is a part of being "black."

"What are you doing in Third Ward at night? Somebody'll think you're just looking for black pussy."

He chuckles as he pulls off. "I am. Mine."

I asked for that one. "Not yet it isn't."

"Just say the word." He won't be happy until I'm the third black Mrs. Dirk Ingersoll.

"I have to get my car."

That's not what he wanted to hear. "We can get it in the morning." Actually, I'm glad not to have to drive all the way out to Missouri City where I live. I'd love to move back to "The Trey," as one of my clients calls it, but I can't afford it.

Can you imagine not being able to afford to live in the ghetto?

Dirk starts telling me about his day, detail by boring detail. I cut him off mid-tale of woe about another poor woman who needs a divorce so she can wind up on welfare. "Why don't you do something else? Legal Services is burning you out."

He goo-goo eyes me. "And you look good enough to eat." His way of letting me know he intends to do just that tonight. "I'd give up everything I have for your body right this moment." He's crazy. Nobody's body is worth the Ingersoll fortune. They own timber, paper plants, and office buildings all over the South.

I stare out the window at the bayou. It's been raining a lot lately, so the water's high, like a shiny black ribbon snaking through the city. I've got a lot of things on my mind. Like where to find some money—the holy grail in private practice. And Michael threatening to blackmail me, the sleazy, slimy, rotten dog. He's just trying to mess with my mind.

Dirk pulls into the driveway. "I thought Ashleigh Lee was supposed to be home." I look at the darkened house and know right away something's wrong. "She is."

I rush up the front steps, fishing in my Gucci bag for the keys. Dirk nuzzles my neck, to my irritation. I'm worried and he's thinking sex. I put the key in the lock, but something tells me to wait. Instead, I walk across the thick St. Augustine grass to the window, peek through the drapes, drop my purse.

"What the hell do you think you're doing?" I burst through the door. A teenage boy jumps up from my sofa, looking like he could pee on himself. I recognize him. "Torrence Robinson, I'll be talking to your mother about this. Now, get out."

He takes off. Ashleigh Lee sits up, almost naked from the waist up, staring at me without an ounce of shame as she calmly buttons her top. I cross to the sofa to slap the insolence off her face. My hand strikes her arm, which she raises to defend herself. I keep trying to hit her. She keeps ducking and covering her head, like this is a game. Finally, I grab her hair. She screams and kicks me in the side. Now I'm really going to kill her.

"Gwen, don't!" Dirk tries to pull me off her. I don't know what's happening. Nor do I know this *woman,* hitting me back with her fists. I want to beat her until she brings my little girl back. He succeeds in holding me long enough for her to escape. I swing at him for stopping me. He pins my arms to my side. All I can do is listen to myself breathing like I just ran uphill with a dead body on my back. Ashleigh Lee deliberately slams and bangs about upstairs. I have half a mind to go up there and beat the shit out of her, and I tell Dirk so. He makes me face him. "What would that accomplish? You can't beat her into submission."

Why not? It worked with me. My mother still tells me I'm not too old for her to knock me down. I believe her. I jerk loose, sick of all this child-psychology crap. "That's what's wrong with kids nowadays. Everybody's afraid of them." I start for the stairs. "She thinks she's grown?"

Dirk grabs me again. "I'm not letting you go up there, Gwen. You're too upset."

I glare at him so hard I'm seeing double. Part of me knows he's right, but that's not the part I want to hear. "What do you know? You don't even have any kids." He lets me go. That was a low blow, but all's fair when you butt into someone else's fight. "You think it's easy raising a teenage girl today? They look like women in the fifth grade. They get their periods when they're eleven. I go out one goddamn evening, and she's getting ready to screw some little nigger right here on my goddamn Haitian cotton couch!"

Which reminds me to check the seat cushions. Dirk watches me like I'm in need of medication. He knows this is not the time to be the Reasonable White Man. Satisfied nothing's soiled, I take a deep breath and come back to the senses that child has a way of driving from me. It's not his fault she wants to be wild. But how is it mine? "You're right, Dirk. I'll talk to her in the morning."

He takes my hands. I notice how much darker mine are. He says, "God, you're beautiful. Even at full rant." I know it's not true. Willette is beautiful. I'm just blessed with Creole looks. Still, it's nice to hear.

I've changed my mind about waiting to talk to Ashleigh Lee in the morning. Dirk feels I should talk to her, all right, but not on his time. Isn't that just like a man? This interracial thing has been a real eye-opener for me since we met last year at an obscure metaphysical bookshop in The Village, a yuppie shopping area across from the City of West University, one of several white preserves in the heart of Houston. Every big city I know has them, places where white folks don't have to be bothered with "us."

The Village is socially verboten for blacks. You might find a few of us working in the shops, because in the South blacks work all over. But black customers are virtually nonexistent. I hate going in places like that. You never know how white people are going to act: if they're going to come out of a bag and treat you like a thief, or if they're going to be cool, take your money, and hope you're a singleton and not a trend.

I knew Dirk was going to find an excuse to talk to me as soon as he spotted me studying the astrology section, trying to find a book a client had recommended. I didn't really want to know anything about astrology, but I was told Ashleigh Lee and I have the same sign—not that I needed astrology to tell me we're too much alike to get along—and since she'd been giving me nothing but the blues from the day she turned thirteen, I was desperate to understand how her hard head worked.

Dirk offered to help me. After we found the book, instead of going about his business, he asked me if I came there often. I laughed and told him it'd taken me two weeks to work up the nerve even to come inside. He laughed. He had a nice laugh, free and easy, like he and life were in on some private joke. It didn't hurt that he looked like a young Robert Redford.

He offered to walk me to my car, which I declined. I didn't want him getting any ideas that he and I were going to have anything to talk about outside that store. I'd never messed around with white men, and I didn't want to. From everything I'd always heard and knew, they just wanted black women for one thing. I had no intentions of making him a "real man."

He walked me out anyway, telling me this funny story about a woman who'd come to Legal Services wanting to have her husband legally castrated. He'd been underweight all his life, and she'd heard that not having a "thing" would make him fat and easier to get along with. I feil out laughing. The next thing I knew we were making plans for dinner—that night. And lunch the next day. And eventually breakfast.

He was the smoothest, most persistent white boy I'd ever met. I didn't know it was because he'd had "experience." To tell the truth, I was probably ready for a white man, I just didn't know it. Not for the usual "woe is me, look what my black man done done to me now" reason. I was just tired of competing for the same tiny pool of black men of means.

Here's the truth: black men with money can pick and choose. I might be light-skinned with good hair, but I've been around the track, I'm no spring chicken, and—as one brother informed me—I've got "luggage"—a child. To a white man I'm a new experience. To a brother I'm same-old, same-old. So I told myself to go where I was appreciated, although I must admit I was ashamed to let anyone—not even C.C. or Willette—know for the longest I had gone "that way." When I told them my reasons for seeing him—not that I owed anybody any explanations—they readily understood. It's the numbers thing. It's frightening.

It has been interesting being with Dirk. He's cool enough not to try to be "black," which would get on my last nerve. And though he claims to love me, the same cannot be said of his feelings for my people. Not that he'd ever admit to disliking blacks. It just comes out. For one thing, he's a registered Republican in a state where being in the Grand Old Party is tantamount to saying you hate niggers.

Ashleigh Lee's got both the TV and the stereo going when I start to knock at her door. In light of her most recent behavior, I change my mind about extending this little courtesy and just walk in. She's on the phone. "Hang up," I tell her.

She twists her mouth and tells the person she has to go, hangs up, and stares at me like I'm taking up valuable time. I fight the anger expanding my chest preternaturally. I can't keep blowing my top every time she does something. "Do you want to talk about using protection?"

She looks insulted. "I wasn't going to let him do anything."

I wasn't prepared for that one. "What do you mean, you weren't going to do anything? You were *doing* it. If we hadn't walked in, you probably would've done everything there is to do."

"That's not true. I was going to stop him."

Now I've heard everything. "How, Ashleigh Lee? He's a teenage boy. You think he can stop on a dime?" She shrugs. "Do you want to get pregnant? Or a disease? Do you want boys to talk about you? I don't understand this." I really don't. "I get you everything you *think* you might want, and this is how you repay me. Sneaking boys in here, letting them do whatever they want. Don't you have any shame?"

Her black-brown eyes regard me like I'm something under a glass. "Do you?"

My chin automatically draws into my neck. "Just what's that supposed to mean?" I get right in her face. She stands her ground, though she does look away.

"Nothing." She pokes her lip out sullenly.

"You're not having sex in my house, Ashleigh Lee. You're too young. I'm not ready to be a grandmother, and I'm not going to be one before my time."

"I wasn't having sex." Her eyes slice at me. "I haven't had sex, I'm not going to have sex. Are you happy?"

I hate the way she turns things back on me. "No. I don't want you doing whatever you called yourself doing tonight either. Leading boys on can get you in a lot a trouble too."

She smiles. "You mean like being a cocktease?"

I know this is a challenge to see how I'll react. "Yes. And since you apparently know so much about it, you know how dangerous it is. I don't want you doing it anymore. You got that? Otherwise, I'm telling your father." Her expression instantly sours. "You won't be Daddy's little angel anymore." She wants her father to think she's perfect. "Do you understand me, Ashleigh Lee?"

"Yeah." Her eyes hold mine a second. I look away. She looks as if she hates me.

3

Willie Shalandar's victory party is spilling out into the lobby by the time Dirk and I walk into the downtown Hyatt Regency. It takes us twenty minutes just to get into the ballroom. The high spirits are infectious. I feel good knowing I played a key role in his election.

When we finally make it inside, Dirk leaves me to get drinks. I head straight for C.C. and Willette. They have their heads together in a corner. It could be my imagination, but Willette doesn't look that happy to see me. My heart leaps to my throat. Does she know?

"All riiight," I say, skinning their palms. "The Three Musketeers do it again. Where's our boy?"

"Daddy's still upstairs." Willette smiles like I'm her long-lost friend, and I relax. Some important-looking white people come up to congratulate her. C.C. finishes her answer. "Marvella got food poisoning at lunch." I cluck sympathetically. "Don't worry. He's not about to miss his grand entrance."

Willette notes the time. "Daddy should be on his way down, y'all. I better check the mike." I offer to do it, anything to ingratiate myself. "Gwen, Daddy won't murder his only child if anything goes wrong during his speech. I can't say the same for anyone else." We laugh. She beckons Michael, a few steps away. "Honey, would you give me a hand?"

"Sure, baby. Well, hello, Ms. Parrish."

He smiles like a snake at me, his words ringing with intimacy. I can't help it. He rattles me. "Hello, Michael." My voice sounds surprisingly normal.

"If I didn't know better," Willette says to me and Michael, "I'd think you two were perfect strangers. Wouldn't you, C.C.?"

"I don't know about perfect." Michael lets Willette lead him to the dais through a gantlet of enthusiastic supporters. C.C. touches my arm and I jump.

"Nerves," I joke.

She gives me an odd look. "You better do something about that." What does she mean? Did I give myself away? "After-party's at my place."

I see Dirk craning over people's heads trying to find me. I make my way to him, taking a tip from Willie that it's never too early to look for votes and greeting as many folks as I can. Sam Sprott, an old classmate, almost splashes his drink on me.

"Sorry, baby—" He gives me the once-over. "Umph-umph-umph. You sure look good tonight, Attorney Parrish. When you gonna let me touch you up?" Sam was one of the handsomest, blackest men in law school, so you know he was my type. We went out a few times the first semester, but I was seriously looking for a husband and he was just looking for pussy. Time, booze, and private practice have taken their toll, bloating his still good-looking face. I jokingly pat his paunch and ask him when he's going to deliver that baby. My mistake. He rolls his stomach obscenely. "The women love it. Wanna ride?"

Dirk walks up with my drink. I smile, grateful for him and his impeccable sense of timing. In fact, the thing I like most about him is his uncanny ability to be there when I need him. Especially when my father required emergency heart surgery. Dirk used his family connections to have him treated here at the Texas Heart Institute. He even chartered a private jet to fly him down, and stayed with me and my mother practically every second of the operation. Daddy still brags about sharing a room with an Arab prince, "All expenses paid!"

"Sam," I say, slipping my arm through Dirk's, surprising him, "do you know my fiancée, Dirk Ingersoll?" We generally avoid physical contact in public, usually splitting up at social events until the end, my way of dealing with people who can't deal with "us." Predictably, Sam sneers and moves on. I remove my arm and answer the question on Dirk's face. "He tried to hit on me."

"Nobody disrespects my woman." Dirk starts for him, his jaws tighter than a nun's thighs. I yank on him real hard, praying nobody notices. "Take it easy, Tarzan."

He looks at me, melting. "God, I love you."

"I know. Same here."

"Say it. You never say it. Not even when we're in bed."

I hate this. Men always want you to say the words so that sooner or later they can make you eat them. I do love him. Not like I loved Kwame. That was stone love. Am I turned out? I shiver inwardly. That's Michael's department.

"Tell me you love me and I won't kick his ass."

I laugh. He takes a step toward Sam. "Okay, okay." I make sure no one's listening. "I . . . love you."

He grins like this is a milestone event. "We're going to have to work on your delivery."

We hear a clamor in the back of the room. Willie enters, a bright spotlight bouncing off his shiny pate as he presses forward. He's a tall, ebony black man. His willowy wife, Marvella, is at his side, a happy-face smile frozen on her pale features. I don't know how you do that behind food poisoning. I take my hat off to her, she's a real trooper.

Physically, they remind me of my Aunt Delores' one dating admonition: it takes a white woman—not just a light woman—to break up jet black skin. Otherwise you get brown kids, like Ashleigh Lee. By rights, Willette should be her color. I told Dirk about Aunt Delores' rule. He called it racist nonsense. "You and Willette are the same color." I was shocked. He honestly couldn't see the difference between us. He's a white man; all he sees is dark and darker.

Willie mounts the podium, a grin like a lazy crescent moon on his inky black face. Like some colored Nancy Reagan clone, Marvella gazes at him adoringly. Willette flanks his right side, a taller and younger-looking Marvella. Michael's beside her, looking like the prince of darkness. They don't have children, but if they did, they wouldn't be her color.

Willie gives a rousing victory speech, highlighting the same promise he made during the campaign. "I will be county commissioner for all the citizens of District Five!" That gets a big round of applause from the white folks. They won't have to worry about anything changing but the players.

"I want to thank everyone who helped in my election. Most of all, I want to thank my lovely daughter, Willette Shalandar Rormier, for the magnificent job she did as my campaign chairman. What do you think, y'all? Isn't she great?"

Willette actually blushes. She's not an out-front person, unlike me and C.C. We have to paw the air like dogs at the pound for white people's attention. She gets it automatically by virtue of who she is and what she looks like. They don't say it out loud down here, but having the massa's color doesn't hurt you at all, another old thing that hasn't changed in the New South. It has to do with white folks' comfort level.

He resumes his speech, a line about fighting to expand services to the district. Willette whispers in his ear, interrupting him. He coughs, momentarily embarrassed.

"Ladies and gentlemen, my daughter informs me I've made a big giant boo-boo. And if I don't correct it right now I'm not gonna be able to go home tonight. And if I do, I'm gonna be sleeping on the couch." We all get his drift and laugh. "Actually, there was no mistake, y'all. I was just saving the best for last." He beams at Marvella and hugs her.

She doesn't once break her smile. "This is my wonderful wife, marvelous Marvella Shalandar. She's been at my side for thirty-seven years. I wouldn't be standing here tonight without her love and loyalty."

For a second Marvella looks like her face and her smile are saying two different things, like, my lips love you, my face hates you. It happens so quick I doubt if anyone even notices but me, and I could be imagining things. The crowd roars its forgiveness for Willie being human. They love Marvella all the more for being so understanding. She eats it up. Willette discreetly tugs her sleeve, a signal for her to step back so that Willie can shine alone. The applause is deafening.

I have to hand it to Willie. Unlike most politicians these days, he is what he appears to be—a solidly successful black man with a still supportive wife of almost forty years of marriage, an unflinchingly loyal and beautiful daughter. Too bad about his dog-ass son-in-law. Willie invites everyone to have a good time in his name. "Party till your socks fall down, y'all. Just make sure to have some on when you come to church on Sunday morning."

The band plays and the liquor flows. The only sour note in the entire evening occurs after Willie leaves, fortunately. Charles Garrett, though garnering less than ten percent of the vote, was Willie's closest rival. He and a band of his supporters crash the celebration, using a portable mike to accuse Willie of pulling dirty tricks and smearing Charles' name "in the community." Somebody wrestles the mike away, and security hustles him out while he curses everybody in sight.

C.C. and I happen to be standing at the entrance when security shows him and his raggedy little group the door. I'd just told her Dirk and I are passing on the after-party. He's got a trial setting in the morning, and I don't dare leave Ashleigh Lee to her own devices, even though she's spending the evening with a girlfriend whose mother assured me on pain of death she'd keep a close eye on her.

C.C. elbows me to check out Charles' eyes, so bloodshot they look on fire. He catches me sniggling behind my hand and stops, recognizing me, unfortunately. We go back to my third year in law school, when I clerked at Legal Services. He came in wanting to sue his landlord for wrongful eviction. Amazingly, we won. Back then I just thought he was intense. Now I think he's crazy.

"Tell Willie I ain't throwing down for this, sister." Dirk steps in front of me protectively. Charles quickly figures out we're together. "You yellow bitches are all alike. Ain't none of y'all worth a quarter."

Dirk grabs him by his fatigues, shoves him up against the glass. Charles' supporters can't do a thing to help him; they're already outside, and security's not about to let them back in. "You owe my lady an apology, Mr. Garrett."

Charles balks, and Dirk lifts him off the floor. Charles panics when he sees his feet dangling. "Hey, man, I didn't mean nothin'."

That's good enough for me. We're drawing spectators like flies. I touch Dirk's arm. "Let him down."

Dirk sets him down and smoothes his lapels. Charles looks at him as if he's the Holy Ghost incarnate, then skitters off backwards.

"Shame on you," C.C. says jokingly to Dirk. "You scared Charles so bad he's moonwalking."

4

I immediately notice Kwame's car as I turn Black Beauty into the driveway. So Ashleigh Lee's called her father on me again. No sweat. I'm trained to handle problems. This is just one more in a pile as high as the ceiling, since this was my first day back after the campaign and everybody and their mother was looking for me, from judges to clients on down.

Ordinarily, just seeing my home's pristine, white-on-white interior helps me slough off all the cares and concerns I've picked up like fleas practicing law all day. Lord knows it cost me enough: I bought the most expensive furnishings I couldn't afford.

Not this time.

Like a cop at a pot party, Kwame's spoiling the atmosphere, sitting on my sofa like he owns it, deliberately smoking a cigarette, knowing how I hate smoke in my house. Looking so much like him he could've spit her out, Ashleigh Lee sits cross-legged on the floor in front of him. Knowing a set-up when I see one, I take my time setting my things down, nonchalantly kick my heels off, keeping my voice neutral. "Kwame."

He rubs his nasty cancer stick out in the gorgeous onyx ashtray I keep on the coffee table strictly for show.

"Gwen." He smiles his killer smile, the one that melts your resistance at fifty paces. Luckily, I'm wearing my bullet-proof heart. "You cut your hair."

"Thank you," I say as if he'd complimented me. He hates a bald-headed woman, like most black men. I look at Ashleigh Lee expectantly.

"I want to live with Daddy."

Instant pain makes my heart skip three beats. "No." I turn to leave. "Excuse me, Kwame, I've got to fix dinner."

"She wants to live with me, Gwen. Why can't you accept that?"

"Because—" I almost shout. I take a big, deep breath, lower my voice. "The court gave me custody. I'm her mother. She belongs with me."

He runs his eyes up and down me like I'm wearing my clothes inside-out. I feel my confidence pulling away from the edges, just like it always does whenever he x-rays me like that. "Some mother. Men traipsing in and out all times of night. So busy you're not even home half the time. Ashleigh Lee says—"

Later for being cool. I explode. "I don't give a damn *what* Ashleigh Lee says. I'm doing the job you walked out on. If you don't like the way I'm doing it, tough titty and rubber booty."

"I hate you!" Ashleigh Lee screams at me and runs out. I steel myself. I hated my mother when I was her age. She'll get over it. Kwame slowly faces me, his eyes shiny cold. He looks as good as he did the first day I saw him in Property class. Only aged, like fine wine. "I didn't walk out, Gwen. You told me to take my black pride and shove it up my red, black, and green ass. Remember?"

I'll never forget. It was the worst time of my life. I was sick of being poor and dedicated to "the people." I wanted nice things, Kwame wanted revolution. Neither of us, though, needs a nasty custody battle right now. It wouldn't look good to his constituents or, more important, for my judicial candidacy. I soften my voice. "Okay, Kwame. I admit I've been busy lately, what with Willie's campaign and—"

He blows through his teeth impatiently. "When are you

going to stop sucking out of that white man's nigger's ass and get real?" He sets his hands on his slim hips. Despite pushing forty, he's still lean and hard in all the places I like in a man. I remember what those hips can do. I must be losing it to have such thoughts at a time like this.

"That 'white man's nigger' just got elected to the highest office in Harris County. Maybe if you tried putting your mouth somewhere besides at a microphone ranting and raving at white folks like you're crazy, you could get someplace besides the state legislature."

"You call hanging out with Willette Shalandar and C.C. Hendrix getting someplace? Those bitches are wiping their behinds on you just like they did in law school."

Angry tears spring to my eyes, but I dare one drop to fall. "Per usual, Kwame, only you know the real deal on everything and everybody including my hair, my friends, and every other goddamn thing you feel compelled to criticize me about. Only you don't have any papers on me anymore. This is my house—the one you could never afford." I march to the door and hold it open for him. "I'm inviting you out of it."

He shuts it. "Not until we get this thing settled about Ashleigh Lee."

I pick up the phone and dial 911, tell the dispatcher there's a domestic dispute at my house. Kwame stares at me. I give my name and address and hang up. They're sending a black-and-white.

"You're wasting your time, Gwen. I've got legislative immunity."

I don't care what he's got; the police aren't going to let him stay in my house if I don't want him here. I perch on the arm of the sofa and wait. He remains by the door. In a few minutes the bell rings. Kwame moves aside so I can answer it. Two white policemen stand in the doorway.

"We got a report of a domestic dispute, ma'am. I'm Officer Grogan, this is my partner, Officer Maxwell. What seems to be the problem?"

"This is my ex-husband." I emphasize "ex" and indicate Kwame. "I've asked him to leave my house, he refuses."

"Officer Grogan." Kwame steps right in front of me, smiling genially, playing the Reasonable Black Man. "We were discussing a matter pertaining to our child. We couldn't agree, so she called you all." He shrugs helplessly, like, "You know how it is, man."

I can feel the officers' attitude change toward me. "Is it true she asked you to leave, sir?"

"Yes, Officer." He glances at me. "Uh, can we discuss this outside?" Kwame ushers them to the porch before I can say anything, tells them something I can't hear, but they all three look at me. I feel like Boo-Boo the Fool. Officer Grogan steps back inside.

"State Representative El'Kasid is leaving now. He doesn't want any trouble. Is that satisfactory, ma'am?"

Hell, no. I want his balls cut off and thrown in the street and run over, damn him. "Fine."

The next day I'm still steaming about Kwame, and I wind up late as I wheel into the circular drive of the Shalandar home. It's palatial—what they call a "swankienda" down here—and it's in the heart of black South MacGregor. It's times like these when leasing the Jag pays off, even though the payments are killing me. I know I look good climbing out of it when I greet Willette, who's waiting for me in the doorway.

"For a minute I thought I told you the wrong time," she says with a warm smile and a hug, which I take as a good sign. She's usually not this outgoing, even with me.

"A client came in with cold cash right when I was walking out the door, so you know I had to listen to his tale of woe. My rent is due." I leave my jacket in the car to make my white silk blouse and slim black skirt look dressier. Good thing I wore my pearls today. Willette had said it was going to be a quiet dinner party with a friend of Willie's when she called to invite me this morning.

I'm excited and flattered. I've never been inside Willie's house before, though like lots of other black people in Houston, I've driven numerous out-of-town friends and relatives by it, showing off. Tonight's invitation can mean only one thing. I'm getting my judgeship.

Willette and Michael don't live far from here. Because, to hear Michael tell it, Willette can't stand being more than a mile radius from her father at any given time. Needless to say, I've been to their house many times. It's a gorgeous split-level a block or two over.

When I step inside the marble foyer, Michael's on his way up one side of a humongous double staircase. He gives me a wink behind Willette's back that says, "I know what you look like naked." The dog. Willette guides me around the foyer, briefly explaining the paintings and artwork while I try to ignore Michael's open leer as he watches me from the balcony, like he's the preacher and I'm Sunday dinner. I can't afford to be offended. The possibility of betrayal is clearly in his eyes. He puts his finger to his lips when I get just that message. I hate him. He knows I want him as much as he obviously wants me. That's what I really hate.

Willette accepts my compliments on the house, really a museum, there are so many expensive antiques and collectibles everywhere you turn. When we finally enter the giant family room, her mother rushes to greet me. I apologize profusely for being late. Marvella, ever the professional hostess, assures me it's no problem.

Willie's seated on a big leather couch along with C.C. and Riley Gregoire, whom I recognize from the campaign as the president of the black Teamsters local. I say hello as Willette shows me to a seat across from them. Everyone greets me warmly. Marvella offers me a drink, and I allow myself to relax a little, even though Michael joins us. I'm not worried, since he has to behave now. I steal a glance around, noting that the heavy, masculine decor seems out of place in the skylit black-and-white-tiled room.

Willie's moon-pie face is solicitous when he addresses me. "How's that foot, girl?" I show him. I stepped on a fire ant mound putting up his poster. The swelling's barely noticeable. "Now, that's what I call serving above and beyond the call of duty."

We all laugh, including me, as Marvella flits around like a hummingbird, tending to everyone's needs. It makes me uncomfortable. She seems to be trying just a little too hard. As soon as I set my drink down, she insists on refilling it though I've barely touched it. I try to stop her, but she whisks it away anyway. Willie jokes about "Mother's over-helpfulness," but he's looking at her very coldly. I guess she gets the point because soon she makes herself scarce. At which point Willie leans toward me, grinning like a big black bear. "So, my baby tells me you wanna be a judge."

I hope no one can hear my heart pounding. "Uh, yes, sir. Ever since I was a child, practically." I want to kick myself, stuttering and stammering. He wants to know why. I cross my legs to look more sophisticated. "Every lawyer wants to call the shots at some point. I think I can be as fair as anybody else." Damn, I wish I had said something profound. I laugh nervously. "Private practice is more than a notion."

"Amen to that." C.C. comes to my aid, thank God. "Those mean streets are no place for a lady to have to hustle, Willie. I don't know how people do it."

Michael adds his two cents. "It's not so bad on the civil side. There may not be much glory in real estate, but it pays the bills. Isn't that right, baby?" He squeezes Willette playfully. She giggles like a schoolgirl.

Some practice Michael has. He doesn't even break a sweat. Everyone knows he has a direct feed into the probate courts because of Willie. Every guardian *ad litem* appointment—if the estate is black—automatically goes to the firm of Rormier & Cashion. Ditto for the appraisal work. Segregation does have its rewards.

Willie turns to Riley, a brown-skinned man with thick

glasses and a long head. "What do you think, man?" nodding at me. "You got any questions?"

Riley clears his throat like he's got a fish bone stuck in it, shifts around to get a good look at me. His speech is slow and deliberate as he weighs me through those Coke-bottle lenses. "First of all, is it Miss, Mrs., or Ms.? What's your credentials?"

I feel like the answer is part of a test. "Call me Gwen, sir."

"Unh-uh," he says, elbowing Willie like I said something ridiculous. "I don't call no ladies by they's first names."

I flunked. "Ms. Parrish'll be fine, sir." Coke-bottle eyes just blink at me. "I've been in private practice for five years. Before that I worked in the D.A.'s office for five years, and before that I clerked for Judge Sanders, First Court of Appeals." I want to mention working on law review and graduating in the top ten percent of my class, but something tells me he couldn't care less. He grunts and sits back.

Warning bells go off in my head, sending my anxiety level up like a shot. I'm more than qualified to be a judge, and they know it. Especially when you look at all the nitwits presently on the bench. All due respect, but most of them aren't even cheap imitations of Oliver Wendell Holmes. As I pick up my drink to steady my nerves, Marvella announces dinner. I feel like I got a reprieve.

"Everything's lovely, Marvella," I say, taking my place. The table's formally set with a beautiful centerpiece of fresh flowers. "Can I help with anything?"

She presses me into my seat. "No, dear. How sweet of you to offer." My way of letting everyone know I have home training. I'm between Riley and Michael, who promptly squeezes my knee under the table. I don't believe him. Willette is across the table, looking right down his throat. I ignore him and try to carry on a conversation with Riley. Michael's hand finds its way up my skirt. I knock over my water on him. Everyone assumes it's an accident, but he knows better. I apologize profusely. He gives me a dirty look and excuses himself to dry off. When he returns, he keeps his hands to himself.

The meal is excellent. Marvella's one of those old-fashioned Southern cooks who insists we eat heartily from the platters of country ham, brisket, and fried chicken she sets before us. I can't compliment her enough on the homemade rolls, her specialty. They literally melt when you bite into them. Willette eats sparingly, I notice. I'd really like to imitate her, but I keep succumbing to Marvella's urgings to eat another helping like C.C.

The old men eat heavily too, quizzing me between mouthfuls. It doesn't go well, or so it seems to me. Finally, Willie points his spoon at me. "You know, Gwen, being a judge ain't all it's cracked up to be. Ask Miss C.C. here." She's busy concentrating on her plate and just shrugs. "It's a lotta asking for something by people you don't want to give the time of day to, let alone give 'em what they want. You understand what I'm saying?"

I say I do, but I wonder what he's getting at. "Them judgeships are pretty big jelly rolls." He winks. "White folks keep 'em to themselves for a reason. And that's another thing. How you gonna hold on to your seat? One of them's sure to challenge you. Even C.C. here got an opponent last time."

"That white boy threw everything at me but the kitchen sink," she garbles around a mouthful of peach cobbler. "Even sent out mailers telling white folks that when they punched that card for Cynthia Carmen Hendrix, they were voting for a black woman, 'in case you didn't know.' Good thing I kept my picture off all my campaign literature." Willie's idea.

"The point being," he says, "C.C. barely managed to squeak by. We hope to do better next year, but you can never tell. It's a long ballot, and our people usually get tired before they get to the bottom for the judicial races. Takes a lot of money talkin' to keep the bullshit from walking, I'm here to tell yuh."

I can't disagree with anything he's said, but I know I can

handle it and tell him so. I look to Willette—she's been too quiet. She's looking past me. I'm afraid to look at Michael. He hasn't said anything either. Willie squints at me like he's watching my heart beat. "Look here, Gwen," he says, "you worked hard for me and I appreciate it. I wanna do something for you. Truth is, I can't get you a criminal bench."

I murmur something in response that doesn't even make sense to me, I'm so hurt, and keep eating Marvella's peach cobbler, even though it's rolling around in my stomach like a rock. Michael's leg brushes against me. For some reason, it's particularly humiliating being rejected in front of him.

Riley tries to get that bone out of his throat again. "How 'bout you cut your teeth on something a little more easier, Miz Parrish? You young yet. A young lawyer's a menace to society, I always say."

He obviously wants me to agree. I want to scream at him I'm the same age as C.C. Instead, I swallow the last mouthful of cobbler. And the urge to smash his ugly ass glasses into his face. "Yes, sir."

I stare at my empty dessert dish, trying to be nonchalant even though I'm falling apart inside. I look up. Willie's smiling like he's about to knight me. "I can give you an opportunity, though," he says, "if you're smart enough to see it. I think you will. You're a pretty smart gal."

I force my mouth not to twist sideways. You just don't know, old man. I'm smart enough to see through this doublecross. What I don't understand is why. Terror grabs me by the throat. I want to look at Willette so bad it hurts. Is this her revenge? Does she know about me and Michael? How? She couldn't. Nobody does.

I pop back to Willie saying something about a part-time position on the municipal bench. ". . . I know it ain't much, Gwen. You do a good job, I promise I'll recommend you for the next opening on the state level. What you think, girl?"

They're all waiting for me to say something. His words sink in.

"Thank you, Willie."

I'm a judge. Part-time, but still—a judge.

5

"**G**irl, have you heard the word?" Carlotta Holt, a sister who graduated from TSU a year after me, plops down beside me. I'm waiting for my case to be called. The bailiff gives us a stern look to be quiet, and Carlotta ducks her head apologetically, whispers. "Tommy Shaw's getting the 332nd."

I drop my pen. I'd been doodling curlicues on my client's file to kill time. That idiot? "You are lying." She tucks her head in her neck, her looks saying otherwise.

"*State* versus *Wilson*."

They would call my case right now. The judge doesn't even look up when I approach with my client, a three-time loser they want to charge as a habitual criminal, which means I have no choice but to go to trial. "How do you plead, Mr. Crockett?"

"Guilty," I say, cutting my client off.

"What?" Crockett looks at me like I'm crazy.

"I mean not guilty." Where is my mind? "Definitely not guilty." The judge sets the trial date, and the bailiff leads my client away. He wants to talk, but I don't have time. I've got to find Carlotta. I've got to find out what's going on. Tommy Shaw graduated a year ahead of me at the bottom of the class C.C., Willette, and I nicknamed "The El Stupidos." Only a third of them managed to pass the bar exam first time around, a low even for TSU.

Carlotta's using the clerk's phone. I wait impatiently for

her to hang up, drag her out into the corridor like she's under arrest. We tangle in the throngs a couple of times. She thinks it's funny. I'm serious as a heart attack as I push her into the ladies' room and make her tell me everything, which she does with relish. "Girl, it's all over the courthouse. Plus, I saw him. He's got that stick-up-the-butt 'walk' they get when they're judges already." She demonstrates. That confirms it.

I turn to my bewildered reflection. "Tommy Shaw's going to be a district judge?" We must've been switched at birth. How else could he get the bench I'm supposed to have and I'm stuck with the one he should have? Even part-time, he'd be in over his airhead. I'm entitled to an explanation.

I cross the street to the annex. I would never ask Willie. Or even Willette. I do have some pride. That leaves C.C., taking a plea when I push through the doors of her courtroom. She nods at me expressionlessly. I wait in the jury box, trying to ignore the disappointment threatening to explode in my chest. C.C. rises and motions for me to follow her into chambers. She closes the door behind me and unzips her robe. She knows why I'm here. "Why Shaw, C.C.? He's got the mentality of a gnat."

She shrugs. "White folks prefer us that way. Besides, you don't need to be a rocket scientist to do this job." She drops on the sofa like a load of bricks and kicks off her shoes. "I should know." We both know she's low-rating herself. She graduated number one in our class, right in front of Willette, who was just in front of me. "Look, Gwen, just pay your dues in muni court, keep your name in the hat and out of the media and—abracadabra, presto-chango—you'll be a bigtime, state court judge one day."

She pats the sofa for me to sit, which I do reluctantly. "It's not fair. I wanted that bench. It's because I'm a woman, isn't it? They already have one black female judge, right?"

She reaches for a cigarette. "I keep saying I'm going to quit." Her face disappears behind a cloud of smoke. "The city's not so bad, Gwen. Any chance you get to be referee, it's good experience."

"Not as good as I'd get here." The bitterness in my mouth tastes nasty, like snot running down my throat.

"The game's the same all over. And make no mistake, it *is* a game: bridge in federal court, tonk on the civil side, pitty pat over here, Old Maid at the city. Keep some aces up your sleeve, you'll be okay."

One thing I like about myself is that when I think someone's right, I listen. Except when it's Kwame, but that's how mad he makes me. I take a deep breath, lean back. And giggle.

"What's so funny?"

"I can just see Tommy trying his first case. He'll have to look up the rules of evidence."

"He'll have to ask where to find them first."

The bitter taste returns. "At least he'll be a real judge. Not a Mickey Mouse one like me, deciding who ran the stop sign and putting away drunks."

"I'll tell you a secret, Gwen. To the public, all judges are alike. We all scare them shitless. You'll see." I hadn't thought about it like that. The phone rings and she gets up to answer it. "Judge Hendrix—"

The bad taste disappears as I watch her. She was as thin as a rail in law school, but now my poor friend's going the way of the flesh. Her hair always was sorry because she insists on doing it herself, and it's managing to look even worse these days. I don't know why Willette hasn't said something to her about her appearance. C.C. turns away from me. I see why Michael calls her "Big Bumpity." I'd certainly make a better-looking judge than her. Maybe that's why I got passed over.

She whirls around and looks at me, her face gray with shock, giving way to disbelief. I sit up. "C.C., what's wrong?" She drops the receiver, her mouth opening and closing like a fish gulping water. No words come out.

"C.C.?"

"Willie's dead."

*   *   *

I still can't believe it. I tell Dirk so for probably like the fiftieth time. He's lying on the bed, reading the *Chronicle*. I sit down and pull off my panty hose. It was unseasonably hot today for early spring, and it's such a relief to air out.

When I first moved South, I couldn't believe women—black, white, green, and otherwise—actually wore panty hose every day in ninety-plus heat and ninety-plus-percent humidity. I refused. After showing up at a few functions bare-legged, though, I succumbed to the pressure. You just don't feel "dressed" without stockings on. I pitch the hose in the laundry basket in the closet. I should be more careful considering they're Christian Dior, but I'm too upset.

"Two," Dirk says, like I've just scored the winning basket after double overtime. Great. He's being silly while I'm at my wits' end.

"I can't believe Willie's dead."

Dirk drops the paper and cold-eyes me impatiently. "Believe it, Gwen. He's dead." He shows me the front page with Willie's picture. "See? Plus, we watched the news. Do you want to see the body?"

"Don't be disrespectful, Dirk. The man is dead."

He turns to the sports section. "I forget how superstitious you people are about death. Really, Gwen, I thought you were more enlightened."

This is not the time for his latent racism to rear its stupid head. "How's this for enlightenment, Dirk?" He looks at me. "Go to hell."

"Hmm." He pretends to contemplate what I've said, his mouth pulled down like Emmet Kelly. "Now, that ranks right up there with the Bill of Rights and the Sermon on the Mount."

I smile in spite of myself, which is one of the things I like about him. "That's better," he says. "After all, it's not like Martin Luther King just died."

He's right. I unsnap my bra, a move that catches his full attention. Time for me to pull a couple of his strings. I give my breasts a shake. "You like, Tarzan?" He works his tongue around lecherously, hops up on his hands and knees, panting like he's half crazed with desire, ready to play "our game."

"Me likum plenty, jungle bunny."

I let him lick them just long enough for him to really get into it—then push him over on the bed and run to the bathroom. He kinda balls up and looks at me helplessly. He realizes he's been had. "That's for calling me superstitious." I slam the door and lock it. Kwame and Michael have taught me there's only one boss in the bedroom, and it's not going to be Dirk. I turn on the water for a long, hot shower. I need to wash the funk off. And the sadness.

I'm deliberately knotting my bathrobe at my side when I come back out. Dirk pretends to be engrossed in watching TV. I sit on the bed, let the robe slide off my thighs, rub lotion on my legs in long, slow strokes. His eyes shift to me. Unh-huh. "So when's the funeral?" he asks, trying to be cool. I know he's excited.

He's only asking to be polite. Dirk never liked Willie, considering him the equivalent of the old plantation straw boss, the slave who oversaw the slaves for the massa. Of course, being from the South himself, Dirk understands the absolute necessity for such blacks to exist. This I understand, which only goes to show you what a man and a woman will overlook, ignore, or accept about each other when they're sleeping together.

"C.C. said Saturday." Today's Tuesday. "Poor Willette. She's out of her mind over Willie. I phoned, but she's not taking any calls."

"Playing it for all it's worth, huh?"

I cut my eyes at him, set the lotion aside, and wrap the robe tightly to let him know that whatever hopes he had for getting some just ended with that unnecessary comment. He sighs and goes back to watching TV. I pick up the paper and read the article on Willie's death. "Prominent Black Leader Killed in Freak Accident." You know Willie was important:

he made the front page of both Houston papers without killing, robbing, or raping somebody. The *Post*'s picture of the twisted wreckage that was Willie's Lincoln is grislier than the *Chronicle*'s.

"He proved one thing." Dirk studies the picture, his chin resting on my shoulder. His way of letting me know I run this relationship.

"What's that?"

"A car's no match for a train."

"True." I turn to page fifteen for more details. " 'He was apparently trying to cross the tracks before the train came.' *Apparently*."

"So where was the crossing arm?"

"It was a black neighborhood. There probably wasn't one."

Dirk looks at me like I'm being ridiculous. I give him a look right back that says, like white people don't short-sheet us every chance they get. "Maybe he was in a hurry," he says. "On his way to sell more black people down the river so he could make another million."

"At least he was getting a piece of the action." The way I see it, the only time we stopped being a commodity to be bought and sold out was on paper. Willie was simply operating our version of the stock exchange.

He nuzzles my neck. "You smell good."

I wait a moment, then let the paper slide to the floor. Dirk pulls me to him and gives me a long, passionate kiss. He's not Michael by any stretch of the imagination. His lips aren't thick enough. But it's pleasant. His hand slips inside my robe and massages my breast. I think of that old song about loving the one you're with and ease down in the bed. He unties the robe and stares at my body like it's made of gold.

"You are one beautiful black . . . bitch."

I smile. I bet women get called bitches as regularly as black people are called niggers. As Dirk runs his tongue over me, I think of all the different kinds of bitches I've known—fat ones, stupid ones, trifling ones, ignorant ones.

There was a girl in law school so dark we used to call her "smoky bitch." When he works his head between my legs, I forget about her. It's getting too good.

Afterward, he leans on his elbow, idly tracing patterns on my stomach. My eyes are closed. I'm drifting off. "Gwen?"

"Yes, Dirk."

"Will you marry me?"

The words have a delayed impact. "What?"

"You're familiar with the concept, Counselor. Marriage, a legally sanctioned custom giving rise to legal and moral obligations—"

"I know, I know." He's caught me by complete surprise at a time when he's already batting a thousand in the let's-see-if-we-can-blow-Gwen's-mind department. "Let me think about it."

"Time's up."

"I don't know, Dirk. You're—"

"Financially independent, sincere, warm, intelligent, understanding, sympathetic, and I don't leave my shorts in the middle of the floor. My health is sound and I have all my teeth." I was going to say white.

"I don't know. Ashleigh Lee—"

"Will love me. I'll make her. I made you, remember?"

I don't believe love can solve everything anymore. Dirk has been good to me. But marry him? What would people say? Kwame? Kwame. He thinks Dirk's just a friend because that's all Ashleigh Lee knows, and he let me know through her he doesn't like it. "I don't know, Dirk. You see what my life is like."

"You're blindly ambitious, your daughter can't stand you, your ex-husband is a spear-throwing radical, and you hate practicing law. Now for your bad points—"

I slam my pillow against his head. He grabs his and socks me back. We play like that until we both collapse. Then he starts tickling me. I beg and scream for him to stop.

"Will you marry me or do I tickle you to death?"

The mere mention of death has an immediate, sobering

effect on me. We don't joke about it where I'm from. Talking could make it happen.

"Sorry." Dirk thinks I'm thinking about Willie. "I keep forgetting he was a friend."

Willie was a two-timing, back-stabbing, lowlife son of a bitch for giving my bench to Tommy Shaw. If I were being honest, I'd admit it was his power and influence that drew me to his daughter and then to him in the first place. Thank God I'm already sworn in for muni court, or I'd really have cause to miss him. Still, things could get funky. I need someone to watch my back and keep the wolves from my door. Who better than a rich white man? I may be what they call high yellow, but I'm still getting too old to compete with these young chicks for the brothers everybody wants.

"Yes."

"Yes?"

"Yes, I'll marry you."

The funeral is great. Everyone from the governor on down is there. I'm sitting in the family section, so I have a good view of all the dignitaries. I spend my time scoping them out on the q.t.

The services are being held at St. Mark's A.M.E., the oldest black church in the city, which Willie pastored. It's a beautiful structure with a red tiled roof and blond brick facade. I've been a member of St. Mark's ever since I first came to Houston to go to law school. All the important blacks belong.

Built a hundred years ago by ex-slaves, it's listed on the National Register as a historical site. A good thing too. Downtown developers have lusted over its prime location for yet another skyscraper for years. People are amazed we've been able to resist the ever increasing offers to sell.

St. Mark's seats a thousand, and it's overflowing. Speakers have been set up outside so the mourners and the curious jamming the sidewalks can hear. The choir sings "Swing

Low, Sweet Chariot" and nearly brings the house down. I'm in the front between C.C. and Dirk.

I glance at Willette and Marvella, both in designer black and sitting straight-backed just ahead of me. Willette wears a veil. Seems like it should be the other way around. Head bowed, she gently rocks to the music, so lost without her father it makes you want to just hold her and tell her everything'll be all right after 'while.

Michael catches me looking in his direction and winks. Man, you'd think on the occasion of his father-in-law's death he'd show more respect. Only, if anyone's ready to boogie on Willie's grave, it's Michael. I thought they got along until he told me one night he'd divorce Willette in a minute but for Willie's 3-D threat. "I'll be disgraced, disbarred, and destroyed." I didn't see the big deal. "Just go back to Mississippi," I said. "Your daddy's King Fish." He looked at me like I'd proposed self-castration. "You know that song about how you'd rather drink muddy water before you'll do something?" he said. "Mississippi *is* muddy water."

My eyes stray to Willie's body, lying in a silver casket surrounded by enough flowers to deplete a botanical garden. Jones Brothers Mortuary sure did a good job, considering how bad Willie was torn up, what you'd expect after being hit by a train. From a distance you can't tell they stitched his face back together at all. He looks like he's catching a quick nap.

Willette insisted on an open casket over Marvella's objections. Now I see why. As we file by to take one last look, Willette stops and kisses Willie's lips, a dangerous thing to do considering how poisonous those embalming fluids are. Even Marvella doesn't do that.

I had visions of Willette trying to throw herself in with the casket during the burial, but the gravesite service goes off without a hitch. Well, there is one hitch. Kwame keeps staring at me and Dirk with one of his patented ugly looks. This is the first time he's seen me with him, and he's trying

to figure it out. Good thing we're not close enough for him
to say anything, and we won't be, if I can help it.

Unfortunately, he arrives at Marvella's house afterward
at the same time we do. "Who are you?" he asks Dirk, acting
like he's the secret police or somebody. My heart stops.
Dirk doesn't have a clue.

"Dirk Ingersoll," Dirk says with a smile, extending
his hand.

Kwame shakes it, to my surprise. "State Representative
Kwame El'Kasid."

Dirk obviously doesn't place the name. "Nice meeting
you, State Representative El'Kasid." Dirk understands how
big black people in the South are on titles. "This is my fiancée, Gwen Parrish," Dirk says proudly, taking my hand.
My ears stop up from the explosive pressure I feel.

Kwame looks at our hands, then looks up, his bedroom
brown eyes grinding into me. "Congratulations," he says,
his thick lips splitting into a grin his eyes don't support.
"Here's my wedding present."

"Kwame, don't—" is all I get out, he hits Dirk so fast.
Someone screams as Dirk drops to one knee. Kwame evil-
eyes me and stalks off. C.C. rushes up to help me get Dirk to
his feet.

"Well," she says, "the Zulu Prince didn't take the news
of his ex-wife's remarriage as bad as I thought he would."

"Guess what?"

My law partner, Eddy Harris, looks like he's swallowed
Tweety Bird. I don't want to guess. It's too early in the
morning to play games, especially after being up all night
while Dirk grilled me about Kwame. About four o'clock
this morning, I finally convinced him I couldn't care less
about Kwame.

Our secretary, Pat, sees I'm on edge. "I'll bite. What?"

Eddy refuses to say unless we're both chomping at the
bit. Honestly, sometimes he's a direct pain in the ass. I'd been
through three truly rotten male associates before him—a

pathological liar, a psychopath, and a deadbeat. Then I tried a woman, thinking the extra chromosome was the reason why I couldn't find a reliable, responsible black attorney to practice law with. I soon discovered she liked to masturbate in her office. By that time I didn't care, as long as she paid her share of the expenses and kept her door closed.

Unfortunately, Pat was going to the file room one day when she saw her door wide open, the woman moaning and rubbing on herself. Disgusted, she closed the door, which started a big fight. They were screaming and calling each other names when I walked in from court. The bitch demanded I fire Pat on the spot. Pat threatened to quit if she stayed. That was an easy call. Lawyers are a dime a dozen. Try finding a good legal secretary.

Eddy was looking for space when we bumped into each other again at the county law library one afternoon. I was using the reporter he needed. We hadn't seen each other since the BLA picnic when we whipped "the whistologists," as our opponents arrogantly called themselves. As it turned out, he'd just finished a brief stint in the D.A.'s office. When he agreed the district attorney was a Nazi surrounded by Klansmen, I knew he was my next office mate. We've been able to practice law together for the last five years because we stay out of each other's business, legal and otherwise. He can be a direct pain. Like now, when on top of everything else I've got a king-size headache.

"What, Eddy?" My patience is gone. "What?"

He hands me the newspaper. "They're appointing Willette to fill Willie's term."

"That's not news." I take the paper to the sofa and sit down, which saps all my strength. "Who else would they pick?"

"I should've known you'd know. So how was the funeral?"

"Fine. You should've been there."

"I don't like being around dead people."

"The dead can't hurt you." I skim the long article on

Willie and Willette. "It's the live ones you have to worry about."

Eddy points at her picture. "What does she know about being a county commissioner?"

I shrug. "What Willie knew: where the bodies are buried."

He grins like I'm a first-class chump. "So the dead *can* hurt you."

6

My wedding day. I wasn't this nervous the first time I got married. Kwame was Phillip then, and I wanted to be Mrs. Phillip Lonzo Parrish so bad, I didn't know what to do.

You can be a lion or a wolf in law school, stalking the law on your own or in a group. Phillip/Kwame was definitely a lion. The rest of us preferred the safety of the pack. Slowly but surely I gained his confidence. Mainly by offering to help him in Contracts, the only class we shared our first year and which he had a hard time grasping because, like most of us, he knew very little about commerce, the heart of contract law. If we did, we wouldn't be poor, right?

We studied in the library at first. Later I invited him to my tiny, roach-ridden apartment not far from campus to study for the final. We worked late into the night, and it seemed only natural to ask him if he wanted to stay. We made love in my creaky twin bed. I was in heaven.

When I told Willette and C.C. we'd done "it," they said I was a fool, that he was going with some undergrad chick on the other side of campus. I was devastated but undeterred. I intended to be Mrs. Phillip Parrish before the year was out. On the advice of a girlfriend back home, I got some Vicks cough drops. The plan was to mentholatedly go down on him so much, that by the time I was through, he'd beg me to change my name to his.

He was the one who wound up changing his name to

Kwame Nkrumah El'Kasid, and I wound up getting pregnant. He was ecstatic, I felt trapped. I'd wanted to get Kwame fair and square, with my body and my mind. Willette and C.C. didn't see what difference it made, especially because whenever he'd see me in school he'd smile like he'd invented fatherhood and proudly remind me, "You got life in you, girl."

I was ten weeks pregnant when we stood in front of Judge Bledsoe and got married. He was the only black justice of the peace in Harris County at the time. I felt ashamed, my ankles swelled, and it was so hot, I wanted to take off my cheap little white dress and wring out the perspiration.

C.C. and Willette were the only people I invited besides my parents, who I knew wouldn't come. Daddy thought I was wasting my time trying to be a lawyer ("You need to get a job like you got some sense"), and Mama always followed his lead. She did send me some money, though, which I appreciated.

I miscarried right before school started in the fall. Kwame was heartsick. I was relieved. We'd moved into his hole-in-the-wall. It was bigger—not by much—and cheaper than mine. There was barely room for our books, let alone a baby. I got pregnant again right before graduation, this time with Ashleigh Lee. Taking the bar exam with morning sickness is like crawling over hot coals on your knees and elbows. My only consolation was that Kwame passed first time around, along with C.C., Willette, and I, a real feat. At the time, most TSU graduates flunked it at least once as a matter of course.

Now I sigh deeply, dab on the final touches of my makeup, about to marry Dirk. I purposely avoid looking at my eyes. I check the time—oh, my God, I'm late. I'm going to be late for my own wedding.

As I slip into my dyed-to-match pearl pink satin pumps with rhinestone buckles, my stomach flip-flops. I'm marrying a white man in the heart of the deepest South, which is what Houston is as far as race relations are concerned, like all the Gulf cities—New Orleans, Biloxi, Mobile. Even at this late date, white folks expect you to know your place, and no one down here leads you to believe you're standing anywhere but at the end of the line.

My eyes slip up and connect with my reflection. Are you sure about this? I ask myself. It's not too late to back out. That would be really chicken shit, myself says. You're a lot of things, but you're not chicken.

The wedding goes off without a hitch in Willette's backyard, which looks like a veritable park. Dirk wasn't crazy about the idea, but he's crazy about me and she insisted. We exchange vows under a flowered canopy before two hundred friends and relatives, mainly from his side. My father disowned me when he heard I was actually going to marry Dirk, which I told him was really prejudiced. He hung up on me when I told him our gene pool could stand some rejuvenation.

Actually, Daddy renewed my previous disownership for marrying Kwame, which he accurately predicted wouldn't last. ("She better gon' on and git a job.") My mother sent a beautiful vase in both their names, her card begging for understanding. I tore it up and dumped the vase in the garbage. This was their last chance.

As the ceremony concludes, C.C., my maid of honor, signals me on the sly to look to my right. Kwame's arrived, trying to be inconspicuous as he beckons Ashleigh Lee. She practically skips to him, only too happy to leave, which I agreed beforehand she could do after bribing, threatening, pleading, and cajoling to get her to come. Our eyes meet. I expect his wrath to turn me into a pillar of salt. Instead, he shakes his head sadly. I look away, furious. How dare he feel sorry for me? The minister asks if I'll take Dirk for my lawful husband. I emphatically say, "I do." That was for Kwame.

Dirk and I face our guests as man and wife and are pelted with rice. The photographer takes pictures, notices Ashleigh Lee's absence. "She went with her father," I say, keeping my voice light. Dirk doesn't like the idea. "We're going to have to start being a family sooner or later, Gwen." I give

him a kiss, bless his heart. White man that he is, he thinks
there's nothing he can't do.

The reception's a blast. The champagne fountain flows,
the music's rocking, the chairs have been replaced by a temporary dance floor. Everybody's having a ball, especially
me. Dirk and I received well-wishers for about an hour;
then I kicked off my shoes and started dancing my ass off,
but only on the slow songs with Dirk. He dances too much
like a white boy on the fast stuff, all jerks and fits, totally off
the beat.

Dirk and I take a breather by the buffet table under the
canopy, giggling and feeding each other samples of food.
Michael saunters up. My stomach automatically tightens.
He's drunk.

"Seig heil, man," he says to Dirk, grabbing me by the
arm, "let me borrow your lady for a minute. I need to talk to
her about something." Dirk instinctively hesitates.

"Honey," I say, "why don't you check on how the champagne's holding up? We don't want to run out, not with all
these hollow legs." If lawyers drink like fish, judges drink
like whales. It's the pressure. Dirk gives me a proprietary
kiss and pat on the ass and leaves. As soon as his back is
turned, Michael pulls me behind the canopy and tries to kiss
me. I duck away from him. "Are you crazy?"

"I can't get some sugar from the bride?" He gives me his
loan-shark smile. He's not as drunk as he pretended. I peck
him on the cheek real fast, but he pulls me close. "You can
do better than that." When I resist, he pushes my hands
away, slips his tongue in my mouth, waits for me to suck it.
I do it just to get rid of him. He lets me go. "That's more like
it. When can I see you?"

"You're crazy." I walk off.

He whirls me around and slides his hand down my dress,
kneading my breast and kissing me. I'm caught off guard.
To my surprise, I hear myself moan. He lifts my wedding
dress and pulls my hips to him. "Michael, please don't—"

He backs me against a tree and unzips his pants. *"Michael—"* I shove him backward. He stares at me. He looks crazy, and a chill runs through me. "You're right, baby. I don't have to take it."

A strange smile spreads over his face. "I got you a wedding present." He hands me a key.

"What's this for?"

"Our place." I drop it like it's fire. He picks it up, presses it into my hand, folds my fingers over it, and strolls off. I look at the key, then him. I've got to stop this shit right here and now. *"Michael—"* He smiles expectantly. I throw the key at him. He catches it, looks around, spots Willette and Dirk laughing with Dirk's parents. Shrugs. "I'll give it to your husband to keep for you."

Now, I've seen enough movies to know there're only two ways to deal with a blackmailer: you either expose yourself and face the consequences, or you give the blackmailer what he wants. I hesitate, hold out my hand. He gives me back the key, deliberately brushing his hand across me, and whispers huskily, "We better join your old man and my old lady before they get suspicious."

I let him "join" Willette and Dirk. I head for the champagne fountain. I fill my glass repeatedly and gulp it down, laughing and toasting everyone who comes up. I'm getting drunk, which is my intention.

"Here's to marriage," I say, lifting my glass high. "The only institution in the world run solely by the inmates." The champagne misses my mouth by a mile. As Dirk takes my glass, I hiccup and fall against him. "My White Knight, Sir Dirkalot." Giggle. "Dirkalot and Gwennyvere." He steers me toward the house, saying good night to our guests on the way. "There was somebody else too, wasn't there? Lancelot, Guinivere, and—" I try hard to remember the name, but I can't.

"King Arthur," he says, his voice tight. King Michael. Evil King Michael. Dirk grabs my bags, which C.C. packed and left at the front door.

"Ready, honey?" Dirk smiles at me like I'm twelve. I wish I were. I'd have all this mess ahead of me instead of whirling around me like a hurricane.

"Yep."

I lean on his arm as we walk out the door. Step onto the porch and remember my briefcase. Willette and C.C. teased me about bringing it to the wedding. I don't care. One time, when I left it on top of the car and drove off, it slid off and I drove over it. The only way I've trained myself not to lose it is by taking it everywhere. "Do you have my briefcase?"

"No. Why did you bring it in the first place?"

"I must've left it upstairs," I say, hitting the stairs before he can stop me. "Be right back." A lawyer's briefcase is her life. You can't leave your life lying around just anywhere. My feet tangle in my train, so I ball it up and carry it as I trudge up Willette's long-ass staircase to the room where I changed for the wedding. My briefcase's exactly where I left it, on the floor by the dressing table. I bend over to pick it up. All of a sudden the room starts doing a merry-go-round thing. I've had way too much to drink, and I have to sit down a minute. Instead, I sprawl on the bed and stare at the ceiling until it comes to a complete stop. I sit up. Some-one's shouting. Dirk must be looking for me. The ink isn't dry and he's nagging me already.

"I'm coming, I'm coming—" I stand up. I feel a lot better, walk to the door, and remember I forgot the briefcase again. I go back to the bed, pick it up, and open the door.

"Where do you think you're going?" Across from me, Michael storms out of their bedroom. Willette grabs him. "I'm not through talking to you—" He slings her against the wall and slaps her sideways, twice. Instead of knocking the shit out of him, which is what I would've done, she just stands there and takes it. I shut the door. All these years I had no idea he manhandled her like that. She begs him to keep his voice down, they have guests, assures him she'll talk to C.C.

"You better," he says. "And tell your cunt-sucking, pussy-eating, carpet-munching bulldagger friend she better—"

A door slams, cutting him off. All's quiet. I wait a moment, open my door a sliver. They're gone. I slip outside with my briefcase and run down the stairs. My feet trip on my dress, and I remember the part in the movie where Stepin Fetchit says, "Feets don't fail me now." I want to laugh, only what I just saw wasn't funny.

Dirk is waiting for me in the foyer. "Gwen, what have you been doing?" He's obviously annoyed that it's taken me so long.

"You don't want to know," I say, stone sober.

7

"Honey, where's the mayonnaise?"

This is the third time Dirk's called to me from the kitchen. If I'd known he was going to be so helpless, I'd've fixed his goddamn sandwich myself. I cap my magic marker, set aside the transcript I've been reading, go directly to the refrigerator and pluck the mayonnaise jar from its "secret" hiding place on the door, and hand it to him. "If it had been a snake, it would've bit you."

He smiles sheepishly. As I start back to the den, he stops me by holding onto my sweat top. "Stay, honey. I'm lonely."

Honestly, men. When they have things to do, you don't exist. But try shutting them out for a single afternoon.

He resorts to bribery. "I'll fix you my super-duper, dee-luxe White Boy."

I smile. "Don't you mean po' boy?"

He pulls out imaginary pistols, confidently blows "smoke" from their barrels. "I mean what I said, ma'am. You want a white boy or not?"

"All right," I say warily. Dirk is a great kidder. "Fix me a 'White Boy.' "

"Thought you'd never ask." He picks me up and carries me into the den. I'm laughing and beating on him to put me down, I have work to do. He plops me on the sofa and pulls off his shirt.

"Dirk, it's the middle of the afternoon."

"Yes, ma'am."

I sit up. "I have to read this transcript by Monday."

"Yes, ma'am." He pushes me back and kisses me. I mumble that this is the den. He fumbles at my bra. "Yes, ma'am."

I start feeling that delicious, tingly itch between my legs. I slide down, pulling him with me. "Ashleigh Lee could come in."

"I'm already here."

We jump apart. She smirks from the doorway. I feel like I did when my mother caught me under the stairs with a boy.

"You're supposed to be studying with Pamela Britton," I say, pulling myself together.

"We finished early." She shrugs. "We want to go skating."

Dirk stiffens. Here we go. Tug-of-war, I'm the rope. "Ashleigh Lee, you know how your stepfather feels."

Her dark eyes shine combatively, looking so much like Kwame he could've spit her out. She's got my booty, though. It runs in the family. "I'm not asking him. I'm asking you."

Dirk stands up. "Roller City isn't a suitable place for you to be hanging out. They do drugs there."

"They do drugs everywhere," she shouts. "If that's what I wanted, I could get it at school."

"Unh-uh," I say. "Not for the money I'm paying."

They both glance at me like I'm singing off-key. "No," I say. She pouts. "Because he said so?"

"We both say so."

"I hate you!" she screams and runs out.

Dirk marches after her, and I automatically follow. "Young lady, you don't talk to your mother like that." He catches her arm as she's about to hit the stairs. She snatches away. "Don't you *ever* touch me, sheet."

I jump between them. "What did you call him?"

"Sheet." Her lip curls defiantly. "You know, like KKK."

That's what I thought. My hand flies up. "You apologize, Ashleigh Lee, or so help me, I'll slap you into next week."

"No, Gwen—" Dirk steps between us. "Go to your room, Ashleigh Lee."

You'd think the little bitch would be grateful he saved her

life. Instead, she sneers like he's scum, runs up the steps two at a time. Slams the door. I let the air out of my chest, returning it to normal size.

"It's okay, honey."

"It's not okay." Damn Kwame. He's twisting her like this.

Dinner is a drag. Ashleigh Lee refuses to eat even though I fix lasagna, her favorite. Dirk and I eat in silence while I go over in my head all the ways I've gone wrong with my child. Maybe I should've spent more time with her, but how could I? Kwame never made enough jousting at windmills to support us, not the way I wanted. Why couldn't he have cared about money as much as he cares about "the people"?

Resentment sours the food in my mouth. What about all the things she has, thanks to me? The clothes? God, the clothes. She's always the best-dressed kid in her class, I make sure of that. Not that she cares. She'd wear rags to school if I let her. And what about me? I'm entitled to some happiness.

"Want to watch the news?" Thank God Dirk interrupts me. I was throwing a big pity party for myself. He turns on the set. I refill his wineglass. "Thanks, honey."

Honey. Why can't he call me baby? Honey is for white women. I stare at the TV screen, thinking about Ashleigh Lee. She was a beautiful baby. And so good. Everybody said so. Dirk starts to turn the channel, but something catches my attention.

"Wait." I touch his hand. "Isn't that Charles Garrett?"

Dirk turns up the volume. ". . . Garrett, a longtime community activist, was arrested late this afternoon at his residence—"

"Arrested?" I say to the TV. "For what?"

Dirk shrugs. "Knowing Garrett, he was probably protesting Santa being white."

The segment cuts to Matoomba House, a community center in Third Ward, Garrett's base of operations. His attorney, Warren Covington, a classmate of mine, is surrounded by Garrett's supporters, angry and cursing, vowing to do whatever's necessary to free their leader.

"The facts will show my client is absolutely innocent," he says. The reporter asks him if he expects Garrett to be charged. Warren can feign indignation better than any lawyer I know. "What's the crime? How do you make a train run over somebody?"

Dirk and I exchange a look, glue our eyes to the set. The phone rings. It's my law partner, Eddy. "You heard?"

Heard what? I say. What the hell is going on?

"They got Charles Garrett for suspicion of murder."

This is making no sense. "For killing who?"

"Willie Shalandar, fool. Don't you read the paper?"

Every day, only I had to finish that damn transcript, so I hadn't gotten around to it yet. I hang up and look for it. "Eddy said Charles Garrett's been arrested for murdering Willie Shalandar." Even Dirk's surprised.

I keep trying to get through to Willette or C.C. while Dirk leaves to get the *Post*. Both papers cover blacks in the usual "tell everything bad" tradition, but the *Post* goes for the nitty-gritty. I give up, asking myself, How *do* you make a train run over somebody? I run dish water and wash dishes, trying to figure it out. Dirk returns, tosses the paper on the counter. He has a funny look on his face.

"There's no light on in Ashleigh Lee's room."

I tell him not to worry, she's been sitting in the dark since she was a child. "I'll see if she wants dessert or something," he says. I smile. He has about as much chance of enticing her out of her room as I do of being mayor. Even still, it takes a load off for Dirk to take responsibility for my child. I appreciate him for that. A lot of men wouldn't.

He calls to me to come upstairs. I wish they'd find some common ground besides me. He's standing in her doorway. At least he got her to open up. That's progress.

I step around him and flip the wall switch. "Let's get some light on the subject."

She's not there. "Ashleigh Lee, where are you? Ashleigh Lee?"

"I think she's gone, honey."

You don't know what panic *is* until you've had your child disappear on you. Your heart stops, your mind freezes, terror leaks into your bowels. Fortunately, your arms and legs keep working, so you can at least go through the motions while you relive every minutia of every moment you can think of that'll give you a clue to her whereabouts.

I would've given in to the panic if it hadn't been for Dirk. Three years of legal training, five years of prosecuting every heinous crime imaginable, five more years in private practice dealing with every dreg known to humanity, do nothing to allay the anxiety of my child's disappearance. He suggests we try Kwame, completely logical given the circumstances. A simple telephone call confirms she's there. I'm relieved and furious with Kwame for not letting me know.

"She said she had your permission," he claims.

"C'mon, Kwame, this late at night?"

"You've done stranger things."

"Like what?"

"Like marrying that white boy."

Dirk and I have our first serious argument on the way to pick her up. He hints—ever so gently—I consider giving her up.

"She's fifteen years old, Gwen. She's old enough to know who she wants to live with."

"I don't want to talk about it."

"She wants to live with *him*. Tonight should convince you if nothing else does."

"I said I don't want to talk about it."

"Honey, I know she's your only child, but—"

That's it. "What do you know?" I snap. "It's easy for you to tell me to give up my child. You don't have any. She's my daughter. She stays with me."

"That's it?"

"No, this is: it's none of your goddamn business."

He whistles through his teeth, jerks the car around the next corner so hard, the tires skid. I don't care if he's mad. He can scratch his ass and get glad. Ashleigh Lee's not going anywhere, even if I have to chain her door and tie her down.

"I don't understand you, Gwen," he says. "You can be so level-headed about everything but Ashleigh Lee."

"Yeah, well, that's what being a mother does to you, Dirk. Nature made it that way so that even if your child looks like a monkey you'll still love it."

"You don't have to be sarcastic. I'm just trying to help."

"You're just a regular helpful Harry. I guess that's why you play work for Legal Aid." I hate the things I'm saying to him, but I can't help it. My emotions are revved up. I don't know any other way to come down.

Dirk's so mad, he soars onto the Loop, not a good idea on Saturday night. All the crazies are out. I keep my ass off the freeways on the weekends. Houston drivers take those car stunts on TV seriously. A car cuts so close it doesn't look like there's space left between us. Dirk hits the brakes and blows his horn. The driver waves, goes on about his business. Almost getting killed snaps me back to reality. "Let's get off this damn thing before we're a goddamn statistic."

Dirk frowns. Cursing is another thing he's been getting on my back about. Too bad, cursing is who I am. Otherwise, I'd go straight to murder.

Kwame stays in Kashmere Gardens, one of several black enclaves in Houston. His little matchbox bungalow looks just like all the other ranch-style tract homes in this subdivision. Several street signs are missing, so I guess at the turn when the time comes.

Dirk parks out front. I ring the doorbell. Kwame opens the door, deliberately leaving the ghetto screen—my name for those bars that make each home look like a private jail—between us. I feel like I'm on a conjugal visit.

"Where is she?" Kwame and Dirk eye each other like

hunters after the same game. I don't have time for their macho shit. I call out to Ashleigh Lee. "Where are you?"

The floor creaks. Ashleigh Lee appears beside Kwame, chewing gum, which she knows I despise, looking like a cow chewing its cud. Now that I know she's safe, I want to reach through the bars and strangle her. "Get your things and let's go." She just looks at me and blows a big pink bubble. I poke it, and it splatters it all over her nose and mouth. "I said let's go."

She starts whining. "Why can't I stay here with Daddy? You don't need me. You've got Dirk the Jerk."

I glance at Dirk. I'd forgotten he was with me. His face is red as a beet, his mouth an angry straight line. Kwame doesn't say a word. I would've slapped her head from her shoulders for being so rude, but he doesn't believe in hitting a child, naturally. My theory is that they don't always remember the rules, but they do remember the pain of breaking them.

"I said get your things, Ashleigh Lee, and let's go. Now."

She realizes I mean business, stomps off, and grabs her backpack. "I'm sorry Ashleigh Lee barged in on you, Kwame."

He unlocks the bars to let her out. "No problem." They exchange one of their secret smiles. "She knows she's welcome here anytime." A pang of envy stabs me. My father's not close to me or my half-brothers and -sisters. He's too busy telling us what we "need" to do.

Dirk trails us to the car. Before I let Ashleigh Lee set foot inside, I make her apologize for calling him out of his name. She mumbles something resembling "I'm sorry." Dirk starts the car. "Call me anything you want, Ashleigh Lee. Just call me if you need anything."

She turns her head and stares out the window.

8

Life has a way of picking you up in Kansas and setting you down in Oz. It doesn't just happen to the Dorothys of the world either. Take Charles Garrett. A month ago he was our resident community activist. A professional "civil rightster," he was a black man with power, within certain limited circumstances, for certain limited purposes. That is to say, anytime you needed a ready-made protest, you could count on Charles and his loyal band to picket the transgressor of the day's locale, waving homemade signs and shouting epithets. His payoff was that he got to say things to and about the white man the rest of us can only whisper to each other and then only behind tightly secured doors.

Everybody but Charles' troops thinks it must be a bad joke that he's suspected of murdering Willie Shalandar. Naturally, they're calling it a set-up. Those of us who are supposed to be in the know, namely the black legal community, don't know what to think. I spoke with a couple of my white folks about it in court this morning, and they don't either. The police and the D.A.'s office isn't saying a word, so rumors are running faster than cheap panty hose.

Charles' arrest is having a strange effect on black Houston politics, though. Willie Shalandar was revered in some quarters, feared in others, but respected by all for his ability to "talk to" white folks. Charles, on the other hand, is one of "the people." We may be like crabs in a barrel when it comes to holding each other down, but usually when it comes to trouble, we can solidify faster than Jell-O. Probably because in our heart of hearts, we know none of us, no matter how successful, is ever immune to the capriciousness white people call justice.

But this time we're split, irrevocably. I'm in the group that's educated and upwardly mobile, inclined to believe the charges. The side adamantly maintaining Charles' innocence is by and large inarticulate and emotional, hardworking but unemployed or underemployed. It's like Charlotte Wilson, a former colleague still in the D.A.'s office, said to me during a recess, "We, the educated people, have to understand what's going on so that we can enlighten the rest of us."

I run into Warren Covington, Charles' attorney, a former University of Houston star basketball player, in the coffee shop. The years have added poundage around his middle that looks good on him. Everything about him is big, including his dick. I know because he never lets an opportunity pass to so inform me or any other woman who says more than hello to him.

"Warren, what's happening?" I push my tray along the cafeteria line just ahead of him.

"You, baby. Every day and every way." He flashes even white teeth and busses me on the cheek. I'm not a lawyer to him, just another chick to be hit on.

"How'd your boy Garrett wind up behind the eight ball?" I'm being nosy, so I overlook his cretin behavior.

"They got an 'anonymous tip.' D.A.'s full of shit on this one, baby." He pays for my coffee and roll; we move to an empty table by the register. He gives me the once-over before we sit down. "Damn, baby, you got a nice playground. That white boy's putting a new shape to it."

Warren's idea of a compliment. "Don't call my husband a white boy, Warren." It sounds like he's calling him a nigger. Warren tucks his chin indignantly and sips his coffee, spots Oscar Gantt and waves him over.

"Hey, man, caught you on the box Saturday," Oscar says, turning a chair around and straddling it. Oscar has a friendly, round face and is what I've heard described as a "shit-colored nigger": yellowish-gold skin and freckled. "I hope you got your cash up front."

Warren wipes his mouth with his napkin and grins, happy to forget my presence. "Better believe it. I officed with ol' Percy Lewis when I first started out. Humph. Percy knew more ways to get money outta niggers than the IRS." Percy Lewis is now disbarred, which Oscar and Warren lament. "Yeah," says Warren, "ol' Percy always said to get as much outta them the first time round 'cause you'll never see 'em again."

I interject. "Maybe that's why they take their business to white lawyers. They think we're all out to fleece them." Warren and Oscar exchange a look that says I probably believe in the tooth fairy too.

Oscar attempts to set me straight. "Black people take their business to the white man 'cause the judge is white, the jury's white nine times out of ten, and so is everybody else in the legal system."

"It's changing," I insist. "More blacks are turning from the white boys and bringing their business to us."

Warren slaps his knee. "Now, ain't that just like a woman? Man, not more than five minutes ago, she told me not to call her husband a white boy."

Oscar tilts his head to the side, like he's recalling something. "Hey, yeah, congratulations, Gwen. Heard you got hooked up. Didn't know the lucky man was one of the enemy." He and Warren dap, like they're blood brothers or something.

I push away from the table, ready to defend Dirk and me to the death. "I'm not for any bullshit this morning, fellas."

Warren's hands spring up like I'm about to shoot. "Hey, baby, you like it, I love it. It's for damn sure his shoes ain't gonna be under my bed." He turns to Oscar. "Done any fishin' lately, man? How 'bout those Astros?"

They chat about catfish and baseball. I get the hint and split. Anyway, I've found out what I wanted to know. If an anonymous tipster busted Garrett, then somebody saw Willie's murder.

If anyone had told me by the end of the day I'd no longer want to be a judge, I would've told them to check my dreams all the way back to childhood. Yet I'm sitting in muni court for the first time and all I want is out.

In the first place, it smells in here. I have the night arraignments, and the courtroom's crammed with life's flotsam and jetsam. I look over the sea of faces looking at me; every one of them looks like a possible ax murderer. Which makes me keep my eye on Hershel, the police officer acting as my bailiff. Though fully equipped, he wouldn't last a hot second if all these potential criminals got the urge to go on a rampage. Now I understand why the legal system works only because of the high level of cooperation of the accused.

"Is it always this packed?" I whisper to my clerk, Fern, a petite white woman with mousse-packed hair and horn-rimmed glasses. She nods and continues to sift through two six-inch stacks of charges in front of her.

"When I call your name," she says to the audience, jarring me into what I hope is my judicial demeanor, "just answer present." Easy enough. Only instead of just answering to their names, every third person wants to tell me their story instead, which drags out Rosemary's job. Why can't people follow directions? Good thing the Russians don't know how stupid we really are.

She finally finishes accounting for everyone, and I begin to take the pleas: not guilty, guilty, guilty with explanation. Guilty with explanation is at least entertaining. Like the man telling me the reason he ran three red lights in a row is because he's color-blind. When I ask how he's managed to avoid a collision all this time, he says God has given him special powers that protect him at intersections. I do all I can not to bust out laughing while I read the complaint.

"Too bad the other driver didn't have his special powers," I observe. "You wouldn't have sideswiped him." I find him guilty and impose the maximum fine. I'd like to strip him of his license and impound his car, but I have no such power to keep the truly dangerous off the roads.

Fern politely informs me during the break that if I continue to listen to every individual citizen's sad little tale, we'll be here all night. When I retake the bench, I move things along. Even still, we don't finish until midnight. A rookie police officer escorts me to my car. Thankfully, he's not much of a talker. I'm too tired and I have a blinding headache. As I pull out into the street, I wish I could put my car on automatic pilot. I can just hear my "guilty with explanation" explanation after I run over somebody. "You see, Your Honor, God gave me the power to drive while I slept in the backseat. . . ."

As I pull into my driveway, I notice most of the lights are on, even though it's one-fifteen and anyone with any sense is sound asleep. It's sweet of Dirk to wait up. I drag myself from the car. The cool air tastes of petrochemicals and God only knows what else the city lets the big companies dump in the atmosphere. No wonder they're so desperate for a cure to cancer.

Dirk is nodding off in the easy chair in the family room while a slasher stalks a white woman on TV. I turn off the set and kiss his forehead. He squirms but doesn't awaken. He looks so vulnerable. It's strange: Attila the Hun, Hitler, and Dracula, everybody looks the same way in their sleep.

I go back into the kitchen and take out two pieces of bread and reach inside the fridge for a slice of cheese, all the dinner I can manage this late. Spot Dirk's note on the door. Willette wants me to call her. I forget it when I discover—happily—the plate he's left me. I let the refrigerator door slam without thinking. The noise wakes him.

"Hi, honey." He wipes his eyes, yawning big. "How was it?"

I take a bite of roast beef. "A zoo. I hate it."

"See my note?"

"I'll call her in the morning. I'm tired."

"She said it's important."

"It can wait." I have Willette to thank for the most miserable night of my legal life so far. Dirk kisses me good night and goes to bed. I scrape the mashed potatoes and green beans into the disposal and think about the note. It really could be important. Willette rarely calls me at home. In fact, Willette rarely calls me. I reach for the phone. It takes so long for her to answer, I wish I'd followed my first mind and waited until morning. I pray Michael doesn't answer. Willette finally picks up.

"Willette, Gwen. What's up?"

She doesn't sound the least bit sleepy. "Meet me at Daddy's office in the morning. Ten o'clock."

9

I've never been inside Willie Shalandar's private offices.
I've been to the Shalandar Building before, a three-story
structure in the heart of Third Ward, but never beyond the
lobby. It's a landmark black people in Houston like to point
out to visitors—like the Shalandar home or where the president
of TSU lives or rich Dr. So-and-So's house. You know
you've arrived in Houston society when your home's on the
"tour."

I pull into an angled parking space, looking up at the towering
SHALANDAR BUILDING sign as I get out. The only buildings
I know in Detroit with black people's names on them
were usually put there by white people. I'm proud Willie's
was named by him and that it houses Houston's first and
only black savings and loan. Willie Shalandar wasn't just an
astute politician; he knew how to turn a buck.

It's only nine forty-five in the morning and it's hot already.
I ran the air all the way, but my silk blouse clings to
my back anyway. I glance at the other corners of the busy
intersection. A pharmacy is directly across from me, all its
windows grated with metal, a fact of life in the ghetto, even
a relatively decent one like this. I'm told that before integration
this was a booming, commercially prosperous section
of Third Ward. That's hard to imagine looking around
at the fraying drabness.

I approach a glass door stenciled with GULF SAVINGS AND
LOAN ASSOCIATION and SHALANDAR ENTERPRISES, INCORPORATED
in flaking gold lettering. The door swings open like

magic, startling me. I enter, automatically on guard. Michael lets it swoosh closed behind me. I should've known. He looks me up and down like I dressed just for him. "Marriage ain't hurting you at all, baby."

I ignore him and walk to the elevator, passing the savings and loan to my right. It takes up the entire first floor, heavy fiberglass drapes lining the glass wall that separates it from the small lobby. A customer comes out. Michael glad-hands him and shows him to the door. I reach for the elevator button, but he covers it up.

"I want you, baby. Real bad."

I push his hand out of the way. "I'm on my way to see your *wife*."

"I know. It was my idea."

"For what?"

His hand grazes me suggestively. I shiver involuntarily, follow his eyes down. My nipples are straining against the flimsy fabric. I look up, my face on fire. He smiles knowingly.

"Meet me at 'our place' when you finish so I can get rid of this." He grabs my hand and forces me to hold his erection. I try to pull away, but he won't let me. "You've missed it, haven't you, baby?"

I yank away, looking around to see if anyone's watching. Twelve years of living in the South, you learn how quickly people add two and two just seeing you talk too long together. "No. It's over. I'm married."

"Don't make me drop a dime on your old man too."

"He won't believe you."

Michael scoffs. "Say, baby, do I look stupid? That white boy'll go crazy when he hears the kind of stuff I know about you." His eyes run down my body, leaving a blaze of guilt in his wake. "Like how I make you come and come—"

I reach out to slap the shit out of him. He catches my wrist, twists it behind my back just enough to let me know he could hurt me if he wanted to. "Play that shit with whitey." He brings my hand to his face, opens my palm, and gently kisses it. "Noon."

"I hate you."

"I know."

I don't know if I've lost my mind or if I'm crazy to begin with. The truth is—and I make it a practice not to lie to myself, thereby being straight with somebody—I do want to see Michael. I need what my best friend back home calls "body buffing."

The ride up to Willette's third-floor office gives me time to pull myself together. The elevator's so tiny I'm surprised when the doors open and I step directly into a beautiful reception area, richly appointed with heavy, masculine furnishings. The secretary, a dark-skinned elderly woman with thick glasses and a tight salt-and-pepper natural, greets me.

"I'm Delzenia, Ms. Parrish. Please have a seat. Commissioner Shalandar is on the phone." Willette's gone back to her maiden name for obvious political purposes. "Can I get you anything—coffee, tea?"

A gun to shoot Michael with.

She invites me to a big leather armchair by the window and brings me a glass of water. The light goes off on the telephone. The door opens behind her desk and Willette walks out, smiling and wearing a lemon yellow dress that hugs her slender body. Her blond hair is parted and pulled back behind her ears into a bun. She looks crisp and professional, although in my opinion yellow is a color better left to the darker sisters. Like red. It belongs to them.

We hug warmly. At her invitation I follow her into "Daddy's office." It has that same expensive, masculine decor. Willette obviously hasn't changed a thing, not even the picture on the credenza of her in a bathing suit with a banner reading MISS HOUSTON 1970 across her chest. Father Time has been kind—she hasn't changed a bit. And they say yellow women crack early.

I pick up the picture. The inscription reads, "To Daddy, with undying love, Willette." I tell her I never knew she was into beauty pageants. She sets it back in its place, just so. "Ever since I was a child. It was Daddy's idea. He thought it would give me poise." She smiles like she's giving away a secret. "It was our . . . hobby."

We chat about pageant life while Delzenia brings her a cup of tea and another glass of water for me. My encounter with Michael has left me thirsty for some reason. Willette's green eyes have a way of looking right through you as she talks, and I wonder if she has any idea about us. For reasons I don't comprehend, she's always tolerated his alley-cat ways ("Crawling the streets, sniffing for pussy," as Stacey would say). I wish I could be that cool, calm, and collected about men. I raised so much hell the one and only time Kwame stayed out late when we were married, he never made that mistake again. If Dirk even *looked* like he was going to do anything, he'd be grabbing hat.

Delzenia buzzes Willette to take a call. Willette excuses herself, ends the conversation quickly, smiling apologetically as she hangs up. "I honestly don't know how Daddy did it. Just being commissioner is about to drive me up the wall."

I can't imagine anything getting the best of Willette and tell her so. "That's sweet of you to say, Gwen. You always did think I was Superwoman."

"You are. We all are. We have to be. Liberation for us would be staying home and doing nothing. Nobody works harder than black women. Except maybe Hispanic women. With men like ours you have to."

She gives me a look. " 'Ours'?" I smile sheepishly, forgetting my husband's white. I think it's good I don't think of his color. The problem is that for the past twenty minutes I haven't been thinking of him at all. In the back of my mind I'm in bed with Michael. This is crazy.

Willette looks at me expectantly. ". . . I said, I want you to be my administrative assistant, Gwen."

"Assistant?" I'm caught completely off guard. I better watch that.

"Each commissioner is entitled to one. I can't ask C.C.

Michael thinks we spend too much time together as it is. Can you believe he's jealous of her?"

I shrug. "Men always try to separate you from your friends and family." I remember what Michael said about C.C. at my wedding. "It's a control thing."

She dismisses the possibility, returning to the subject at hand. "The salary's excellent." She names an amount that exceeds what I made in private practice last year by half. No more hustling for clients, passing out cards to niggers who think you're trying to hit on them, and when I'm done, a *real* judgeship. Now, this is how you repay somebody. ". . . You get lots of perks. The taxpayers are very generous when it comes to benefits. Excuse me—" Delzenia buzzes again. Willette tells her not to disturb us for the next five minutes. Which means she expects my answer right away. "So, what do you say?"

What do I say? "Hell, yes. Thanks, Willette—"

"Don't thank me yet. You don't know what you're in for."

"Nothing—I repeat—nothing is worse than private practice."

She laughs. "We'll make a great team," she says, escorting me to the elevator. We set a start date two weeks from now, all the time I need to close down my practice. She needs me like yesterday.

"I can give Eddy everything but my rape trial in front of Judge Filzer. It won't take more than a week to try."

"You want me to talk to Filzer?"

"You know her?" Willette's never set foot inside anybody's courtroom as far as I know.

"No, but she knows me. Daddy toted water for all the judges when he was in the legislature. They came to him for their raises, and he always delivered."

I decline anyway. "My client's counting on me. He's got a good case. I can go out with a bang."

Delzenia informs Willette the mayor's on line three. She gives me a quick hug and returns to her office. I board the elevator and wave good-bye to Delzenia, a big Kool-Aid smile on my face. After the door closes, I hoot and holler like a kid who just got his own candy factory. You never know what's going to happen in life, but it's all to the good.

Michael greets me with a grin and an enormous hard-on, completely naked when he opens the door.

"I can't do this—"

He takes me in his arms and kisses me until I'm dizzy, which is all I need. I'm crazy to respond like this, but my body isn't listening. Still kissing me, he works my clothes off and pulls me to the bed at the same time. I feel the edge of the bed behind my knees, tumble backward. Before I hit the mattress, Michael is inside me, moving, moaning about how much he's missed me and how he's going to tear it up. I clutch his back and hang on for dear life.

We spend the next hour and a half in bed. Michael gets his nut off. I roll over on my stomach, wanting to vomit up all the guilt I feel. He slaps my behind ("a love tap") and asks me to hand him his watch. I reach on the nightstand and give it to him, avoiding his eyes.

"Talk to me, baby." He forces my head around. I look at him. He's relaxed, pleasant even. He lights a joint, drags deep, passes it to me. I don't indulge normally, but charge up just to make Dirk's sad face go away. I hold the smoke as long as I can and exhale, coughing like I have T.B. Michael laughs. "So, what's it like being married to a white man?"

My head feels like it's encased in a bubble. I am blasted. "Black man, white man, *man* man," I hear myself say in a strange, unattached voice. "You're all canines." I imagine a pack of dogs with faces of the men I know—Dirk, Michael, Kwame—chasing me. I giggle uncontrollably.

Michael lies back, blows smoke into the air, listening to the music he's found on the clock radio. I look around. The apartment's tucked in the back of one of the look-the-same complexes that spring up along freeways like thistle. This one's in Fifth Ward. Good choice. Third Ward niggers don't go into Fifth Ward even to slum. I laugh. Whoever heard of previous slum dwellers slumming?

"Nice decor," I say sarcastically. "Early rent-to-own?"

He chuckles. "That's funny. I always did like your sense of humor, baby."

I reach for my panties, holding the sheet up to me. "I'm just a barrel of laughs."

"What do you think you're doing?"

I fasten my bra. "What does it look like?"

He unhooks my brassiere, pulls it away, and buries his head in my breasts, taking turns sucking each one. I slide into an ocean of desire.

"You like that, don't you, baby?"

"Yes, Kwame—"

Michael stops, looks at me. "What did you call me?"

I try to focus. "What *did* I call you?"

He looks mad about something. Well, he can just get glad. After all, I'm the blackmailee. He smiles cruelly, his eyes cold slits.

"You called me Kwame."

"You're crazy. My husband's name is Dirk." And I'm living out his worst nightmare: I'm in the arms of a black man. Funny, but I really don't think he'd care as much if Michael was white. I wonder if white women with black men live with the same fear—that they'll go back to black. I smile. "Dirk the Jerk. And you're Michael the—Ichael." I laugh, rolling over and doubling up. "Oh, no. I've got the sillies—"

Michael pulls me on top of him. "I can make you stop." He pushes me down his body. "Give me some head."

I check myself in the rearview mirror after I get in my car. I don't look like I've been with another man. As I merge with the Gulf Freeway traffic, I think about Michael's parting words. He expects me to meet him like this on a regular basis. That's why he urged Willette to hire me, so he and I can be seen together and nobody'll suspect.

Some idiot cuts in front of me. I hit the brakes, inches

from rear-ending him. That's my life right now, a series of near collisions. If I can just hang in there until I can get my judgeship, Michael can kiss my ass. If I could get on the federal bench, that would be even better. Of course, I have a snowball's chance in Houston for that. They practice voodoo politics for federal appointments. You have to be one of their sho-'nuff, absotively safe Negroes before they'll let you do something for *life*.

I did ask Michael what he had against C.C. before I left. "She's a back-stabbing, lowlife, skanky bitch."

"Oh," I said. "You tried to hit on her and she turned you down."

He got a real ugly look on his face. "I wouldn't touch that bulldagger on a bet." I dropped the subject. Black people get irrational on the subject of homosexuality. I remember when rumor had it at TSU that the three of us—me, C.C., and Willette—were lesbians. When somebody told me that shit, I was insulted. How could I be gay? I was married. They said Kwame had "a little sugar" in him too.

I forget about Michael as I park behind Dirk's Porsche. Glancing at myself in his car window, I imagine how cool we must look with a Porsche and a Jag in the driveway. As I approach the back door, I hear Dirk and Ashleigh Lee having a hell of a laugh. Progress. I open the door, hoping to catch the punch line. Freeze. They're in the middle of the kitchen, faced off like rival serial killers.

". . . I told you," she growls, "I didn't take your damn chain." Nostrils flaring, she's every bit her father's child.

I slice between them, facing Dirk. "What is going on?" He's flushed with anger.

"He said I took his stupid ass chain."

I turn to Ashleigh Lee. "You watch your mouth." My mother always said profanity was the effort of a feeble mind trying to express itself forcefully. I agree. Except that it's better than knocking the shit out of somebody every time you get mad, which is what Ashleigh Lee looks like she wants to do. I turn back to Dirk. "What's she talking about?"

His blue eyes level with me. "My gold chain with the eagle is missing."

"The one your mother gave you?"

He nods. "I just asked her if she'd seen it. She got hysterical."

Tears stream down Ashleigh Lee's face. "He said I stole it!"

"That's not true, Ashleigh Lee, and you know it—"

I raise my hands like a referee. I feel more like the punching bag. "*All right*. Ashleigh Lee, go to your room. I want to talk to Dirk."

She slashes her eyes at him. "I know you're going to believe him. You always do."

When she's gone, I turn on Dirk like he stole something. "What do you mean accusing my child? If she said she didn't take it, she didn't take it."

Dirk looks at me like I've said I could fly. "If she didn't, who did?"

"You lost it."

"I distinctly remember putting it in the case the last time I wore it. Last week, to the bar association golf tournament."

"So why does that mean my daughter took it?"

"Because—" He starts to say something, hesitates, says it anyway. "I think she's into drugs."

"How dare you?"

"Open your eyes, Gwen." He tries to take me by the shoulders, but I twist away. I don't want his white hands on me. "You're killing Ashleigh Lee with your love."

"Oh, so you've lived here exactly four months, and now you're an expert on me and Ashleigh Lee. You think you know everything. Just like every other know-it-all white boy on the planet. Only you don't know shit about doo-doo."

So much for my good news.

10

"**O**bjection," I say, jumping up with the last syllable. "Counsel's leading the witness."

Judge Filzer pushes her glasses up her beak nose. "Overruled."

Goddammit, this is the fifth time this bitch has let the assistant D.A. get away with putting words in the complaining witness' mouth. I roll my eyes to let the jury know the judge is full of shit. The well-dressed brother in the front row nods sympathetically. He doesn't fool me. He'll be the first one back in the jury room to vote against my client, just to show the white folks he doesn't favor blacks.

The complainant finishes her sad tale of woe while I doodle on a legal pad, looking disinterested for the jury. I know her story inside and out. She's a young white girl with stringy brown hair and a terrible lisp, pure "p.w.t." My black client, Jimmy Sadler, made the mistake of hitting on her outside of Billy Bob's, a neighborhood icehouse in the Heights. Poetic justice gave him the clap and a rape charge.

This is my last case before I start working for Willette. Filzer appointed me. Jimmy's a two-time loser—robbery and theft—so we had to go to trial. I want to get it over with, but I ain't rolling over and playing dead. My client may be a thief, but he's no rapist.

For the record, the white girl, Patricia Boudreaux, points out Jimmy on cue from the D.A. "Yeth-thir, that'th him over there, thitting next to the colored woman."

My mouth twists on reflex. I've been "she," "that woman,"

"little lady," and even "honey," and I keep right on step-pin'. But "colored" drives me up the wall. It's almost the goddamn twenty-first century. My man on the jury snorts indignantly too.

The assistant D.A., an arrogant silver-spoon asshole, obviously graduated from one of the white law schools, turns to me like I'm something on six legs. "Pass the witness."

I look at the judge. She nods, giving me permission to cross-examine. I approach the complainant. She plays it for all she's worth, sort of shrinking down in the chair, like I'm going to jump on her. White women kill me. They're always playing Scarlett and making us Beulah. Even the trash.

"Miss Boudreaux, my name is Gwenlyn Parrish. As you know, I represent the man you just pointed out at counsel table as allegedly raping you. Do you understand?"

"Yeth, ma'am."

"I want to ask you about what happened before you were allegedly raped, if you don't mind."

She sits up, jutting out her weak little chin, her dignity wounded. "Wasn't no *alleged* rape, ma'am. He raped me, sho' 'nuff."

I haven't heard a white woman this ignorant in a long time. I have a hunch. "Ms. Boudreaux, where are you from originally?"

"Where wath I born?"

"Yes, where were you born?"

"Pottsville, Lou'siana."

"Are there any black—colored people in Pottsville?"

She smiles shyly. "Mostly colored. 'Thept for the white folks out in the county."

"So you grew up with colored people, is that correct?"

"Oh, yeah. Alla my friends was colored. We wath the only whites in the neighborhood."

I study the jury as I ask the next question. "How long have you lived in Houston?"

Her face screws up as she thinks. " 'Bout eight-ten months, I reckon."

"Did you move here directly from Pottsville?"

"Yeth, ma'am."

I smile. "You homesick?"

She relaxes. "Truly. I mith my people so much I could cry sometimes, ma'am."

"By 'people' do you just mean your immediate family?" She doesn't understand. "Your mother, father. Or are you including everyone you grew up with?"

She smiles happily. "Oh, ev'rybody. I mith ev'rybody."

"Were you homesick when you went to Billy Bob's that night, the night you say you were raped?"

"I *was* raped."

"But you were lonely that night, weren't you?"

She turns sullen. "Ain't no crime being lonely."

"If it were, Ms. Boudreaux, the jails would be overflowing."

The D.A. jumps up, the first opening I've given him. "Objection to counsel's sidebar comments, Your Honor."

Judge Filzer sustains him. I apologize, zero back in on the complainant. "You were lonely and you were looking for company at Billy Bob's, right? Somebody to talk to."

Her watery blue eyes dart around the court, even lighting on my client. "I th'pose tho."

"That's when you met Mr. Sadler."

She gets defensive. "He talked to me first. I wasn't payin' him no 'tention."

I can't resist it. "You weren't studdin' him, were you?"

She takes the bait. "Wasn't studdin' him a'tall. He was kinda like givin' me the eye, tho's I kinda smiled at him. Next thing I know he was thittin' up under me."

"You talked."

"Yeah, we talked for a while."

"What did you talk about?"

The D.A. twists in his chair, deliberately making noise, trying to break the jury's rapt attention to her. It doesn't work. They're following her every word. "Loneliness, mostly. Stuff like that."

"Jimmy told you he was lonely?"

"Yeth, ma'am. He's from a little-bitty town like me. Thaid he hadn't lived here that long neither."

"How long did you all talk?"

"Hour, maybe more."

"Is that when you left with him?"

She squirms around in her seat, like her behind itches. "He said he had his own place not too far. Said we could walk to it."

"Jimmy doesn't have a car, isn't that so?"

"He didn't have none that night."

"How far was his place?"

"Two-three blocks, maybe." She looks at the D.A., remembering his instructions too late. "I 'on't recall."

"How long did it take to get there?"

" 'Bout ten minutes, I s'pose."

The D.A. stands up. "Your Honor, I've been pretty lenient, but I don't see where any of this is going."

I look at the jury. As long as they "see," I could care less. They see. "Is that an objection?"

My question throws him off. White people never expect you to question *them*. He looks at me in a new light. I call it "the monkey can talk" look, which is how they look at you when they realize you're not stupid. I turn to the bench. "If the court please, I have a reason for pursuing this line of questioning."

"It does not please the court one bit," Filzer says, scowling over her glasses at me. "I've warned you repeatedly not to take up precious court time with your endless questions. Get to the point."

Of all the reasons I want out of private practice, this is the biggest one. The judges are so goddamn racist and unfair you can't win. Filzer's been on my back *ab initio* to "move it along." As if justice has a time limit. "Your Honor, I have a right to thoroughly examine this witness. This is a serious crime. If my client is convicted—"

"I don't need you to tell this court what your rights are, Ms. Parrish. Move it along." Her bird eyes run me up and

down. It occurs to me what her problem is: she hates me.
I'm standing here in my designer dress and three-hundred-
dollar shoes, defying every stereotype she wants to have of
black people.

"For the record, I object." My eyes lock with hers. "I'm
pursuing a legitimate line of questioning."

"Objection noted. Now, move it along before I hold you
in contempt."

I've been threatened with contempt before. Few black attorneys walking the halls of the Criminal Courts Building
haven't, if they're worth their salt. I purposefully cut my
eyes to the witness, deliberately pursue my previous line of
questioning. "What did you and Jimmy talk about on the
way to his apartment, Miss Boudreaux—"

The D.A.'s on his feet. "Your Honor, I object." He looks
pointedly at me. "Irrelevant and immaterial."

Filzer slams down her pen. "That's it, Ms. Parrish. You're
in contempt of court."

My soon-to-be ex-law partner Eddy just shakes his head
when I walk out of the hold, where I've spent the last four
hours reading the graffiti in the dimly lit eight-by-ten-foot
cell. There are 6,423 dots in the acoustic ceiling. I knew
how many cinder blocks made up the walls, but I lost count
as soon as the bailiff appeared at the door to release me.

I sniff my jacket sleeve. "Damn, it sure doesn't take long
to get funky in the hold. Don't get too close."

Eddy escorts me out. "Don't worry. I don't even want to
know you. I got a case in front of Filzer next month."

"Just remember to 'move it along.' "

I get a standing ovation when I walk into our monthly
BFLA meeting, which embarrasses me. I was being fool-
hardy and irresponsible provoking Filzer like that. Though
it didn't turn out all bad. The D.A. came to his senses and
offered my client misdemeanor assault, which Jimmy
jumped at. It's funny how you can lose the battle and win
the war.

"It wasn't 'bout nothin', y'all." I want to get on to something else. Rendine Carlisle, a heavy-set woman with nut brown skin and thick glasses, disagrees. "It's about time we showed these judges we can't be pushed around. Otherwise, what do you need black lawyers for?" She's a solo practitioner specializing in employment-discrimination cases, always in the paper for raising hell over in the federal courts. Frankly, I never could figure out how you make money off people who've lost their jobs, but she seems to be doing fine, judging by the nugget-size diamonds in her ears and the expensive wool suit she's packed into. Not that you can tell by appearances alone. Blacks are some of the best-dressed poor people I know.

While Rendine regales us with an account of her latest escapade before a fifth-generation racist federal judge, C.C. leans over to me and says for my ears only, "Your boy resigned."

"Who?"

"Brad Yarrow."

"What?" Everybody looks at me. I apologize and urge Rendine to keep talking, which she's only happy to do, a windbag like every other lawyer I know. "I'll be right back, y'all." I pull C.C. up and drag her into Groovey's empty dining room.

"Resigned? When?"

C.C. folds her arms across her flat chest with satisfaction; she knows this is juicy. "Effective this afternoon. Said he's going back to private practice." I lean on a table, my mind whirling with possibilities. "They want to get a new boy in before the general election. Give him the incumbent advantage."

The moment for which I've been praying for the last five years, namely that a bolt of lightning, a hurricane, a plague of locusts, an act of God, would descend on Yarrow and take him out. I honestly try not to hate white people, but I can't stand the Nazi son of a bitch. He ran me out of the D.A.'s office to make an example out of me, and I've never forgotten it. Setting my own example, I've never forgiven him.

C.C. smiles. "Thought you'd enjoy knowing he's biting the dust."

"Not a moment too soon." I was busy erecting my stepping-stone to a district-court judgeship when Brad got in my shit. He didn't like my "attitude," the usual reason we get fired. Which means we're either not grateful enough, simpering enough, or unquestioning enough. Because what goes around comes around, it's getting so everybody has to display the same characteristics to keep their jobs. More so for us because somebody did us a favor hiring us in the first place. To make matters worse, I was one of those "smart ones," a cardinal sin in the South. They like their niggers stupid down here.

"Where's he going?" Not that I care. White boys rarely go solo. They don't have to.

"Hansen and Jarrard." Big-time downtown firm.

"Figures. They hot-wire themselves all the way up and down the system." I notice dark circles under C.C.'s eyes. "You look tired."

"Child, I am. This judge shit ain't all it's cracked up to be."

"Tell me about it." I relate my latest muni-court adventure: I had to pull a gun—I followed the clerk's advice and got one, never thinking I'd have to use it—on a Hispanic defendant who jumped over the bench to get me after I gave him thirty days for beating the shit out of his common-law wife.

"Where was your bailiff?"

"In shock, like everybody else. My man backed up and did the James Brown when I told him I'd shoot his *cojones* off." She laughs, I'm ready to resign.

"Why not? Willette'll have you so busy you won't know whether you're coming or going anyway."

"I can't wait." It's either feast or famine in private practice. I'm ready for a steady diet of dead greens.

*   *   *

Dirk is watching the late news when I get home. Ashleigh Lee's gone to bed. Thank God all's quiet on the home front. He apologized to her for accusing her of taking his chain, which she graciously (for her) accepted. They've been pretty cool ever since.

"She wanted pizza for dinner," he says. "I wanted hamburgers. We compromised on a bucket of chicken. Leftovers are in the oven if you're hungry." I grab a drumstick, gnawing hungrily.

"Didn't you eat today?"

"Unh-uh." No point telling him I spent lunchtime in the pokey. He'd think I'm developing a social conscience, a rarity in the black legal profession as far as he's concerned. He thinks we're all just out for ourselves. I say we have the right to be just like white lawyers, no better, no worse. He sounds just like Kwame talking that smack. Dirk can afford to be Don Quixote, he's got a trust fund. I toss the bone and reach for a wing.

"You need to take better care of yourself."

"That's what I've got you for." I polish off the drumette, wipe my mouth, peck him on the cheek. He snaps off the set and follows me upstairs. I undress while he finishes watching the news.

"Guess what?" I say.

"What?"

"Yarrow resigned."

"Good. Maybe you can get back in now."

I look at him. "I don't believe you said that. The only way I'd go back in the D.A.'s office is if I *was* the D.A." I ball up my panty hose, shoot them into the hamper, take my two points. "Right after the second coming of Christ."

I feel Dirk's eyes on me as I move around the room. God, I hope he doesn't want any tonight. I am not in the mood.

"Why not? You'd make a great D.A."

I yank my gown over my head and stare at him. He must be trying to mess with my mind. All men do that. This must be the white boy version. "There's no way in hell they're going to let me—or any nigger, for that matter—be district attorney."

His lips pinch together into a line. "I wish you wouldn't use that word."

"No—don't *you* use that word." I smile to break the tension suddenly walling us off from each other. "Unless we get in an argument and you call me a nigger bitch, in which case you'll be pushing up daisies."

"For calling you a nigger?"

"For calling me a bitch." We laugh. I slide under the covers and cut my light, fading as soon as my head hits the pillow.

"Why can't you be D.A.? It's a free country."

He's being so ridiculous I don't even bother to open my eyes. "You know, for a rich white man you are totally naive when it comes to how the real world works. Probably because you didn't have to dirty your hands making all that money. They don't let just any white boy be sheriff of Nottingham; you think they're gonna let a woman, let alone a black one? The D.A.'s the chief law enforcer for Harris County, the man with the goods on everybody. Hoover. You know what he did to people and their nuts."

"How will anything ever change if you don't try?"

I cut my eyes at him, turn my head, and sock my pillow. White people always want us to be the shock troops for change. Only after the big change comes, we're still at the end of the line. Like I was after I "changed" the racial and gender makeup of the D.A.'s office. I'd interned there my last year in law school, the only black and female law student in the program. I knew immediately I wanted to work there after graduation, a natural progression for interns. I had outstanding evaluations; everybody got offered a job but me. I filed a discrimination complaint when my supervisor told me Yarrow wouldn't hire me because women didn't make good prosecutors. "They cry." He never forgot he was forced to hire me. It took him five years, but he got me out. "Forget it."

He jumps up, stomps around to my side, turns the light on in my face. "You know what? You're a coward, just like the rest of your brothers and sisters in the law. You're safely ensconced in the Big House, so you don't care what happens to anyone else."

This is one of those moments in a marriage when your reaction determines in a split second whether there's going to be war or peace. My stint in Filzer's holding cell has taken the starch out of me. "That's right. Every man for himself and God save us all." I cover my head to block out the light.

He yanks the blanket off me. "It's not right. I see it every day—cases black attorneys should be trying and don't. Issues black lawyers should be raising but won't. People who need help who get referred to us by as many black attorneys as white ones."

I hop out of the bed now, assuming the black woman's fighting stance: back swayed, fists balled at hips, neck jutting like a chicken. "Wait just a goddamn minute. It's easy for you to talk shit about what black lawyers should be doing. You *have* money. Your people have all the law firms, which you make sure stay white. You get corporate clients and humongous retainers. You get the judgeships, the clerkships, and all the government jobs. You practice law in the twenty-first century, and we're dinosaurs. Nobody got my degree for me but me. *I* worked my ass off for three goddamn years, and *I* sweated the bar exam. I don't owe anybody anything."

He shakes his head. "You're wrong, honey."

"No, you're white."

His mouth turns into that straight line again. I yank back the covers and get back in bed. I don't care. He could walk out of Legal Services tomorrow morning into some big firm on the fiftieth floor of Shell Plaza tomorrow afternoon if he wanted to. I get to work for Willette.

He sighs like the world's on his shoulders, gets in on his side of the bed, and turns his light off. I lie in the dark, eyes wide open, too pissed to sleep. I toss and turn a few times, then get up and walk out into the hall, automatically glancing at Ashleigh Lee's door. Her nightlight's shining underneath. I peek inside to make sure she's okay. She's curled up in her bed, one side of her thick hair shooting straight up. She asked the beautician one time how she could get her hair to stand up the way a lot of white girls wear theirs. Sheila told her to just go to sleep.

My mouth sours with resentment. She should have my hair. I still remember the disappointment I felt when her straight black hair began to knot up shortly after she was born. I did everything to keep those zingboppers out. That's what my mother calls hair like hers, so tight that when you pull it and let go, it goes "zing—bop." I shake my head thinking about all the battles I had with Ashleigh Lee's hair, which I knew nothing about handling. As soon as I could, I turned her hair care over to Sheila, which Kwame wholeheartedly disapproved of. "You're her mother. The least you should be able to do is comb her hair." He said I was going to give her a complex. I told him to comb it, then. That shut him up.

I pull the door closed and go downstairs. It's not often I can't sleep, but when it happens I know enough not to force it. I flick on the TV and settle on the couch. An old blackand-white movie is on, which I just half watch, my mind wandering to what Dirk said. I'm not a coward. It took a lot of courage to be the first black female prosecutor in Harris County. White people didn't trust me; most blacks resented me. I had to devise a ready response when they asked me how I could work for "the Man." "You better be glad I'm there. I can't vouch for these white people, but I know I can be fair." They hadn't thought about it that way.

Kwame still considers me a traitor, which hurt at the time. A lot. We'd just split up by the time I finally got the job. He just knew I couldn't make it without him, always accusing me of trying to be the man in our relationship. Taking a job he despised confirmed it for him.

I snap off the TV and sit up, my mind made up. I'm going to be the first black district attorney in Texas. In the country even. Like Dirk said, nothing beats a failure but a try.

11

Pat buzzes me. "Your ten-thirty appointment's here." I'm not taking any new cases, but I am still doing consultations. At sixty bucks a pop, I can't afford not to. A lot of black lawyers I know don't even charge for them. That's giving away your time and your knowledge—a lawyer's only real commodities. That's insane. But then, we tend to run our law practices like all our other businesses: into the ground: out of ignorance.

I check my calendar and see where Pat's penciled in Freenie Walker. What's a Freenie Walker? Male? Female? I always like to know beforehand. I've learned to be outgoing and friendly over the years, but I'm rarely at ease with strangers. Plus, if it's a woman, I constantly compare myself to see where I'm deficient. I can't help it. I walk out to our small reception area, looking at Pat. She nods at a man sitting on the sofa. He's staring at the ceiling.

"Mr. Walker, I'm Attorney Parrish." I extend my hand.

He stands up, head still tilted backward, looking up. Speaks with a great deal of effort, like someone's holding his vocal cords. "Nice to meet you, ma'am."

"What can I help you with, Mr. Walker?"

I direct him to one of my side chairs. I've met a lot of weird people in the practice of law, but I have the feeling Mr. Walker's about to take the cake. His head appears to be permanently stuck looking up. He looks around while I wonder how he eats or drinks. My walls are bare except for my license, prominently displayed behind me. Three narrow windows near the ceiling let me know whether it's day or night. He turns his head sideways at me, spittle collecting in the corner of his mouth as he speaks. "I want you to stop my wife from having me put away."

I guess Freenie to be in his fifties, with close-cropped hair and dusty brown, deeply creased skin. Aside from the fact that he's inexplicably staring at the ceiling, he looks pretty sane to me. If he's telling the truth, his wife must be a real bitch.

"Why would she want to do that?"

"I don't know. She keeps telling the doctors I'm crazy, and every two or three months she has me committed. They say I'm okay and they let me out. I'm sick of the shit— excuse my French."

I excuse him under the circumstances and encourage him to continue. "She knows it ain't a damn thing wrong with me. She's just trying to get me locked up and outta the way."

After years in practice I've learned to cut to the heart of the matter. "Why does she think you're crazy, Mr. Walker?"

He leans his head to the other side so his other eye can see me. He reminds me of a fish. " 'Cause I can't lower my head."

"I see. Is your condition a result of an accident, or is it congenital?"

"No, ma'am."

"Well, then, what is the nature of your illness, Mr. Walker?"

"I'm not sick, ma'am."

"Then why can't you lower your head?"

Fish eyes regard me. "Attorney Parrish, one day I looked up and saw Jesus, just sittin' up there in the clouds. He smiled and kinda waved his hand over me. I been like this ever since."

"I see. And just when did this incident take place, Mr. Walker?"

" 'Bout twelve years ago."

"And when was the first time your wife had you commit-ted?" He says about two years ago, which means she let this fool get away with this shit for ten years. I was wrong. She's a saint.

"I been to all kinds of doctors. They done run all kinds of tesses to give me." He shakes his head, which is really weird looking up. "They can't find nothin'. Say it's hysterical paralysis."

"I see." I thought I could listen to anybody for sixty dollars, but now I'm having my doubts. "I assume you're not working, Mr. Walker."

"No, ma'am. I can't."

"You've been unemployed since your, uh, illness?"

"Vision. Vision of the Lord."

"Right. But you haven't worked for the past twelve years, is that correct?"

"Yes, ma'am."

"What did you do before you, uh—"

"Seen the Lord? I was an electrician. Damn good one too, if I say so myself. Can't do nothing now, though. Not since the Lord revealed Himself to me in all his glory."

I should know better, but I can't resist asking, "What does the Lord look like, Mr. Walker?"

His eyes look rapturously at the ceiling, hands gripping my chair. I hope he doesn't rip the arms off. "He's Beauty and Light and Truth, ma'am. Too powerful to behold."

"But is he white or black or what?"

My question takes him by complete surprise. He drops his head, looks me straight in the eye, which surprises me too. I press my knee against the button under my desk that will bring Pat. She knocks and enters.

"Excuse me, Attorney Parrish," she says, puzzled at Mr. Walker's unstuck head. "Judge Hendrix wants to talk to you. Immediately."

"Thank you, Pat." I walk to the door, playing along. "I'm sorry, Mr. Walker. You'll have to excuse me. It's an emergency."

He doesn't move, just stares at the floor. "It's a miracle." Slowly he rises, looks at me. "It's a miracle, Attorney Parrish."

"Yes, Mr. Walker, I do believe it is a miracle." I guide him to the door. Pat reminds him about the consultation fee. I wave furiously at her behind my back. Forget the sixty dollars. I just want him out of here. "Good-bye, Mr. Walker." I give him a little push. "And good luck."

I lean against the door just in case he has any ideas of returning. "We need a red light to go on automatically when the crazies come in. Thanks for helping me out."

"You're welcome," she says. "By the way, Judge Hendrix does want to talk to you."

I see the com-line blinking. "Why didn't you say so?" I hurry back to my office to take the call. C.C. must've heard about my decision to run for D.A. I didn't get a chance to run it by her or Willette, who I'm pretty sure will back me, though she's out of town. C.C.'s been tied up trying a big-time murder case. I tear the phone off the hook. "C.C., what's up?"

"You, fool," she says. "Meet me at Glatzmaier's, twelve-thirty." Glatzmaier's is a longtime down-home restaurant downtown where Houston's movers and shakers hang out for lunch.

My office is located on Main in a small building in Midtown north of Elgin. It's convenient to downtown without the hassle of downtown's expensive parking for my clients and expensive rent for me. This side of Main Street is still pretty decent. Going south from Elgin isn't again until you get to Hermann Park and the Medical Center, where it's very attractive. Funny how many faces a street can wear on its way through a city.

Downtown Houston is shabby for the same reasons downtown anywhere is: white shoppers abandoned it. Unlike other big cities whose downtowns are on black and brown life support, though, white people who still need or want to come to downtown here can do so with minimum fear, as long as they stay underground. Because of Houston's tentacle-like tunnel system, you can go all over downtown—

shop, eat, take care of your business—and never see daylight.
Same with going from the Criminal Courts Building to the
Family Law Center to the Civil Courts Building, the only time
you actually feel like you're in a horizontal hole in the ground.
If you enter at Pennzoil Plaza or One Allen Center, it's like
being in one long, winding mall with no black masses to
scare you or offend your sensibilities.

I emerge from the tunnel to the Civil Courts Building to
file the only kind of divorce I handle—no kids, no property.
It's all paper except for one appearance before the judge.
My client could've actually done this herself, which I suggested to save her money, but she didn't want to have a fool
for a client. I can't turn down easy money. The rest of what
I make is too hard to come by. Besides, I'm meeting C.C.
when I leave here.

Per usual, the clerk's office is packed, mainly with law
clerks and paralegals or attorneys like me who can't afford
either or are too cheap or too stupid to, all swarming like
ants. I take number ninety-seven. They're on seventy-eight,
and I consider myself lucky. All I need are certified copies.
People mill about like ants. I lean on the wall by the microfiche and people-watch to pass the time.

You can tell the lawyers. They're "important." Lay people
are dead giveaways, hesitant and uncertain; they approach
the counter like it's a high-voltage wire. A lot of the clerks are
black, nonchalant and typically bureaucratic. All the good-
natured banter between them slows the service. I cringe
whenever the black woman at the first booth calls out a number. She must be the prototype for the stereotype of us: big
lips, big butt, big titties, big flat feet. Beulah. "Eighdy-tree.
Numba eighdy-tree." She sounds so ignorant, I'm wondering
how she got hired. She must really have the right "attitude."

"Umphumphumph."

I look to my right. Barry Caswell looks me up and down
like I'm lip-smacking good. "All this and a lawyer too."

Barry's middle-aged, fat, and bald. It's no compliment
when an old man hits on you. "Barry, how's it going?"

"How else?" He checks his number against the one being displayed. "The private practice of law is a bitch."

"Tell me about it."

"Hear you're putting in for D.A." Leave it to the black dispatch. They say there're three ways to spread information: telegraph, telephone, and tell a woman. Add tell a nigger.

"I'm thinking about it."

"Thought you were handling Willette Shalandar's legal business?" The way his black eyes shine at me behind wire-rimmed glasses, I know he's digging.

"I am." Black people will make up what they don't know about your business, so you might as well 'fess up when you can so your version'll be out there with the lies.

"Ninedy-too. Numba ninedy-too."

I cringe. "She sounds as ignorant as she looks."

"White folks *like* us like that," he says. "Gives 'em something to feel good about themselves." I tuck his observation in the back of my mind to run by Dirk some time. Comes in handy having your own resident white man to explain their behavior.

"So how's your girl?" Henry winks like I automatically know who he's talking about.

"Who?"

"The judge." He leers at me again. "I hear she likes it on the wild side."

"What are you talking about, Barry?" I hope I don't sound as annoyed as I feel. Gossiping men are worse than gossiping women. There's no shortage of either among black attorneys.

He makes sure no one's listening. "They say she was partying with Mac Florty last weekend." My stomach flutters ominously. Mac Florty gives some of the wildest parties in town. Orgies, actually. I can't believe C.C. would be caught dead or alive at one of them and tell him so.

He snorts to the contrary. "Guess you don't know your girl like you thought. Check this out: they say one of Mac's girls got too full of juice and passed out in his bed. Next thing she knows, she wakes up and your girl's chewing on her."

I make my face register every ounce of disgust I feel for such sheer fabrication. "You men are something else."

He thinks I'm complimenting him. "What you mean, baby?"

"I'm not your baby, Barry. I'm not an object or a child. I'm a grown-up human being. I have a name, try using it."

His hands pop up like this is a stick-up. "Whoa, baby— I mean, Gwen, I'm just telling you what I heard. Check it out. This ain't the first time your girl's gone south of the border."

I take a step toward him, and he backs up. "That's defamation of character, Henry. I don't have to tell *you* that."

"Truth's an absolute defense, baby."

"Ninedy-seh'um. Numba ninedy-seh'um."

"Here," I say. I purposely look Barry up and down like the scumdog he is and turn on my heel. I catch him staring at my behind as I walk to the counter. Men. As I wait for my copies, I try to figure it out: why in the world would C.C. be at Mac Florty's? Everybody knows he's a player. The word sounds so quaint. In the old days, as my daughter calls my childhood ("Did they have cars when you were growing up?"), a player was one step removed from a pimp though just as glamorous—they both had the money, the big fine cars, the baddest clothes. Like the pimps, they were to be avoided like syphilis. Otherwise, you could get "turned out." Whatever that meant, it was a fate worse than death. The pimp turned you out for profit. The player, for his pleasure.

Mac Florty. I shake my head. I suppose some women would say he's handsome, in a down South kind of way: big, barrel chest, flamboyant dresser, gold star capping his front tooth. The kind of lawyer who'll forge the client's *and* doctor's signatures. He has one of the biggest personal-injuries practices in town.

"Beulah" slides my papers to me and calls the next number. As I turn away from the counter, Barry smiles smugly, still waiting by the microfiche. Unfortunately, I have to pass him on my way out.

"Check it out," he says confidently about C.C.

I don't reply. Otherwise, I'd tell him to crawl back under his rock.

Glatzmaier's is an institution, which is why they can still get away with sawdust on the floor and steam tables. It's always noisy and crowded, mainly with influential white people who haven't forgotten their "roots." Several lawyers and judges greet me while I wait for C.C. I'm not exactly basking under the recognition, but it does make me feel good that so many important people know who I am. I've done my share of ass-kissing, and of course, it doesn't hurt that I'm president of BFLA. Come election time, a lot of these white boys'll be looking for black votes and'll have to "koom-bah-yah," as my law partner Eddy would say.

Old Judge Sowell enters with another white man who looks vaguely familiar to me. Sowell greets me warmly, taking my hands in his, soft gray eyes smiling down at me. He reminds you of that handsome old guy on *Dynasty,* only Sowell's better-looking.

"Gwenlyn, you look as lovely as ever. Do you know Harry Chase?"

That's who he is. Chase just settled a twenty-five-million-dollar p.i. His client was black. They always take the big cases to the white boys and hire you to look over their shoulders. I shake his hand, clammy as his eyes are cold. I am of no significance to him. I remember the first time someone white looked at me like that. A girl I went to junior high with. We were inseparable in school. Then one day I ran into her downtown. Happy to see her, I greeted her as I would in school. She looked right through me and walked right past me. Next day at school she acted as if nothing'd happened, like we were as tight as ever. I've never forgotten how it feels to be rendered invisible. I want to strike back.

"Judge Sowell, I'm thinking of running for district attorney. What do you think?"

That gets Chase's attention, all right. Suddenly I exist. Genuinely startled, Judge Sowell recovers magnificently. "Gwenlyn, don't you think you should cut your teeth on something a little less—shall we say—daunting? District attorney is one of the highest elective offices in the county, you know."

In other words, nigger, you're getting out of your place. Bitter resentment drips into my stomach. "I have five years' experience in the D.A.'s office. Plus another five years as a criminal defense attorney. Brad Yarrow never even tried a case before he became D.A."

Sowell glances at Chase. I'm not supposed to know that much about white folks' business. "Have you discussed this with Willette Shalandar?"

"As a matter of fact, I work for her."

C.C. walks up. "Judge Sowell," she says, smiling brightly. "Hello, Harry. Sorry I'm late, Gwen." She links her arm in mine, exchanges pleasantries with them.

"Gwenlyn tells me she's considering the D.A. slot, C.C.," says Sowell. "You need to talk some sense into her."

C.C. laughs merrily, hugs me to her. "Don't worry, Judge. She has plenty of sense. Don't you, Gwenlyn?"

We go our separate way from Sowell and Chase, stopping to chat with people we know before we finally make it to our table, in the back by the kitchen door. I start to protest. We always get the worst tables, as if we should just be glad we get to come in the first place.

"Be cool." C.C. slides onto her chair and studies the menu. "Everybody's watching." She smiles extra bright at the waiter serving our drinks. "What you having, girl? Everything looks so good," she says loud enough to be heard, grinning bigger than Lionel Hampton entertaining white folks. I hate it when she does her "happy nigger" routine. We all have to cheese up so whatever white folks we're dealing with know we're harmless. C.C. gets ridiculous with it. It makes me lose my appetite. I tell the waiter I just want a salad. When we return with our food, I have a plate of lettuce, C.C.'s loaded down with fried catfish, shrimp and oysters, a baked potato cascading with butter and sour cream, and a plateful of cornbread. She closes her eyes, savoring each bite.

"Umm, this is good. Want some?"

I decline. I've gained ten pounds since we graduated from TSU. Willette looks exactly the same. C.C.'s put on at least forty, probably why she's still single. "I ran into Barry Caswell at the clerk's office," I say, ready to gauge her response. "Why is it that men can have bellies hanging over so far they have to prop them up, but we have to be slim and trim?"

"I heard that," she says, slathering another piece of cornbread with an inch of butter. "I can't stand tubba-wubbas myself. I don't care what kind of degree they have or how much money they make, fat ain't where it's at."

I think about what Barry said, wondering if I should ask her about it. "I know one thing," I say. "If there is such a thing as reincarnation and I have a choice, I'm sure not coming back as a bitch. I want to have all the fun next time around."

She belly laughs, slapping the table and carrying on. It wasn't *that* funny. I check my watch: it's going on one-thirty. She's going to have to be getting back on the bench soon, which means if she ever stops feeding her face, she'll be getting to the point of this meeting. To my surprise, she orders another round of drinks. I decide to ask her straight up about Mac Florty. "I hear you're partying on the wild side now."

"Yeah?" She polishes off the last of the shrimp, sandwiching it between two oysters, popping the whole thing in her mouth.

"Grapevine has you getting down with Mac Florty."

"Yeah." She smiles sheepishly. "That was dumb." Then

her lips poke out like platters, pouting like a kid snitching cookies. "I'm supposed to have some fun."

"With that lowlife, jack-leg creep of a lawyer?"

She shrugs. "Thanks for letting me know my business is in the streets." She lifts her glass to me. "One good turn deserves another: they sent me to tell you you can't have the D.A. Get it out your mind, girl."

Dirk badgers me all the while we're washing the dinner dishes until I give him the real reason I've changed my mind about the D.A. spot.

"The downtown boys said Harris County isn't ready for a black female district attorney, okay? It's that simple." Until the oil boom in the seventies, Houston was ruled by seven white men. Prosperity forced them to "democratize," that is, the septumvirate—my word—expanded to include representatives of the "nouveau whites," who wanted in on the action. I would've been a long shot even with their blessing, but if the white vote had splintered and I got all the black and brown votes and a few white ones, I could've forced a runoff and cut the necessary deals to win.

"You're just going to accept it? You're not even going to try?" The look in Dirk's eyes is hard to take, like somebody thinking you're made of gold and you're nickel underneath. "Damn it, Gwen, how can you just knuckle under like this?"

"Because I'm not knuckling under. I'm playing by the rules—which I did not make."

"You're not doing anything to change them either."

I slap the dish towel on the counter and stomp into the family room. Ashleigh Lee takes one look at me and gets up to leave. She knows the fight signs by now. Bumps into Dirk. He has to remind her to excuse herself, which she does with a smirk. As soon as she's out of earshot, he starts in on me. "Gwen, I think you should reconsider—"

I cut him off at the pass. "Don't say another word to me about it, Dirk. I'm sick of your white-liberal-goddamn-goody-two-shoes-holier-than-thou missionary ass. It's easy for you to tell me what I should be doing when you're white and you will always be white."

"What's that supposed to mean?"

"What I said. You could leave tomorrow, fade back into your white world, and brag to your buddies about all the black pussy you've had, they'll call you a real man—"

His hand slams the side of my face, throwing my head sideways. My ears ring. The imprint of his hand stings my cheek. My feelings turn blood cold. Dirk's eyes turn panicky, as if he just realized what's happened.

"My God. Gwen—I—forgive me, honey."

He reaches for me. I signal him like a traffic cop not to touch me, massage my face. "Kiss a monkey's ass, Dirk."

"I'm sorry—"

"I don't want to hear it. And believe me when I say that I now know from firsthand experience that any time a man can't stand to hear the truth from a woman, the first thing he does—regardless of his race—is to hit her."

BOOK 2

—∞∞∞—

Boston No Trump

12

I've been so caught up in my own life, I've forgotten there's a world out there where things are happening too. Events have a way of slapping you back to reality, though. Especially when it comes to politics. I've been working for Willette exactly two days, and I'm exhausted. As her administrative assistant I'm expected to be everywhere she is and isn't, ready with all the answers. Like the lone wolf, she covers a lot of territory.

She gave me the office directly across from hers, and it's substantially larger than the one I had in my practice. The walls are soft, steely blue, and silver mini blinds shade the large picture window. It's certainly nice having a window you can see something out of other than the sky. She let me pick out my own furniture, which I make contemporary and distinctly feminine. The only thing I brought from my old office is my law license, which I haven't even had time to hang up.

I'm familiarizing myself with her files when Willette comes in with a dictaphone she wants me to start using. I take one look at the tiny tape recorder and want no part of it. "It's faster than writing," she insists, holding it out to me anyway. "Delzenia likes it better than having to try to figure out your chicken scratching."

I take it reluctantly. "Trust me," she says. "You'll wonder how you lived without it." Same way I lived without all the other machines around here. The office is fully automated. I hope never to have to operate the computer. I suspect it's

smarter than me, and I don't want to find out for sure. I like
the fax the best. I like the idea of sending a letter to someone
instantly instead of having to wait on the mail. Eddy and I
considered ourselves blessed when we were able to get our
own copy machine instead of having to run out the building
to the copier place in the next block. It was embarrassing
having to duck out on your client for ten minutes to copy
their records.

Today Willette's wearing a yellow linen suit with an elec-
tric blue silk blouse. Her straight blond hair's pulled back
into a long ponytail. I feel dowdy by comparison even though
I'm wearing an expensive, hundred percent cotton dress
and my Bruno Maglis. She always has that effect on me and
probably every other black woman.

"By the way, we're meeting with the D.A. this afternoon
on the Garrett matter," she says. "Take plenty of notes."

I've been so busy I'd forgotten Charles Garrett stands accused of murdering her father. "Testing," I say into the
recorder. "Testing one, two, three." I play it back, I sound
stupid.

Both Willette and I are rudely reminded Charles isn't
your run-of-the-mill accused killer when we arrive at the
D.A. building and about a hundred of his supporters are out
front protesting. "They got the wrong man, sister," one of
them shouts at her. "Or is it 'Oreo'?" Willette displays no
emotion whatsoever, just heads up the steps to the entrance.
I follow, shocked by their disrespect.

Someone shoves a sign in her face that demands Charles'
release, accusing Willie Shalandar of selling out the black
community. I want to tell them all to go straight to hell, but
when I see their "leader," a Mandingo warrior built from the
ground up with Medusa dread locks scowling at me, I know
he's just looking for an excuse to go off. I'm not about to
give it to him.

Once we're inside the marble-columned lobby, the black
security guard apologizes for the disturbance. "They know

better'n bring that mess in here, Miz Shalandar," he brags, escorting us to the elevators.

As the car rises, I feel like I should say something. "They wouldn't've harassed white people like that."

Willette stares coldly. "We never treat them like we treat each other."

Brad Yarrow actually gushes as he shows us into his office, sucking up so tough to Willette I hardly recognize him as the cold-blooded creep who "invited" me to resign five years ago. I remember asking him if I had a choice. "Yeah," he said, icicles hanging off every word. "You can be terminated." Now he's acting like we're long-lost friends.

Sitting in the same spot where he handed me my head, I can't help but note how much he's aged (like LBJ his last year as president) and how little the office has changed (still government mint green, Kmart decor). He gets to the point. "Willette, we've got to do something about these damn protests. It's making us look bad, like we're being partial in our investigation of your father's death." I almost laugh. If he was any more "impartial," he'd be kissing her feet.

"I understand, Brad." Willette's voice is smooth and low. "I don't like the division it's causing in the black community either."

Just to mess with him, I want to ask Yarrow where they are in the investigation. Which is nowhere, from what I hear on the street. However, my orders are to be seen, not heard.

"I'm between a rock and a hard spot here, Willette. Garrett's a flake and an opportunist, but a lot of your people can't see through him. Frankly, we underestimated his influence."

"I agree, Brad," Willette says, to his visible relief. "But I want my father's killer brought to justice even if Garrett's supporters tear this building down brick by brick."

Yarrow clears his throat, squirms in his chair like he's scratching his behind on the seat. "Willette, I worked with your father many years trying to build trust and confidence in your people that the D.A.'s office is fair to every citizen, regardless of race."

Now it's my turn to clear my throat. If I don't, I'll bust a gut. He ignores me. "I don't want to see all our efforts to bring people together thrown away." His eyes narrow just enough to hint at a threat. "I don't have to tell you it's in your own best interest to keep a solid black vote behind you. You'll have to run next time around, and your people have long memories."

If Willette's the least bit concerned, she doesn't show it. She stands and picks up her portfolio—her father's, actually—terminating the meeting. Yarrow scrambles to his feet. White people like to be the one to dismiss some-body. I follow her to the door, loving every moment. She shakes his hand, "We'll be in touch," and walks out.

"Thank you, Commissioner." He casts a wary eye at me. "Gwen, nice to see you. How's it going?"

"Fine, Brad." I'm grinning like a monkey. "Just fine."

It's a little after seven and the spring sun's still shining high when I climb in my Jag. The light is strange this time of day. Everything has an Old World, Mediterranean patina. I turn the ignition. Nothing happens. I pump the accelerator a few times, try it again.

"Problem?" My heart skips three beats. Michael's smil-ing down at me. I've been congratulating myself on my suc-cess in avoiding Michael since I've been there.

I turn the ignition again. "What do you know about cars?"

He leers. "I know how to drive one." I hope I look appro-priately disgusted. Willette left only moments ago. I forgot my Daytimer and had to go back it and get it.

Michael swings the door open, forcing me over. "What do you think you're doing?"

"Rescuing a damsel in distress," he says, taking over.

"Rescue somebody else." I scoot out the passenger side. "I'm calling Dirk."

"I'll help you dial." He follows me back to the Shalandar Building.

"That won't be necessary."

He shrugs. "I need to check on something myself." He unlocks the door, follows me to the elevator. I hope he doesn't try anything. We ride the elevator in silence. I'm practically hugging the wall to keep my distance from him, which amuses him. The door opens, he steps aside. I hurry to Delzenia's phone and dial. He mashes the switch hook.

"What do you think you're doing?"

He takes the receiver from me and hangs up.

"Michael—"

He kisses me so deeply my head spins. I wish I could understand the desire he conjures up in me. I *promised* myself to have nothing to do with him—and yet here I am in his arms, my body feeling things I have no control over. His hands move over me like he owns me. He forces me to feel the length of his hardness.

"Michael, please, don't—"

He covers my mouth with a kiss as he carries me into the ladies' room and sets me down, flicks the light, smiling at himself in the mirror as he backs me into the vanity.

"Get up there."

"Are you crazy?"

"Get up there before I put you up there." I refuse. He picks me up and sets me on top of the counter.

"Put your arms around my neck."

"No. Let me go—"

I try to slide off, but he shoves me back, forcing my legs apart with his as he unzips his fly.

"Michael, stop it—"

When I beat on his chest to keep him from entering me, he pins my arms. I'm too ashamed to look at him, so I bury my head in his chest while he rocks me. "You like this, don't you, baby?"

I don't say anything. I can't. He forces my knees to my chest, pumping me harder and harder against him. "Tell Daddy how much you like it."

"I . . . love it."

That same prostitute who told me a man either looks

good or dicks good taught me more about men than men. But the one thing she could never explain was how her pimp got her to voluntarily stand out in sub-zero weather, if necessary, and sell her body to get him money. Now I know. She was turned out. So am I. Only the reasons differ.

Afterward, Michael has the audacity to insist on waiting outside with me until Dirk arrives. "This can be a pretty dangerous neighborhood, baby." Tell me about it. My dress has unsightly wrinkles across the front. I hurry and get in the car before Dirk notices. Michael leans in my window and greets Dirk.

"She's doing a helluva job, man." Michael winks at me. I feel like the ground he's standing on. "I can personally attest to that."

I've been in the office all morning, dictating letters to Willette's constituents. On top of everything else, my job is to get done all the things she promises people in all those meetings she attends and speeches she gives. She's right about the dictaphone. I wouldn't have a chance without it against the small mountain of correspondence I have to respond to.

I remind myself to stop frowning. Aside from the ten pounds I gained when I quit smoking after I married Kwame—he hated it—so far I've been able to fend off the worst ravages of Father Time. If we can keep the weight off, most black women can look good longer than our white counterparts, most of whom need every device known to man to keep from looking old and wrinkled early.

I finish my letter to Ms. Hattie Whitfield, advising her that while Commissioner Shalandar would very much like to solve her problem, her authority is limited to those matters under Harris County's jurisdiction. As such she has no authority to fix her streetlight . . . blah, blah, blah.

Willette taps on my door, peeks in. "May I come in?"

I welcome the interruption. "What's up?"

She sits posture-perfect in the chair across from me.

"Charles Garrett and his new lawyer are holding a press conference at Matoomba House at three. I want you to go and find out what they're up to."

"He fired Warren?"

"That's what I heard. I'm going to ask for a special prosecutor to investigate my father's . . . death. I want you to research the law before I submit the request to Yarrow."

"Special prosecutor?" I sit back, surprised. "They don't like to do that."

"Why not?"

"It's giving up control. No D.A. likes that. They're control freaks." I've never known Yarrow to appoint someone outside the office to handle a case—unless it has political implications—like this one. Or in conflict with his interests— like this one. She might be on to something.

"He's going to do this." Willette's pert little mouth clamps tight, her green eyes like death rays. "He won't dare sweep Daddy's . . . death under the rug just to save a few black votes," she says.

I agree. "But I think he's worried about a lot of black votes, not a few, Willette. You should be too. Look at Jesse Jackson. He's King of Niggers." Of course, kings come and go in the black community. She looks at me, seeing something new apparently, smiles slowly. She's really beautiful when she smiles. "Daddy was right about you, Gwen. You do have good political instincts."

My cheeks warm. I don't accept compliments well, especially from a dead man. "Willie said that?"

"He said you see with a third eye."

Third eye? "I didn't think Willie paid that much attention to me. I'm just a spear carrier."

She chuckles, loosening up for the first time since I've been working for her. "*Au contraire,* Ms. Parrish. Daddy paid a lot of attention to you. He said you were going places, if you stopped tripping yourself up."

Like jumping up and down for a district judgeship before I'm ready. Or thinking even for a second I could be D.A. Or sleeping with her husband, even if it is against my will. She turns serious. "Daddy had a thing about people's eyes. 'Eyes,' " she says, sounding so much like Willie it's spooky, " 'tell you everything you need to know, baby girl. Eyes.' " I want to rub mine—for a second she even looks like him. "Daddy said we come here with three sets of eyes."

I'm getting the heebie-jeebies behind all this mumbo-jumbo, having been in Houston long enough to develop a healthy respect for hoodoo, which a lot of people around here still believe in, especially the ones from Louisiana.

"The ones you see the world with, the ones the world sees you with, and the third eye." The likeness to Willie disappears, thankfully. "That's where your instincts come from. It sees everything whether you're looking or not."

"That's only five," I say, trying to joke.

She overlooks me. "Most people can't use their third eye. Daddy said you're a natural."

I forget trying to be funny. "Willette, this is—you know—scary. Can we change the subject?"

She laughs, her eyes don't. "Daddy had a favorite saying about eyes." My heart trips an alarm. Did Michael tell?

"Really? What's that?"

"Every shut eye ain't 'sleep."

I know this one. "And every good-bye ain't gone."

13

Matoomba House is in a rundown section of Third Ward. I have to park quite a distance away, since the street in front of the ramshackle structure is crowded with cars on both sides. On the way to the building I pass a lot of unemployed black men wandering up and down the sidewalks, looking for something to do. I see lots of kids too, which surprises me—they should be in school. At the rate the country's going, what are they going to do ten years from now when you'll need a degree just to flip burgers?

Looking around, I see a once proud neighborhood of big two-story houses and manicured lawns now neglected and abandoned, everything dead or dying. Except the trees. They're oak. They preside majestically over the deterioration, magnificent canopies entwining across the wide boulevard, creating a long green archway. Nature's no respecter of poverty. I love it.

Matoomba House is the only community center in Houston formed and operated solely by blacks, mainly through the efforts of Garrett and his followers. They "expropriated" a house destined for demolition, renovating it themselves. That it looks mammy-made and uninviting doesn't diminish its occupants' pride in it one iota.

I climb the center's rickety stairs and wonder if I'll break a leg. I'm walking tippy-toe by the time I reach the porch. Why don't they fix the goddamn steps? A big, burly brother man with gray cat's eyes and a mean mouth guards the door, arms like hams folded across his big chest.

"What it is, sister?"

I'm tempted to say it is what it is, but I don't want to start anything. "I'm here for the press conference. I'm representing Commissioner Shalandar."

"Say you is, huh?" He gives me the once-over, his head bobbing jack-in-the-box-like. "Upstairs. To the right."

He holds the door for me. Thank God it's not hot outside. Air conditioning, now a necessity in this hellfire climate, did for the South in the twentieth century what the cotton gin did for us in the nineteenth. There's none to speak of in this joint, just tons of open windows and ceiling fans. It's not unpleasant, but I take my jacket off before I head upstairs as a precautionary measure. I sweat like a pig.

At the top of the narrow staircase I turn right as instructed and enter the back of the conference room, formerly two small rooms converted into one big one. The sheet rock joining the new walls wasn't completely patched and looks tacky. A long table with a portable podium stands at one end of the room, and neatly spaced rows of folding chairs run its length. They got a good showing by the media, for most seats are taken.

I sit in the back, deliberately low-key. After all, I am from the enemy's camp. Even though it's three-twenty, techs are still setting up equipment. I knew better than to rush. Twelve years of rushing to the courthouse has taught me when it's going to be "hurry up and wait."

The door opens next to us. Of all the people I don't expect to see, Kwame enters, followed by the guy with the Medusa dreadlocks who led the protest at the D.A. building the day Willette and I went to see Yarrow.

Or maybe I shouldn't be surprised. This is Kwame's kind of case: David versus the White Man. He stands at the podium, Medusa Dreads at his side. Everyone hushes. In a black leather battle jacket, blue jeans, white shirt, red, black, and green skull cap on his head, Kwame looks good.

"Good afternoon, ladies and gentlemen. We apologize for the delay. I'm State Representative Kwame El'Kasid.

I'm going to be taking over the defense of brother Charles Garrett. Unfortunately, within moments of obtaining his release for suspicion of murder—for which, I might add, there's not one shred of evidence—Brother Garrett was re-arrested on a felonious charge of possession of cocaine, which is also without merit and part of a conspiracy to harass my client. Under the circumstances, the press conference is canceled. Thank you."

Medusa Dreads single-handedly keeps everyone at bay as Kwame walks out under a fusillade of unanswered questions. I duck before he can see me, slowly easing up after he's gone.

I catch up with Willette at the Hou-Tex Human Relations Foundation banquet. She's on her way out to attend another function. She'd already heard about Garrett and Kwame. I get stuck taking her place at the head table, sitting between the Reverend Joseph Blakely, chairman of the foundation, and the Reverend Robart Cleets, the director and his arch enemy. Each has large black followings, luckily on different sides of town.

I'm so sleepy I want to drop my face into my mashed potatoes. They look like a pillow. I have to force myself to maintain my "honored-to-be-here" look. Occasionally, either Reverend Blakely, a squat man with satiny black skin and a bald head, or Reverend Cleets, tall and paunchy with cat-eye glasses, says something to me. If I have to smile one more time at either of them, the corners of my mouth are going to stick in my cheeks permanently.

The speaker, an Uncle Tom from way back, drones on about how great minority progress is. I disagree. A few of us are better off, but a whole lot more whites are. How is that equality? Damn, Kwame, he'd know. He says they always find one black person to agree with them that President Bush is doing a great job. Who cares what the other twenty-nine million, nine hundred and ninety-nine thousand, nine hundred and ninety-nine think?

I snicker at the thought, and the reverends look at me. I hiccup, excuse myself. I downed three Wild Turkeys in rapid succession at the reception to settle my nerves after seeing Kwame. I'm feeling no pain as I sip another Turkey and wait for the speaker to sit down, which he does finally. The audience of approximately five hundred, evenly divided between blacks and whites, gives him a rousing round of applause. I clap politely.

I check out the rest of the dignitaries at the head table, stifling another urge to giggle. Kwame wouldn't be caught dead in this den of inniggerty. Along with several prominent whites, there are our two black city councilmen, a high black mucky-muck in the federal government, and, of course, the Honorable Judge C.C. Hendrix. She smiles, and I wave, accidentally knocking my drink on Reverend Blakely, who jumps off his seat.

"Oops. I'm so sorry," I say, reaching for my napkin to help him dry off until I realize it's his crotch that's soaked through. He snatches the napkin and sits back down, blotting himself under the tablecloth while I continue to apologize. The awards presentation begins—practically everyone in the audience'll get one—and I start hiccuping uncontrollably. Reverend Jones offers me water. Not to be outdone, Reverend Blakely pats me on the back. They're drawing attention, so I ease off the dais as Houston's only black assistant police chief receives a standing ovation and a plaque— for being Houston's only black assistant police chief.

I'm still hiccuping when I reach the lobby. They say the Shamrock Hotel's decorated with sixty-three shades of green. I'm the sixty-fourth. At least that's how I feel until I step out into the silky night air. Like magic, my hiccups disappear.

"I see you couldn't take it either," a man says behind me. I turn slowly: this could be Jack the Ripper. I squeal with delight when I see Tallmon Anthony, an old running buddy from TSU. We had a lot of classes together and a lot of laughs. Talk about a sight for sore eyes.

We sit in the back of the bar, catching up on each other's life. It's been years since I've seen Tallmon, and I fuss at him for being a stranger. "I've been checking you out," he says. "You don't exactly let any grass grow under your feet."

True. "It's harder to hit a moving target." I smile, taking in his face. He looks good: brown sugar black, a neat, low 'fro, tailored suit, monogrammed French cuffs. "The practice of law isn't hurting you one bit."

He smiles like he knows the secret to eternal youth. "I got out of that rat race a long time ago."

I salute him. "So what are you doing now? Don't tell me if it's illegal."

He chuckles. "Hardly. I'm the minority subcontractor to a white firm in Austin that heretofore did all the state's bond work. Your ex-husband made them slice the pie in the legislature."

"Affirmative Action Man strikes again." Damn Kwame. Lately he's been turning up in my life like a bad penny. I sip my Turkey and remember something Mama used to say about watching your pennies and your dollars'll grow. She loved Kwame's funky drawers. Still does, quiet as kept. "Kwame or no Kwame, you're handling white folks' *big* money," I tell Tallmon. "I'd say you've died and gone to black lawyer heaven." I smile. "Remember how we thought the streets would be paved with gold, people would be lining up to give us their money when we got out of law school?"

He remembers. "We were all going to be driving Mercedes in a year and living on South Mac Gregor." He winks at me. "I was hoping you'd be there with me. But you only had eyes for Kwame."

I crack up laughing. "Love makes you blind, dumb, and crazy." We trade war stories about our respective divorces. Tallmon's ex didn't go to law school, which doesn't surprise me. Most brothers are too insecure to marry lawyers.

He strokes my hand, resting on the table beside my glass.

Looks deep into my eyes. I don't believe it. His "love lights" are shining. "Kwame never understood you."

"I have a husband for that now, Tallmon."

He scoffs. "A white boy? You need a soul brother." I pull my hand away. "Did I say something wrong?"

Just that Dirk can't satisfy me because he's white. "No." I stand up. "Look, I have to go, Tallmon."

He tries to take my hand. "Gwen—"

"It's late. My husband'll be worried."

He gives me a long, penetrating look, like he's trying to decide if I'm serious. "I'll walk you to your car."

"That won't be necessary."

He leaves some bills on the table for the check. "I'm old-fashioned like that."

We walk past the banquet room. They're still giving each other awards. When we reach my car, Tallmon takes my keys and opens the door. I get in and roll down the window, smiling one last time for the road. "It was nice seeing you again, Tallmon."

"Really?" He looks at me like I'm disappearing before his very eyes.

"Really." I rev up the Jag. "Take care."

I watch him through the rearview mirror, watching me drive off. I don't feel sorry for him. If he's anything like all the other thirty-eight-year-old divorced men I know, he's got child-support payments up the ying-yang and an ex-wife who's a bitch. He's obviously got more money to spend than the average brother, but that doesn't mean he's going to spend it on a woman. Most guys nowadays prefer to give you service instead.

I kiss Dirk's forehead. He's nodded off in his easy chair reading the latest issue of the *Poverty Law Journal*. He smiles as his eyes open to me.

"Hi."

"Hi." I sit in his lap and give him a kiss. He responds instantly, which reminds me I haven't exactly been meeting his needs lately. I've been too tired. But I had plenty of time to think on the long drive from Third Ward, and I resolved to do better by him. And to get Michael out of my life, one way or another. And Kwame off my mind.

"Honey, Willette called," he murmurs, ready to do whatever I want. "She said it's important."

"Everything's important with her." I get the phone and sit back on his lap while I dial. We kiss until she answers. "What's up?"

"Forget about researching the law on the special prosecutor. Meet me and C.C. at Benihana's at one tomorrow." I'm surprised, but I trained myself a long time ago to leave office matters at the office.

"Cool." I hang up, lingering on Dirk's lap, kissing him.

"Let's go to bed," he says huskily.

I have a better idea. I straddle him, giving no further thought to Willette or Michael or affirmative action.

I get to the restaurant before Willette or C.C., so I order some sake and watch the Japanese chef do his knife thing for the white couple across from me. They "ooo" and "ahh," though it just looks like he's making mincemeat out of everything to me.

A pretty Japanese waitress sets my drink down and asks me if I'm ready to order. "I'm waiting for the rest of my party." She bows and disappears. I hate being bowed at. Any self-respecting black person should after three hundred years of bowing and scraping ourselves. I try the sake. It's warmer than I thought it would be, and it tastes like lighter fluid. Willette and C.C. walk up as I make a face.

"I'll have whatever you're drinking." C.C. laughs. They sit down on either side of me. Willette wastes no time getting to the point after the waitress takes their drink order, spring water for her, sake for C.C.

"Yarrow granted my request for a special prosecutor." I ask how she pulled off the impossible. "I'm the third-party beneficiary to all the chits Daddy had on him."

Basic contract law comes back to me. "The 't.p.b.'—as Prof. Denton used to say—has as much right to enforce the contract as the original parties." Must be the sake.

Willette looks at me. "I'm submitting your name to be the special prosecutor."

The sake goes down the wrong pipe. I start choke-coughing. C.C. slaps me on the back, her eyes twinkling. "You all right?" My coughing subsides. "Whad'd'ya say? Wanna be special prosecutor, sister?"

Are they kidding? Somebody just said the magic word and the genie showed up with my three wishes.

14

The parking lot attendant brings my car first, since Willette and C.C. rode to Benihana's together and we parked at different times. We hug and kiss like schoolgirls before I get in, excited for me. As I drive off, I notice Willette suddenly lash into C.C., blessing her out for something. Probably her drinking, which got out of hand at the restaurant after she told the waitress to take "that thimble" and bring her a "glass for grown people" for her sake. C.C. looks like she's crying. Poor C.C. Whoever made up the expression "sober as a judge" must've just been trying to cover for them. Most of the ones I know drink like fish.

Late-afternoon traffic is as bad as it gets downtown, but I don't care. See what happens when you live right? Just last night I resisted a man most black women would kill to be with, I swore to get Michael out of my life, and I renewed my commitment to my husband. So I—Gwenlyn Parrish Ingersoll—get to be special prosecutor on the most important case in Harris County. In Texas even, and it's big damn state. Of course, I'll have to be approved by the black leadership just so everybody gets a chance to piss on my appointment, but I'm a sure thing. Willette wants me. And of course, I'll have to take my marching orders from Brad. I can even stomach him to be special prosecutor.

There is one fly fluttering around my soup. His name is Kwame Nkrumah El'Kasid. If I had a suspicious mind—which all lawyers do, a natural outgrowth of all that endless questioning in law school—I'd think Willette deliberately sets us up to go to war, retaliating against me for Michael. Only she doesn't play with you before she kills you. Michael could've suggested me. He seems to be telling her what to do more and more these days. He's the kind of person who'd pull your nails out finger by finger and then offer you a manicure, but what would he gain from throwing me and Kwame at each other? Michael hates even the sound of his name, claiming I called him by it once in bed. If I believed in ghosts, I'd say Willie wants to sic me and Kwame on each other. Doesn't have enough entertainment where he's at. Nah, this is just one of those ironic tricks Fate plays to keep you on your toes. I don't care. This is my ticket to stardom and it's "All aboard!"

Willette and C.C. probably had me in mind for special prosecutor all along. I'm a damn good lawyer, and C.C.'s seen me in action enough times in her court. Willette undoubtedly made me her assistant so I'd be taken seriously when she submits my name. They know me and Kwame. We both trained in the fight-tooth-and-nail school of trial advocacy: the winning attorney walks out over the loser's body, left to lie in a pool of blood on the courtroom floor.

I turn onto Main, changing my mind about going back to the office. I'm going to break the good news to Dirk. I park in the lot next to his building, two blocks down from my old office in Midtown. Gulf Coast Legal Services occupies the entire top floor. The lobby bustles with the usual activity, except the bustlers are blacker and browner than downtown. I expect the elevator to be crowded with poor people in desperate need of legal advice, but it's not. The Hispanic woman chatting with the black woman riding with me work for Dirk, judging by their shop talk. When we get off, I'm surprised to see how idle the waiting area is. The poor must be getting the Republicans' message about leaving these Legal Aid lawyers alone if they know what's good for them.

I identify myself to the receptionist, a young black girl who immediately takes me back to Dirk's office. They all know he's married to a black woman, so she's not surprised to see me. We execute a series of turns through a labyrinth of offices with cheap wood paneling and green carpet until we come to Dirk's door, which is open. He's on the phone. As soon as he sees me, he smiles and waves me in. Contrary to the outer drabness, his office is nice, spending his own ducats to make it "befit" his position as director. I peck his cheek and take in his wonderful view, high enough so that Midtown looks like interesting concrete blocks scattered among tufts of greenery.

Dirk hangs up and reaches for me. "This is a surprise."

"I thought so. I've got another one." I give him a kiss. "Guess what?"

"What?"

"Guess who's going to be special prosecutor?"

He frowns. "Not you."

Not exactly the reaction I expected. "You're supposed to be proud of me."

He turns away, runs his hand through his hair, worry lines webbing his face. "I'm not."

That knocks the wind out of me. "May I ask why?"

He stares out the window, like he's thinking about jumping. "You know why. Your ex-husband's representing Garrett."

I don't get it. "And your problem with that is—what—he's my ex-husband?"

"This isn't funny, Gwen. You'll have to deal with him."

"I have to deal with him now. We have a child together, remember?"

"You know what I mean."

"I know. Kwame and I will be adversaries in every sense of the word now. Or don't you think we can put aside our mutual loathing and be professionals?"

That throws him. He smiles a tiny bit. I slide my arms around him. "Don't you trust me?"

Pure, unadulterated, insane jealousy flashes in his eyes. "I love you. Just like he does."

I laugh. "Don't be silly. Kwame hates me."

"If he hates you so much, why hasn't he ever remarried? Men do—unless they're still in love with their ex-wives."

"And I suppose their ex-wives remarry because they're still in love with them."

He looks at me hard. "Sometimes."

I shake my head. "Here I thought I was bringing good news. Dammit, it *is* good news. You're not going to ruin it for me with your stupid jealousy, Dirk."

"My jealousy's all I've got."

"Then you better keep it to yourself."

Dinner is a disaster. I tried to salvage the day by making everybody's favorite food, spaghetti and meatballs for Dirk the Jerk, lasagna for Ashleigh Lee. The meatballs taste like cardboard; the lasagna's dried out and rubbery. Watching them pick through what amounts to garbage just to keep from hurting my feelings strikes me as funny. I snigger, breaking the silence that's prevailed since dinner began. They look at me like I pooted.

Ashleigh Lee looks concerned. "Mom?"

"Are you okay?" Dirk asks.

"I'm fine." The kitchen looks like a war zone. I haven't touched a pot in weeks, and in one night I think I can be Chef Boyardee. That's funny. Dirk takes out the champagne I splurged on and opens it, pops the top and fills my glass. I can't resist smoothing the pretty baby hair at Ashleigh Lee's temple. At least she got that much from me. She moves her head away. "I'm not a baby."

"No, you're not," I say, wishing she was. "By the way, I'm going to be the special prosecutor on the Garrett case. Cool, huh?"

She stares at me like I said I was going to go running naked. "I can't believe you." Jumps up from the table. "It's bad enough the kids at school call me zebra because of you. Now you're going to beat up on an innocent man."

I knew Kwame was brainwashing her. "Did your father tell you to say that?"

"Daddy doesn't have to tell me what to say. I have a mind. I can think for myself." She actually bares her teeth at me. "Unlike you."

I stand up slowly. "What's that supposed to mean?"

"Everybody knows Aunt Willette and Aunt C.C. do all your thinking for you. I guess that makes you one dumb bitch, doesn't it, Mother?"

I'm too hurt to answer, sink in my seat. Dirk steps between us. "You don't talk to your mother like that, young lady."

"What're you going to do about it?" She glares at him, eyes like knife slits. "You're not my daddy."

There are no more hateful words a stepfather can hear or a stepchild can utter. Dirk doesn't flinch an inch. "Apologize to your mother this instant, Ashleigh Lee."

Fury emanates from her like waves of heat. "Get out of my way," she says, pushing him.

"Apologize."

She tries to force her way around him. He takes her arm. "Take your white hands off me!"

"Apologize!"

She tries to twist loose. "Let—me—go—"

He holds her. *"Apologize."*

She swings her free fist and pops him in the mouth. Everything happens so quickly, I'm moving like in a dream, useless and out of sync. "Ashleigh Lee—?"

Blood sprouts from his lip. Seeing it makes her crazy, as if she realizes for the first time he bleeds too. She tears into him, fists waling on him like paddle wheels. Dirk tries to restrain her, but she fights him like a wild woman, grabs the champagne bottle. I spring to my feet. "Ashleigh Lee, are you crazy?"

She whirls around and looks at me like I'm something oozing from a backed-up sewer. "You married him and you ask me that?"

"I've had enough of this," Dirk says. "Go to your room.

And stay there until you can conduct yourself in a civilized manner."

She smirks, taking her sweet time setting the bottle on the table. Supremely arrogant, she spits in his face. He slaps her. I scream and jump on him, trying to kill him.

I told Dirk I was going to take a nap, but I can't stop replaying the terrible fight in my mind. Ashleigh Lee's behavior was despicable, and so was mine. What to do now is the question. Corporal punishment's out of the question. Grounding won't work, she's a loner. She's too big to spank, though Dirk swears that's what she needs.

I shiver with shame when I think of her spitting in his face. After things settled down, I couldn't stop apologizing to him. He said it's okay, but I know he's deeply hurt. He left awhile ago saying he needed some fresh air. Ashleigh Lee's in her room. My head is pounding so bad it feels like boulders crashing around inside. I refuse to take anything. I want to suffer. It's my punishment.

The doorbell rings. I sit up, lie back down when it stops, hoping they'll go away. It rings again. I step out into the hallway, going downstairs to answer it. Ashleigh Lee comes out of her room, takes one look at me, and ducks back inside. Fine with me. I won't be ready to look at her for a long time.

Whoever's at the door lays on the bell. I call down that I'm on my way, but they won't let up. I'm furious by the time I reach for the door. Something tells me to look up. Ashleigh Lee's watching from the balcony, a little smile on her face. My heart leaps to my throat. I pray she hasn't done what I think.

"Where is he?"

Kwame pushes past me into the house. "I'll teach him to touch my child." When he's like this, there's no use trying to tell him he's got it all ass backward. I have to get him out of here before Dirk comes back.

"Where is he?"

"Hi, Daddy." Ashleigh Lee runs down the steps.

I step in front of him. "Don't you think you should get the full story before you fly off the handle, Kwame?"

Nostrils flared, he taps his foot impatiently. "I don't need any explanations. Nobody puts his hands on my child."

"He's not here, Kwame."

He charges past me, stalking all over downstairs looking for him. "It's bad enough you married him. But when you let him put his hands on my daughter, you've gone too far."

Ashleigh Lee follows us around on this pointless trek, enjoying this like nothing else. He's about to go upstairs. I block his way. "That's it, Kwame. I want you out of my house."

He backs up, looks at me a moment. "No problem. I'm taking my daughter with me. Get your stuff, Ashleigh Lee."

Music to her ears. She runs up to me, expecting me to move. "You're not going anywhere," I tell her. She looks at Kwame. I tighten my eyes at him to let him know I mean business. "Do you want to hear what happened or not?"

We glare at each other, neither intending to ever back down. Ashleigh Lee tugs his sleeve. "Daddy—"

He reluctantly turns his glower from me, smiles reassuringly at her. "Go on upstairs. Your mama and I are going to talk."

It's pretty clear she doesn't want to leave us alone. "You're going to take her side. You always do. You never believe me. She let him hit me. Aren't you going to do something about it?"

I'm struck by what she just said. He always takes my side? He never believes her? That sure is news to me. He tells her in no uncertain terms to go to her room. She deliberately stomps up each step. We watch her slam the door, then look at each other.

"All right," he grouses. "Start talking. And make it good."

I take a cleansing breath, like I did after each contraction trying to get Ashleigh Lee born. "She got out of line during dinner. She said—something to me that Dirk didn't think was appropriate."

"What?"

"Something she's heard you say a thousand times, I'm sure. That Willette and C.C. do my thinking for me."

He looks genuinely surprised. "Gwen—I never have and I never will run you down to Ashleigh Lee."

And rats don't like cheese. "You'd run me down over and under if you thought it would get you points with her."

"Why on earth would I do that to my child's mother?" He shakes his head. "That's what you think of me? That I actually sit around with her every chance I get and run you into the dirt? You think that's why she likes me more than you?"

Blam. Right in the breadbasket. He always did know how to counterpunch. I've had to learn how practicing law. "She 'likes' you because she doesn't live with you. You're prince charming, the good guy—'Daddy.' "

"Fine. Then let her live with me. I'll be happy to be the villain if that'll straighten her out."

"Then you agree she has a problem?"

"Everybody has problems. Her biggest one is you."

Me? He starts pacing like a caged lion, ready to tear somebody—anybody—apart. "And that—man you call your husband. Nothing you've said excuses him for hitting my daughter."

"She spit on him."

He halts, looks at me, shocked. "She what?"

I repeat it real slow. "She—spit—in—his—face."

His eyes narrow suspiciously. "Why?"

"He insisted she apologize for calling me a stupid bitch. She didn't want to."

"She would never—"

"She would and she did. I thought she'd be proud of my appointment as special prosecutor. She wasn't. That's when she called me—what I told you. Dirk got upset and tried to get her to apologize. She went crazy on him and grabbed a wine bottle. I made her put it down. That's when she spit on him. No reason. No provocation. He . . . slapped her without thinking." This is the part I'm not proud of. "I—I jumped on him. She had to pull me off."

Kwame stares at the floor, listening carefully. Looks up at me. "After all that I don't expect there's a whole lot left of him for me to deal with after the two of you got through with him."

I don't want to, but I smile. "He held his own." I shrug. Actually, Dirk looks like something the cat dragged in. Between Ashleigh Lee's fists and my nails, we chewed his face up pretty bad.

At least Kwame's calmed down. "I don't like him touching her, Gwen. For any reason. She has a father. I'll deal with her when she cuts up." He heads to the door, pauses, and looks at me, sad for his child. "If that's the 'whole' story, I'm ashamed of her for doing that, spitting on him." He sighs deeply. "I'll talk to her."

"We'll both talk to her."

He looks at me. "Maybe we should do it together. A united front. Let her know we both mean business."

This is new. He always wants to do his own thing with Ashleigh Lee. "Fine."

"Good." He reaches for the doorknob. "By the way, congratulations. I didn't know you were going to be the special prosecutor." How could he? I just found out myself. He opens the door and smiles that smile. "That's not going to stop me from kicking your ass."

I smile confidently. "You can try."

He chuckles. "See you in court, Attorney Parrish."

"Parrish Ingersoll."

His mouth turns down. He steps out on the porch. "I mean it about us working together with Ashleigh Lee for a change. It can't hurt."

"No," I say. "It can't."

He grins. "I'm glad I didn't have to do something stupid tonight."

"I'm glad you didn't either."

"Well, good night."

"Good night."

As he turns to walk down the steps, his jaw connects with

Dirk's fist, which appears out of nowhere. Kwame falls backward through the doorway, smashes against the floor. Ashleigh Lee screams, "Daddy!"

"Dirk, how could you—?"

He takes his eyes off Kwame and glares at me—long enough for Kwame to jump up and slam his face sideways. They clinch, slugging it out, crashing around the foyer.

"Daddy!"

Ashleigh Lee starts to go to Kwame, but I drag her up the stairs, push her back into her room, and close the door. Dash to my closet, knocking shoe boxes off the shelf until I find what I'm looking for. I hear the sound of my living room being torn up. I run downstairs and fire the gun I'm holding, aiming at the floor where they're wrestling each other to the death. They break apart, surprised. Kwame takes one look at the gun, jumps to his feet, hands raised. He knows me. "Gwen, don't do anything crazy."

Dirk staggers up. He can't believe his eyes. "Honey—"

"Shut up, Dirk. Get out, Kwame. Right now. Or I swear the next bullet'll be between your eyes." He knows I'm not kidding. Daddy taught me how to shoot when I was thirteen years old. Kwame slowly backs to the door. Ashleigh Lee calls out from the top of the stairs. "Take me with you, Daddy."

"Get back to your room, Ashleigh Lee," I say, keeping my eyes on Kwame. "You're not going anywhere."

"I'll call you, baby." Kwame takes his eyes off the gun, smiles at me impishly. "See you in court, Attorney Parrish."

He chuckles, closing the door behind him. I lock it, put the safety back on my gun, and remove the clip. "I'm going to bed." Dirk follows me upstairs, head hanging. He looks like he got run over and backed over. "I'm sorry, honey. I don't know what got into me."

Must be a full moon. "Where'd you learn to fight like that?"

He half smiles. "Marines."

Dirk goes into our room. I walk up to Ashleigh Lee, staring from her doorway, her dark eyes radiating pure hatred. "I hope you know I wasn't really going to shoot your father, Ashleigh Lee—"

She slams the door in my face and locks it.

15

"If Charles Garrett is responsible for my father's . . . death, I want it proven in open court with solid evidence. I'm recommending Gwen because of her outstanding record in the D.A.'s office and in private practice."

Houston's pillars of the black community—all male other than Willette—look as stern as biblical prophets seated around the big oval table in her conference room, eyeing me like they're trying to decide if they should bet on me to win, place, or show—or at all. Harrison McIlroy's to my right. He and Robert Morrison, across from us, are Houston's two black at-large councilmen. At one end of the table is Councilman Vashti Burton, who represents District A, which encompasses Third Ward. Bigelow Washington and Francois Pierre watch me from the other end. Bigelow's president of the school board. Francois runs Houston's largest black automobile dealership and heads the Black Chamber of Commerce. I smile politely at the mention of my name and wait for their questions, which Willette told me not to worry about. She intends to make chopped liver of anyone foolish enough to oppose her. Nevertheless, I'm prepared for anything from cross-examination to the Inquisition.

"Gwen's a triple threat, gentlemen." Willette smiles at me supportively. I smile back. The top dog in Houston now is a black bitch. It hasn't felt this good working with her since law review.

Willette sings some more of my praises. "She's thorough, she's fair, and she's honest."

"And handpicked by you." Bigelow's watery, bloodshot eyes stare at me. "People already think Garrett's being set up."

"Is that what you think, Bigelow?" Willette looks at him so hard he starts to squirm unconsciously.

"Of course not, Willette," he says quickly. "I'm just telling you."

Her gaze imprisons him a moment longer, then sweeps the table. "Gentlemen, need I remind you this is an unprecedented opportunity for us to clean our own house for a change? Charles Garrett has pimped and preyed on the poorest, most impressionable of our people long enough. We're lucky to have someone like Gwen, who can handle this matter professionally and expeditiously." My heart beats a thousand times a minute as I anticipate her next question. "Does she have your support?"

Now, in the game of politics, the only black commissioner in Harris County beats three city councilmen, one school board president, and the Chamber of Commerce any day. They know they'll all need her long before she'll need them; they just want to see if she knows. She looks each man in the eye one by one, starting with Bigelow. They all agree to support my appointment as special prosecutor—until she gets to Francois Pierre.

"I don't know, Willette," he says. His narrow face, pencil-thin mustache, and slick black hair make him look like a pale little rat. He's from Orange originally, a little town next to Beaumont on the way to Louisiana whose claim to fame is a lot of mulattos who marry only each other to preserve their Creole looks. Francois smiles pointy little teeth at me. "No offense, Miz Parrish, but this is a man's job. Especially going up against Kwame El'Kasid. He'll make you yell aunt and uncle."

My smile back is stiff and artificial. I want to tell him to go straight to hell and stay there. Black men are some of the biggest sexist dogs on the planet, most of them wanting us liberated just long enough to help them free themselves; then it's back to the kitchen and the nursery.

"Far as I know, Frank," Michael says, waltzing into the room like he owns it and everyone in it, "there aren't any restrictions on her law license because of her sex. Sorry I'm late, darling." He gives Willette a proprietary little kiss to let everyone know he's the power behind the throne. I'm as surprised to see him as everyone else. He winks at me like everything's in the bag. "As far as Mr. El'Kasid is concerned, who better knows how to handle him than his ex-wife?"

Someone gasps. The pillars are shaken.

Kwame and I divorced when Ashleigh Lee was three, so it's not common knowledge that we were married. Thanks to the black dispatch—Bigelow looks like he wants to pee on himself wanting to tell this juicy tidbit—it will be now.

"Isn't that some kind of conflict of interest?" Francois demands, seeing daylight in his effort to block me.

"No," says Michael. "It's insurance. Which is why I suggested the idea in the first place."

Michael suggested me?

"My wife raised the same concerns you've expressed—"

Willette didn't want me?

He smiles proudly at her, like she's his star pupil. "I persuaded her that appointing Ms. Parrish is in everyone's best interest. What's it going to be, my brothers? Do we speak to the Man with one voice on this?"

Willette's eyes meet mine for an instant. She didn't say anything about Michael being here, let alone about him being the one who championed me to be special prosecutor. I understand the look on her face. It says exactly how I feel and then some. Like the bully just stomped your beautiful sand castle just to show you. What can either one of us say? We're both turned out. Michael smiles graciously all around. "If there are no further objections, it's settled. Thank you all for coming."

"I don't have an objection," Francois says. "I do have a question." Politicians. Just when you think they're dead, you have to drive another stake through their wily hearts. "Garrett's the only suspect, right?"

Michael and Willette look at me. "That's correct," I say.

"Then what do we need a special prosecutor for? It's gonna cost us a lot of goodwill with the downtown folks. We might need it for something down the road."

He has a point. Garrett's people are going to scream like poked pigs, Yarrow doesn't care. Untold numbers of blacks have been sent to TDC on far less evidence.

Michael coaxes Willette. "Tell them, baby."

She responds a little too obediently for my tastes. "My father," she says, her eyes misting ever so slightly, which no one picks up on but me, "always said the only thing a white man respects is money and the number of votes you get."

"We've got plenty of money," Michael boasts, making Willette cringe.

She clears her throat. "My intentions are to be elected to his seat by a landslide. That can't happen with Garrett's people running around calling me a sell-out. If, on the other hand, it's shown by clear and convincing evidence beyond a reasonable doubt that he did in fact murder . . . my father, no one will blame me for wanting his head on a stake."

The pillars nod understandably. Everybody in the room has sold out at one time or another, except me, only because I haven't had a chance.

Michael beams at Willette like she's his child and she just recited the alphabet for the first time. So Willette wants to be Queen of Niggers? I imagine the two of them running the black Ship of State.

"I'll be back," I tell Delzenia the next morning as I head to the elevator. She purses her lips and nods, eyes glued to the letter she's typing. Until I move out, she can't move up. I'm starting to feel like a rich relative she's waiting for to die. I step into the elevator, push the button to the first floor. Michael slides in, leering at me greedily. I'm almost certain Delzenia noticed as the doors closed.

"So," he says, moving in on me, "don't you want to know why I did it?"

I'm practically pressed against the wall trying to avoid him. "I don't care."

He looks at me a moment. "No, I guess you don't. You just want the job." His hand settles on my breast. "Make a big splash."

"Stop it, Michael. Somebody could get on."

"We'll solve that." He pushes the stop button. The car jerks to a halt.

"Are you crazy? I have to get downtown." I try to reach around him to start the elevator. He covers the button. "Unh-uh. Not until you show some gratitude. I just made things possible for you." He kisses my neck. "You do the things you're supposed to do, I'll keep making them possible."

He pulls me to him, holding me like I'm the one thing in the whole wide world he needs. I will my arms to just dangle. It's always a battle between me and my body with Michael. It's straining to answer his call. I feel for the elevator button until I find it. The sudden downward pull of the car surprises him. He lets me go, flicks the stop button again, locking the doors.

This is starting to get on my nerves. "I don't think it says anywhere in the rules of blackmail that the blackmailee has to be grateful. They just have to be afraid. Let me out of here before I forget to even be that."

He gently kisses my lips. "You don't have any reason to be afraid of me, baby. Unless—"

I lose my patience. "What do you want now, Michael?"

He smiles, his eyes lazily running me up and down. "I want you to beg for it."

I laugh in his face. "Please." I shove him aside, open the door, and walk out into the lobby. Beg? Never.

He calls out behind me. "You will. You'll see."

16

I got along well with the police when I was in the D.A.'s office, though they were all suspicious of me. They automatically assumed I automatically sympathized with black defendants, which was true to the extent that I felt my first obligation as a prosecutor was to be fair, in and of itself a novelty in the D.A.'s office. Everybody else cared about their conviction rate.

The only time I had trouble working with a cop was when I dismissed his case against a young black defendant he planned on turning into a snitch. It just so happened I knew the boy's older brother, a hardworking, honest mechanic where I took my car. The detective knew his case was weak, but he wanted me to press it anyway so Petey—the younger brother—would agree to narc. I dropped the charge altogether for Petey's promise to enroll in community college and get a job. The detective wanted me riddled with bullets. He went to my supervisor and—I heard—raged about "that black woman" who'd thrown his case out. The supervisor asked me about it, and I told him the case was weak and the defendant deserved a chance to turn his life around. The other prosecutors did the same thing for young white boys every day of the week. One of the main reasons we're filling up the prisons. He let it go. Today, Otis—the older brother—and Petey own a garage near the Galleria. They service only Jags.

I won the police over by doing something I learned from Nicky Lathan, a star basketball player I dated for a hot second while we were at Western Michigan. He was between white girls. He used to tell me all the time, "Just be a woman, baby." In other words, put a man's needs first, act like I was a second-class citizen, you know, the kind of shit a lot of sisters were doing at the time. After he went back to the white girl who had his nose open, I realized he meant that the way you get a man to come around is to make him feel like a man. To do that you have to "be a woman." So I let the police officers I worked with teach me, even when I understood a procedure better than they did. The police are the D.A.'s clients, and clients are the same all over. What they really want is for you to fight for them, even if you lose.

I prosecuted every case like it was my only one. Pretty soon I got a reputation among the officers for being one of the better assistant D.A.'s on staff. It didn't hurt that I'd go out with them to serve search warrants or make drug busts, things most assistant D.A.'s couldn't be bothered with.

"Howdy."

A friendly good ol' boy knocks as he enters the temporary space I've been given in the D.A.'s office, closing the door behind him.

"Officer Polawski?" I ask.

"Check."

"I thought you had a partner," I say, immediately on the alert.

"I do. Doesn't like women." He pulls up a chair. "Thinks they ought to be at home."

"Don't tell me," I say. "He carries a club and has a big, hairy chest."

He snickers. "Like to see her pull off the hairy chest part."

"She doesn't like women?"

"Says you're all a bunch of pussies." He grins like a gopher. I refuse to give the son of a bitch the satisfaction of seeing me blow up. I pick up the receiver and dial police headquarters. "What's your supervisor's name?"

Polawski turns white as a hot flash. "Uh, maybe I can talk some sense into her."

I hand him the phone. "Tell her she's got five minutes to get her ass in gear."

He places a call, speaks with his back to me in a hushed whisper, like I care what he's saying. Hands the phone back. "She's on her way."

Turns out the bitch is black.

I'm riding in the backseat of an unmarked police car on the way to view the scene of Willie Shalandar's alleged—convince me—murder. The police brief me why they suspect foul play. It so happens, ten days after his death they received an anonymous call.

"Somebody saw it? You've got a witness?"

The black female detective—her name's Rosie Grady—looks at me like she can't stand to breathe the same air with me. "Not exactly, Ms. Parrish Ingersoll . . . ma'am."

"Ms. Parrish will do, Detective Grady," I say. She's been wearing me out with that shit ever since I made her haul her big ass to my office. When she showed up, I understood why she hates women. Though she's definitely not what old folks used to call "homely," she's made up her mind she's not ever going to be beautiful. In the company of men, she's not constantly reminded of all her "holes," real or imagined. Someone like me brings them all out like I'm rubbing her nose in her shortcomings.

Rosie's mouth does an ugly twist when I put her in check about my name. She's determined to have the last word. "Well, you never know what people want to be called these days, they got so many names."

"I heard that," I say with a smile. I'm determined to kill the bitch with kindness. "Since we'll be working together, how about you just call me Gwen? I'll call you Rosie, and I'll call you—" I look at her partner, Polawski. I didn't catch his first name.

"You can call me Dan," he says, pretending to concentrate on driving but, like a man, smirking at the prospect of a cat fight.

"Anything you say, ma'am," Rosie says in that purpose-fully bland voice public servants reserve for those they truly despise. "Like I said, we got a call. The tipster wouldn't say how they knew, but they said somebody pushed the victim's car in front of the oncoming train."

I sit back and think. Willie was a notorious creature of habit. Even so, somebody would have to be pretty damn good to plan a murder by train, and Charles Garrett is not exactly a rocket scientist.

I ask the sixty-four-dollar question. "So what makes you think Garrett had anything to do with it?"

Rosie tightens her eyes so hard they practically disap-pear. She thinks my question is shit. I may reconsider killing her with kindness and just kill her. I'll get my chance, which I learned from practicing law will come around. All I have to do is wait on it. Right now I need what she knows. She knows it.

She takes her sweet time answering. "The tipster told us to check out Garrett's car. It wasn't a whole lot for the lab to work with, but we did get a match with the paint from the victim's car with the small dent we found on Garrett's bumper."

Figured it was dumb luck. Contrary to what we see in movies and cop shows, in real life most criminals catch themselves. Houston's finest isn't about to cut loose their air conditioning and Shipley doughnuts to chase somebody down in the Texas heat. Too bad Hollywood doesn't like lawyers. We'd be heroes too.

"This is too good," I say, thinking out loud. "Charles Gar-rett pushes Willie onto the tracks and lets the two-nineteen do the rest. The almost perfect crime." I get a horrible image of Willie. *"Dang—"*

Rosie reads my mind. "Never knew what hit him."

I half chuckle. Police are notorious for their gallows hu-mor. Rosie seems to appreciate that I liked her little joke. She half smiles.

"Did you talk to Garrett?" I ask. "Is he alibied?"

She gets real country on me, like I think she's ignorant. "Well, now, *Gwen,* ma'am—we'ins didn't want to hog all the glory, gettin' him to confess and all, all by our lonesome."

Okay, ask a stupid question, get a stupid answer. "So in other words," I say, "you tried to question him and he told you to kiss his ass and talk to his lawyer."

Dan laughs. "Bingo," he says.

We've just turned onto South Mac Gregor, one of Third Ward's unofficial boundaries. This part is being rapidly gentrified, which Dirk calls a polite way of saying white folks are reclaiming the ghetto. He's currently battling the city on behalf of some woebegone residents of Allen Parkway Village, a public housing project presently occupying prime downtown commercial property in what's left of old Fourth Ward, Houston's first victim of gentrification.

We enter the part of Third Ward where the rich blacks live. Where I intend to live. From the way Rosie is trying so hard not to be impressed, I can tell she harbors the same dream. Who wouldn't? These are mansions with estates attached, built by rich Jews who fled to Southwest Houston when integration came. We stop at Ardmore, which runs parallel to the old HB&T Railway line, about five minutes from Willie's home. It's ironic that a railroad line could run through such a fine neighborhood. I guess they didn't think much better of Jews than they did of blacks back in those days.

Dan pulls the car over, and we get out to look around. The first thing I notice is that there are no crossing arms. Just signs and traffic lights. I look down at the ground.

"If you're looking for skid marks, there aren't any," Rosie says. "Or any other signs that the commissioner was doing anything but waiting for the train." She idly stubs some gravel with the toe of her shoe. "As a matter of fact, till we got the tip, Traffic was treating it like a routine car-train accident."

"There is such an animal?" To my way of thinking, nothing's routine about a train and car colliding.

"Oh, yeah," Dan corrects me. "Harris County's got the highest incidence of these kinda collisions of anywhere in the country." Now, that's deep. Did the killer know that?

I look around at all the tiny glass fragments scattered about like gravel. "I don't think I want to know the kind of people who consciously cross in front of an oncoming train."

Dan shrugs and, like the good ol' boy that he is, sticks a match between his teeth. It dances around his mouth as he talks. "You'd be surprised how many you do know. They all think they can beat it. Sometimes they do, sometimes—blam—crunch city."

I try to imagine it's night and Willie's and Garrett's cars are lined up waiting for the train. "You said there was only a small dent and a little paint on Garrett's car?"

Rosie rolls her eyes for no particular reason. She was being cool for a hot second, but now she's got her ass on her shoulders again. "That's right . . . Gwen."

"What evidence of contact is on the commissioner's car?"

"None," she admits reluctantly.

"None?"

"None," Dan reiterates.

"I want to see the pictures of the vehicles."

Rosie insolently shifts her hips to one side, doesn't make a move. Dan and I glance at each other, reading her body language clearly. She's none too happy, about what I don't know.

"I'll get 'em," he volunteers, glad to have an excuse to head for the car. Men like to watch bitch shit, but they don't like to be in the middle of it if they can help it. When he's out of earshot, I decide to straighten her out once and for all.

"Listen, Rosie, let me tell you something for your own good." Her eyes tighten, like she's been waiting for this. Good. "I'm not one of those blacks who feels loyalty to other blacks just because they're black," I say. "If you don't give a damn about me, I don't give a damn about you." She opens her mouth. "Let me finish, because when I do, there's not going to be anything more to say. If you show your ass to me one more time in front of that white boy—or anybody else, for that matter—I'm going to report you for having a 'bad attitude.' We both know that's the Bismark for *us*." She stares at me, breathing hard. "When I get through telling on you, they ain't gonna let you carry the shovel behind the mounted patrol. And even if they don't believe me, I'll make sure it goes in your personnel file and follows you to your grave. I'm a lawyer. I've forgotten more ways to plant things than you'll ever remember." She's mad enough to chew rivets, but she holds herself. In a move I know will offend her, I get right up in her face, make my voice dead serious. "You mess with me, I'll cut your titties off."

"Here you go, Gwen—"

I turn and smile brightly at Dan, who is holding a large manila envelope out to me. "Thanks, Dan," I say. I look at the photos inside. Dan tries to figure out what he missed while I sift through the thick stack of black-and-white photos one by one. She was right about Willie's car. They shot his classic black Mercedes from every angle possible. Not a scratch anywhere. In contrast, the front bumper of Charles' car—a brand-new red Ford pickup—is scratched and dented. "This doesn't make sense."

"Well, now, Gwen," Dan says with a shit-eating, white boy grin, "if I had a nickel for every case I worked on that made sense, I'd be a poor man."

I smile politely at him, shielding my eyes from the hot glare of the afternoon sun. He has pale white skin and hair as red as crawfish. Spiny red strands shoot from his nose, which somebody broke for him. It's covered with webby broken veins from guzzling beer, probably at the place where he got his nose job.

He and Rosie couldn't be more opposite. I wonder what he really thinks of her. Or me, for that matter. They've learned to keep their true feelings to themselves, which I hate about the "New South." In the Old South you knew where you stood, always at the bottom or at the end, but it was your place alone. Now you've got to try to figure it out just like up North. Dan's right about one thing—the only

person who ever understands a crime is the perpetrator.
Sometimes even they don't know.

There's a smaller envelope in with the pictures, the crime-
scene photos. They're morbid and fascinating, like all pictures that capture death. Willie's car was almost cut in half
by the train. What remains intact is a twisted wreck.

"Somewhere in all that metal is the commissioner," Dan
says, studying the pictures over my shoulder. "Found his
head down the road a piece."

I close my eyes to erase the image of Willie's head rolling
around loose. "I haven't heard that expression in a long
time," I say, massaging the sudden throb in my temples
from looking at the pictures. "My father used to say he was
going down the road a piece whenever he went to the bar.
Every Friday night."

I hand the pictures back. I prosecuted a lot of murder
cases when I was in the D.A.'s office, and I've defended
quite a few. Every time it comes to viewing the victim's remains I get the same weird feeling, like I'm dancing with
the corpse, my recurring nightmare as a child. I'd always
tell my mother the next day, sometimes still shaking inside.
She'd smile like adults do when children say something sincerely stupid. "The dead can't hurt you. It's the live ones
you have to worry about."

17

If I can just keep to the middle, tell everybody what they want to hear, be all things to all people, I can make it. At least that's what I tell myself on my way to Ashleigh Lee's school to meet with her counselor. She's having "problems."

Kincaid School is in River Oaks, the most exclusive school in the most exclusive neighborhood in Houston. Ashleigh Lee's been going there since the second grade, over Kwame's running objection. He thinks she should be in one of the "better" public schools. If it's a public school, it can't be better. As far as I'm concerned, it's just as easy to rub elbows with rich kids as it is poor ones.

Ordinarily, the parking lot would be crowded with expensive late-model cars and I'd have to circle a couple of times to find a space, but school's been out for thirty minutes, so it's not a problem. I head straight to the administration building. It's so hot, heat ricochets off the asphalt. Kincaid is pretty, like a miniature Ivy League school, all vine-covered and plush-looking. Nothing like Cass Tech, my old high school in Detroit. It looked like an automobile factory. All the buildings at Kincaid have been completely refurbished except for the natorium and the library—they're brand-new. I glance at the bronze donors plaque, proud to see my name, one of the few blacks to make a sustaining contribution to the construction fund even if it is killing me financially.

Cool, soothing air envelops me as soon as I step inside

the lobby. I enter the dean's office, announce myself to the school secretary. I'm not for any bullshit this afternoon. Dirk and I have tickets for the Alley Theater's annual gala tonight. I need to get home to wash my hair, which takes a long time to dry in this high humidity.

"Hello," I say, entering the conference room like I own it, something I learned from court. "I'm Gwen Parrish, Ashleigh Lee's mother."

I stop in my tracks. I thought I was meeting with her counselor. Instead, a half dozen people are sitting around the conference table, scrutinizing me like I'm Jack the Ripper's mother. Ashleigh Lee's seated in their midst, looking like a habitual criminal on her last strike, all contempt and fear.

"Mrs. Ingersoll, we spoke on the phone. I'm Cathy Hardesty." A well-dressed black woman with short salt-and-pepper hair and thick, muddy-looking makeup, Paliachi cheeks and Cleopatra eyebrows, rises to greet me.

I take the only empty seat, slowly sitting down next to Ashleigh Lee, my warning bell going crazy. I know a hangin' jury when I see one.

Hardesty gives me a fake smile and introduces Ashleigh Lee's teachers—three white women and two white men, one of whom is Mr. Reddison, the math teacher. Ashleigh Lee "hates" him. "Are you aware your daughter has skipped class thirty-two times this year?"

Did I know she could speak Chinese? "No, I am not."

"Of course, we're talking about different classes at different times." She smiles politely. "Never the entire day."

"I see." Red. I'm trained to observe and to listen, but I'm so mad I can't do either. I should've let Dirk come with me like he wanted to do.

"In addition to cutting my class twelve times this semester, Ashleigh Lee failed to turn in the last three assignments, and she's missed—" Ms. Vaughn, the English teacher, stops to check her grade book. Hers is the last in a litany of sorry reports. "One, two, three quizzes. In addition to flunking the midterm."

Ashleigh Lee swivels away from me and stares out the window like we're all wasting her time. "Why wasn't I told about this sooner?" I ask indignantly.

Ms. Vaughn looks to Hardesty. She's ready for me. "Mrs. Ingersoll," she says, her voice modulated, like I might go berserk, "I have a record of each phone contact we made to your office this semester—five in all—none of which were returned until yesterday."

Damn, have I been that busy?

"These are copies of notes that were sent home with Ashleigh Lee from her teachers advising you of her deficient status." She hands me slips of NCR paper I've never seen. "And this is a letter I wrote you two months ago advising you of the problem, urging you to contact me." She pinches the envelope with her thumb and forefinger like it's contaminated. "It was returned."

"I changed offices—"

"It was addressed to your home."

I don't even have to look at Ashleigh Lee to figure this one out. "I've been very busy," I say lamely, looking around for sympathy. I might as well be looking for gold.

"Mrs. Ingersoll," Hardesty says ever so kindly, "perhaps our program's too . . . rigorous for your daughter."

I shove away from the table. "Are you trying to say my daughter's too dumb to be here, Ms. Hardesty?"

My frankness startles her. Functionaries don't like it when you speak plain English. The white people avert their eyes. They'd rather have to separate fighting dogs than us. "Mrs. Ingersoll, no one's saying Ashleigh Lee is dumb."

"They'd better not." I eye each one of them in turn. "Ashleigh Lee had to be tested like just everybody else to get in here."

Hardesty puffs up like a rooster. "I assure you, Mrs. Ingersoll, we've been more than fair to your daughter. We've tried to help her in every respect."

Where does she get off with that "we" shit? Of all the Uncle Tom niggers in the world, I hate this kind the most. I've had enough. "Ms. Hardesty, are you familiar with the expression, 'Money talks and bullshit walks'?" Mr. Reddison and the other male teacher snigger, the white women gasp. I couldn't care less, not after all the money I'm giving this school. "I want to see Dean Kerr."

Ashleigh Lee looks like she has the world on a string as we walk outside. I'm furious. "What the hell do you mean embarrassing me like that? Did you see how much groveling I had to do to keep you in this goddamn school?" Actually, Dean Kerr was very understanding, especially when I mentioned I'm a sustaining contributor.

Ashleigh Lee shrugs. "Nobody asked you to."

I stop and look at her. The only thing keeping me from slapping her is the fact that somebody might see me. She keeps walking. I don't care who sees me. I snatch her arm, make her face me. "*I* asked me to. Fifteen years ago when I brought you into this world. I swore I'd work my fingers to the bone if I had to so you could have everything I didn't."

She plays her hole card. "Then why don't I have a father?"

I let her go. She was too young to remember how it was with Kwame. I've never low-rated him to her and I never will. Naturally she idolizes him and I'm a bitch. She waits at the car for me to unlock the door, pats her foot impatiently. When I unlock it, she opens her door, arrogantly tosses the thousand little braids she's started wearing lately, which I hate. She looks like an African. That's it for me.

"Ashleigh Lee, if you don't straighten up—and I mean 'p.d.q.'—you can forget about that trip to L.A."

Her brown eyes register disbelief. "But you said I could go to the reunion—"

"I said maybe." They've been planning this trip for four months. Kwame promised to take her to Disneyland, and he has a thousand relatives in California—plus he said he'd teach her to drive on the way.

Deep furrows accentuate her scowl at me. I don't care. "If

you're mad, Ashleigh Lee, you better scratch your ass and get glad. And attend class and get your grades—otherwise the trip's o-f-f. Off."

I've had a taste for whole fried trout all morning. The Groovey Grill has the best. That's because black folks know how to season food. But they're not open for lunch anymore. The way things are going, they won't be open at all.

After the Groovey, I like Cap'n Benny's. It's not seasoned the way I like, but the fish is fresh and it's fried with cornmeal, the only way to cook fish if you know what you're doing. They have three locations, each housed in actual boats. I prefer the "black" one on South Main.

Cold air whacks me in the face when I step inside. Ordinarily, the hull can hold fewer than twenty people, sitting at the counter or standing at a long shelf on the wall. Lunchtime, twice that'll pack in. Fortunately, it's late afternoon, the job slaves are back in the mines, so it's pleasantly empty.

I slide onto a stool at the counter and place my order with Laurzel. She and Rosco, the oyster shucker, have been working here so long people think his name is Benny and she's his wife, since they're both black. Rosco winks and offers me some oysters, which he knows I hate. Like eating raw eggs. Betty automatically sets iced tea in front of me and calls out to Enrique, the Hispanic cook, to "drop my whole cat."

"And get the seasoning right this time, Enrique," I tease, waving hello. He smiles back with snaggled teeth. *"Sí, bonita senorita."*

Laurzel gives me a look. "He couldn't season right if you held a gun to his head."

"He sho' can fry fish for a Mex," Rosco says.

"I heard that," I say, sipping my tea. I don't load it down with sugar like everyone else, a dead giveaway I'm not from the South.

"Hey, hey, whatchew say." Rosco beams when the door opens. I look to see who rates such a big greeting. Swallow hard. It's Kwame. There are over three hundred thousand black people in Houston, and he has to be the one I run into today.

"What's happening?" he says to me, taking the stool to my left, cool as ever. He and Rosco dap. Laurzel presents her cheek to be kissed, smiling like a schoolgirl when he obliges. "Give me the whole cat, Laurzel."

"How about some gumbo to go with that, sugar?" she says, like she's coaxing her favorite child. "It's delicious."

"Whatever you say," he says, knocking the foam off the beer she serves him. He takes a big gulp. "Ahh. That wet my whistle."

She sets my fish before me. "Umm, looks good," he says, reaching for a fry. I slap his hand. He smiles mischievously. "So it's like that."

"It's always been like that," I say, eating. He knows I never did like people in my plate. Not that that ever stopped him when we were together. No matter how much I put on his plate, he always reached in mine for something. The first time he asked me to lunch, we went to this broken-down fish shack around the corner from the law school, my suggestion since he was on grants and loans just like me. We both ordered the deluxe fish sandwich and fries, got our food, and sat at the broken-down picnic table out front. I was shy about eating in front of him. The first thing he did was to reach for my fries. I shielded them instinctively.

"Selfish-hearted." He laughed and took one anyway. "You must be an only child."

I wished. I'm the oldest of nine. "I don't like people in my food, that's all."

"I'm not 'people.' " He seemed to look right through me with those beautiful dark eyes of his. My heart didn't stand a chance, keeled right over. Then he smiled. I felt stingy and like I was making a bad impression for being so picky. "Here," I blurted, shoving my food over to him. "You can have the whole thing." C.C., Willette, and I laughed about that for days. There I was—poor, starving, a first-year law student just like him—and I'm giving food away. I *must've* been in love.

". . . I said, how's your husband?"

It takes me a moment to stop strolling down memory lane and turn my feet back to present. Kwame stares at me, amused, like he knows something about me no one else does.

"Fine."

He spoons the last of his gumbo from the brimming cup Laurzel gave him. "You were right," he tells her. "This is better than it was, and it's always good." He toasts Enrique. *"Muchissimos gracias, señor."*

Flattered, Enrique insists Laurzel give him some more when she serves his catfish. That's how it's always been with Kwame. People are either giving him things or doing things for him for which he never fails to show his appreciation which they lap up. Like now, he can't compliment the fish enough. Golden-fried and crackling hot, it steams when he bites into the creamy white meat. Laurzel, Rosco, and Enrique beam.

"So," he says to me, "I hear you're not letting Ashleigh Lee go to California." Figured he'd bring up either that or Garrett. "May I ask why not?"

I lay my fork down, wipe my mouth with the cheap paper napkin, crumple it, and drop it in my plate. I remind myself that I'm still a lawyer, and lawyers don't answer questions. "Didn't she tell you?"

"She did, but I didn't understand it. First she said because of her grades, then her teachers. Don't you think you're being too hard?"

If he'd stop playing Father Perfect, I wouldn't have to make up the difference all the time. "You don't have to live with her every day."

"We can change that real easy."

I look at him, expecting to see a smart-aleck expression. Instead, his brown eyes are "blue," like that country song.

"No."

I sound harsher than I intended. We both look down. He

breaks the awkwardness. "I better change the subject, then, before you go off. They haven't seen you act your color in here."

"You don't know that."

"Yeah, I do. They still let you in here." This isn't right. The ground feels like it shifted or something. We shouldn't be this . . . friendly.

"So," he says, feeling the awkwardness too, "how's the case coming? Got any exculpatory evidence you want to give me?"

Garrett. I'm back on solid ground. I know this Kwame. "No."

"Why not?"

"Because there isn't any. Everything points to your man."

"Come on, Gwen. I know you well enough to know you've looked at this case inside out and backward. There's nothing there but air and you know it."

"Don't sell air short, Kwame. People pull stuff out of it all the time."

"They're called magicians. Which is what you're going to have to be to get a conviction."

Playtime's over. Neither one of us is smiling now. "I've got a rock-solid case against your client."

"A solid circumstantial case. You need a witness to convict him."

"I have one."

He's genuinely surprised. "Who?"

"Whoever snitched on him in the first place."

He pushes his plate away, annoyed. "Like I said, you need a witness. Why don't you do the right thing instead of the white thing for once and throw this crap in the trash where it belongs?"

"Are you saying Willie wasn't murdered?"

"I don't care. My client didn't do it and you know it."

I jump off the stool, ready to fight. "Some of us do care."

"You know I didn't mean it like that—"

I grab my purse and head for the register, pay my bill, and leave as Laurzel rings Kwame up. "Everything all right, sugar pie?" I hear her purr at him on my way out.

"Great," he says, in a hurry to catch me. "Wait up, Gwen. We're not done talking—"

I swing the door open. "Yes, we are, 'sugar pie.' " I stomp outside, mad that I'm mad. The sun doesn't help any, beating down on my head like it's a tom-tom. Neither does the gravel parking lot. I can feel every stone through these leather soles.

"I said to wait up." Kwame blocks my car door.

My hand goes to my hip. "When are you going to learn I don't have to do one single, blessed thing you say?"

Surprisingly, the question knocks the steam out of him. "You don't," he says, moving aside, a strange look on his face. "I'm sorry. I was way out of line."

Now the steam gets knocked out of me. "Did you just— apologize?"

"Yes," he says. "I was wrong. I wouldn't have jammed another lawyer like that." He smiles a little. "Yes, I would've. But not you. I really do want us to be friends. For our daughter's sake."

Hot tears spring to my eyes from I don't know where. "How dare you, Kwame." I turn my head so he doesn't see, fumble with my keys.

"What?" Bewildered, he tries to stop me. "What did I say?"

"Get out of my way." I shove him back, get in the car, slam and lock the door, quickly wiping my eyes with both hands.

He knocks on the window. "Gwen, what did I say?"

I have to roll the window down or suffocate from the heat. He leans inside. "Gwen, please—I don't want us to keep ending like this. Can't we talk about it?"

I shift into drive. "The only discussions we'll be having from now on will be in the courtroom, Mr. El'kasid." I speed off, my wheels spitting gravel at him. I don't stop for traffic when I pull out onto Main. I don't even see it. Tears stream down my face. I'm not making sense even to me.

I curse the light I'm forced to stop at. "How dare he turn into the man I've always wanted him to be after all these years." I pound the steering wheel. "Not after all the changes I've been through. Oh hell, no."

I don't even remember getting on the South Loop. Now I'm sailing off it onto the feeder, going God knows where. Stella Link's coming up. Another light, maybe I'll come to my senses. Only I have to slow down first. If I stay in the middle lane, I can still get back on the freeway and go home. Or I can turn onto Stella Link and drive along the bayou to the office. *The office.* I have to meet Willette. Damn Kwame. I screech to the right. The car hits something—rolls over it. A big something. My heart jumps to my throat. I slam on the brakes and jump out. There's a bicycle under my front wheels. "Oh, my God—"

Tasting nothing but terror, I look under the car. No one's there. The bike wiggles. I stand up and run around to the passenger side. A little white boy, eight, maybe nine years old, kneels on the curb, trying to free it. I swear I never saw him.

"Are you—all right?"

I'm afraid to touch him. He's looking at me like I murdered his bike and he could be next. He scrambles to his feet. "Yes—I—yes."

He looks fine. No visible injuries, abrasions, contusions, nothing that looks like he just got hit by a car. I don't know what to say. He stares forlornly at his bike. At least I can help pull it free. It's a miracle it's in one piece. I roll it around to make sure it's operable.

"Thanks," he says, taking the handlebars from me.

"Are you sure it's okay? I can buy you a new one. What's your name? I'll come home with you. I need to tell your parents what happened." You see, Mr. and Mrs. White Folks, I was so upset with my ex-husband for being nice, I almost ran your son over.

"That's okay."

The kid hurries away, walking his bike across the street, which was what he was probably getting ready to do when I hit him. Thank God someone taught him bicycle safety. If he'd been riding instead, they would've been pulling him from under my wheels. I look around guiltily. What if someone saw us? I don't think so. Traffic's still fairly light; no one's on the street. They don't do a lot of walking during the day. It's too hot. I look back at the boy. Safely across the street, he glances at me fearfully, hops on his bike, and takes off. I stare after him, imagining my future. Nobody would believe I didn't see him. I'd be disgraced. Lose everything.

What if he goes home and tells? Should I follow him? I look around again. Nobody saw it. Why should I? He doesn't know who I am. Nobody does, unless I do something stupid, like tell on myself. I check my fender. No trace of the accident. I get in the car, check the mirror to see how I look. The same. Somebody honks for me to move on, which I do very carefully. Now I know how Charles Garrett feels.

18

I exit the elevator and breeze past Delzenia. "The commissioner in?"

She nods, typing. "She's with Judge Hendrix. They're waiting for you." I almost say sorry, I got held up running over somebody. Instead I open Willette's door—just as she extricates herself from C.C.'s cloying embrace, obviously irritated with her.

"Hello," I say. "Sorry I'm late—"

They quickly move apart, assume "normalcy." I enter slowly, playing off what I saw, but remembering what Michael said to Willette on my wedding night ("tell your cunt-sucking, pussy-eating, carpet-munching bulldagger friend").

Willette and C.C.? No way. Must've been my lyin' eyes.

"I had an accident."

Willette's immediately concerned. "Are you okay?" She glances at C.C. as she sits at her desk. C.C. stands by the fireplace, looking at me like I'm a defendant she's waiting to hear the facts about. "What happened?"

"It was nothing. Just a fender bender. This is for you—" I hand her my report on Charles Garrett, taking a seat across from her, not about to tell them I almost killed a little white boy. A white boy. They'd put me under the jail. We don't get away with killing white people. It's the Eleventh Commandment. I joke about the accident. "You know Black Beauty don't take no shit."

Willette doesn't hear me. She concentrates on the report, reading greedily. C.C. laughs, walks over, and sits down.

"You and that damn Jag. I've never seen a woman love a car like you do." Her eyes linger on me. I don't like it. I'm starting not to like her. "I hear you're ready to wrap things up."

We watch Willette, but she's oblivious to us. "I think so."

C.C. breathes an exaggerated sigh of relief. "Thank you, Father. The way they cut up at Emancipation Park this weekend, I say the sooner Charles Garrett is set up—" We both laugh at her gaffe. "Talk about a Freudian slip. In any event, the sooner they ship him to Huntsville the better."

"What happened at Emancipation Park?" Between home and working on this case I have no idea what's happening in the rest of the world.

"Your people called themselves rioting," she says scornfully. "It was supposed to be a 'peaceful show of support' for Garrett. That lasted about a minute. Then the police had to start knocking heads."

"You mean they kept their itchy fingers off their batons that long?" I'm serious.

C.C. stiffens defensively. "I think the Houston Police Department showed uncharacteristic restraint."

"You mean they didn't kill anybody."

"Yes," she says, indignant. "That's progress and it's to be commended." I want to commend her—on her transformation from a black person to staunch defender of the white establishment. I just now noticed. On top of her usual mammy-made hairstyle, she's even starting to look like a Tom (they actually come out and call themselves Republicans now): body rigid, nose upturned, nostrils flared, eyes cold, mouth turned down whenever it's not minstrel grinning. Some kind of spiritual rot underneath it all. She snorts haughtily. "That's what Garrett gets for talking so much shit."

It sounds funny hearing her curse now that she's "Judge Negro." She looks at me, her face a lewd sneer. "I hear Kwame's telling people he's got something special for the special prosecutor."

"Be serious." He would never say anything like that,

though he is being nice for a reason. Good thing I didn't fall for it. Other than getting so rattled I almost ran over somebody. "I've got Mr. Garrett *and* his lawyer by the short hairs."

"It certainly looks that way." Willette hands the report to C.C. "Excellent."

I warm all over. "Thank you, Willette. It's circumstantial, but it's tight as—"

"New pussy," C.C. cackles, reading. Willette and I exchange a look, silently agreeing to ignore her remark.

"I've ordered the detectives to keep looking for witnesses," I say. "They're turning over every stone. If we have to go to trial without one, well—" I shrug. "Many a cell at TDC is filled with people convicted on slimmer reeds."

"What about his alibi?" C.C. asks.

I check my watch. The grand jury's about to adjourn. "In an hour his wife will be indicted for aggravated assault," I say. "We hold on Garrett till she's convicted, and there goes what's left of her credibility."

"Who'd she assault?" C.C. asks.

"The special prosecutor," I reply.

"Very clever." Willette smiles, her green eyes radiating so much pure admiration I'm embarrassed.

"I got lucky." And almost maimed for life but for the quick thinking of Detective Rosie Grady, my new ace boon coon, tight and mellow. We'd gone to Garrett's house to interview his wife. I shiver recalling how hateful Sue was, standing in her doorway, potato in one hand, peeler in the other. She swore up and down Charles was with her when Willie got killed. And if we didn't believe her, we could kiss, suck, and lick her black ass. The more she talked, the madder she got, waving that peeler like a switchblade to emphasize her point. I asked her if anyone could verify that she and Charles were together all night besides their children—six stair steps all under the age of seven, crowded around her, watching like Brazilian street urchins. She got insulted. "I'm sick and tired of y'all calling us a lie. I don't have to lie. Bitch, you a lie. Lying on my husband."

I cut her off, thanking her for her cooperation, which she apparently didn't appreciate because as I turned to go she slashed my arm with the peeler just like it was a potato. She was getting ready to "peel" me again, but Rosie caught her hand and tried to wring it off her wrist. That's when she ordered her kids to jump us. They wore us out, kicking and hitting and biting. Rosie had to pull her gun and threatened to shoot Sue. They got hysterical. "Don't shoot our mama! Don't shoot our mama!"

I didn't want her arrested in front of her kids, so Rosie and I left, limping and bruised, and drove to Ben Taub to get checked out. On the way, I started thinking about how it must've looked—us battling a bunch of kids and their mama—and started laughing. Rosie busted out laughing too, so hard she almost couldn't drive. We got tetanus shots at the hospital and licked our wounds. Turns out Rosie likes Wild Turkey too.

I rub my forearm. The long, thin scab is beginning to itch and drop off. "Never," I tell C.C. and Willette, "underestimate what a potato peeler can do." They laugh.

Willette turns serious. "I noticed the lab report hedges on the paint. There's not an exact match?"

I'm glad she brought that up. "No, but we're not talking dye lot differences. They're at least ninety-eight percent sure the paint's from the commissioner's car."

"Humph," says C.C. "Two percent's enough for Kwame to see daylight."

Concern surfaces on Willette's face. Damn C.C., she always did like to stir the pot. Fun, long as you're not the one she's messing with. I need to reassure Willette. "I wish I could tell you we have a perfect case, Willette. There's no such thing. And you know it, C.C. What we do have is as close to perfect that I've ever seen. The lab boys don't know why the paint doesn't match one hundred percent, but it happens. Metal on metal, alloys form, you get impurities." I shrug. I'm not worried. "Did you notice the fibers? Garrett must've used a blanket over his fender when he pushed your father onto the tracks." I shake my head. "You have to give him credit. His murder scheme was almost perfect."

"Unfortunately." C.C. glares at me pointedly to check out Willette. Her face is frozen with pain. I want to snatch every one of my stupid words back. "Willette, I'm so sorry. I only meant—"

She flicks her hand dismissively, vanquishes the sadness. "I understand. You've done an excellent job, Gwen."

I quote Willette as I peel onions—with a knife—while Dirk tosses a salad. " 'You've done an excellent job, Gwen. The downtown boys will be impressed.' My shit is going to be gold."

He doesn't say anything, not the reaction I want. "Did you hear what I said, Dirk? I'm on my way."

"Are you taking the case to the grand jury?"

"Yarrow is." Still annoyed about that, I toss the onions in the pan. They hit the hot oil with a crackle. "Day after tomorrow." There are just some nuts we'll never get to crack. The grand jury—the *sanctum sanctorum* of the criminal justice system—is one. I bet there's only been one black grand juror—they have to have one black face—in all of Harris County, and he's (black women are too unpredictable) the safest, most loyal, white folks-loving Negro they can find.

"They're using you, honey."

Doesn't he think I know that? "Use me, just don't abuse me," I say, adding bell pepper and garlic to the onions. The aroma cools me out. "I've got an idea. Let's go down to the Riviera. We can leave after Ashleigh Lee gets out of school." I slide my arms around his waist and rub against him, my sure-fire way to get him to agree to death by mutilation, if necessary. "What'd'ya say, Dirky?"

He disengages himself, carries the salad to the table, arranges the knives and forks, his back purposefully to me. Don't tell me my mojo isn't working. "Is something wrong, Dirk?"

"I don't like the way they're using you, that's all."

I came home tonight to celebrate. Like a man, Dirk's doing his damnedest to make me reach for my boxing gloves. "Haven't you heard anything? The world's divided into users and the usees. Anyone can wind up in either category at any time, including you. C'mon, baby." I draw him close. "Be happy for me."

I stand on tiptoes, kiss his lips, forcing them apart with my tongue. He wants to be cold, but I feel his body relax. I press harder against him. A dam breaks: he moans and kisses me back, his hands all over my body, ready to do it right here on the table. My chicken conveniently clamors to be turned. I slip away from his arms with a smile. Got my mojo working, all right.

My getaway idea has been an unmitigated disaster. The five-hundred-mile ride south was bad enough. I might as well have been locked in the car with fighting cats the way Dirk and Ashleigh Lee hissed and spat at each other nonstop. I was hoping things would improve when we got out into the fresh Gulf air. I was wrong. They're not speaking to each other—or me, since this was my idea.

He's fishing in his dinghy someplace; she's holed up reading or sticking pins in her voodoo doll collection. I'm doing my Otis Redding thing at the end of a long, old dock, toes making little circles in the water, staring out across the Gulf at Padre Islands, the main draw for the snowbirds who flock to South Texas every winter. Less than a mile off, they look like floating forests.

These same weather refugees used to fill up places like Dirk's old mainland resort until the islands became an exclusive retreat for the "touristas." His place looks like it did in its fifties heyday: two strings of tiny wooden cabins, each with a view of the Gulf, lining a long drive that leads up to the "Big House," a stately clapboard castle sitting high up on the windswept promontory of his private peninsula. He bought it on a whim, closing it to the public, updating only the Big House. He likes having a time warp all to himself.

The only way me or Ashleigh Lee could've come here back in the good ol' days would've been as maids, an irony that swirls about me like the constant watery breeze making my hair look like I stuck my finger in a light socket. Poor Ashleigh Lee. Hers hasn't shown up since we got here. I think about all the things my mother used to say about hair like hers. "Rising like baking powder," "looking like a mosquito around the edges," or "Where's that chil' going with those kooka-burros?" If she called somebody's hair "bee-bees and buckshot," it was hopeless.

The rhythm of the waves, the salty breeze, the hot sun, all combined makes me sleepy. I make a pillow with my hands and lean on the rail, nodding off. Damn Kwame. He put a curse on my child's hair.

"Mom!" That's why she's yelling at me.

I wake up, look around. Ashleigh Lee's waving at me from the front porch of the Big House. "What?" I call.

"Telephone!"

I pad up the narrow dock, over the stony grass, up the porch steps. "Who is it?"

Ashleigh Lee shrugs. "Ms. Shalandar."

My heart thumps in my ears when I take up the receiver and hear Willette say, "We got the indictment."

19

Tony's is one of the most expensive restaurants in Houston. The night is velvety warm when we pull in front, and the black parking valet helps me from the car like I'm royalty. Now I understand why we're the Mercedes-Benz of servants. After three hundred years of training, no one can be as elegantly obsequious as us.

I feel like a star entering under Tony's trademark long red canopy. Inside, Willette waves to us as the maître d' ushers us to her table. She and I hug, Dirk shakes hands with Michael and Judge Zachary Tyree and his wife, Minnie. Judge Tyree's up for reelection and is the chief administrative judge for the Harris County civil courts, no-man's-land as far as I'm concerned. You don't go there unless somebody's got your back. Minnie is a gray-haired little white woman with a kind face and a sweet smile, both of which belie her hollow leg and dirty mouth. I always get a kick out of her.

Rumor has it that Judge Tyree, a country boy from West Texas, married Minnie for her money, which he parleyed into several fortunes over the thirty years they've been together. All I know is I got stuck sitting next to him at a Democratic fund-raiser a few years back, and he squeezed my knee every time he punctuated a sentence. So when Dirk steers me to the seat next to him, I deliberately drop my purse. When Dirk bends to pick it up, I switch places—winding up next to Michael, of all people.

The moment we're seated, C.C. and her date—if you can call him that—show up. Judge Tyree stops in mid-sentence;

Willette and I cut eyes at each other. The guy looks like she scraped him off the sidewalk: he has a head full of wormy-looking dreadlocks, he's wearing a grimy T-shirt and raggedy baggy pants, and he has a dirt ring around his neck. His too small jacket and power tie are compliments of Tony, no doubt.

"Hi, everybody," C.C. says, all schoolgirl breathless and slurring badly. "Sorry I'm late. This is Winston Hershell. Say hello, Winston."

"Hello." He flips the tie hanging around his neck like a noose. Where I'm from, they'd say his teeth have butter on them they're so yellow. C.C. beams at him like he's the best thing since sliced bread. "I forgot to tell him we were coming here." She giggles, pinches his cheek, and twiddles his ear. "We were busy coming. And coming—et cetera, et cetera."

The judge clears his throat, Dirk shifts uncomfortably, Michael looks bored. Mortified by C.C.'s behavior, Willette looks at me. I shrug. What's there to do? C.C.'s obviously laying on full. Minnie, slow on the upturn, finally gets it. Slaps her knee laughing and cackles like a hen laying an egg. "Sounds like a mighty scenic route you were on, Judge Hendrix. I wouldn't mind taking it, but Tyree'd probably get lost." She and C.C. snicker lasciviously. "It's been a while since he's driven into the forest by himself."

"Now, Minnie," says the judge, "that's not true. We went up to Big Bear just two weeks ago."

Everybody stares at him. Poor thing, he didn't get it. I can't help it. My shoulders start shaking. Before I know it I'm laughing. So is everyone else, including the judge, uncomfortably, rightfully suspecting the joke's on him. That breaks the ice. While Willette goes over the wine list with the sommelier, Michael asks the judge about his cattle ranch, Minnie and C.C. swap dirty jokes and booze it up, and Dirk, having discovered Winston plays in a reggae band, engages him in a deep discussion of the relative merits of reggae as it's played in the islands compared to what we hear stateside. It all sounds like thumpa-thumpa to me.

I'm enjoying the hell out of the night—until Michael's hand squeezes my thigh. I turn my body toward Dirk, now arguing with Winston over who's the better musician— Jimmy Cliff or Bob Marley. He's been in the doghouse, coming with me tonight is his only chance of escaping anytime soon. He smiles at me and holds my hand, which I rest in my lap. Until I feel Michael's hand again. He's stroking my thigh. I immediately set Dirk's hand on the table. Good thing he needs it to make a point to Winston.

I want to give Michael a look to stop it, but he's yukking it up with Judge Tyree like nothing in the world is happening. So I casually sip my wine and carefully pick his hand off my leg, giving it a swat to let him know I mean business. He feels around in my lap. Shocked, I catch my breath and press my legs together. (Where's a dime when you need it?) I would have to wear a mini. His fingers wedge my thighs apart and do their job on me. I'm dying from disgust and desire. Twisting away doesn't help. His fingers just follow me.

I assume I'll get a reprieve when the food comes, since he'll need both hands to eat. He doesn't. I've got to stop this before I go off. This is supposed to be my victory celebration of the successful investigation of Willie Shalandar's murder. I'm a cinch to get the conviction, so everybody tells me anyway. I should be leading the conversation around me instead of smiling like an idiot, afraid if I open my mouth a moan'll escape instead of words. Dirk glances at me. I avoid his eyes, pretending interest in the new art museum C.C.'s telling Willette about in Montrose, a trendy gay area. Minnie's telling Michael and Winston a dirty joke about two camels and a dog; Dirk and the judge are talking about a new Texas supreme court decision. I feel depressed. My life's finally going the way I want, and Michael's hand between my legs reminds me at what price. When I push my chair back, he snatches his hand away. "I'm going to the ladies' room."

I splash cold water on my face and try not to look at myself, return to the table, and apologize. "I—don't feel well."

Immediately concerned, Willette orders Dirk to take me home, which he's already on his feet to do. I peck C.C.'s cheek good night. She holds on to me and whispers, "You just need a good lube job up the old tailpipe, you'll be all right." I just look at her. A drunken smirk smeared across her face, she's disgusting.

On the way home, Dirk rattles on about *Dameon* v. *Swallow,* the case he was talking to Tyree about. He's really excited, thinks it's on all fours, legalese for gotcha. "Just think, hon," he says, "if the court of appeals agrees, I can make some new law." Make law, not love. Real lawyers live to "make law." The black lawyers I know live to make a buck, style and profile. They think *stari decisis* is something you get vaccinated against. I can't remember the last time I discussed a fine legal point with Willette or C.C. or Eddy or even Michael, or any other lawyers I know. I think it was in law school.

Dirk looks at me. "How you feel?"

I roll the window down and lay my head in the breeze, the light scent of refined oil and things that crawl the bayou at night wafting in the air. "I have a headache." And a heartache, which I can't tell you about. You're it.

He floors the accelerator, jetting down South Braeswood like it's the freeway. "That seems to be a refrain lately," he says resentfully. He's mad that I haven't given him any since we got back from Riviera. He and Ashleigh Lee were well rested, so the trip back was even worse. I wasn't about to reward him for that.

I don't like the way he's skimming through lights. "Dirk, don't jeopardize my life because you're in a snit."

He laughs unnaturally. "You call watching your wife play footsie with another man all night a 'snit'?"

My God, he saw us. What about Willette and the others? I stay cool. "He was drunk."

"You could've stopped him."

I sit up. "You could've done more to make our trip to

Riviera pleasant instead of a nightmare, but you didn't."
I learned from my first marriage that when you're dead
wrong, attack. A tactic Kwame used quite successfully on
me. "You made it a thousand-mile round-trip argument with
Ashleigh Lee instead."

"She was arguing with me."

"She's fifteen."

He falls silent, jaws tighter than jeans. He hates being
called childish. I sit back. At least I distracted him from Michael, who I fully intend to curse out so bad he won't want
to come near me with a pole. This is it. I mean it. Dirk means
too much to me.

We say not a word the rest of the way home. When we
walk in, Dirk slams his keys on the counter, jaws still tight.
The sound wakes Ashleigh Lee, asleep on the sofa in the
family room. I glare at him and tell her to go to bed. She
stumbles upstairs half-asleep. I run water in the sink and fill
a glass. I'm probably the only person in Houston who
drinks water directly from the tap. Dirk looks like he wants
to say something, but I turn my back and sip my water.
When you're on the offense, you have to stay there until you
decide to forgive the other person for what you did or they
apologize. He stomps upstairs.

I sift through the mail. There's a letter from Dirk's mother,
bless her heart. I couldn't ask for nicer in-laws, especially
compared to the set I inherited with Kwame. Floyd and
Leona Parrish made Ma and Pa Barker look like flower children. Kwame took me to visit them exactly one time and
only because I insisted. They live in Texas City, a little burg
forty miles south of here where feudalism Texas-style still
rules the day as far as blacks are concerned. Same holds true
for every other little town in Texas. The blacks are generally uneducated, hardworking, and poor, living at the behest
of the white folks.

The night I spent with Floyd and Leona, Floyd's red eyes
glared at me coming through the door of their modest little

frame house, which he built himself. His way of saying hello, so I was told. Leona was pleasant enough—until Floyd refused to go up the street and get her a "soda water." All hell broke loose. Floyd threatened to get his shotgun, and Leona pulled out her butcher knife. Kwame assured me they threatened each other like that all the time, but I didn't sleep a wink. I kept envisioning how the ropy scar down the side of Floyd's face probably got there. Before we left, Leona pulled me aside and passed along a little tip for keeping Kwame in line. "Throw some hominy on him. Takes the skin out by the plug. He'll straighten up and fly right."

To his credit, Kwame never even looked like he was going to get physical with me like that, which is miraculous considering the violence he must've witnessed growing up. Which makes me mad all over again when I think about Dirk slapping me and Ashleigh Lee. On the theory that every dog gets one bite, he's had his one and only time to ever do that.

"What are you doing?" Dirk's voice is conciliatory and low. He's come back downstairs, tail between his legs.

"Reading a letter from your mother."

"Really?" He moves closer, using the letter as an excuse to slide his arms around me. I let him, but I'm cold as ice. "What'd she say?"

"The usual. Everyone's fine. Your dad says hello."

He nuzzles my ear. "So give her a call. She'd love to hear from you. You're her favorite daughter-in-law."

"I'm her only daughter-in-law." I try to free myself.

He turns me around and kisses my face. "I'm sorry, Gwen. You know, popping off about Michael. I know you can handle yourself."

"Thanks for the vote of confidence." I feel myself warming to him, forgetting the bitterness I just felt about him hitting me. And the guilt over Michael.

"I don't know what I'd do if I lost you, Gwen. I don't want to be a three-time loser at marriage." He lifts my chin and forces me to look into his eyes, oceans of love and understanding. "I can forgive you for anything. Except—"

I place my finger to his lips. I know what he's going to say. Men are like that. White or black, they don't like to share.

20

Now that Garrett's signed, sealed, and delivered, all I have to do is get ready for trial, set early September before the Honorable Timmons Maday, the youngest and most rabid law-and-order judge on the bench. If Timmons had his way, they'd take prisoners straight from the courthouse to the firing squad and skip all that coddling in between. When Kwame found out Garrett's case was assigned to him, he promptly declared motion war, raining paperwork down on me and Timmons in torrents. No one expected Kwame to roll over and play dead, but he's exceeding his usual zeal. He tells everyone otherwise, but this really is getting personal.

Thank God I have the resources of Harris County and the state of Texas behind me. So far just my fee is over fifty grand, and other than Garrett's arraignment I have yet to step inside the courtroom. I'm almost embarrassed by all the money I'm making off this case (Willette's still paying me as her assistant). She says it's part of the game.

"By rubber-stamping you," she explains, "my fellow commissioners get a big chit on me early. I let them as a way of reassuring everyone I'm no maverick." Her sly smile reminds me of Willie. "Besides, what's to complain about? The county's getting a first-rate prosecution, and Charles Garrett can't scream discrimination."

I've known Willette a long time, but watching her do her commissioner thing is not only a study in politics, but a real trip. For instance, she definitely has Willie's ability to take the heat. That is to say, no matter how irate the taxpayers, unruly the department heads, or arrogant the white people, she never loses her cool during commissioner's court. This morning's a prime example. For an hour and a half we had to sit and listen to a gallery full of blacks from northeast Houston rant and rave about a granddaddy-size landfill some garbage company put in the middle of their neighborhood, they say because they're black. Though the site is in the county, their subdivision is in Houston's "extraterritorial jurisdiction" (in other words, the city did a land grab on the county), and the city issued the permit, two important facts the commissioners don't lose sight of, including Willette. They don't want this tar baby.

To maintain the appearance of fairness—nobody really cares how things actually are since most of what government does is always unfair to somebody—presiding Commissioner Judge Hennessy allowed each and every black person to say their piece, no matter how unintelligible, nonsensical, or offensive.

After the last resident has been heard from, Hennessy informs them that since the county didn't issue the permit, commissioner's court has no authority in the matter. Bang. The public session is closed. The residents grumble bitterly.

"Judge Hennessy, may I be heard?" Willette asks.

"Yes, Commissioner Shalandar," he says hastily. He knows a riot-conducive situation when he sees one.

"It saddens me," she says, speaking directly to the overflow of angry blacks, "that in this day and age, our neighborhoods are still being used for dumps." Lots of amens to that one. "My heart goes out to you all. I just want you to know I support your fight." Her eyes majestically sweep the semicircular dais where she's seated with her co-commissioners. "I'm sure I speak for my colleagues when I say that if the county had had anything to do with this travesty—and I want to reemphasize that we do not—I can assure you today's outcome would be very different."

The residents lap it up, deeply gratified by her show of support. When they first showed up en masse and mad, the commissioners were ready to call in the national guard. Now that Willette's not only pacified them, but shown the white boys a way to get some brownie points, each one eagerly speaks in support of their battle. She's a hero. I can see her mentally adding up the chits.

She signals me to follow her to a vacant conference room behind the commissioners' chambers. It smells like stale sweat. Her White Shoulders instantly dispels the odor.

"How'd we do?" she asks, pushing a renegade tendril back up into her topknot, much more attractive than the bun she started off with. Michael told her to start using what she's got to get what she wants on the court.

"Your colleagues ate it up."

She dismisses them with a wave of her hand. "I mean the citizens. Daddy says never let a constituent leave empty-handed. Give them your words and your time."

"In that case," I say, "get ready to be canonized."

"Good." She peeks out the door and makes sure no one's eavesdropping in the hallway. "Daddy says you can't be too careful." That's the second time she's quoted him in the present tense. Hmm. "There's something I need to discuss with you."

My legs feel rubbery. Michael.

"C.C. is becoming . . . a problem." She looks at me, then looks away uncomfortably. I let out a sigh of relief. Not Michael. "She's getting more—attached than I can stand."

I take a chance. "I hate to be the one to tell you this, Willette, but rumor has it, you know, she's going the other way now."

Willette chews her pretty lip for a moment. "I heard the same thing."

"In that case, you should let her know her business is in the streets."

She gives me a sharp look. "Because I'm her best friend." I don't answer. I don't have to. She rubs her eyes under her glasses. They look tired. "I think—she tried to hit on me."

"The day I walked in?"

She nods, turns, and bows her head. A little sob escapes her. "What's wrong with her?"

She sounds absolutely wretched. I'm desperate to cheer her up, so I tell her about the time Kwame and I were married and a friend of his accused me of going with his wife. He'd dogged her for years and she'd had enough, so she told him she was leaving.

Willette tries to smile. She knows me well enough to know this is going to be funny.

"So what happened?"

"I told him I wasn't going with his wife. I didn't like her perfume."

She cracks up. I'm on a roll. "Kwame said, 'Man, I know Gwen and I know Susan. They might be going with somebody, all right, but it for damn sure ain't each other. You can take that to the bank and draw interest.' "

Willette laughs so hard I have to give her a Kleenex to dab her eyes. "Thanks," she says. "I needed that."

So do I. This thing with C.C. is a drag.

"Wait, Ashleigh Lee."

My daughter is so hardheaded and long-legged I can't keep up with her in this primeval forest she insisted on visiting for our weekly outing, a tradition I've maintained with her since she was a baby, though admittedly these last few years I've missed more dates than I've kept. I'm determined to make it up to her. When we pulled into the Houston Arboretum, I told myself I should be glad she still wants to do things like this. Now that I'm trailing her into what looks like the Forbidden Forest, I'm not so sure this isn't a set-up.

As if reading my mind, she pulls me down a vine-covered path. "You're not going to get lost, Mommy." I'm just glad I insisted on a map at the visitors center. "Trust me."

Famous last words.

I'm not the outdoors type. I like to see grass and trees, that's all. Whenever I watch a scene with people romantically rolling around in the grass, all I can think of is whether

something's crawling on them or what if they roll into
dog doo? Give me the great outdoors behind a big picture
window.

"Ashleigh Lee, you wait!"

We've been out here five minutes and I'm sweating like a
pig even though it's mid-morning and only in the seventies,
which is about right for early June. By the end of the month
it'll be in the eighties by sunrise. Another reason I don't like
to be outside is I perspire easily. I couldn't pass myself off
as Southern belle if I wanted to. The authentic ones—like
Willette—don't have sweat glands.

I stop to look around. This place looks like a swamp. Ashleigh Lee would pick a time nobody's here but us. "Man,"
she says, disgusted with me. "Can't you just relax? Ax mur-
derers aren't lurking behind every tree."

Relax? In the Black Lagoon? Forget it. I continue to trail
behind her along a narrow wooden walkway over ugly,
boggy soil that probably turns to quicksand when it rains.
She kicks a stone to let me know she doesn't appreciate my
attitude. A little brown bird flutters skyward. "I knew this
wouldn't work," she mutters.

What wouldn't work? Genuinely suspicious now, I catch
up and grab her arm. "You knew what wouldn't work, Ashleigh Lee?"

She yanks away, looking so much like her father he
could've blown life into her. Am I in there anywhere?
"What are you up to?"

"All right," she says angrily. "Daddy said to try to understand you. You're going through a lot of changes."

"What?" I grab her again. "Since when is your father so
understanding?"

She breaks away and moves out of my reach. "Ever since
you stopped."

Now I've heard everything, confirming once again that
despite the almost grown woman's body she's walking
around in, she's still just a kid. Her logic is shit. "And when
was that, Ashleigh Lee?"

Her lower lip quivers. "When you married that white man."

She makes Dirk being white sound like a congenital malignancy. "That 'white man' is my husband. Somebody I care a great deal about. Just like you."

Tears shake in her eyes. "You don't care about me. If you did, you wouldn't have married him."

"Wait just a cotton-picking minute. You don't have a right to tell me—"

"I have every right!" she screams.

I look around. All I need is to draw attention. "Ashleigh Lee, lower your voice."

She goes crazy. "That's all you care about, isn't it? If somebody hears us, if somebody sees. If you're so worried about how things look, why'd you marry that cracker?"

My patience spool winds out. "That's it, Ashleigh Lee. I've had all the nonsense I'm going to take from you. Let's go."

I start back in the direction we came from. She just stands there, arms folded across her chest. I march back up to her, push her ahead of me. "I said let's go."

She practically drags her lip all the way back to the car while I spit and sputter I'm so mad. Who the hell does Kwame think he is telling my daughter to "understand" me? Like he's Mr. Wisdom and Light all of a sudden. When I needed him to act like he had some sense, he was out fomenting revolution.

So much for our nature walk.

"It's for you."

Dirk covers the receiver with his hand, holding the phone out just as Ashleigh Lee slams the door to her room so hard the windows rattle. I grit my teeth, tight. "I don't want to talk to anybody."

He points the phone at me. "Hey, don't take her out on me." He's right, but who else is there?

"Who is it?" I frown at the phone. He knows I hate answering blind.

"They wouldn't say."

He slaps it in my hand and walks out. Great. All I need is for him to get his ass on his shoulders. I take a deep breath, raise the receiver to my ear. "This is Gwen Parrish."

"Ms. Parrish, you don't know me." The voice on the other end sounds like it's in a wind tunnel. So much for fiber optics.

"Who's this?" I dig around the fridge, looking for something to salve my frustration. Fall upon Sara Lee cheesecake like it's insulin and I'm a diabetic.

"I have some information on Charles Garrett."

There's a good-size quarter left. I lift it out of the tin, intending to eat it all. "Who is this?"

"Check out the deed on that landfill your people were complaining about." I drop the cheesecake, look around frantically for Dirk, nowhere to be found when I need him.

"Who is this?" The line goes dead.

"Who was that?" Dirk asks, walking in as I hang up.

"I don't know," I say, unable to take my eyes off the phone. I can't get the voice out of my head. I can't place it, but I know I've heard it before.

Monday morning doesn't come soon enough. A complete one-eighty considering how I feel about Mondays. Unfortunately, I have several errands to run after I drop Ashleigh Lee off at school, which only makes me more anxious to get to the clerk's office before I get jammed up taking care of Willette's business the rest of the day.

It's almost noon when I step off the elevator to the fourth floor of the Civil Courts Building. I quickly discover how rusty I am when it comes to finding stuff in the gigantic ledgers where they record all the land transactions in Harris County, so I catch the eye of "Sweetness"—a black male clerk—helping another confused citizen navigate one of the enormous tomes. I let him know I need him next and wait, leaning against the chest-high counter, looking around. Things have changed. Ten years ago, you saw one, maybe

two blacks working the counters. No fags. Now both groups
are everywhere.

The one I'm waiting for has plenty of sugar in his tank.
The others aren't as obvious. Good thing the average white
Harris County taxpayer doesn't know about this sea change
in race and sexual orientation in county personnel. They'd
be hard pressed to say which one they abhorred the most.
They could kill two birds with one cross burning.

Finally free, Sweetness switches my way. He's young,
immaculately groomed in a pinstripe shirt, dark trousers,
power tie. Dark spots on his face from a bad case of acne are
his only physical imperfection. A real nice-looking brother.
I tell him what I need, and he plucks out a volume I didn't
even know was there, flips it to the middle, runs a well-
manicured nail down several pages, expertly scanning each
entry, stops, and pronounces, "This is it." We match the legal description with the one on the landfill application,
which I kept only by the grace of God. The protesters passed
out copies of the commissioners meeting. Willette automatically gave hers to me to throw away.

"The owners are listed as Fealty Realty, trustee," he says.

"Damn." I'm right back where I started. "A real estate
syndicate."

He slams the big book shut. "That's what it looks like."

It'll take a thousand years to track down all the owners.

"Anything else I can help you with, ma'am?" His smile is
beautiful, genuinely friendly.

"Thanks," I say. "You've been most helpful."

I weigh the pros and cons of telling Willette about my
anonymous call as I drive to the office. It's not like I found
out anything. Indecision always makes me hungry, so I stop
at Louisiana Po' Boy's, a rundown Creole delicatessen in
Midtown. The parking lot's packed. I smell the salad onions
as soon as I walk through the door. I like their sandwiches
best. They bake their own French bread, and they pile on the
meat and cheese. Judging by the line winding down the hall,

a lot of other people agree. This is one of those rare in-
stances of true integration in Houston: downtown white
boys, black construction workers, rich, poor, and in-between,
men, women, we all wait patiently. This is not McDonald's.

Afterward, my stomach growls every time I look at the
big sandwich sitting on top of my briefcase on the passenger's side of my car. I think my mouth is watering. I fixed
breakfast for Dirk and Ashleigh Lee, but I didn't get a
chance to eat because I had to help her finish her science
project, which she didn't tell me was due this morning.

I pull into my space in front of the Shalandar Building,
tense automatically. Michael's navy blue BMW is here, which
means he's back from Mississippi, where he's been for the
past three weeks helping his father run for reelection. The
old boy finally got some opposition after all these years.

The office is uncharacteristically quiet. Everyone must've
gone to lunch. The phone line flashes but doesn't ring. I almost pick up, realize the phones are on call forward. The
light for the next line comes on. Someone else is here. I look
at Willette's door. It's closed. I hope it's her. I need to deal
with Michael, but not this soon. I'm not ready.

I sneak into my office and ease the door closed. If Willette's here, she'll understand. She always eats by herself in
the office. I look at my greasy Po' Boy, feeling guilty. She
might have a salad and soup at the most.

I kick off my heels and prop my feet on my credenza. It
feels good to air out under my skirt. I unwrap my sandwich,
but I forgot to get a drink. Damn. I can't eat without liquids.

I pad across the reception area and fill my coffee mug at
the water cooler. I take a sip on the way back to my office. I
have to admit it does taste better than what the city of Houston supplies. I'm just inherently opposed to buying water on
top of the outrageous water and sewer rates the city charges.
I take my water back to my office, pause. I hear Willette in
hers. Cool.

I munch on my sandwich and study the note I scribbled at
the clerk's office. Fealty Realty. That's just too cute. I fish

for the white pages to see if it's listed. Nope. Nothing in the yellow pages. Must've been a crank call after all.

". . . I'm warning you, Michael." I stop chewing, cock my head to one side. That was Willette. "This is the last time—"

Her voice is shrill, uncertain. I've never heard her sound like that before. Michael laughs contemptuously. I can't understand what he's saying. I press my ear to the wall. That only makes it worse. I remember the glass I keep in the credenza for my Wild Turkey. I set it against the wall. Their voices are amazingly clear.

". . . No, Michael," Willette says. "Not another dime."

"I can always divorce you and get my half."

"It'd be worth it to have you out of my life once and for all."

He laughs. "No way, bitch. I said for better or worse. 'Better' better come quick. Come here." Silence. "I'm tapped out, baby," he says softly, like he's making love to her. "Take care of it." More silence. The door opens and closes. I snatch the glass away, feeling guilty about eavesdropping, wondering what the hell that was about.

21

"Hello . . ." My voice is hoarse with sleep.

"Gwen?" Willette sounds scared. "I need you to make a run."

"What's up?"

"It's C.C."

The only thing worse than getting called in the middle of the night is having to go out in it, especially in Houston. The air has a nasty aftertaste. They let them dump anything in the air here. Why not? The South's never been a place that valued human life. They had slaves, remember?

At least the drive along Brays Bayou compensates for the inconvenience. There's little traffic and the lights are synchronized. I can cruise for the most part. My window's down, catching the sensuous Gulf breeze, Magic 103's on the radio. At night they play all the mellow stuff. Right now it's a ballad about adultery.

I almost turn it off. It's too close to home.

Once you get used to the air, you can smell the bayou. It smells swampy, which is what most of Houston was before it was settled. The developers have paved over so much of the natural drainage, to catch the runoff from the monsoons that strike like clockwork every spring and fall, the main bayous like Brays have been turned into miles of big, open, concrete sewers. Still it floods, so bad sometimes the water comes up over the hood of your car. Talk about your man-made problems.

C.C.'s a woman-made problem. We're always more complicated. Willette said she was making a fool out of herself at Councilman Scott's house, and she didn't trust her to drive. I don't understand why they just didn't send her home in a cab.

Larry Scott's district encompasses South Park, a sprawling lower-middle-class to poor area that spills southeastward from Third Ward like ink. Martin Luther King Drive, the main drag, is a hodgepodge of liquor stores, churches, fast-food joints, and people's homes, mainly Crackerjack box-size pre-fabs built after the war.

Larry's house is not about to be outdone when it comes to doing the dog, however. Lit up like it's Christmas, his swankienda (i.e., swank hacienda) rivals anything you'd find in Third Ward. So many BMWs, Cadillacs, and Benzes crowd his driveway and the street, there's no way I'm going to find a space anywhere close. Needless to say, there are no fried-chicken joints on his block.

I'm not dressed to party, but knowing Larry's crowd they're dressed to kill. Dirk was already mad I was running out of the house at one o'clock in the morning. If I'd done more than slip into leather pants and a cotton top, wash my face and run a comb through my hair, he probably would've followed me. He watches me like a hawk now. We went to Don's Seafood last night for dinner, and this brother walked up to me and said, "Don't I know you?" I said no, and he went about his business. Dirk had a fit. He's been around enough black men to know that "Don't I know you?" is the same as "Didn't I do it with you?" The guy was being totally disrespectful, but I still had to get Dirk straight. "If he did 'know' me, he wouldn't hardly forget me." That shut him up.

I check my reflection in the copper mail slot while I wait for somebody to answer the door, layer on a quick coat of lipstick, fluff my hair, check my eyes for matter. Lean on the bell again. I hope Larry doesn't answer. I went to his office once to help get a stop sign for a group of his constituents.

They hired me when he wouldn't return their calls. He literally chased me around his office. When I bumped the door trying to get away, the secretary knocked to see what was going on. That's when I slipped out, surprising them both. I've kept my distance ever since. I don't like his definition of constituent service.

A brother with a bald head and bulldog face finally opens the door. Music blares behind him. "Hey," he says, peeling my clothes off with his eyes. "Fresh meat." I give him my patented "touch-me-and-your-dick-falls-off" look, walk into the mammoth foyer. "I'm here to pick up Judge Hendrix."

He's staring at my behind. "Oh, really."

"Yes, really." I turn up my nose, march to the large living room—gasp, step back. He grins, enjoying my instant revulsion. "Just—tell her—I'm here."

I ease back to the door. Rumors have floated around for years about Scott's parties, but I 'clare 'fore Jesus (as a client used to say), I've never seen anything like this in my life. They're having an orgy in there. "Join the party, baby," Dog Face says, stripping me naked with his eyes. "I need somebody to sit on my face."

He needs a foot up his ass. "Just tell the judge I'm here."

"Suit yourself." He saunters into the living room, pulls the doors shut. I turn away, pretending to study a Jacob Lawrence print, secretly calling C.C. everything but the Child of God. The doors slide open.

"Gwen Parrish, I didn't know you liked to indulge."

I turn to Martine Hornsby, the biggest gossip in our law school class. It'll be spread all over town before nightfall I was here. "You still don't. I'm just here to pick up Judge Hendrix."

She and Dog Face must be the only people in there with clothes on. Fifteen years ago she was one of the prettiest girls in school. Now her walnut-colored looks are haggard, her heavy makeup clownish. She tosses Miss Clairol blond hair off her shoulders, looks me over admiringly. "Girl, what is your secret? You look good."

"I live right."

She laughs. "I heard that. C'mon, I'll take you to her."

My instincts tell me to get the hell out while the getting's good, but I have no choice but to follow her. I gotta get C.C.

"Still flying the friendly skies?" I ask only because I don't want to think about what's going on in the living room as we pass by.

"Have to, girl." Martine worked as a flight attendant all through school. She had enough seniority so she only had to fly one or two days a month. "Can you believe after all these years I still don't make enough money in private practice to cut it loose?"

"Yeah."

We enter Scott's black and white Art Deco kitchen. "Save me some, Artie." She grins seductively to a brother in a crumpled leisure suit picking over platters of fried chicken. His jacket is unbuttoned, revealing his hairy belly. He sticks a drumstick in her mouth and tells her to suck it. She giggles, remembers me. "Hold that thought, sugar." She pats the erection bulging in his pants and heads for the back door. He grabs me as I follow. "Hey, don't I know you?"

"No," I say emphatically. He must believe I'll do something bad to him, because he lets me go quick.

Martine chatters away as she leads me out to the enclosed pool. It feels like a sauna. After twelve years of practicing law, I didn't think I could be shocked. Then I saw the naked people crawling over each other like worms in Larry's living room. Now this: several naked men—some of our leading citizens—sitting around the pool, blowing mounds of coke and getting blow jobs from naked, more than willing young girls. The men are so blasé they could be getting shoeshines. Martine stops to toot. I've seen enough. "Where's C.C., Martine?"

She lifts her head, a dot of white powder on the tip of her nose. "Damn, that's good 'caine. Want some?"

One of the men checks me out as he casually comes in a

girl's mouth. I look away, too disgusted for words. "Get C.C. *Now.*"

She shrugs, wipes her nose against her arm, and leads me out the other end of the pool house. Points to a candy-striped canvas cabana. "She's in there. Larry was kicking her ass."

"What? Didn't anybody stop him?"

She puts her head to mine like we're schoolgirls sharing a secret. "That's how he gets his nut. Good seeing you, girl." She winks. "Gotta get back to the chicken. I'm hungry."

She laughs and steps back into the pool house, peeks back out. "Oh, yeah. Larry said to take her out through the garage. See you."

The garage is the least of my concerns. I stare at the cabana. My instincts tell me not to go in there. I walk to the door; Willette's counting on me. "C.C.?"

Nothing.

"C.C., are you in there?" I step into darkness. She's huddling in the corner. A moonbeam strikes her face. My voice catches. "My God—"

"How could you be caught dead in that . . . hellhole?" I set a cold washcloth on a mean-looking cut just above C.C.'s right eye. "Those people are night crawlers."

She pushes my hand away and holds the pad. "I thought we agreed, no lectures."

That was to get her to the car. "Anybody who gets me up in the dead of night for bullshit gets to hear what I've got to say about it."

"Yeah, yeah, yeah," she says resentfully, and walks out into her living room, leaving me standing in the bathroom by myself. I'm not letting her off the hook. Slumping in an easy chair, she scowls at me through puffed-up eyes. "I don't want to hear it, Gwen."

Jaw swollen, blackened eyes, busted lips, a big knot in the middle of her forehead—she looks like Larry tried to beat the living shit out of her. My heart hurts for her. "Just let me run you to the Medical Center." She looks like I suggested slitting her wrists. "You can use my name. We need to see if anything's broken."

"I'll be all right." She slowly lifts her legs to the ottoman, her face wrenching in pain.

"You don't know. You're not a doctor." She stares at me with her good eye. It's shot through with blood. "I know."

I stare back. I don't know this person. "C.C., please."

"Larry never hurts me, okay?"

I have to sit down. The closest thing is the coffee table. I don't care. *Essence* and *Ebony* fall to the floor. Everybody's so black and proud. I look at C.C., eyes closed, head back. Where's her pride? "I don't understand this at all, C.C."

"Get me a joint."

She points at her rolltop desk. I was with her when she found it at a flea market. It's beautiful now, though I thought it was a piece of junk at the time. We spent many a weekend refinishing it, hard, dirty work I never intend to do in life again.

"Look under the inkwell."

They say cops and judges have the best dope. There are six neatly rolled, plump joints inside her little stash. I bring two, the clip, and matches. After what I've been through tonight, I intend to fire up right along with her. At first all I do is cough and sputter—the weed's strong. Pretty soon I'm cool, though, inhaling like a pro. Kwame taught me. I never did any drugs until I met him. He used to smoke constantly. I laugh. "And he says I never do anything he tells me."

"Who?" C.C.'s not feeling any pain either. Thank God.

"Kwame."

"Good ol' Kwame." She smiles. "I bet he's sittin' up someplace right now wondering what his little Gwen-Gwen is doing."

I scoff. "Kwame isn't hardly sitting up anyplace wondering about me, C.C."

"Girl, please. You got that nigger's nose open so wide you can drive a Mack truck through it. Yours is too."

That cracks me up. I roll over onto the floor laughing. C.C. just grunts. "You two ain't fooling nobody. Never have, never will."

Right. I sit up. "Don't try to change the subject. This isn't about me and knucklehead Kwame. It's about you." All the marijuana in the world can't make me forget my first sight of her. Blood streaming down her face, clothes damn near beaten off her. She refused to let me help her until I said Willette had sent me. We stumbled around the backyard after that looking for the stupid garage. I was all for taking her through the house, but she wouldn't have it, didn't want to offend the other guests. Offend, my ass. Can you believe that? I pass her my joint. I'm high enough. "C.C., what the hell were you doing tonight?"

She stares at the ceiling, blowing smoke in little balls like smoke signals. "Just call it my—initiation."

"Into the Marquis de Sade club?"

Her eyes level at me coldly. "That's funny. You won't be laughing when somebody warms up that big boo-boo of yours." She holds the joint out to me. "You wanna be a judge, don't you?"

I smoke it to keep from looking at her. She looks wicked. "Not that bad. Ain't gonna be no days like that for me." I give her the joint back. She takes a long drag, blows a billow of smoke.

"That's what I said. You have to pay the piper."

"Not if you don't dance."

She cackles harshly. "Then they chop your legs off. Know why?" she said, smiling like a little devil.

"You tell me."

"So you can join the gang. You have to be part of the gang. You're in the gang, you can't tell."

"Tell what?" I don't know what the hell she's talking about.

Her expression turns ugly evil. "Anything."

"You're crazy," I tell her, standing up. "What do you have to eat? I've got the munchies." She shrugs, lights another joint. I check out the refrigerator. Bottled water and low-cal salad dressing. "I see you're back on your diet."

I open the cabinets. "Mother Hubbard ain't got nothing on you." All I find are some rice cakes in the pantry, take one out and bite into it. Stale. "Ugh." Carry them back to the living room, munching all the way. They taste pretty good by the time I take my place at the coffee table.

C.C. waves a cloud of smoke away, hands me the joint. "So," I ask, curious, taking it, "does the gang have secret hand signals and passwords and stuff like that, like the Masons? Daddy always wanted to be a Mason. They wouldn't let him in. He said 'cause he worked at G.M. You had to be a Chrysler nigger." That makes me laugh. "The Ford niggers had a better idea. I forget what it is, though."

Dead serious, her eyes bore into me. "You don't get it, do you?" She shakes her head like I'm hopeless. "You never have and you never will."

I snigger, then bust out laughing. "That's what you said about me and Kwame."

"He doesn't get it either." Her mouth twists in disgust; he's apparently hopeless too. "You two deserve each other."

"I'd like to know what two you're talking about. I have a husband. His name is not Kwame. It's Dirk." I smile. "Dirk the Jerk."

She moves close, grinning eagerly. "So tell me, is it true what they say about white men?"

Even if I knew what she was talking about, I wouldn't tell her. "Is it true what they say about judges?"

She doesn't like that. "What?"

"You're all crooked."

I see the scales weighing in her mind whether to tell me or not. She renders her decision. "In our own way, yeah. No tacky envelopes stuffed with money like they do up North, though. Here it's bank loans and junkets to remote and exotic places. Need something? Anything. All I have to do is make a call. Folks are ready, willing, and able to render up any service I need. Law firms own banks, banks own judges, judges own your fate. Everybody lives happily ever after."

My eyes drift around her condo. I always wondered how C.C. could afford living in Southampton, one of Houston's ritziest neighborhoods, the new BMW, big diamonds on her hands, vacation in the Alps last year, all on sixty grand a year.

She pats me playfully. "That's why you've gotta be a member of the gang, Gwen-Gwen. They're not gonna let you make mud pies with clean hands."

I look down at my hands, imagine them dripping filth. I squeeze my eyes tight. I don't like that picture. Open them up, they're normal again. "Thanks," I say. "I get it now."

"Don't thank me. Thank Willette."

I stare at her. She's trying to say Willette doesn't trust me. I know better than that. Willette trusts me with her life. She wouldn't set me up like this. This is C.C.'s demented shit.

Which is why I stood up at that point and said I was going home. I'd smoked as much dope as her, but she didn't try to stop me from possibly wrapping myself around a tree. A small but telling point. Not that I would've stayed. She was pretty frosty when she walked me to the door.

I have to pull Black Beauty to the curb. I can't drive anymore. I'm in no condition: both the spirit and the flesh are weak. Maybe if I get out, get some fresh air, stretch my legs, I can make it. I open the door and stand up. Nausea slaps me twice. I lean against the car to steady myself. Sweat pops out on my forehead, my teeth chattering. I need to call Dirk. Where the hell do I tell him I am? I look around. The neighborhood looks familiar. One house in particular. I straighten up. Walk toward it, staring like I see a ghost. I walk up the short walkway to the small porch. Ring the doorbell, no one answers. I reach inside the burglar bars and bang on the door. A light comes on. I look around. This is the street, all right. Cleburne. Jack Yates High School is across the street. Footsteps hurry downstairs. The front door opens.

We stare at each other through the burglar bars. Why is Kwame not surprised to see me? He unlocks the gate, holds it open for me as I enter. I see myself in the hall mirror. My eyes look wild, which surprises me. I know exactly what I'm doing.

"Gwen—"

I kiss him. At first he just stands there, like a stick. I kiss him harder. A little moan escapes from him. He crushes me to him, kissing me hungrily.

"Gwen—" he says softly, picking me up. He carries me up the steps. I want to stay in his arms forever.

"Why didn't you call me?" Dirk demands. "I've been out of my mind." That makes two of us. "I was just getting ready to call the police."

"I'm sorry," I say, keeping my voice low. "C.C. was in bad shape when I picked her up. I couldn't leave her."

"Why didn't you call me and let me know you were okay?"

Perfectly logical questions. "I don't know. We started smoking dope—"

"My God, you were doing drugs? Are you out of your mind? What if something had happened? Do you know how it would've looked?"

"Very bad if I'd run off the road and killed somebody."

I'm trying to sound really sorry. He's not buying it. "You still could've called. You know I would've come and gotten you. I don't understand how you can be this irresponsible."

Kwame comes into the kitchen. I turn away, tangling in the phone cord. I can't look at him and talk to Dirk. He moves around, making coffee, watching me. He knows who I'm talking to.

"We'll talk about it when I get home."

"Which is?"

He's deliberately being difficult. "I'm on my way, okay?" I hate that Kwame heard me snap at him.

"I'm sorry, honey," Dirk says, softening immediately. Men are strange. "I've been out of my mind the whole time you've been gone. I didn't know what had happened to you. You know how I am. Why do you do these things to me?"

I glance at Kwame, guilt splintering me to pieces. "I have to go, okay? I'll see you soon." I hang up, twist my hands awkwardly. I can't seem to move my feet.

"Good morning," Kwame says, laying strips of bacon in a pan in a neat row.

"I, uh, good morning." I head for the stairs. "I'm—going to get dressed."

"Fine," he says. "Breakfast'll be ready by then. Eggs easy over, light toast, coffee black, right?"

That gets to me. He still remembers after all these years. He always was a big breakfast fan, which he cooked when we were together. Sunday mornings he'd lay out a feast, to us anyway, considering how little we had.

Shame, guilt, pride—I'm like a chameleon on a piece of plaid, I don't know which way to feel. I flee without saying anything, tear upstairs to his bedroom, gather up my clothes, trying not to look at the bed. Or remember what it was like to sleep with him after all these years. My scalp suddenly tingles; hot sensation runs through my body. It was beautiful.

I hurry into the bathroom to forget. He left a towel and washcloth out for me, even a toothbrush and toothpaste. That's too thoughtful. Unexpected jealousy makes me look in the medicine cabinet. More toothbrushes. I smack the door shut. He is one of Houston's most eligible bachelors, handsome, intelligent, financially solvent. I'm just the ex-wife, the one who did all the hard work trying to civilize his ass. Getting him ready for another woman to ride into the sunset with was more like it.

"I have to go." The breakfast he's prepared looks very inviting. My stomach growls noisily.

Kwame smiles. "Sit down—please." I slide into one of the two dinette chairs. He pours coffee. "Never let it be said that a woman left my home on an empty stomach."

"Is that your motto?" I sound like a bitch, why'd I say that? He's not married. I am. He sits down across from me, takes my hand. "Yes, I have 'friends.' But there's only ever been one woman for me."

I pull my hand away. "Kwame—"

"You don't have to say anything. Your actions spoke loud and clear." He smiles mischievously. "Especially that third time."

Shame sets my face on fire. "That was a mistake, Kwame—my coming here last night. I was high." I flash on us making love. "I was totally blasted."

He's offended. "I see."

No, he doesn't. I look him straight in the eye. "I must've wanted it to happen or I wouldn't have come here. But it was a still a mistake. Never to be repeated."

"So I guess I should cancel that talk I was planning on having with your—husband."

I spring to my feet. "You wouldn't, you can't—"

"I was kidding, Gwen," he says quietly. I breathe easier. "I'm assuming you'll tell him."

I shake my head, look away. "He doesn't deserve to be hurt like this. He's my husband. I love him."

"You said you loved me." His eyes narrow. "Or was that the dope talking?"

I can't take any more questions. "I'm sorry."

I head for the door. He stops me as I try to unlock the door gate. "What exactly are you sorry about? Because you came here? Because we made love?" He forces me to look at him. "That you love me?"

"I don't, Kwame." I shake my head no. "That's in the past. I'm married. I intend to stay that way."

"I see." He lets me go, bitterness lacing his voice. "You'll have to excuse me. I'm not used to being a one-night stand."

"Oh, you can dish it out but you can't take it."

"Meaning?"

"The toothbrush supply in the medicine cabinet." I know I shouldn't be saying this, it just comes out. "Very thoughtful."

"It is thoughtful," he says, looking at me closely. "Especially when your daughter regularly forgets hers."

I'd forgotten about Ashleigh Lee. I feel like a fool. "I've got to go. Dirk's waiting for me."

As I fumble with the stupid gate, he takes me in his arms. "You don't love that white boy and you know it. He doesn't know the first thing to do with a woman like you. I made a lot of mistakes when we were together. I can make it up to you now. I understand what you need. We can be a family again."

"I have a family."

He lets me go. I cut him deep, I don't know why. He turns away and picks up a document from the hall table. I recognize the blue back instantly. "In that case, you better take this with you."

He holds the legal papers out to me. I instinctively hesitate. "What is it?"

"A copy of a petition I filed. I was holding off service until we had a chance to—work things out."

I grab the pleadings, scour the first page, shocked. "You want custody?"

"Ashleigh Lee wants it. She's old enough to know who she wants to live with, Gwen."

My mother's version of the birds and the bees is my recurring thought as I drive home. "Men are like dogs. They get what they want, they go on about their business." In my heart of hearts, I honestly believed Kwame was different. I was wrong. I feel like the stuff you wipe off the bottom of your shoes before you go into somebody's house. Gwen-Gwen's done it again.

BOOK 3

———— ⊶∞∞∞⊷ ————

Save Your Hearts

22

I'm standing by the automatic doors in the lobby of the Holiday Inn Downtown, waiting for Dirk. He's coming from his office, so I drove my own car to Thurgood Marshall's annual Law Day Banquet. A lot of people I know have already begun to arrive, including Kwame, who came alone. Which is why I don't want to walk in by myself.

He tried to talk to me. "Gwen, let me explain—" He can never explain trying to take my life from me. And he'll never make me believe this is all Ashleigh Lee's idea either. "Just ask her—please." I wouldn't give him or her the satisfaction. I just look at him. He always did have more nerve than a brass monkey.

I wish I'd followed my first mind and waited in the bar, but that would only draw one of Dirk's "looks." Which I've been getting a lot of since the night I stayed out all night. Unfortunately, he called C.C.'s house trying to catch me before I "left," claiming to tell me to bring some doughnuts home. She told him I hadn't been there. I didn't know who to be mad at more, him for trying to check up on me or her for lying. Needless to say, he was fit to be tied when I walked in, demanding to know where I'd been, accusing me of seeing another man, which of course I denied. "He's black isn't he? Isn't he?" he kept asking me. I got tired of it, so I went on the offensive. "No, Dirk, he's white. Is that all right?" That threw him. Later he came in while I was taking a bath and offered to wash my back. It was a peace offering, so I let him.

.

A porter accidentally bumps me with his dolly. "Sorry 'bout that, ma'am," he says. "You all right?"

"It's okay." I look up at him. "Mr. Turntine?"

A former dope-dealing client grins with snaggly teeth. " 'Torney Parrish, I been readin' 'bout you. You here for the big wang-dang dullah?"

I laugh. "I haven't heard that in a long time, Mr. Turntine." I look him up and down, impressed. He's wearing a crisp red uniform trimmed with gold braid, a far cry from the county whites he had on the last time I saw him—eight years ago in court, the judge popping him twenty-five years for trying to sell a boatload of marijuana. Literally. "I thought they'd put you under the jail."

"Got out on good time. It's three for one now." Devil's Island looks like Club Med compared to most Texas prisons, which is why they're under court order to finally improve. The quickest way is to dump prisoners back out onto the streets. He proudly shows me pictures of his wife and five kids. "These here is what keep me straight."

"You've got a beautiful family." His chest swells with pride. "What's the word on the street?" I only ask to make conversation, so I'm surprised when he eyes me like he really wants to pull my coat. He looks around carefully.

"Don't say I told you," which means this is going to be deep. "Your boy ain't long for this world."

I draw my chin in, puzzled. I don't know who he's talking about. "Who?"

He checks over my shoulder, then stoops down like he's arranging suitcases. "Ain't you got that big drug case against Garrett?"

"I've got the murder case. The D.A.'s handling the drug prosecution."

He shrugs. "They can't shoot up no dead man." He's referring to the fact that capital punishment in Texas is now by lethal injection.

"Somebody's put out a contract on him?"

"Word."

"Who?"

"I ain't hip," he says. He stands up. "If I was him, I'd be careful 'bout the company I keep, know what I mean?"

"The police have him under surveillance twenty-four seven," I say. "That should help."

He opens the door and spits on the ground, pushing the dolly outside. "The laws ain't gonna stop nobody gettin' kilt they want kilt."

"Are you saying the police are setting him up, Mr. Turntine?" Not that I put it past the HPD.

"I ain't sayin' I ain't sayin'," he says.

I slip him a twenty. "Thanks, Mr. Turntine. Buy those kids some ice cream on me."

A big grin splits his face. "Thanks, 'Torney Parrish. You good people."

Dirk walks up, an open question about the black man I'm talking to in his eyes. This is ridiculous. What would I want with a snaggle-toothed porter with five kids?

"Sorry I'm late, hon," he says, kissing my cheek and sliding his arm around my waist possessively, like he's a guard dog and I'm a bone he's daring anybody to take, which make me uncomfortable.

"It's okay," I say. "Dirk, this is one of my former clients— Maxie Turntine. Mr. Turntine, this is Dirk Ingersoll—"

"Nice meeting you, Maxie," Dirk says, smiling broadly now that he knows the deal, extends his hand. "Was my wife as good a lawyer as she claims?"

He's obviously surprised I'm married to Dirk—like I'm the last black woman he expected to see with a white man, let alone marry one. "Yes, sir. Better." He tips his hat like I'm a stranger. He obviously knows a jealous man when he sees one. "Nice seein' you, 'Torney Parrish."

I check myself in the full-length, three-way mirror in the anteroom of the ladies' lounge, all pink and gold fluffiness, thick mauve carpet running up the wall, globe lights illuminating the mirror, everything designed to make you feel pampered and revered. I feel like the walls are closing in on me. Which is why I escaped here to begin with.

Dirk's acting so stupid. He wants every man in the banquet room—especially Kwame—to know I'm his, so he's constantly at my side, either holding my hand or draping his arm around me every chance he gets, all of which he knows I don't like in public. He even rested his free hand in my lap while we ate. People don't like their faces rubbed in this interracial shit, white or black.

Dirk keeps insisting Kwame's staring at me—which he is—so Dirk spends half his time shooting evil looks his way. He spends the other half watching me to see if I'm staring back. It's past ridiculous and I told him so. He just kept right on pawing me. I told him I was going to the ladies' room. He didn't like the idea, but he couldn't rationally object either. I wouldn't be a bit surprised if he's waiting for me when I come out.

I smooth a couple of wild hairs in my brows. Is this what life is going to be like with him from now on? I had considered telling Kwame about Garrett's life being in danger, but with Dirk acting so crazy, it's out of the question. Besides, Kwame's probably already heard about the death threats. He's one of the "peoples."

I lick my finger to dab my brows. Freeze. The air stirs behind me, like someone came in, I didn't see who. I look around the anteroom through the mirror. I feel it again. I turn around. No one. I face myself. I look the same—basic black evening dress, diamond earrings, black pumps. I take my lipstick out. My hand trembles unaccountably. I will it to stop. I'm being silly. Nobody's in here but us chickens.

The door swings open. A white woman walks in. She smiles at me, I smile back. If she just knew how glad I am to see her. She crosses to the stalls. I finish touching up, start toward the door.

"Excuse me, sir," I hear her say, "you're in the wrong facilities—"

"Uh, sorry. I thought this was the men's room."

My heart skips several beats as I turn to see Dirk hurry to the door, his face bright pink, utterly embarrassed. I make a point of opening the door for him, glaring at him like he's lost his mind. His eyes avoid mine as he walks out as if nothing happened. I drop the handle, let the door glide closed behind him, and stare. He actually followed me inside the ladies' room to see if I was really here. Or to see if I was here alone. Either way, it doesn't look good for the home team.

The white woman comes out and checks herself in the mirror as she finishes drying her hands. She's plenty pissed. "I have half a mind to report him. Imagine mistaking this for the men's room. Where are the urinals?"

"I agree," I say, mortified all the way to the ground.

"You were lucky he didn't do anything."

"Yes, lucky," I say, walking out.

23

The cold light of day has a way of separating fact from bullshit. When I returned to the banquet room last night, Dirk was all sheepish grins, like I'd caught him masturbating. I wanted to believe that Dirk hadn't been spying on me, so when he told the people at our table how he'd mistakenly wandered in the ladies' room, I laughed right along with everyone else at how funny he made it sound. When he finished his story, he said, half seriously, "Men, we need to organize. We may have more toilets, but theirs sure are prettier." From that point on he was Perfect Man. Witty, charming, solicitous, appropriate. He even stopped giving Kwame the evil eye. It was one of the best evenings we've spent out together in a long time.

After we got home, he fixed nightcaps and served them in bed. Then he wanted to make love. It turned out to be the most satisfying experience we've shared recently. Only he kept asking me if I loved him, and how much and to show him. By the time he finally came, I was going through the motions. I couldn't help it. All this time I'd forced myself to forget how good it was with Kwame. I have the curse of knowing again.

I have to get out of the office: the walls are closing in on me again. I spent the morning briefing Willette on the agenda for tomorrow's commissioners court meeting. I'm as meticulous as she is when it comes to making sure she's prepared. As the only black and the only woman, she's held to a higher standard of performance than the white boys. We both want to make sure she meets and exceeds it every time out.

I press the elevator button and wait impatiently, tapping my foot and drumming my fingers. Delzenia sarcastically asks me if I'm rehearsing. "All that noise you're making, it must be music."

"It is," I reply when the doors open. "It's called 'Who's Fooling Who?' "

I leave the cool dimness of the lobby and walk out into bright, warm sunlight, smiling grimly to myself. My father says you can't fool a fooler. Which one am I? The smile falls off my face. Michael's sitting in my front seat.

"Are you crazy? How did you get in my car?"

"It was open." That's a lie. "Drive, baby."

I pull away from the curb. "Would you mind telling me how you managed to break into my car without setting off the alarm? I'm sure my insurance company would like to know."

"Trade secret." He shrugs lazily. "I used to steal cars and joy-ride when I was a young whippersnapper." He stares at my thighs. Unbeknownst to me, the slit in my dress has fallen to the side, completely exposing them. I move to cover up. He stops me.

"I'm enjoying the view."

I'm prepared for him this time. "Look, Michael, I'll take you anywhere you want to go. But I want you out of my car." I mean it. "It's over."

He eases down in the seat, making himself comfortable. "I'm hungry, baby. You wouldn't put a man out on an empty stomach, would you?"

Against my better judgment, I agree to eat lunch with him "for old times' sake." I suggest the Museum of Fine Arts. Few if any blacks go there even though it's free. Surprisingly, he doesn't object. More surprising, he goes along with touring the da Vinci exhibition. I myself try to catch the new shows whenever I can.

Michael belittles the drawings because they're not in

color. Standing over my shoulder, he whispers, "I could watch a black-and-white TV for this." He sticks his tongue in my ear. I recoil, glancing around quickly to see if anyone noticed. Thankfully, everyone came to see a master's artistry, not nigger shit. I give him a warning look. He shrugs, his face registering unmitigated boredom. I made a big mistake bringing him into the galleries. I should have gone straight to the sandwich shop so I could be rid of him.

"Let's go," I say, walking out. He follows me, stopping occasionally to comment on something that catches his interest, always a nude of some kind. I ignore him. We pass the gift shop. It's crowded with people milling about, leafing through art books, looking at souvenirs, which is how I'd be enjoying myself if Michael wasn't with me.

"Say, baby, isn't that your old man?"

"Where?" My heart pounds like a trip hammer. How could Dirk know we'd be here?

"In the gift shop."

I'm afraid to look. If it is Dirk, we are through, period, *finito*. I can't have him running behind me like this. I force myself to very casually turn my head, scanning the shop through the big glass window. I don't see him.

"I guess that wasn't him after all." Michael enjoys that I almost peed on myself big-time. "Must be seeing things."

I jab my elbow in his ribs. "That's not funny, Michael."

He grabs his side dramatically. "Damn, baby, that hurt. You're going to have to kiss me to make it well." He reaches for me, but I slip from his grasp and run down the stairs. He chases me. I squeal and run to the sandwich shop door. By the time he catches up with me, we're laughing and out of breath.

We order chicken sandwiches, chips, and two glasses of white wine at the window, taking our trays outside onto the patio, which is completely enclosed by a high brick wall except for the glass wall that separates it from the sandwich shop. I choose a table near the little fountain, quietly bubbling and gurgling. It's very restful. Tall trees shade us from the sun. A white woman and man talk art over ice cream bars at another table. They don't notice us.

Michael chews his sandwich and looks around. "This isn't bad. Not bad at all."

I take a good look at him in the clear light of day. He's shallow, vain and, when he wants to be, thoroughly crude. How could I have ever found him appealing in any shape, form, or fashion? Then I realize. He made me forget Kwame, for a while anyway.

"My dick is hard, baby." His smile is somewhere between a leer and a lopsided grin.

"You're disgusting."

"Touch it."

"I most certainly will not."

He shrugs, studies me over his plastic wineglass. "You're going to owe me for this one."

I drink what's left of my wine. I feel much more sure of myself now that we're on neutral territory. "I don't owe you a damn thing, Michael Rormier."

"How quickly they forget, Ms. Special Prosecutor Administrative Assistant." He smiles cunningly.

"Willette picked me, not you."

"I picked her."

He has a logic all his own. It's rooted in his penis. "I don't care," I say. "I owe you nothing."

He scoots his chair close to mine, slips his hand under my dress. "Stop it, Michael." I glance at the white couple. "They're looking at us." Which they are, like they're at the zoo watching the gorillas.

He nuzzles my ear. "Then let's go to our place."

"No." I push his hand away. He reaches back up my skirt. The white couple gets up to leave. The man smirks; the woman looks at me like I crawled out from under a rock. My face burns with shame.

Michael squeezes my thigh. "Then how about right here? Nobody's watching now." I slash him with my eyes, pick his hand off, and stomp to the door. I hear him laugh and my face burns. I know he's watching my behind.

My mind's losing its peripheral vision. I see things, but the edges are missing. Especially at home. I open the front door after a very long day and it's "s.o.s." Same old shit. Dirk and Ashleigh Lee are arguing so loud, they don't even notice me until I slam my briefcase down. They pause, each one looking at me for instant support.

"Gwen—"

"Mom—"

Dirk's really steaming. Ashleigh Lee looks like she's ready to fight. I don't know how I'm going to pull this off, but somehow I have to split myself in half, which will satisfy neither one. They each want all of me.

"What is it this time?" I ask wearily. Their endless arguments are grinding me down.

"Tell your daughter she's not permitted to watch X-rated movies."

"Tell him I can watch what I want." She looks at him like he's bird crap. "He's not my father."

I'm proud of him, Dirk doesn't even flinch. I start to open my mouth, but he cuts me off. "I may not be your father, Ashleigh Lee, but I am an adult and your mother's husband. You will respect me for that. When I tell you not to do something, I don't need your mother to co-sign it. Do you understand?"

I want to voice my support for what he's saying, but he stops me again. "No, Gwen. This is something Ashleigh Lee and I have to get settled once and for all."

Ashleigh Lee's lower lip is sticking out so far you can set a plate on it. "They don't do anything on cable you and my mother don't do."

Wrong. My body tingles involuntarily. Michael is the dirty movie.

"What your mother and I do behind closed doors is none of your business," Dirk tells her. "This is a school night. You have homework, I know."

She cuts her eyes from him to me and back again, turns on her heel, sashays out. Handle it, Dirk, handle it. My maternal alarm goes off. Something, something just ain't right, as the song goes. She gave up a little too quick. I watch her leave. Knowing Ashleigh Lee, it will reveal itself. I peek into the oven out of habit.

"I didn't save dinner for you," Dirk says rather stiffly. "I didn't think you'd be hungry after your big lunch at the museum."

So he was there. I open the refrigerator and stare, stalling. I don't know what he saw. I know better than to tell on myself, I'm a lawyer. Even if the police found me standing over the dead body with a smoking gun in my hand, I'd deny everything. "Michael thought he saw you," I say, my voice deliberately light. "Why didn't you join us? By the way, what were you doing there?"

His face reddens. "Uh, we—had a board of directors meeting. An emergency. Something came up."

He's lying.

"Really? What?"

"A new Picasso acquisition," he says defensively. "We had to get our bid in or be out of the running." Trapped, he can't bust me without busting himself. The only question now is, How long did he follow me? I give the screw one more turn to find out.

"I thought you had a pre-trial conference this afternoon." I take out bologna and cheese, the last thing I want to eat after a hard day working.

"That's why I left," he says. "I had to get downtown."

Thank you, Jesus. I want to take a big, deep breath of relief, but I can't. He's watching me. "Too bad," I say. "I could've used some art appreciation." One of our first dates was at the Museum of Fine Arts. I impressed him with my knowledge of the Pre-Raphaelites. "Michael is a big lummox when it comes to art."

He takes over making my sandwich. "Most black men are. Their minds are too gutterized to appreciate art."

I look at him. "Did you say ghettoized?"

"That too. You know what Earl Butz said—all they want is a tight pussy, loose shoes, and a warm place to shit. Ha-ha-ha." He notices I'm not laughing. "What?" he asks innocently. He sets my sandwich on the table, pours me a glass of wine. "You know I'm bad at jokes. Did I get the punch line wrong?"

"You got it right, all right," I say, sitting down. "I just never thought I'd hear you say something like that about my people."

He kisses my cheek, pours himself a big glass. "Black men aren't your people. They're your enemy. What have they ever done for black women other than create problems?"

I want to disagree, but I remember all the changes I went through getting rid of Michael this afternoon. He was serious about doing it on the patio, so I agreed to go to "our place" just to get him out of the museum, but I told him I had to use the rest room first. He was so busy ogling a nude statue he didn't notice me duck back out and sneak behind his back to the door. He saw me at some point because I heard him calling me as I boogied across the street to the parking lot, but I kept on stepping. I drove right past him on my way out. He gave me a hateful look. I didn't care. Now he knows I mean business.

"Can't think of a thing, can you?" Dirk says smugly. He stands behind me and massages my shoulders. I stare at my sandwich. "You know what I think the solution to the racial problem is? Send black men back to Africa."

I look at him like he's crazy. It's the jealousy talking. "That's racist, Dirk."

He smiles. "It's not racist. It's just radical."

24

I sit on the edge of the bed, turning the little cellophane packet over and over in my hand. The doorknob turns, and the door slowly opens.

"What are you doing in my room?" As far as Ashleigh Lee's concerned, I've breached national security.

"Come in and sit down."

My voice sounds unnaturally low. I'm serious as lung cancer. She strolls in, her every movement radiating resentment. I'm ready to blow my top. "Whose is this?"

I toss the packet to her. She fumbles catching it, sees what it is. Her sullenness changes to terror.

"Mom, I swear—"

I stop her. "Don't. God may strike you dead, which will be the least of your concerns before I get through." My voice goes up a notch. "Is that yours?"

"Mom, I sw—*no*, it's not mine. I don't know where it came from. Honest."

I just look at her, really look at her, for the first time in years. True, she has her father's eyes, his nose, mouth. But there's something there that looks like me too. And then there's the part that's all her own. The part I want to strangle. Her fingers twiddle the miniature baggie. She catches me watching, sets it on her dresser. "I'm gonna ask you one last time, girlfriend. That your 'caine?"

"Why are you talking to me like that?"

"Because," I say, "this is how I talk to lowlives."

She turns away. "It's mine, okay?" She faces me, her

courage restored. "I got it from a kid at school. I wanted to see what they were all talking about." School? I'm paying for her to meet drug dealers at school?

"Are you crazy?" I yell, lunging at her. "Do you think I'm going to have a drug addict for a daughter? I'll kill you myself." I throw her on the bed, wrestling with her while I climb on her chest, panting and grunting, battling to pin her arms down. She tries to hit me. I try to knock the pure "d" shit out of her. Neither of us says a word. I'm saving my energy to kick her ass until the cows come home if I have to. I nail her arms with my knees, my hands dangerously tight around her neck. She's crying and snotting up the bedspread. I don't feel an ounce of pity for her.

"Dry it up." She snuffles back tears. "You want to be a lowlife? You want to see what they do? I'll show you—" I move off her so she can sit up. She coughs and sputters like I really hurt her. Sneaks a glance at the phone.

"Unh-uh. Daddy's not riding to the rescue this time." I yank her to her feet. "You want lowlife. I'm gonna give you lowlife."

I cut in and out of the late afternoon Eastex Freeway traffic like a madwoman. Glance at Ashleigh Lee, clinging to the ceiling strap and her seat. She's scared shitless. If she says one word, I'll probably turn the Jag over I'm so mad. A car cuts in front of me. I hit my brakes, jump to the next lane, clipping somebody else.

"Mom!"

"Pay for your ride, girlfriend, get your bumps free."

I take the Lyons Avenue exit off the expressway and drive into the heart of darkness—Fifth Ward. Every big city has one. Buttermilk Bottom, Southside, Watts. The sho'nuff, stomp-down ghetto. Houston's is just countrier.

Crosstown traffic forces me to drive like I have some sense, which admittedly I'm short of right now. I've been pushed over my line. Whoever pushes me this far had better run, not walk, to the nearest exit. Kwame found that out the hard way when he left me to battle a rat by myself when Ashleigh Lee was a baby.

As we drive into the Fifth, I see Ashleigh Lee looking at the scenes around her, fascinated. She's so suburbanized, the closest she gets to seeing real street life is on TV or the movies. Buses belch black exhaust fumes and job slaves at every stop, the latter trudging in from the new Big House downtown or Miss Ann's personal plantation in River Oaks where the old-money white folks live. Nasty-looking prostitutes compete with each other hustling johns. Knots of used-up black men idly swap lies and cheap wine. Dusty little kids play in the street or anyplace else they can find for their homemade games while fat women fan themselves to no avail on the handkerchief-size porches of shotgun houses.

The houses are all gray and peeling. I've been inside a few, invariably coming away wondering how whole families can live in a chicken coop. I'm always afraid to sit down. Roaches jump off everything. One time I had to go to a client's house not too far from here to find out why he hadn't shown for arraignment. I made the mistake of laying my purse down on the table while I tried to explain to his grandmother if he didn't show up that afternoon, the judge was going to give him more time for bail jumping. I went directly from her house to court, set my purse on counsel table next to my briefcase, flipped it open to get a pen while I argued with the D.A. not to throw him back in the slammer, and out trooped this big black son of a bitch. I was too through. The D.A. cut my client some slack. He felt sorry for me.

I turn on a dead-end street and park in front of a house that looks like it's been firebombed. It looks as good as any. I hand Ashleigh Lee a ten-dollar bill and tell her to get out. Her face is a question mark. "What for?"

"Do what I told you."

I get out and casually lean against the car. She stands a few feet away, trying not to worry about the junkies eyeing

us from across the street. They look like living ghosts. I
must look like damn-it-I'll-bite-you, since they keep their
distance. I've got my pistol just in case things get funky.

A dusty-covered boy with hair so knotted up it looks like
woolly beads rolls up on a skateboard. He can't be more
than ten or so, but his eyes look like he's already walked the
Valley of Death. "Y'all looking for something?"

"She is," I say, nodding at Ashleigh Lee. "Aren't you,
girlfriend?" She wants to dissolve into tears. I look at her
like I dare her to spill one drop. She nods shakily. The kid
sizes her up and down, skeptical. "That right, baby?"

Her eyes plead with me to rescue her, but she can't speak.
So she's not so big and bad after all. "That's right," I say. "You
know where we can get something?"

"Whatchew want?"

"The lady."

He's surprised, probably figured her for a Mary Jane girl.
He checks her out again as he talks to me. "How much?"

"A dime," I say. Signal to her to show the money, wadded
in a ball in her hand. He snatches it up, makes sure it's a ten.

"Be right back."

He picks up his board and pimp-walks up the steps of the
house in front of us, looking around carefully before he
knocks on the steel door. I look at Ashleigh Lee as a tear
slides down her cheek. She cuts her eyes away and wipes it.
I want to take her in my arms and beg her to forgive me for
doing this, but if I do and she winds up like the "haints"
across the street, it'll be on me. She can hate me till her dying day as long as that doesn't happen.

Metal scrapes metal, the door cracks open. The kid does
some fast talking. The door slams, he gives us a thumbs-up.
A moment later he trots back down the steps.

"Enjoy, baby," he says, slipping the packet to Ashleigh
Lee. She refuses to look at it. When I thank him for his as-
sistance, he asks me why we're wasting our money on such
a small purchase.

"My daughter only likes a hit every now and then," I say.

"Yeah?" His eyes are dead cold as he smiles at her, a stone hustler already. "Ask for Q next time. I'm always around."

She glares at me. "Can I get back in the car now?" She doesn't wait for permission. Q has the nerve to still try to rap. "You're kinda cute, baby. What's your name?"

She turns up her nose, locks the door. I tell him to go hit on somebody his own size. He gives me a dirty smile. "You my size."

I start up my car. "Boy, if you don't get away from me—"

He grabs his crotch, "I got your boy," laughs and skates off. I glance at Ashleigh Lee. She stares straight ahead, her body rigid, unforgiving. I start to pull off. Somebody pounds on my trunk.

" 'Torney Parrish!"

I nearly shit—somebody knows me? Maxie Turntine runs up to my window. I almost don't recognize him out of uniform. "Whatchew doin' on my side of town, 'Torney Parrish?"

"Uh, I'm looking for a client, Maxie."

"Who? I know eb'body in this neighborhood."

"Actually, I don't have time. I've got to get back to my office."

"That your daughter?"

"Uh, yes. Ashleigh Lee, this is Mr. Turntine—he's a former client of mine." He smiles big at her. "Hi."

She ignores him. I smile apologetically. "She's not feeling well, Mr. Turntine. Well, it's nice seeing you—"

He looks at her closely. "Lotta that goin' 'round. Gettin' so bad, you blow your nose 'round here, people ask you how much you got." I laugh politely. He means coke. Which means he probably saw the deal go down with Q. I don't say anything. There's nothing to say.

"She's sho' easy on the eye. Like her mama," he says, admiring Ashleigh Lee. Runs his hand over Black Beauty. "Y'all better be careful 'round here. They'll have your car sittin' up on cinder blocks with you in it."

"I heard that. Well, I have to be going, Mr. Turntine."

"I hear another one of your friends got her nose runnin'."

"Charles?"

He shakes his head. "He been gone." He says that like it's common knowledge about Garrett's drug habits. I had no idea. "One of your good buddies. Gave me probation last time I was in her court."

C.C.? He nods solemnly. "She be makin' this run on a regular basis. Won't be long 'fore somebody busts her, know what I mean?"

Recognizes her—or worse. Is she crazy or what? "Look, Maxie, I gotta get back south. I'll see you, okay?" I fish in my purse with my free hand for some money.

He steps back. "Unh-uh, 'Torney Parrish. This one's on me. Sho' hope your daughter gets over that . . . cold."

Downtown passes in a blur. My mind's whirling. What did I do to her? She hasn't said a word since we left Fifth Ward, just looks straight ahead, arms folded, knees together, body slouched. I can't tell what's going through her mind. I can only pray one day she understands I did this for her own good.

Some days it seems like half of Houston is doing coke—including the doctors, lawyers, and judges. It's hard enough knowing C.C.'s deep into cocaine, let alone stupid enough to buy it out in the open. If she doesn't want to be a judge anymore, she should just resign. Give the slot to somebody who does. Like me.

I shove C.C. to the back of my mind, look over at my child. If C.C. wants to self-destruct, all I can do is get out of the way. I won't let Ashleigh Lee destroy herself. I want to tell her that, make sure she understands, but I don't want to turn her off any more than she is. "Still want to see what the kids are talking about, Ashleigh Lee?" I try to sound normal.

"No." She rolls the window down, throws the little packet out. I could melt, I'm so relieved.

* * *

"Daddy wants to talk to you."

Ashleigh Lee lays the phone down and walks away as I step from the bathroom, where I've been since we walked in the door, running from both ends—diarrhea and vomiting—behind a bad case of child poisoning, my physical reaction to the latest traumergency my child's inflicted on me.

"Hello." When I hear Kwame's voice, I understand the meaning of fit to be tied.

"What is she talking about—you took her to buy drugs?"

My stomach gurgles ominously. "I found cocaine in her room."

"Cocaine?" He sounds like I felt when I found it.

"I wanted to scare the shit out of her so she won't do it again."

He doesn't say anything for a moment. "You could've at least told me."

"Like you told me about asking to change custody?"

He sighs patiently. "You could've really hurt her. She's only a baby."

"She's not a baby, Kwame." He doesn't see her on the precipice of adulthood. His feelings got hurt the first time she got her period.

"She's not an adult either. Are you so jealous you want to make her grow up?"

My stomach shudders. "I'm jealous? We'd still be married today if you hadn't been so jealous you didn't want me to work." I'm losing my peripheral vision for sure. Why else would I say something so idiotic?

"I wasn't jealous, Gwen. I just didn't want you standing over me every day telling me where to go, what to do, and who to do it with."

My hands automatically ball at my hips, and my voice rises. "Only because I didn't want to starve to death waiting on the revolution only you red, black, and green niggers could see. We were better off waiting for the second coming."

He sighs again. I hate it when he's Reasonable Man and I'm the Bitch. "That's history. Let's talk about today."

Men always want to stick to today, because if they ever look back they'll see all the little piles of doo-doo they've left in other people's lives.

"There's nothing to talk about, Kwame." A cramp doubles me over. I have to get to the bathroom. "I'll see you in court."

25

I haven't seen Marvella Shalandar since the funeral. When she opens her door and greets me, I'm surprised at how frail she's become. To my embarrassment, she notes my reaction and apologizes for how she looks.

"I've lost my appetite since Willie passed." This from a woman who loves to cook and eat. I tell her she looks wonderful. She beams because she's vain, invites me in. I follow her to the family room. From behind she looks like a walking skeleton.

"I'm so glad to see you. I don't get much company."

She's so lonely. I feel sorry for her. "Your daughter comes by to see you, I know."

She gives me a bit of a look, something strange flickering in her pearly green eyes. "Humph," is all she says, leaving me to get iced tea. I use the opportunity to look at the pictures of Willette scattered around the room, all of them recent and with Willie, looking like a youthful Marvella. She has her skin tone and, of course, her eyes. You don't run across green-eyed black people often.

"I used to do a lot of entertaining," Marvella says, setting two frosty glasses on the coffee table. "Not anymore." She sips her tea, looks around wistfully. "She won't let me." Her voice trails off. "She" must be Willette.

I can't imagine not letting your mother have company, so I don't know what to say. I check my watch. "Guess I'm a little early. I came from the office. Willette's coming from downtown."

Marvella seems to scowl at the mention of her daughter's name, which surprises me. I always thought she was her heart. "She works too hard," she says. Her voice loses its characteristic sweetness. "She doesn't listen to me. I'm just a silly old woman." She leans forward like she's telling me a secret. "He thought so too. I fooled them. Humph."

She laughs and claps her hands, downright giddy over her private joke. I make sympathetic noises like I understand. She stops laughing all of a sudden, and I still don't have a clue as to what she's talking about. She looks at me sharply, like she's taking my measurements. I squirm uncomfortably, clear my throat. A sudden smile brightens her face.

"Lord today," she says. "Child, where are my manners? How would you like some nice iced tea?" Her face darkens. "He used to load his up with sugar. You don't put a bunch of sugar in yours, do you?"

Before I can tell her we've got tea in front of us, she dashes off to the kitchen. I see why Willette doesn't want her around people. Marvella ain't wrapped too tight. I check my watch again. Almost six-thirty. Willette left word with Delzenia for me to meet her at her mother's for dinner. Delzenia said it was urgent. All I can think of is that Michael must've told her about us. At least we'll be in private when she goes off.

"How's the Garrett case coming along? She doesn't tell me a thing." Marvella sets the two new glasses of iced tea on the table. If she notices the other two, she doesn't say anything. "Bless his heart, you don't really think he did it, do you? It was an accident."

You know you're in trouble when the victim's wife is on the defendant's side. "The evidence doesn't point in that direction, Marvella."

"Humph." She takes a seat and sips her new tea, humming softly to herself. It's probably easier for her to consider Willie's death an accident as opposed to knowing somebody—Garrett—hated him enough to kill him. She stares at me with those eel green eyes of hers.

"Have you talked to him?"

"Garrett?"

She smiles at me like I'm three. "Of course, baby. Who else?"

"Uh, no, ma'am. I haven't."

"You should."

I'm about to ask why when Willette sweeps in. She kisses Marvella's cheek and greets me. "Sorry I'm late, Gwen." She's not, she's right on time. "Mother, leave us, please."

"Don't you want to eat? I spent all afternoon cooking."

"I told you not to." Willette inserts a tape into the VCR, focusing on the TV screen. "*Excuse us,* Mother."

Marvella makes a disapproving clucking sound, like she pities Willette. I feel sorry for Marvella. I've never seen anyone black talk to their mother like that. Marvella's eyes grab mine. She mouths, "Talk to Garrett."

"Mother—" Willette warns, her back to us.

Marvella smiles cheerily at me. "Nice seeing you, baby. Come back and visit me." Willette gives her a look. Marvella scoots out. I'm embarrassed for both of them. Willette sits down in front of the TV. "You'll want to see this, Gwen."

What I want to do is give her a piece of my mind. For two cents I'd do it too. Marvella's her mother. You don't dog your mother, especially in front of people.

"Here," she says, totally absorbed. I pull my eyes from her long enough to glance at the TV. Black-and-white snow bursts into images. It's some kind of party. People standing around, laughing, talking, having a good time. They look vaguely familiar. The scene changes, and the same people are crawling all over each other, naked, having group sex. My God, it's Larry Scott's house. I feel dirty already. I lurch toward the set. I see myself. I'm in the middle of the orgy.

"What the hell—?"

"Watch."

She doesn't need to tell me to do that. My eyes burn into the TV. I don't know how they did it, but they've made it look like I'm part of this sex sty. The scene changes. I'm standing in the pool house like I approve of all the fellatio going on around me. Cut to the cabana. Willette freeze-frames me standing over C.C., huddled in a dark corner with her clothes torn off. It looks like I could've done it.

"I don't know how they did it, Willette." My blood is boiling in my veins, I'm so mad. "Any reputable lab can find every slice and splice of that tape."

"I know," she says. "I didn't want anybody to see it. Not even Michael." Which explains why we're meeting here. I check over my shoulder to make sure Marvella's gone. I don't want anybody to see this garbage either. Thankfully, there's not much more and it doesn't get any worse.

"If this is someone's idea of a joke, it's not funny worth a damn," I say. "Whoever did this is going to pay dearly."

"I don't think they were joking," she says. "It was hand-delivered to me during commissioners court this morning. From the 'Friends of Charles Garrett.' " She looks at me like I automatically know who they are.

I shake my head before any words come out. "Hell no, Willette. Kwame?" All's fair in love and a custody battle. He knew I was there that night. And he's definitely a friend of Garrett's.

She shrugs noncommittally. "Or it could be Garrett. He's not exactly your everyday garden-variety snake either."

To our surprise, Marvella chooses this moment to enter with two glasses of iced tea. "I thought you all might be thirsty." I thank her and set mine down next to the other two. Unfortunately, sweat from Willette's glass dribbles onto her silk suit. She explodes. "You cow! How many times have I told you never to serve me without a napkin? Look what you've done."

Marvella looks like she could kill Willette, and I don't blame her. The problem is, Willette looks the same way. I can't take any more. "You should lighten up, Willette. It's only water."

She ignores me. "Get out, Mother. Right now. Don't come back in here unless I tell you to."

"Humph," Marvella says, marches out with the glass. Willette makes sure she's gone, then turns on me, teeth gritted together, eyes slits. "Don't you ever take sides with my mother against me. Ever."

I've seen Willette all the way live out the box before. I'm not afraid of her. I know her secrets. "Then don't you ever talk to her like that in front of me," I say, matching her evil eye to evil eye. "Ever."

We glare at each other like gunslingers waiting to draw. She "blinks"—taps her fingertips together lightly, reels her anger back in. "Fine." She ejects the tape. "Here, do the honors of getting rid of this."

I don't hesitate. "Gladly."

"Believe half of what you see and none of what you hear."

It's an old saying. It pops into my head as I pull out of Marvella's driveway while she and Willette wave good-bye at the door. I wave back and blend in with the cars driving by on South Mac Gregor. With Willette's arm around her waist, they look devoted to one another. If the passersby only knew. I know I didn't. Not until today. She could be pinching her for all I know.

"Believe half of what you see and none of what you hear."

I glance at the videotape, lying on the passenger seat with my purse. You got that right, old folks. Destroying it is probably as useless as trying to kill all the roaches in Texas. If you see one, hundreds are in the woodwork. I don't flatter myself there are that many copies in circulation. But it's for damn sure this isn't the only one.

"Believe half of what you see and none of what you hear."

Kwame didn't do this to me. It's not his style. He likes to

wipe up the courtroom with you, out in the open, straight up and down. He's a warrior; this is ninja shit.

Michael definitely has the ninja mentality. Only it doesn't go with him either. Not at this point. If he hurts me, he hurts Willette. She needs me.

"Friends of Charles Garrett." My enemies by definition. Behind C.C. and Willette, who needs friends? If it hadn't been for them, I wouldn't've been at that stupid party.

I take South Main instead of the freeway. Even with all the lights, it's the most direct route to Missouri City when it's not congested. Black commuters aren't any different than white ones when it comes to eating exhaust fumes. Fortunately, most people have made it home long before now.

I stop at a gas station on Hiram Clarke. I'm not riding another block with this videotape. I park at the phone booth, pick it up, and start pulling tape from the cartridge. It's more tedious than I thought. My mind drifts to Willette.

Humph.

She came by Kwame's and my apartment one day to study Commercial Paper. Kwame was in St. Louis at a Black American Law Students Association board meeting, planning how to jack up the National Bar Association for being a bunch of Uncle Toms. He was BALSA president that year and chief strategist. I begged off going. My policy was, you can't help anybody if you flunk out of law school. He was a natural when it came to the law, and he didn't care about grades as long as he passed, which he always managed to do. I just knew it would catch up with him on the bar exam, but he passed that too, though just barely. At the swearing-in ceremony he held up our licenses and asked me if I saw our scores anywhere. That shut me up.

Anyway, Willette was exhausted when she arrived late, unusual for her. She's as punctual as a clock. Frankly, I had been looking forward to going to her house as always—and air conditioning. Our place was hot, cramped, and tacky, but she'd insisted. As soon as she walked in, she collapsed on our only armchair, a relic I'd found at Goodwill and re-upholstered. "You act like somebody was chasing you," I joked, clearing the table for our books.

"I went roller skating." In a long cotton shift, hair divided in two braids, she looks like she just came off the reservation, not a skating rink.

I laugh. "You mean you were watching people skate." Willette is the most unathletic person I know. She's just naturally blessed with a slender frame, bird appetite, and a fast metabolism.

"I need to lie down."

I take a close look at her. She's right, she doesn't look well at all. Light-skinned people look pale when they're sick; black people turn gray. Willette looks—filled out, her skin clammy. She staggers toward the sofa, actually a love seat. "Try the bed," I say, steering her by the elbow. "You can stretch out."

I take her into our bedroom, only a shade bigger than our full-size bed, turning off the light so she won't notice the dingy walls I've tried scrubbing to no avail. She stands at the foot of the bed and weaves like she's going to fall. "I'm—so dizzy . . ."

She gasps, doubles over like a giant pain is ripping through her, and topples onto the bed.

"Willette!" I head for the phone. "I'm calling the doctor—"

"No," she whispers, crawling toward the headboard, settling among the pillows. "I'm okay."

"No, you're not—" I say.

"*I'm fine!*" she screams. Another pain grips her. Her green eyes look black, threatening. Like she'll kill me. "Leave me alone," she hisses. "Close the door."

I pace outside my bedroom door for thirty-five minutes, crazy with worry. I stop. I thought I heard Willette grunt? Or was it a groan? Whatever it was, it was more animal than human. I tap on the door. "Willette?"

Nothing.

I knock harder. "Willette, are you okay?"

"I'm fine," she says, her voice so faint I can barely hear her. "Open the door."

I hesitate. She doesn't sound fine. She sounds . . . strange. I open the door. She stands a few feet away, her dress blood soaked, holding something in her hands. "Willette, what in God's name—?"

The thing in her hands makes a soft, mewling sound.

"Get out of the way."

She walks past me into the light, her hands waist high, holding a tiny baby, perfectly formed, covered with blood. The umbilical cord dangles along the floor, dragging the afterbirth. I watch like a paralyzed fool as she crosses the kitchen, trailing blood to the bathroom, closes the door. The snap of the latch locking echoes around me.

"She had a baby," I say, waking myself up from shock. I run to the door. "Willette!" I pound and bang. "Open the door. You shouldn't be alone at a time like this. Let me help you." Right. Like I know something about birthing babies. "Willette—"

The toilet flushes. The sound electrifies me.

"WILLETTE!!!"

She opens the door. Stares at me, her green eyes calm as the sea after a storm. Her hands are empty.

"What did you do?" I ask, stupidly searching my closet of a bathroom.

"I came this far," she says simply. "I had to finish it." Something pops. We look down. Blood pools around her feet.

26

When I was growing up, we called wearing a hat tipped to the side of your head cocky-like, ace-deuce. That's how my world's looking right now. Tipped to the side, only I'm not being cocky about it.

The Houston Black Lawyers Association meeting has just broken up, held the first Tuesday of every month in the Moot Court Room at Thurgood Marshall Law School. There are over six hundred black attorneys in Houston—the largest black bar in the country, including Detroit. About thirty or so show up, a heavy turnout since we'll be making endorsements for the upcoming judicial races. Most everyone's carrying buckets for somebody, so we voted to create a judicial endorsement committee to make recommendations. To everyone's surprise—including me—I declined to be on it. I said I'm too busy. Really I'm getting tired of being in the middle of mess.

I'm on my way to the Wunderbar, where I agreed to meet Harry Jordan for drinks. Harry's a former classmate and transplanted Yankee, so we've always been *muy simpático*. However, the real reason I accepted is because he said Kwame hangs out there in the evenings. I'm hoping he comes in tonight. I want to talk to him about Charles Garrett. And why, with the trial only weeks away (and locked up, so everyone says), Willette's mother wants me to talk to him.

The Wunderbar is one of the few places in Third Ward that caters strictly to professional blacks. No hoods, hooks, or hardheads allowed. I don't come here often. The atmosphere's a little too sedate. The front of the building is shrouded with palms and elephant ear philodendron. A red canopy leads up long steps to the glass entrance. The club's divided into three sections. The middle third is completely visible upon entry. You pick it if you want to see and be seen. If you want or need to be discreet, you can sit at the bar or in the back room.

Harry's with a group of six black attorneys—all men—commandeering the middle section. One by one their eyes fall on me as I enter. I'm on a mission tonight, so I don't mind being the only woman. I just have to remember to laugh as hard as everyone else at the dirty jokes, maybe tell a risqué story myself. I know all these guys to some degree or another. Somebody wolf-whistles as I walk up. Harry cracks, "Shake it but don't break it, Ms. Parrish."

I laugh, taking the seat he offers. "Is that any way to talk to a colleague?"

His eyes feast on my cleavage. "It is if they look like you."

"Right on to the right on," says Paul Whitfield, one of the few black attorneys working in a downtown law firm. He's Harvard-trained but a TSU undergrad. Neither experience has managed to smooth all his Fifth Ward edges.

"Pour whiskey!" Sonny Fonner—they call him "Cowboy"—shouts at the bartender, waving his glass. A pretty cocktail waitress moseys up to the table. "How're y'all doing?" she says brightly. Sonny orders a round for everyone. I have white wine, which he scoffs at. "In San Antone," he says, "we'd run you out of town on a rail drinkin' sissy stuff like that."

When Kwame walks in, he spots me immediately. I turn my head, pretend interest in Fred's race against some sister for National Bar Association secretary last year.

Sonny's eyes light up. "I remember her. She wore all those tight sweaters and no bra. Perfect little titties. Made you want to just bite one. Man, you lost in a landslide—"

Everyone falls out laughing.

"How's everyone?" Kwame says, looking at me. They greet him like he's royalty. "Gwen."

My breath catches. I hate that. "Kwame."

Harry invites him to join us. "Next time," he says. "I'm meeting someone."

Kwame takes a seat at the bar. My heart sags a little. I hate that. Harry eyes me watching Kwame. The bartender already has a drink waiting for him, and the cocktail waitress leans her chest in his face every chance she gets. You'd think he was a dentist the way she keeps showing him all her teeth.

"What are you waiting for?" Harry asks me.

I give him a blank look, refusing to admit he's peeped my hole card. Harry smiles knowingly. "You've been waiting for him all night."

I look down, my cheeks on fire. "It's not what you think. I need to talk to him." I stare at Kwame. He stares back a moment.

"What's up?" Kwame says, standing over me.

I'm sitting "in the corner in the back in the dark" in the back room of the Wunderbar. The other tables are empty, and the only light is courtesy of a Schlitz malt liquor sign. It's very discreet. Harry told him I wanted to see him.

"I want to talk to you about your client."

"I see." He pulls out a chair and sits down. If he's disappointed, he doesn't let on. "What about him?"

"There's a contract out on him."

"I heard that rumor. I assumed you started it."

I don't believe he said that. "Why would I do that?"

"To put shit in the game."

We stare at each other. It occurs to me how much we think we know each other and how little we really do. "I want your permission to talk to your client. In your presence, of course."

"No can do."

I'm not surprised. "Why not?"

"He fired me."

Ace-deuce.

Matoomba House looks spooky at night. Located on the fringe of Third Ward, it occupies a huge lot surrounded by towering pine trees. I'm not all that eager to get out of my car. It doesn't look like anyone's around, though Kwame said there should be. This is a self-appointed, self-help community center. Their hours, like their programs, are strictly their thing. They can afford to be iconoclasts about everything because they don't take one nickel from the government, an amazing feat for a black organization. Garrett says he doesn't need a sugar tit. His arrogant, abrasive, blacker-than-thou manner gets on the last nerve of Houston's black leadership—"blackeys," as he calls them, which I thought was kind of clever—not to mention white folks'.

Which is why it's so strange that all of a sudden, according to Kwame, there's such a growing groundswell of support for Garrett by the very black people he's talked about like dogs all these years and vice versa. Which is why Kwame got fired.

" 'Nothing personal,' " Kwame says, mimicking him. " 'You're a righteous brother.' "

I don't get it. "Why fire you this late in the game?" Kwame shrugs his shoulders. Getting fired is a drag. He downs his drink in one gulp. "The killing thing is he's hiring a white boy."

He has my total sympathies. "What makes you think the 'blackeys' are rallying behind him? And why don't I know about it?"

He shrugs. "Be glad. That means you're not one of them." I would've been insulted a month ago. "Larry Scott called me two days before Garrett fired me. Told me not to worry about my fee and to make sure the brother had everything he needed on his case. 'Money's no object, man.' " Music to a lawyer's ears. You get as much justice as you can afford. Which explains why black people generally come up short.

"Then Garrett fires me. Like that." He snaps his fingers. "The Garrett Defense Fund—"

"Defense fund?"

"The Charles Garrett Legal Defense Fund, to be exact. One of its founding members—the Honorable Willette Shalandar. How you like them apples?"

I don't, not one bit. Kwame takes my hand. It feels so . . . comforting, strong. His black brown eyes hold me. "You're in the cross fire, Gwen. Watch your back."

I pull my hand away. I have to stay angry with him if I intend to stop him from getting custody of Ashleigh Lee. "I'll do better than that," I say. "I'll watch my sides and my front."

"Kwame?"

A woman appears in the doorway. She's tall and dark, pretty, very feminine. I'm instantly, overwhelmingly jealous.

"Carolyn." Kwame smiles and beckons her. "This is Gwen."

She smiles warmly and extends her hand, which I want to shake like I want cavities. "I've heard so much about you," she says. Kwame's talked about me to her? "Your daughter's so beautiful. And so nice and well behaved. You can't say that about a lot of teenagers nowadays." Or Ashleigh Lee, not the one I know. "She's had lots of home training, I can tell."

I barely touch her hand to shake it. "Thank you—Karen, is it?"

"Carolyn."

"How about having a drink with us, Gwen?"

"No, thanks," I say, standing up, gathering what's left of my dignity. "Three's a crowd."

I feel like a complete and total grade A number one fool. I made such a monumental mistake sleeping with him after all these years. I still don't know how or why I did it, other than being high, stupid, and out of my mind. I deserve having this woman rubbed in my face.

* * *

I knock on Matoomba House's door hard enough to wake the dead. And with the feeling I'm a complete fool.

"Who is it?" a man's voice finally says.

"Helen Saulsberry," I lie.

"Who?"

"Helen Saulsberry."

I pray whoever I'm talking to is just as wary of opening the door to strangers as everybody else these days.

"Whatchew want?"

"I'm looking for my nephew. Charles Garrett? I just got in town. This is the only address I have."

Silence. Footsteps walk away, more footsteps walk back toward the door. I hold my breath, prepared to run if I'm busted.

"He ain't here," a different voice says.

I exhale slowly. "Can you give me directions to his house? I'm from out of town."

The new voice hesitates. "He down on the island at his mama's. Twenty-fifth Street. Number one twenty-eight."

Dirk was not happy when I called and told him I was driving down to Galveston this late at night. I ignored what I heard in his voice. "Did Ashleigh Lee do her homework?"

"Yeah. So when are you coming home? I don't like my woman runnin' the streets like this."

"Your 'woman'? Since when am I your 'woman,' Dirk?"

"Since I put my name on it. That's since when, baby."

I look at the receiver for a second. "Dirk, why are you talking like this?"

"Like what, baby?"

"Like a . . . black man."

"Isn't that what you want?"

I don't believe we're having this conversation. "If I'd wanted a black man, Dirk, I'd be with one."

"I'm glad to hear that, baby. 'Cause you got something a whole lot better—"

"Whatever you say." I hang up on him. He's tripping, and

I don't have time to deal with it right now. I've got to get some answers. I jump in Black Beauty and take off down the Gulf Freeway, snapping on "Quiet Storm" to keep from doing too much thinking. Things are too deep. Unfortunately, the d.j.'s taking requests and dedications. Dirk, Ashleigh Lee, and I listened to the same segment on the way back from Riviera—that disaster. She complained about having to listen to the "we-be's" all night. I asked her what she was talking about.

"We-be's," she repeated. "You know—'we be dis' and 'we be dat.' That's what the kids call them at school."

Dirk sniggers. I cut my eyes at him and straighten her out. "Those are your people they're talking about. Which means they're talking about you too." She just shrugged.

Galveston is about forty miles south of Houston and is the largest island off the Texas coast. Niggers have been there since slave days. The white people in Galveston would probably like nothing better than to deport them all to the mainland so they can gentrify the entire island, but they can't. So they simply pretend fifty percent of the city's population doesn't exist, deny them jobs and decent housing, and hope they'll leave on their own.

I hold my breath driving over the causeway—the only way in or out of the island from the freeway. There's nothing but concrete, asphalt, and air between me and the Gulf of Mexico, and that's not enough. The water looks black and endless.

I stop at a gas station and ask how to get to Twenty-fifth Street. The Iranian attendant looks at me like I've told him I'm selling sand. Fortunately, some black kids playing the video machines overhear me and set me straight. Two blocks over from the main drag I find where Garrett's mother lives. In a huge public housing project, specifically, in the next to the last building on the ground floor. The neighborhood is typically rundown. I'd like to see a well-maintained slum.

Garrett answers the door, surprising both of us. He recovers quickly, dropping his eyelids so much they look closed.

"What do you want?" That's a good question. I don't know.

"To talk," I say. "Pow-wow. Rap."

He smirks sideways, steps out on the tiny piece of a porch. "I got a mouthpiece for that."

He's being real ugly. I'm going to have to go toe-to-toe with him. "You've gone all the way live too. A black lawyer isn't good enough for a real 'down' brother like you."

He glares and deliberately shoots a stream of spit past my arm. I don't flinch. "I have this theory," I say, observing the target area. "Men have more spit in their mouths than women." I look at him. "What do you think?"

His jaws tighten. I could be jeopardizing the entire prosecution doing this. But if it's true that Willette's backing his defense, my shit is counterfeit anyway. Besides, I'll deny this conversation ever happened.

"Did Kwame tell you about the deal I'm offering?"

That gets his attention. "What deal?"

I step down to the sidewalk and walk off. "I guess he didn't get a chance before you gave him his walking papers. Oh, well."

He catches up and spins me around by my arm. "What deal?"

"I'll have to discuss it with your new lawyer. Who is it?"

His eyes dart from mine. "They haven't told—I don't know yet."

I pull away, looking at him like he's got cooties. "Tell him to call me when you do." I take my time getting to my car, his eyes on my every step.

"Hold up."

I unlock my door and get in.

"I said hold up." He snatches the door from my hand like he intends to kick my ass.

I might've pushed him too far.

"Yes?" I say innocently.

"What's the deal?"

I look him up and down. "Sorry," I say, starting my car. "I'll have to talk to your lawyer." Pulling off slowly, I reach for my door. He refuses to let go, trotting alongside me, desperate to find out all of a sudden.

"Tell me. I can run it down when I talk to him."

I stop at the corner. We look ridiculous. "Hmm, I don't know, Mr. Garrett. This could be unethical, talking to you alone." I'm stalling, trying to think of something that'll make him bite.

"Hey," he says congenially. "We ain't discussing the case or anything. I know better than that."

I look around a long moment, letting him stew. Up and down the street people sit like they're in a stupor, trying to cool off. "Okay," I say like I really should know better. Reach for my door, which he gladly releases. "The murder charge for the drug charge."

"No way!" He slams the car roof with his hand. I jump. I obviously hit a nerve. "No way! I ain't going down like that." He paces menacingly, eyes bugged out like he's just two minutes off me. "I'll tell you what you can do with your goddamn deal—"

I lock the doors just in case. "Mr. Garrett, I've got enough evidence on you to put you under the jail. I'm not handling the drug charge, but I hear it's just as solid. Which means you're going to have to cop to something or say good-bye to your friends and family for a couple of lifetimes."

"I'm not taking no deals," he says emphatically. "You can tell them that for me. If I go down, a bunch of folks are going down with me. You can take that back to the city with you. Tell your girl the commissioner, Charles say he don't play that shit."

I give him a last look. "I'll do that, Mr. Garrett." I mash the accelerator, burn rubber at him. Pissed, he picks up a rock and throws it at me. Black Beauty leaves him in the dust.

* * *

The drive back to Houston is long and dark. Texas is so big that there's nothing but highway between cities. This time of night it's just you and the occasional trucker. When I'm alone like this I have no choice but to remember . . .

The emergency room doctor told me if I hadn't brought Willette in when I did, she would've bled to death. I snorted to myself. I'd had to threaten to call her parents and tell them what she'd done to get her to go. She begged me not to.

"They'll know sooner or later," I said, losing my patience with her. "Look, Willette, I'm not going to argue with you anymore. You're bleeding like a pig." She'd gone through every pad I had.

"Okay," she said weakly.

I grabbed the phone and called for an ambulance. "She's hemorrhaging—"

"Gwen—"

Willette could barely keep her eyes open. I gave the dispatcher my address and hung up.

"Don't talk, Willette. The ambulance is on the way."

"Gwen, I have to ask you . . . when they come to take me . . . let me use your name—"

The red circle underneath her was spreading wider and wider. I didn't want her to die in my bed.

"Sure. No sweat."

She—I—wound up having a radical hysterectomy. They took everything. Tubes, ovaries, uterus, everything. Willie thanked me "for using my head" after I told him she was having emergency surgery and why. I'd panicked and called him when the doctor said she'd have to go under the knife. Willie thought it best that we continue the ruse she and I created under the circumstances. He asked me to keep him posted on her progress. He couldn't risk the publicity—or questions—by showing up at the hospital. I asked him if he was going to let Michael know what happened.

"Michael? What for?"

"He is her fiancé. He has a responsibility, Mr. Shalandar.

He should be here." I personally wanted to kill Michael for letting her do this.

"I see your point." Willie did better than I could have. He wasn't even mad at him. "I'll take care of it."

"What about Mrs. Shalandar?" I asked. "Shouldn't—doesn't she want to be here? I know my mother would, and I'm not her only child."

"Mrs. Shalandar's out of town. Her mother's doing poorly. Cancer. They don't expect her to live." I felt so sorry for him. Rain was pouring in his life.

"I'll call you as soon as I hear something," I promised.

"Miss Parrish?" My eyes popped open. It took me a second to remember I was in Ben Taub's waiting room. The doctor smiled at me. "Your sister's fine. She's in recovery."

I ran to the phone and called Willie.

"Praise God!" he cried. "I . . . can't talk anymore."

The receiver banged to the floor, and I heard him sob convulsively. I hung up, leaving him to console himself.

He had Willette transferred to a private hospital the next day. I saw Michael that afternoon in the student lounge, flirting with two first-year students. To be fair, they were doing most of the playing, having a good time describing what color black they wanted their babies to be. ("If it doesn't pass the paper bag test, I'm not bringing it home from the hospital.") I try to ignore them and get ready for Con Law.

"I bet you make some pretty babies, Michael," one of them said.

I looked into his face, saw him grinning proudly, totally flattered. I realized he didn't know a thing.

"They can look like Great Googa-Mooga," he said. "I love babies. I want ten of them."

27

I'm late coming in the office this morning.

"Hey," Delzenia says dryly. She seems a little saltier when I ask for my messages, but it could be me. I ain't in the best of moods. I see Willette's door is closed. Her line's lit up, though.

"Is she in?" I ask as I pick up my messages.

"She's on the phone."

I head to my office, sifting through my calls on the way. There's an urgent one from Marty Guggenheim, one of the top criminal defense attorneys in the city. Charles Garrett's new attorney. I'm in no hurry to talk to him. I kick the door closed with my foot, take a seat at my desk, and return my former law partner's call.

"Eddy Harris." His voice automatically puts a smile on my face.

"Gwen Parrish Ingersoll," I say, mocking him.

"How's it going, Gwen Parrish Ingersoll?" I can hear him smile through the receiver.

"Fine," I say, sorting through the mail out of habit. Practicing law, you try to kill as many birds as you can with one stone.

"I didn't ask how you looked."

I smile all over. "I needed that. What's up?"

"Not much. I keep hearing all kinds of things about your love life."

I lay aside the letter I'm skimming. "What kind of things?"

"Nothing specific. Just that you're on the wild these days.

I was just checking to see if there's any fire behind all the smoke."

"Not even a cinder, Daddy."

"Keep it that way. I gotta get to court. Some of us do have to work for a living."

"Yeah, well, I'd like to be in the group that doesn't."

"I thought you were. Hear Willette tell it, all you do is sit on that pretty behind of yours all day."

"She said that?"

"Would I lie?" No, not to me. All lawyers lie, though. It's called representing our client's interests. But even we have to have somebody to come up for air with. That's what Eddy and I do for each other. Still, I can't believe she'd say that about me. Or stab me in the back.

"I've been working like a dog, Eddy."

"Well, you better tighten up, Fifi. They don't call female dogs a bitch for nothing."

The light goes out on Willette's line. "I'll remember that. I'll be talking to you."

"Do that."

Willette is waiting for the elevator when I come out. "Gwen," she says with a nod.

"I need to talk to you, Willette."

She looks at her watch impatiently, then the floor indicator. "I'm on my way to commissioners court. Check my calendar and see if I've got any time this afternoon."

The elevator doors open. A beefy-looking white sheriff's deputy steps up to her. "Gwen Parrish Ingersoll?"

She gives her patented how-dare-you look, indicates me. "That is Ms. Parrish Ingersoll." She makes a point of reading his nameplate. "Deputy Wynem."

Sensing she's not his average, run-of-the-mill nigger, he tips his hat respectfully. "Sorry, ma'am." He looks at me. "Ms. Parrish Ingersoll?"

"Yes."

"This is for you." He hands me a citation and petition. I

sign for it. He notes the date and time, tips his hat, wishes us a good day as the elevator doors close on him.

"What is it?" Willette doesn't disguise her irritation.

"An amended custody petition."

When I was in private practice, I kept a short list in the back of my head of attorneys I'd call on if I ever needed one. Doctors probably do the same thing. After all, you know the ones with the high A.Q.'s. Asshole quotient.

I would never take my business to a white lawyer. I know how they feel about their black clients. Only you can't tell black people that. They believe they'll have a better chance in front of a white judge or jury with a white boy. The fallacy is that by time you get to court, it's all over but the shouting. Whatever's going to happen was decided in chambers, in the office, or over the telephone.

People always want to know if they really need a lawyer. I have two stock answers. One, "Does the other side have a lawyer?" Or two, "Would you operate on yourself?"

So when I get Kwame's amended custody petition, I know it's time to follow my own advice. Which is why I'm now waiting in Amelia Anderson Gerhart's reception room, killing time leafing through old *People* magazines. Amelia's the only black board-certified specialist in family law in Houston. We met a few years back on a panel on minority women and the law.

"Girl," she gushes, showing me into her office, "when my secretary told me Gwen Parrish Ingersoll was waiting to see me, I asked her what the hell she was keeping you waiting for. How've you been?"

Amelia's about the size of a gnat, but her booming voice makes her seem bigger. "I'm hearing all kinds of good things about you. Have a seat."

She buzzes her secretary not to disturb us, which I appreciate. Nothing's more annoying than your lawyer taking a call every five minutes while you're spilling your guts.

"I need a lawyer, Amelia." I hand her the pleadings.

She reads each petition. Looks at me. "Is he serious?"

I shrug. "As malignant lung cancer."

She sits back in her chair. "In that case, you better tell me all about it."

I relate everything that's happened between me and Ashleigh Lee.

"You actually took her to buy drugs?"

"I wanted to scare her."

"You scare me."

I deserve that. "Does that mean you won't represent me?"

"Huh," she laughs. "Somebody represented Charles Manson."

I'm depressed and downhearted when I leave Amelia's office. She leveled with me, unlike a lot of lawyers who tell clients what they want to hear just to get their business. My case is assigned to Judge Earl Ray Pollock, a shriveled-up good ol' boy who hates everybody. "Even still," Amelia says, "the high point of his docket is when uppity niggers come in with something really juicy."

"Like me and Kwame."

"Like you and Kwame. Then he becomes Super Solomon—and sticks it to both parties." Family law—like criminal law—is essentially cowboy law in Texas. Everybody from the judges on down shoot from the lip and asks questions later.

"Then there's the publicity," she points out. " 'Shalandar Aide Takes Daughter to Buy Drugs.' Whatever professional plans you had for the foreseeable future you can cancel."

As I cross the street to my car, I slap the legal papers against my thigh so hard it stings. Now that she's damn near grown and most of the heartache and hard work is over, all of a sudden I'm not good enough to raise her. My throat constricts with resentment. He's not going to just take my child away from me, even if she says she wants to go. I know Ashleigh Lee. If I don't fight to keep her, she'll think I don't care.

* * *

"Peace, be still."

Reverend Hadley bows his head and closes his eyes, swaying in time while the choir hums softly in the background. "Peace, be still."

He opens his eyes; they seem to flash right through me. "Everybody's busy trying to sidestep the bad," he thunders. "What we need is some of that water-walking faith our Lord had. Peace, be still, my children. Peace, be still. Sing it."

He moves to the side of the podium as the choir sings out. Hollow Ridge Baptist Church has the best choir in the city, although saying it could start a fight in some quarters. This isn't your average black church, which is why I like to visit. Reverend Riley Lee Hadley is young and energetic, with lots of progressive ideas about taking God to the people through day care, youth groups, singles nights, seniors days—he doesn't just sit back waiting for the people to find the Lord or him. We met when he offered to be a character witness for my knuckleheaded client Duwain Tomkins, star quarterback at Prairie View A & M by day, strong-arm robber by night. His specialty was ripping off little old white women. His dual career came to a halt when one old biddy not only refused to give up her purse, she ran after the car and memorized his license plate number as he sped away.

Hollow Ridge gets criticized for holy rolling and talking in tongues—some of the congregants can really cut loose—but unlike the "ee-lights" in my church, they've got real Christian fellowship here. I felt a need for that this Sunday morning.

Even Ashleigh Lee showed some enthusiasm when I told her we were going to Hollow Ridge instead of attending services at St. Mark's. She was dressed and ready to go when I called her down to breakfast. I didn't have to nag her about moving in slow motion one time. She even invited Dirk to come with us, which raised both eyebrows. Naturally, he declined.

"You never go to church," she said. "How are you going to get into heaven?"

"I'll worry about that when I get there," he replied. "She's being too nice," he whispered to me behind his hand. "Better watch your step." I told him to stop being so suspicious.

She asked me if he's an atheist in the car.

"No," I said. "He just doesn't believe in going to church." Thank God. Aside from the office, it's practically the only place I can go now without him. Which tells me how much he hates church.

She asked me if I knew any black atheists. I had to admit I couldn't think of any. "I guess when you were real and actual slaves like our people and then you're freed, you *know* there's a God," she says. I'm impressed by her insight and tell her so, though I question what she means by "real and actual."

"You know," she says, "not storybook, made-up slaves or so long ago that people have to just take your word that you were slaves."

"I see." I really didn't, but it didn't matter because we were actually having a pleasant conversation for the first time in a long time. I really enjoyed it. However, one thing neither of us talked about was Kwame's custody petition or the hearing that's set next month, right on the heels of the Garrett case. Amelia suggested having it continued. I just want to get it over with. I wanted to ask Ashleigh Lee how she could do this to me after all I've done for her, but I couldn't. I was afraid she'd tell me.

"Well, hello, Attorney Parrish. Long time, no see." Reverend Hadley's smile is warm and genuine. Service is over and he's wishing everyone Godspeed. "Ashleigh Lee—girl, I swear, you get prettier and prettier."

She smiles shyly. "Thank you, Rev. Hadley."

"Thank you," he says, taking both our hands. "Attorney Parrish, if you ever need a new home, Hollow Ridge would love to have you and your lovely daughter."

I run into LaTina Baker, another former client, on the way to the parking lot. There are over a half million blacks in Houston, and some days I feel like I know most of them or they know me. We stop to chat. I ask about her ex-husband, whom I helped her to divorce. "We got back together," she laughs. "I'm ready to cut him loose again. How about it, Attorney Parrish?"

"Once was enough for me, Ms. Baker." I look around for Ashleigh Lee. She "disappeared" when we walked outside. "I don't practice law anymore. Excuse me."

I check back inside. She's nowhere to be found. I go back outside to see if she's in the car. As I cross the parking lot, I see Marie Odum run out of the fellowship hall, a separate building from the main church, look around frantically, spot me, and hurry over. Reverend Hadley introduced me to her and her husband, Arnell, the last time I was here. He's a building contractor, and she teaches school. As I recall, they have three pimply-faced teenage sons. I automatically stop. Something's wrong.

"Attorney Parrish—thank God I found you."

"What's wrong?" I ask. Dread fills me.

"Everything's all right—now. Rev. Hadley and Arnell's with the children. I don't know how to tell you this."

"What happened?" I grab her arms, scaring her, I know. "Where's my daughter?"

She starts blubbering. "I hope you explained the facts of life to her. I talked to the boys myself. I assure you I didn't leave it to Arnell. I even showed them how to put a rubber on."

I stare at her, absorbing the meaning of her words. I release her and run to the fellowship hall. She races alongside me. "I hate to be the one to tell you this, Attorney Parrish. I think your daughter needs help."

I bolt through the door, my heart pounding like drums. "Ashleigh Lee, where are you?"

"We're in here," calls Reverend Hadley.

Marie leads me to one of the small Sunday school rooms off the main auditorium. It's lined with folding chairs, a Bible in each seat. Her husband, the reverend, the three

Odum boys, and Ashleigh Lee stand in a loose circle in the middle of the room.

"What's going on?" I rush toward them. The boys' eyes drop to the floor. Ashleigh Lee pokes out her lip insolently.

"I'm gonna whup their behinds when we get home," Arnell says. "That's what's going on. Feeling up a young girl in the church and God knows what else—"

"*What?*" I drive my eyes into Ashleigh Lee.

"Let's not make more of it than it is, Mr. Odum," says Reverend Hadley.

"She told us to do it, Dad," the oldest boy says defensively. He looks eighteen or nineteen. "She let us."

"She can't 'let' you do anything." I walk straight up to him. "She's only fifteen years old."

He gulps hard, holds his ground. "She called us sissies. She started taking her clothes off before we had a chance to say anything."

The youngest son pipes up, his voice cracking naturally. "She said she wanted to live with her daddy and you won't let her. She said she was going to embarrass you until you do. We didn't want to do it." He looks at his mother, tears of shame in his eyes. "Honest."

What can you do when your daughter entices three boys to fondle her in a church, doing some of anything so she can live with her father?

Dirk knows something's wrong as soon as we come in. I don't have to tell Ashleigh Lee to leave us.

"What is it this time?" Virtually everything about him says I-told-you-so.

I pick up the receiver and punch in the numbers with my index knuckle. No point in breaking a nail on top of everything else. "Kwame, this is Gwen. I've come to a decision about Ashleigh Lee. I'm not going to fight you on custody."

28

Dirk believes the way you snap out of the blues is m.y.a. Move your ass, physical activity, his surefire cure for whatever ails you. He suggests we both take the day off. Since it's Monday, it doesn't take much to convince me. He, on the other hand, is a workaholic, so it's a real sacrifice on my behalf when he tells his secretary he won't be in.

I laid around all Sunday evening, not saying a word, sipping Wild Turkey straight, staring at whatever came on TV. The only time I roused myself was when Kwame came for Ashleigh Lee. I walked her to the door, kissed her good-bye, and wished them well. He tried to say something, but I slammed the door in his face. When I plopped back down in front of the TV I heard something crack. I think it was my heart. Before I knew it, tears were running down my face like rain. How could I have been so wrong? And if I was that wrong about Ashleigh Lee, what else am I totally screwed up about?

How can you succeed at anything if you fail as a mother?

Dirk did the right thing leaving me alone. When your livelihood consists of solving other people's problems, it's a given you can solve your own. Every now and then he asked if I wanted anything, dinner, the Sunday paper. Can you bring my child back? I didn't want to think or eat or move. I had my hands full just breathing, lifting my glass, watching TV. Around midnight he called me to bed. I would've sat there all night, drinking and blinking at the screen.

I had one helluva hangover when I got up this morning.

Dirk wouldn't let me sleep it off. He whipped off the covers and pulled me from bed. I didn't resist or fight. I didn't care—until he shoved me into the shower and turned it on. I screamed when the cold water slammed me. The water striking me so unexpectedly triggered another round of blubbering over Ashleigh Lee. I'm not a crybaby. As a matter of fact, I rarely cry about anything. But I was crying a river.

Dirk pulled me out and held me, petting me, telling me everything was going to be all right. We sank to the floor with me sprawled across him, wailing and thrashing about. I was like those women you see on the news, convulsing with grief over the loss of a child. Nothing will or nothing can console you. You just run out of tears, which I did after a time, the pain going into remission to metastasize at a later date.

Dirk helps me to my feet. When I see myself in the mirror, I want to cry again. My eyes are bloodshot and puffy; my face has these hideous red welts across it. My lips are cracked and taste like salt and snot. I look inside out.

I just want to loll in bed and continue to feel sorry for myself. I feel entitled under the circumstances. Dirk has other plans. He comes into the bedroom and informs me he's loaded our bikes onto the car and packed a picnic lunch.

"It's beautiful outside. M.y.a. On the double."

I'm not the outdoors type, I'm not a sports enthusiast, and I could care less about grown men playing games of any kind. I'm not a team person and I'm not a jogger. But I will ride a bike. Dirk and I rode all the time before we got married. Which seems like years ago instead of a few short months.

Houston isn't noted for paying attention to the quality of its citizens' lives. People coming here from other parts of the country once were appalled by the primitive municipal services. Native Houstonians—sensitive, arrogant souls that they are—couldn't stand carpetbaggers talking about how lousy life was here even after they made a pile of money. Torn-up streets that flooded if it rained for more than ten minutes, no libraries, no place to recreate. "A park would be nice" were fighting words. Green spaces were for development only.

All that changed a few years back. Except white folks couldn't give themselves all the parks and give the minorities none. Times had changed. In the black and brown neighborhoods they found any vacant six-by-ten-foot space, stuck up a sign, and proclaimed it a park in the name of whatever minority person was up for immortality. In other places they were so hard up for open spaces they turned strips of land along the bayous into parks. It's not as bad as it sounds. The bike-and-hike trails running along them are magnificent. You can run, ride, walk, or skate for miles and miles right through the heart of the city.

Dirk and I use the one that parallels Brays Bayou. It's the most scenic, and it doesn't have that many stops. Considering how ill-mannered, ill-tempered, and downright perverse Houston drivers are, you come to really appreciate a four-foot-wide lane through some of the prettiest parts of the city, no cars allowed.

We've been pumping along the winding, rolling, tree-strewn path for over an hour. I do feel better in spite of myself. Dirk's a couple yards ahead. Ahead of him a young white girl peddles leisurely. She has an exceptionally wide behind. She gets off the bike path at the intersection of Almeda and North Mac Gregor, the demarcation line for Third Ward. We stop at the corner so Dirk can tighten his chain. While he tinkers, I watch the girl. She's riding with the traffic now. An old blue station wagon drives up beside her, loaded with black men, laughing and heckling her. One of the men leans all the way out the window and shouts at her. She ignores him, maintaining her slow, even pace. The men roar with laughter. The guy hauls off and slaps her on the ass.

"Can you believe that?" I'm stunned.

Dirk watches his wheel rotate. "What?"

How one human being can strip another of her dignity

and think it's funny. Which makes me realize I've still got mine, with or without my child.

"Nothing."

We sit on a blanket under a huge oak tree, watching children toss popcorn and bread crumbs at the ducks who make their home in a large rectangular pool that's part of 388 acres composing Hermann Park. On the other side, an old man "waters" his dog. That is, the dog's on a long leash, swimming down the middle of the pond. The ducks take it all in stride. I lean back on Dirk, shielding my eyes from the early afternoon sun with my forearm. "I love Hermann Park," I say.

"I love you." Dirk runs a wildflower along my face. It tickles. I complain but not too strenuously.

"Any more chicken left?" he asks.

I reach for the box, rattle the crumbs for the answer. Ants have already infiltrated its grease-stained bottom.

"Oh, well," he says, fondling me. "How about the dessert?"

"In front of all these people?" I tease. "A shy Aryan type like you?"

He frowns, pushes me away, jumps up and grabs the Frisbee, runs back a few steps. "Catch."

I have to leap to my feet in order to snare it before it hits the ground. Which he did on purpose, obviously annoyed, which I don't understand anymore. It's getting so he doesn't want to be reminded he's white at all. That's funny. Black people want the same thing.

I whip the Frisbee at him under my leg, paying him back. He snags it just in time. We play aggressively like that, back and forth, until he and the heat wear me out. "That's it for me." I toss the disc on the ground and flop down. "I'm taking a nap."

"I want to check out the new big cat exhibit." He sounds still pissed off.

"Nothing's stopping you." I lie down on the blanket and

turn my back. Now I'm pissed. He takes off in the direction of the zoo in long, angry strides. Everything we do ends like this lately—each of us going to our own angry corner.

Now that I'm by myself, I can't sleep. I sit up and pull my knees toward my chest, lace my fingers around them, and people watch. It's amazing how tranquil it is in the heart of Houston. This is truly an oasis.

I slip Dirk's Walkman on to check the time. He's got it tuned to Magic 103, which surprises me. He usually likes classical music. The announcer gives the time at two fifty-five, telling everybody to stay tuned for the news. I start taking off the headset. I'm not ready for the real world yet. I hear him say, ". . . was found this afternoon. The police have listed his death as an apparent suicide." Curious, I set the earphones back in place. Black people usually have to get in line behind all the things that kill them besides themselves. "Charles Garrett was recently indicted for the murder of Willie Shalandar, the first black ever elected county commissioner. Garrett had subsequently been charged with delivery of a controlled substance and was out on bail awaiting trial on both charges. . . ."

Charles Garrett dead? Suicide? No way, José.

29

The reporters are waiting on me when Dirk and I get to Willette's office. We came straight from the park.

"Have you heard about Garrett's apparent suicide, Ms. Parrish?"

"No comment."

Who hasn't by now? Dirk strong-arms a couple of them so that I can get out of the car.

"What effect does his death have on your case?"

"No comment."

What do you think, dummy? I've heard of prosecuting somebody in absentia, but dead is ridiculous.

"What's Commissioner Shalandar's reaction to Garrett's death?"

Your guess is as good as mine. "No comment."

We finally manage to get to the door of the Shalandar Building, squeeze in while the security guard holds the media at bay, waste no time getting to the third floor. The tranquility of the office contrasts starkly with the chaos downstairs. Delzenia looks me up and down, disapproving of my skimpy shorts and halter top. "The commissioner's waiting to see you."

I peck Dirk's cheek. "I'll see you at home." I knock and enter Willette's office.

"Gwen. Good—"

Willette sees how I'm dressed, checks out the reactions of Larry Scott and Harrison McIlroy, both looking at me, their faces stony masks. I'm surprised to see them here. Especially Larry. Worms don't usually associate with eagles.

"We were at Hermann Park," I say apologetically, self-conscious about how I look, especially in front of Larry. "We rushed right over as soon as we heard."

"I understand," Willette says. "Sit down."

I turn to close the door. I notice C.C. leaning casually on the cabinet behind me. We nod. She pushes her chair toward me. I ease into the seat. I feel like I'm at a table of card sharks playing with a marked deck.

"We were just discussing the circumstances of Garrett's . . . death," Willette says, looking at me.

McIlroy unconsciously rubs the bald spot on the back of his head. "I'll tell you one thing," he says, obviously picking up where the conversation left off. "Black folks don't go 'round committin' suicide."

Larry Scott's lips curl into a leer as he takes in my body. "You remember what Dick Gregory said. We have to jump *up*."

"I agree," says C.C. "We're stronger than that. That's why we invented the blues."

I shake my head. These people are supposed to be our best and brightest—a county commissioner, a district court judge, a city councilman, a labor leader—all talking that smack, "Black people don't—" No wonder we're in trouble.

"Did you want to say something, Gwen?" Willette asks. The others look at me with varying degrees of tolerance.

I clear my throat. "Just that you shouldn't rule out suicide. The only things we don't do that white people do are things we can't afford." I cut my eyes to Scott. "They don't have a monopoly on perversion, and we don't have one on pathology."

Scott yanks on his lapels indignantly and issues me a look to kill. I don't care. I think he had something to do with that tape. "I had a friend," I continue, "whose mother blew her brains out with a shotgun while we were at church. My girlfriend came home from Sunday school, went down in the basement, found her lying in a pool of blood."

McIlroy glowers at me, angry that I'm deviating from the party line. "How do you know it wasn't no accident? Sounds like you were just a kid."

"It wasn't an accident," I say quietly, still affected after all these years. "Her mother left a note."

Willette and C.C. exchange a look I can't read. "This sounds like one of those chicken-egg arguments," C.C. says. "I think the best thing to do is for Willette to issue a short statement saying that with the death of Charles Garrett, the special prosecution of his case has ended."

"I agree," says Willette.

"And dat'll be the end of dat," McIlroy states.

Scott stands up, ready to go. "No disrespect intended to either of the deceased, but this does wrap things up in a neat little package." He dusts off his hands for emphasis.

I don't get this. They don't believe in black suicide, but they believe Garrett killed himself. "What if the autopsy report says otherwise?"

Scott and McIlroy look like I'm peeing on their parade. I ignore them. "Willette, don't you think it's a little strange for Charles Garrett, of all people, to take his life? What if his people don't buy it?"

"What is this?" says McIlroy, exasperated with me. "She's talkin' out both sides of her neck." He mocks me again. " 'Black people commit suicide'—but he didn't."

"I'm being as inconsistent as you are, Mr. McIlroy."

"I spoke with the coroner before you arrived, Gwen," Willette says. "Barring anything unusual—which they don't expect to find—they're going to call it suicide by strangulation."

He hanged himself? I shake my head, trying to match the image of him swinging from the end of a rope with the man who threw rocks at me the other night. Willette exchanges another look with C.C., who stands over me, forcing me to look up. "I think you better go with us on this, Gwen. You were the last person to see him alive."

I gasp. "How—?" Did you know?

"It doesn't matter," she says reassuringly. "You wouldn't want it said that you harassed him into killing himself."

I jump in her face. "Be serious. I suppose I kicked the chair out from under him too."

C.C.'s pupils look like pin dots, she's so mad that I have the audacity to get in "her Honor's" face. "I don't know how you did it," she says, so cold ice cubes could be falling out of her mouth. McIlroy and Scott smirk obnoxiously. Men love to see women fight.

C.C. and I narrow-eye each other. I don't know about her, but I'm ready to get it on. All the bullshit I've been through lately is backing up on me. I need to punch somebody out.

Willette steps between us. "That's enough," she warns. "From both of you." She turns to Scott and McIlroy. "I'm going to talk to the media now. I'll be in touch. Gwen, you stay." C.C. and I roll eyes at each other one last time as she departs. Willette throws up her hands helplessly after they're gone. "What am I going to do with you two? The last thing I need right now is for my two best friends in the whole world to fall out."

I drop my head, ashamed. I feel her green eyes scouring me. "What's wrong, Gwen?"

Everything. "Ashleigh Lee went to live with Kwame. It was her choice."

"You poor thing." She takes me in her arms and holds me. "Ashleigh Lee's your heart." Standing me at arm's length, she looks at me compassionately, her beautiful face glazed with sadness. "I know what it's like to lose the person you love more than anyone. Cheer up," she says, smiling for my benefit. "Kids always think they want to live with the absent parent. She'll be back."

My spirits soar with hope I didn't know I had. "You think so?"

She laughs. "This is Kwame we're talking about. You couldn't live with him but a hot second."

"True," I laugh, desperate to believe her. "Thanks for

understanding, Willette. I'm with you a hundred percent. I'm sorry about going off on Larry. I believe he put that tape out on me."

"I understand," she says. "I inherited him from my father. Scott and McIlroy gave Daddy advice for years. They think they're supposed to do the same for me whether I ask or not. For the record, he swore up and down he didn't do it. I believe him, Gwen."

I wouldn't believe him as far as I can throw him and I can't pick him up. But I'll go with her on it. She's being really sweet. It's not a side she shows often. When she does you know she means it. I appreciate that. She tosses me her raincoat to cover up with.

"Let's throw the media hounds some bones."

Most of the questions are for Willette. She answers them deftly and succinctly. Print and TV reporters are packed like chitlins into her office, hanging on her every word. Time flies. Their last question is for me.

"Ms. Parrish Ingersoll, will you be resuming your regular duties as Commissioner Shalandar's administrative assistant now that this matter has been brought to a close by the death of Charles Garrett?"

I don't flicker an eyelash. "Full-time. Effective immediately."

"That's correct," Willette adds, beaming at me. "Ms. Parrish Ingersoll has done an outstanding job for me in every respect. I don't know what I'd do without her." Her voice softens, and she looks straight into the camera. "In closing, let me just say that my heart just goes out to the Garrett family. I know what it's like to lose a loved one under tragic circumstances. God bless you and keep you safe."

There aren't many people who could extend condolences to the family of her father's murderer. I don't think I could. Willette is amazing.

My phone's been ringing off the wall all evening. More reporters with follow-up questions. Now I see the advantage of an answering machine, which Dirk promises to get me. Until he does, he's stuck answering the phone, something neither of us had to do when there was a teenager in the house. Ashleigh Lee would answer the phone before it rang if she could. Dirk looks unhappy when he hands me the receiver this time.

"Gwen, it's Eddy." That explains the look on Dirk's face. If I never talked to a black man again, it would be too soon for him. That includes my father. "Can you talk?"

Dirk is making coffee. His back's to me, but I know he's listening. "No," I say. "I didn't get the message about the meeting."

"We need to talk," he says. I catch the urgency in his voice.

"I think I left that file at the office, Eddy."

"Meet me at the Wendy's around the corner from you in ten minutes." He hangs up.

I pretend he's still on the line. "Gee, Eddy, can't it wait until tomorrow?" Dirk sets my coffee in front of me, watching me closely. "Okay. See you in a few."

"You're going out, I know." Dirk doesn't bother to disguise his jealousy.

I grab my keys and purse. "Eddy needs a file. He's a real pain. I've been gone for two months, and he's still trying to find shit."

"I'll go with you—"

"Stay." I hold up my hand like a traffic cop. "You've got three briefs to read, remember?" Thank God he's arguing a big motion tomorrow.

Eddy's sitting by the window on the lookout for me when I pull into Wendy's. He opens the door on my side.

"What?"

"I don't want you running off the road," he says.

"It's that bad?" I slide to the passenger side, and he drives around the drive-thru and out onto the street. "Why the cloak and dagger?"

"Somebody's following me." It couldn't be Dirk. "Don't

worry, I lost 'em." His mouth turns down into his customary smile. "Nobody tails me for long."

Eddy was in intelligence in 'Nam. He knows all kinds of little tricks to fool the enemy, whoever that is. I sit back and try to relax. The Jag feels funny with somebody else driving.

"So what's up, Eddy?"

He pulls into a Kentucky Fried Chicken and parks. "You need to know what's going around town about you."

I yawn big-time. "Just so they get my name right, I don't care. You know that."

"This is serious, Gwen." He's as solemn as he was the first time we played cards together. I straighten up and pay attention.

"Supposedly you and C.C. were getting down at a party and things got rough. You knocked her around and wound up dragging her out kicking and screaming."

I exhale long and deep. That's it? "Eddy, Eddy, Eddy— my good, good friend. We're going to laugh about this one day. Right now I'm too tired."

"Cool," he says, his feelings hurt. "I was just trying to help."

I pat his arm apologetically. "I appreciate it, Eddy. Really. But you know I don't go that way."

He grins mischievously. "That's what I told the person who told me that garbage. C.C. doesn't wear your kind of perfume." Something catches his eye. "Say, is that your old man?"

My head whips around. "Where?"

Eddy doubles over laughing. I sock him in his side. "That's not funny."

Dirk's in bed reading a brief when I come in. I give him a quick kiss and head for the dressing room to change.

"That didn't take long," he says casually.

I slip my gown on over my head and come out. "Halfway up the block I remembered the file was in my trunk," I say.

I turn my light off and scoot down, pulling the comforter over my head to block out Dirk's light.

"Good night." I yawn, exhausted.

"Willette called."

"What'd she say?"

"Don't lie to your husband."

I don't think I heard right. "What did you say?"

"She said for you to meet her at nine o'clock," he says innocently. "Sharp. Where are you going?"

"Downstairs. I want some milk."

I throw the cover back and hurry to the garage. Place my hand on the hood of Dirk's car. The engine's as warm as mine. I heard him right.

"Come in."

I take a seat while Willette makes notes on her legal pad. "Just a moment," she says.

I watch her write. She has perfect penmanship: neat, tight, exquisitely formed letters. Beautifully controlled, like her. She puts the pen down and removes her glasses. She smiles, but her eyes are flat, dull green. They avoid mine.

"We've known each other a long time, Gwen, so I'll cut to the chase. Things aren't working out as I thought they would."

She replaces her glasses, picks the pen back up, and writes. I'm having a difficult time breathing. "Are you— firing me?"

"Yes."

"But why?" My head's in a whirl. I don't get this at all.

She stops writing, leans back in Willie's big wing-back chair, gazes at me. "My . . . advisers insist. I'm sorry."

"Scott?"

She nods. "He hates you. What'd you do to him?"

"Nothing." Then it comes back to me. "I turned him down. That was a long time ago. He can't still be mad."

She shrugs. "He said he's sending the tape to KHOU."

"I knew it." I start pacing. "Let him send it. KHOU of all people'll be able to see it's phony."

"Not . . . C.C.'s part."

C.C. So this is about protecting her. "I see." I stand up. I can't feel my legs. "How much notice do you want?"

"Larry wants you off the premises right now. We'll send your things. Delzenia has your severance check. I'm being very generous under the circumstances. I'm . . . sorry, Gwen. I can't help you. Ever."

She picks up her pen and writes, filling the page with beautifully formed lettering. I turn wooden legs to the door, willing them to walk out.

30

"Nothing's promised in life," my father used to say. "Especially tomorrow."

When I was in private practice, I'd get calls all the time from people who'd lost their jobs. My advice was, "Look for another one." I wasn't very sympathetic when they wanted to tell me how they got "de-terminated" or " 'strimi-nated against" or just plain mistreated. Needless to say, I have a new understanding.

Dirk is neither surprised nor disturbed when I break the news. Of course, I can't tell him the whole story. He'd probably go gunning for Larry Scott. "Did you hear what I said, Dirk? I'm through. Finished."

He spears a stuffed shrimp from his plate and bites into it. He insisted on meeting at Don's Seafood for lunch. I wanted to crawl into a hole. "Frankly, Gwen, I'm relieved."

Frustrated by his reaction, I fold my arms across my chest, ready to tear into him. "I don't need you to be 'frank' right now, Dirk."

"No," he says. "You need sympathy. I sympathize."

"You could've fooled me."

He shrugs. "Goldfish don't swim with barracudas."

That hurts. Before I can catch it, a lone, angry tear slips from my eye, plops on my napkin, spreads out like an amoeba before it's absorbed. I stare at it. Kwame. Ashleigh Lee. Now Willette. "I feel like such a fool. Everything I wanted is gone. The judgeship." My voice cracks. "My daughter."

"I'm still here."

I look at him. Try to smile. "I don't know why."

He smiles unhappily. "I don't know either sometimes." He reaches across the table for my hand. His is warm and strong. "Gwen, has the thought ever occurred to you that you wanted the wrong things in the first place?"

Wrong to want my child? Status? Power? "No."

He pats my hand. I feel like a child. "Think about it. I had the privilege of living twenty-four hours a day with Ashleigh Lee. She's a spoiled, obnoxious, selfish, self-centered brat."

His words hit like hollow-point bullets. "You never liked her."

"She's not likable."

"I don't have to listen to you run down my child. I know she's not perfect. Neither are you. You never tried to understand her."

"That's not true. She and I understood each other very well. She hates me."

I stand up. "I don't want to talk about this anymore. You don't care about my feelings."

"Gwen, sit down." He looks around the restaurant pointedly. I'm drawing attention.

"Let them look," I say. "You might as well have an audience since you're kicking me while I'm down."

I head for the door. He follows me. "Gwen, I'm sorry."

"Forget it, Dirk. I've already added you to the list of things that have been a disaster for me lately."

I've been everywhere the last month looking for a job. In addition to the fact that I need and want to work, I am totally dependent on Dirk, which I can't stand and which he thought would be right down his alley. It's not. He still can't keep track of me. When I'm home he calls a hundred times "just to say hi." When I'm out—which is often, since I'm not the kind of person to sit around all day watching soaps—he tries to cross-examine me on every minute. I don't know which one of us is going to go crazy first.

Of course, I have a standing offer to work for him at Legal Services, which I have no intentions of ever accepting. I could do the job, but I couldn't take being in Dirk's line of vision all day long. He's a jealous man. I refuse to let him control me the way he did his first two wives. I have no intentions of having to ask for "cigarette and tampon" money, as a friend of mine in Detroit describes being financially dependent on a man.

Pounding the pavement these past weeks has made me face real reality. I thought I had chits I could call in when the time came. Huh. I found out real quick from the County Attorney, Houston's Legal Department, and the Texas Attorney General's Office that whatever favors I'd done for anybody in the past are in the past. It's always the same response: "Have you talked to Willette Shalandar?"

You have to be "blessed" to get certain positions on the public dole. If you're black, the anointment comes from Willette since she's straw boss now. Before that it was Willie. I found out from my last interview—for the equivalent of legal adviser to Animal Control—Larry Scott's put the bad mouth out on me. Apparently, he doesn't intend for me to ever get another job in Houston. I don't even try the big white firms or corporations. I know better, despite graduating in the top ten percent of my class. They don't hire blacks unless it's politically advantageous. I couldn't be more politically disadvantaged.

Most of the black attorneys I've run into have been sympathetic; they just don't have any jobs. Few, if any, black firms hire employees other than secretaries, rarely paralegals or even law clerks, let alone lawyers. You need corporate retainers, government contracts, or big fat p.i. cases for that. We don't get that kind of business even from black people. And they do have some with money here. Texas has more black millionaires than anyplace else.

It gets down to going out of my mind from having nothing to do or making that call. I chuckle grimly as I dial. I sound like a commercial for drug rehab. Pat answers. Greets me warmly. I ask for Eddy. He comes on the line immediately. It's no questions asked.

"Your office is waiting for you. Haven't changed a thing."

I know attorneys who go in and out of private practice all the time. They get fed up with "feast or famine" and take a job. Then they get fed up with somebody telling them what to do and the limited income of a job. They can't get rich working for somebody, but they might if the "big case" comes through their door. So they spin the wheel again.

I thought I'd left the private practice of law behind me as I skipped my way down the yellow brick road to what I thought was my judgeship. Like they say, I thought like Lit. Fortunately, Eddy doesn't hold it against me. He even gave me back the cases I gave him when I started working for Willette. I'm grateful to have some open files. It allows me the illusion that I'm not starting all over from scratch. Eddy said people still call the office looking for me. I thought he was just telling me that to make me feel better until I actually got a phone call my first morning. I was thrilled.

A. J. Coyt is the kind of client who thinks he's as smart as any lawyer. The kind who figures seven years of school was a waste. All you have to do is watch TV. He comes through the door telling me how he wants his case handled.

"And when we go to trial, you need to fix as many of them errors as you can so we can get reversed on appeal and I can get me a new trial." He grins at me with evenly spaced, gapped teeth, winks slyly. I return neither his smile nor his wink. His mother is with him. She looks worried, as well she should be.

"A.J.," she whines, "maybe you should just listen to Ms. Parrish. Me and your daddy think—"

He bolts up in the chair and roars at her. "How many times I done tole you, Mama—that nigger ain't my daddy. Humph."

Mrs. McDaniel smiles a pathetic, apologetic smile at me. "Mr. McDaniel's the only father the boy ever knowed. I married him when A.J. was six months old. He a good man."

" 'He a good man,' " mimics A.J., stuffing himself back down in the chair. "Humph."

As far as I'm concerned, the most immediate problem Mrs. McDaniel has is recognizing that this tank-head rascal sitting next to her is not a boy. He's forty-five years old and a three-time loser, and the D.A.'s planning on prosecuting him as a habitual criminal on his latest burglary charge. Of course, he's innocent.

"Looka here," he says, sitting up. "I gotta take me a pee. Where's the can?"

"A.J.!" Mrs. McDaniel, a sweet little woman with silvery gray hair and the same thick-lipped, gapped-tooth smile, is genuinely embarrassed. "Where are your manners?"

He looks at her dully. "Humph."

I give him the directions to the men's room.

"He really a nice boy," she says, anxiously twisting a tissue with bird-claw hands. "He just had a lot of bad breaks." Yeah. Breaking into people's houses and getting caught. "Mr. McDaniel and me, we've tried to raise him best we could." Her eyes fill with the sorrow A.J.'s brought her over the years. "Lawd, I just don't know what's gonna happen to him when we pass on. I just don't know."

Usually when a relative dies, you try to keep the survivors from putting all their money in the ground with him—like buying a twenty-thousand-dollar casket knowing they'll need it to live on. I want to warn Mrs. McDaniel against sinking what money they have into her son's case.

"Mrs. McDaniel, have you considered that A.J. may have done exactly what the police are accusing him of?" She looks genuinely surprised at the possibility. "I'm not saying I don't believe him, Mrs. McDaniel. It doesn't matter what I believe. You're paying me to give him the best defense I can. I'm just saying that if he's convicted—and that's always a fifty-fifty chance—he's gone for good."

She wrings the tissue's neck. "Lawd, Lawd, I just don't know what to do. I wish Mr. McDaniel was here."

I always leave the discussion of my fee for last. I'm not as bad as I used to be, but I'm still uncomfortable asking for money from strangers even when I'm entitled to it. Eddy gets around it by setting a picture of his wife and two kids on his desk so that he can always see their faces.

"Since your son is unemployed, I assume you and Mr. McDaniel will be responsible for my fee."

"I don't work," she says.

"I see. What does Mr. McDaniel do?"

"Humph." A.J. steps back in the room. "Hard time."

I look from mother to son. "I beg your pardon?"

A.J.'s face splits into a vicious grin. "He doin' twenty years at Huntsville."

After they leave, I tell Pat about how Mrs. McDaniel intends to use her Social Security to pay for her son's lawyer. "Some people don't just put their money in the grave, they want to jump in too," I say. Pat shakes her head. "That poor woman." She answers the phone. "Harris and Parrish, Attorneys at Law."

Harris and Parrish. It's like I never left. Needless to say, Dirk wasn't happy about me not using his name. Then again, he's not happy about my decision to go back into private practice. I'd say because he has the least possible control over me. He says he just doesn't want me to be unhappy. I was most unhappy doing nothing.

Pat looks at me oddly. ". . . Yes, she's in. May I ask who's calling? . . . One moment, please." She puts the phone on hold.

"Judge Hendrix."

I take my time answering the phone. "This is Gwen Parrish."

"Gwen, C.C." Her voice sounds gravelly around the edges. "Got a minute?"

"Sure. What's up?"

"Not much. I've been on vacation in the Bahamas."

"Must be nice."

"It was great, just great. I just got back in town and I've got work piled up the boo-boo. I need a vacation from my vacation."

I laugh politely. She pauses, waiting for me to say something. I don't. "Anyway, I heard about what happened to you. I'm sorry. I thought you were doing a bang-up job."

"You didn't think so the last time I saw you."

"I had no idea things would go down the way they did," she says quietly. "I'm really sorry, girl."

For weeks I've thought of nothing but giving C.C. a piece of my mind to last her a lifetime. But she sounds so pitiful, it hardly seems worth it. "Yeah, well, shit happens."

She agrees. "Listen, Gwen, I called for another reason. I need a favor."

I burst out laughing. Make C.C. a member of the Brass Monkey Club of which Kwame Nkrumah El'Kasid is the founder. "What is it this time, C.C.? Assassinate the president? Rob Fort Knox? How about crap in the mayor's lap?"

"I understand how you feel, Gwen. You don't understand how tight things get on you when you're a judge. Be glad you're not going to be one."

A pain shoots through my temple. "I think I could've learned to live with the downside."

"Yeah, but you never know who your friends are. Everybody wants something from you. It's gotten so every time I meet somebody, the first think I ask myself is, 'What does he want?' The only people I can trust go way back. Like you."

I remind her of her tight, mellow, ace-boon-coon former employer of mine.

"We fell out."

"I see." That's nothing new. The three of us have been playing musical friends since law school. Willette never loses her chair. "What is it you need, C.C.?"

"Just company, girl. Somebody to talk to."

* * *

"Hey, slow down. You're moving too fast."

Eddy and I almost crash into one another. He's on the way in, I'm on the way out.

"One of us is for sure," I laugh. It's always good seeing him. He's my rock. I hold the door and let him walk in. He looks bushed.

"You're working yourself into an early grave," I warn him. "You can't make all the money. Leave some for the rest of us."

He laughs. "And hear Marsha's lip?" His wife of twelve years, she helped put him through school. As soon as the ink dried on his license she "retired."

"I don't feel sorry for you." Actually, I do. My friend's hair has turned completely white in the five years we've been together. Private practice is sapping all of his juices.

"I don't either," Pat chimes in. "What else is a man good for other than to work himself to death on a woman's behalf?"

Eddy shakes his head good-naturedly while he signs the pleadings she holds out to him. "I don't know why Marsha ever spends her time worrying about either one of you." Pat's and my eyes connect. We didn't know she's jealous of us. "If she heard you talking now, she'd put y'all on retainer."

Not that greedy bitch. Talk about somebody wanting it all, getting it, and keeping it. "She won't evv-ver have to worry 'bout me," I say, opening the door. "I don't go for broke-ass niggers, which is what you'll be when she gets through with you."

"True," he says. "Where're you going so fast?"

I avoid his eyes. "I have a meeting." Two, actually, but I can't tell him about C.C. The only condition he had when I came back here was never to mention her or Willette in his presence. I told him the story behind those rumors he heard. He has no use for either one of them.

"Why aren't you meeting here? Who is it? Are you coming back?"

"Eddy—" My harsh tone startled both of us. I smile. "You sound like Dirk."

It's a little after nine by the time I get to C.C.'s. She peeks through the crack between the door and the night latch, recognizes me, opens up just enough for me to slip inside, locks and bolts the door. The condo is dark, and there's a faint putrid odor coming from somewhere. C.C. acts like she's three sheets in the wind, swears she's completely sober. Just scared shitless.

"I'm so glad you came." Her eyes dart about the room like she doesn't even trust the furniture. "I thought you changed your mind."

Her nails dig into my arm as she walks me to the couch. "Ow, C.C. What the hell is wrong with you?" I pry her fingers loose.

She smiles sheepishly. "Sorry 'bout that."

"Turn on some goddamn lights." I reach to turn the switch on a table lamp.

She stops me. "Don't." Pressing a finger to her lips, she beckons me to follow her as she tiptoes to the bedroom. Her eyes have this wild, wounded look, like she's about to flip out. I hesitate. I should've known she'd be up to her shit again. She waves frantically for me to come. I follow very reluctantly. I smell something really foul the closer we get to her bedroom.

"What stinks so bad?"

She throws the door open, and a hideous smell rushes out. I plug my nose, gasping for air through my mouth. There's a bird cage sitting in the middle of the floor, two dead birds inside. "What the hell—?"

"They were my birds. Somebody poisoned them."

I scoff. "You were in the Bahamas. Were they supposed to order out?"

"I left them plenty of food and water. I was only gone a week." The birds look like they've been dead that long.

"Why would somebody kill your birds, C.C.?"

She slumps against the wall. "Because . . . they were my friends. I don't have any friends. I told you."

After the price I paid in her behalf I can see why. "I can't take this smell." I shut the door and head back to the living room. "You can't just leave them in there. Your neighbors'll complain. I know I would."

She lowers herself to the sofa, rubbing her hands like she's Lady Macbeth. "They're my friends."

I leave her hunched on the couch and go back into the bedroom. I hold my nose to stave off the stench and pick up the cage. It's heavier than I thought, which means I have to let go of my nose. The smell's so bad I can taste it. My stomach threatens to heave up its contents. I swallow everything back down, running out with the cage.

"Where's the garbage?"

C.C. acts stricken dumb.

"Never mind." I remember passing a big dumpster in the parking lot, carry the cage down there, tossing it inside, dead birds and all. When I return, C.C. is lying in a fetal position, sucking her thumb, staring into space. I unlock the sliding door to the balcony, pushing the panel back as far as it can go. Houston's notoriously stinky night air smells fresh by comparison. I throw open the windows in the bedroom and the bathroom, find some herbal tea and fix it. C.C. doesn't say a word. I make her sit up and drink the tea. She sips halfheartedly, sets the cup down, covers her face with her hands.

"I'm scared."

"Of what?"

"You don't understand. Nobody does."

"I might if you give me a chance."

"I can't."

"Okay," I say, taking my cup to the sink. "In that case, I'm going home. It's been a long day for me too."

She jumps up and runs after me like the bogey man's going to get her. "Don't go." How pitiful she looks compared with the stern image she projects on the bench every morning. "Please, Gwen." She throws her arms around me like she's holding on for dear life. I can't leave her like this. I pat her back to calm her. "It's okay, C.C., it's okay."

After a moment I begin to notice her grinding her pelvis against me, ever so softly. I don't believe this. She presses harder—there's no mistaking what she's doing now. I shove her backward. "What the hell do you think you're doing?"

She stumbles against the kitchen table. I head for the door, pissed. "I'm sorry! I'm sorry, Gwen," she wails, grabbing my arm. I shake her off.

"I don't play that freaky-deak shit, C.C. You know that."

Her mouth twists to an ugly snarl. "Oh, really, Miss High and Mighty? The woman who'd cross hot coals on her knees if she had to. You think you're better than me? I've got news. You're not."

I just look at her, my sympathy vanishing without a trace. She realizes she said the wrong thing. "I didn't mean it, Gwen. I—I'm so upset."

She blocks the door. "I came over here," I say, "because I thought you needed a friend. You need a keeper."

She bows her head, lets me pass.

BOOK 4

—∞∞∞—

Cut the Cards

31

It's so hot outside you perspire just looking at it. These are the dog days of summer. I don't know why the middle of August is called that. Probably because you shouldn't send a dog out in this heat.

Summer is a dog for another reason when you're in private practice. Business falls off. It's too hot for people to move, let alone cause each other legal problems. I've been in the office all morning and my phone's hardly rung. This is the first time in a long time I've been able to read the entire newspaper without interruption. Pat buzzes me. I spoke too soon.

"Your husband. Line one."

I sigh, glance at my watch. It's close to lunch. Lately, Dirk always finds an excuse to call this time of day. Ever since his cousin filed for divorce, he's been watching me like a cat watches a mouse hole. Barby—her actual given name—caught her husband cheating. She thought she was "cheat-proof," so she's really taking it hard, calling and crying on Dirk's shoulder every chance she gets. No doubt warning him not to let the same thing happen in the process.

Dirk suggested we start carpooling to "help stop pollution." It didn't make sense (to him) to drive two separate cars downtown every day. I didn't even explain, I just said no. Now he calls wanting to know what I'm doing for lunch, where I'm doing it, and who I'm doing it with. I've just about had it.

"This is Gwen Parrish," I say, answering the phone like I don't know it's him.

"Hi."

"Hi, yourself. What's up?"

"Just checking on lunch," he says. "Want to go to This Is It?"

"You hate soul food." And just about everything else about black culture. Except the women.

"They've got things that aren't loaded with grease."

I laugh. "The lemonade? No, thanks. Pat's going to get sandwiches."

"Pat's going to be there?"

Now he's really getting on my nerves. "You know she always eats in. Look, I've got to go. I've got a client," I lie.

"This close to lunch?"

"They were late. I'll see you at home."

"Love you."

"Love you too." I just don't like you very much. It's the jealousy. It's eating away at my feelings like acid. I grab my purse and head for the door. Pat asks me where I'm going.

"To get some soul food."

The Cadillac Grill is on one of the many residential streets in Third Ward that were severed like roots from a tree when 288 went in. In fact, the block it's in ends right at the freeway, just like in a cartoon. The restaurant itself used to be somebody's home. I always get the feeling I'm entering their front room when I walk in. Tables are crammed together, barely seat two people at the most. It's crowded with working people and professionals. Personally, I think the food is better here than This Is It, which has been "discovered" by white people. Cadillac's fried chicken alone'll make you hurt yourself. It's one of those dead man's recipes that's been handed down since slavery.

I look around for some place to sit. I think I'm out of luck, then I see Michael grinning at me. His is the only table in the place with an empty seat. I blame Dirk for this. I wasn't think-ing about soul food for lunch until he mentioned it. I'd sit down with the devil if I had to—my mouth is fixed for chicken.

"Watch those hips, baby," Michael tells me as I squeeze into my seat. The wall's behind me.

"Forget you." I accidentally bump the man seated to my right, jarring the food off his fork. That's how tight it is in here.

"So, how's it going, Michael?" I'm only asking to be polite. I haven't seen him since I told him to get lost. He made himself real scarce after that, staying downstairs to run the savings and loan. He already has his food—smothered steak, greens, macaroni and cheese, corn bread, iced tea.

"Great, baby. Here." He offers me a bite of his steak. I try to take the fork, but he insists on feeding it to me. I look around, hoping no one notices, futile in a place this small with people this nosy. I keep things light.

"How's Willette?"

Instead of answering, he reaches over the table and feels my breasts. "Michael!"

"Your breasts are bigger than this, baby. What'd you do?"

My face is on fire. Only he would notice I'm wearing a bra that doesn't "project" me as much, the desired effect for the dress I have on. He removes his hands when the waitress appears.

"What would you like, baby?" he asks.

"A less obnoxious you."

"That's not on the menu," he says.

After lunch, he insists on walking me to my car. After fondling me that one time, he kept his hands to himself. We even managed to have a decent conversation, mainly about the political no-man's-land I'm in, thanks to Larry Scott. "He wants to ride you out of town on a rail," Michael concludes. Tell me something I don't know. "You should've given him some, baby. I would've understood."

He takes my key and opens my door. As I get in, he reaches and puts the key in the ignition. Then kisses me. I notice Rudy McLemore and Tim Howard leaving the restaurant as

he does. They're classmates from TSU and notorious gossips. Of course, they see us. Michael slips his tongue in my
mouth. I bite it—hard. He jumps back, wincing with pain.

"Thanks for lunch," I say, starting my car.

"When can I see you?" he asks, talking around his
tongue.

"Never."

"That's too long, baby."

I pull off. I'm not thinking about Michael.

I've got a show-cause hearing at one-thirty in front of
Judge Lassiter. He's a cool white man. I worked on his campaign when he first ran for the family law bench. I take a
seat in the jury box after saying a few reassuring words to
my client in the hallway. A young woman, she's had a lot of
surgery recently for which her doctors have given her a lot
of pain medicine. Her husband's accusing her of being a
prescription junkie. He wants their eight-month-old baby. I
spoke to his high-priced attorney from one of the top firms
last night to see if we could settle out of court. "No judge is
going to take an eight-month-old baby from her mother," I
cautioned him.

He told me he'd see me in court.

Judge Lassiter calls our case. I step forward. He looks up
when he says my name. I smile, he looks away, addressing
my opposing counsel. "Mr. Hammond, good to see you."

"Thank you, Your Honor."

Judge flicks his eyes over me. "Ms. Parrish." I have the
feeling I've done something wrong, I can't imagine what.

"Afternoon, Judge."

"What seems to be the problem, Mr. Hammond?"

This is definitely a bad sign. Whoever gets his version of
the truth in first usually gets over. By time Hammond finishes, my client sounds like an ax murderer. I snort indignantly. Lassiter gives me a sharp look. He finally lets me
speak.

"I've heard enough," he says, cutting me off halfway.

"I'm going to order temporary custody be granted to the petitioner."

My client makes an unworldly sound. Lassiter raps his gavel. "There'll be no more outbursts like that, young lady. Prepare the order, Mr. Hammond. I'll set the final hearing in ninety days."

Air rushes into my lungs. I don't believe this. "Judge Lassiter, may I be heard?"

He frowns at me. "No, you may not, Ms. Parrish. It's in the child's best interest to be with someone who's in the physical and mental condition to properly care for it, as your client most decidedly is not."

I notice we're not on the record. Foolishly I thought this was going to be short and sweet—a piece of cake—so I neglected to make sure the court reporter recorded everything. "Would you mind putting that on the record, Judge?"

He acts like I asked him to eat shit. "I've made the proper entry on the docket sheet, Counselor." He adjourns the hearing and leaves. Hammond struts over and congratulates his client. My client is completely bewildered. "What happened, Attorney Parrish? You said not to worry. Does Charlie get to take my baby?"

I don't know what to say. That's exactly what Lassiter allowed. I advise her not to speak until we get outside the Family Law Center. Once we're alone on the marble plaza, I try to explain what happened. I don't do a very good job. I have no earthly idea why Lassiter put his foot up my client's ass to his kneecap. My stomach shudders queasily. Unless . . . it's really me he's after.

"Don't worry, Ms. Warren. I'm appealing this all the way to the Supreme Court if I have to."

She shakes her head, dazed, like a bomb victim. "You told me not to worry." Tears run down her face. "I'm getting me another lawyer, Ms. Parrish."

I can't say I blame her. Larry's juju strikes again.

Before I got poured out of Lassiter's court—that's what the white boys call it when the equivalent of a building falls on you—I thought I was killing two birds with one stone scheduling this meeting on a day I had to be downtown anyway. A little voice tells me it's still not too late to postpone it. I push through the door to the D.A.'s building. The only legitimate excuse I could give Yarrow for canceling now is that I need to get in bed and pull the covers over my head. Dirk, Michael, Lassiter, what next?

I tell his receptionist I'm here to see him and leaf through *Time* magazine on the deterioration of the (white) American family. Soaring divorce rates, unwed teenage mothers, drugs, shacking up—all the things they talk about us like dogs for doing. Brother Malcolm's chickens are coming home to the roost. I lay the magazine aside. I've got my own problems. The main one being how to get Larry Scott off my back.

"Mr. Yarrow will see you now."

"Gwen, how are you?"

"Great."

Brad squints at me behind his thick bifocals, motions me to sit. "Thanks for coming in." Like I had a choice. "I just wanted to chat now that your special prosecutor duties have concluded. You know, wrap up any loose ends, that sort of thing."

I smile politely. Past experience has taught me to let him run the ball. "So, is there anything I should know about the investigation? Inside—or out?" I tell him I can't think of a thing. It's all in my report, which I've already forwarded to his office.

He clears his throat. "Um, yes. I've got it right here." He reaches behind him to the credenza. "Everything seems to be in order. Very professional."

Surprise, surprise. The monkey can be professional. He scans my report, looks up, his eyes shifting to a point next to my face. "Uh, don't you want to tell me about your meeting with Garrett the night before he died?"

I shrug. "It had nothing to do with the case." I'm not surprised he knows about it. If he thinks I'm going to spill my guts, he better think again.

"Well, now, that's not for you to decide, young lady."

"Thanks, Brad. Nobody's called me young since I turned forty."

He turns cherry pink, drops all pretense of being nice. "I want to know what that meeting was about, Gwen."

I don't flinch an inch. "I told you, Brad, it has nothing to do with the case. He's dead. Case closed."

"I could take you in front of the grand jury."

"Cool."

He stares at me, and I stare right back, casually swinging my crossed leg. He smiles coldly. "You're through, Gwen. You know that, don't you?"

"So I heard."

"Good. I've been waiting a long time for you to fall flat on your ass," he says. "By the time they're done with you, you won't be able to catch a cold. You're gonna starve."

"How's that going to happen when I have a husband who works every day?"

"Do you?"

"Last time I looked."

"Don't look too hard."

I stand up. "Is there anything else, Brad?" He scrambles to his feet. They like to dismiss *you*.

"Just this. I'll be in the cheering section when you go down."

"Fine," I say. "Just don't hold your breath."

32

"This came in the mail. I thought you might want to see it." Pat hands me a thick envelope marked PERSONAL AND CONFIDENTIAL as soon as I walk in. It's from the State Bar Grievance Committee. I drop to the sofa and rip open the envelope, my heart tripping double-time as I read.

Eddy comes in. "What's happening, y'all?"

Pat gives him his messages. I hand him the grievance.

"What's this?" His face compresses into a deep frown as he absorbs its contents. He stares at me. "Are they for real?"

Snatching the letter back, I can't resist being sarcastic. "Well, let's see—it looks for real." I sniff the envelope. "Smells for real." Quote the letter. " '. . . Your conduct in regard to the investigation of the murder of the Honorable Willie Shalandar and subsequent prosecution may be adjudged to have been conducted in an unprofessional manner, blah, blah, blah . . .' " I stretch a smile across my face. "Gee, I think they're for real, guys."

Pat looks at Eddy like she could kill him. He wants to go through the floor. "Talk about asking a stupid question," he says. "Sorry, Gwen."

"No, I'm sorry." I've never had a grievance filed against me, though I know plenty of lawyers who have. Having to answer to the grievance committee is like being called to the principal's office when you're a kid. You're scared even if you didn't do anything. Michael, Yarrow, now this. I really should have stayed in bed today.

"It's a set-up," Eddy says.

"Stevie Wonder could see that," Pat says, giving him a dry look. "In my journalism class they always say to look for the who, what, when, and why behind everything."

Eddy looks at her surprised. "You're taking a journalism class?"

She sniffs indignantly. "You think I intend to be a legal secretary the rest of my life?"

He looks at me. Lawyers need secretaries as much as doctors need nurses. Tarzan may roam the jungle getting all the glory, but it's Jane who holds down the fort.

"Larry Scott is the who," I say, pursuing her point. "What and when—my head on a platter *now*. Why? They think Garrett told me something."

"Did he?" Eddy assesses me, holds his hand up. "Don't tell me."

"Don't worry," I say. "You'll be getting the star treatment next." I toss the grievance on Pat's desk. "I wouldn't wish this experience on my worst enemy."

"Speaking of which," he says, "your girl's name is all over the complaint. You think she had something to do with this?"

I shrug and shake my head. "Anything's possible. They made her dump me."

"Hi, hon." Leaving as I enter, Dirk busses me on the cheek. "Bye, hon."

"Where are you going?" I intentionally waited until I got home to tell him about Yarrow and the grievance—skip Michael. I didn't want to talk over the phone. I've been rode hard and put down wet all day. I need to be petted and told everything's gonna be all right after 'while.

He back steps playfully. "I left you a note. Gotta meet Jim at the gym. Jim—gym, get it?" He gives me another quick kiss. "We're going to the ACLU meeting together afterward. Don't wait up." He swats me on the behind affectionately. "You look tired."

He drives off, waving good-bye as he rolls into the street.

I shut the door, feel instantly sorry for myself. "So much for pouring my troubles out to my husband." I pick up his note saying he's going to play racquetball. It's just as well. I tortured myself all afternoon trying to decide how much to tell him, especially since I haven't told him everything from the get-go. I didn't know what was going to be worse—telling him about all the trouble I'm in or the truth about how I got into so much trouble. Criminals face the same dilemma dealing with their lawyers.

I set the note aside and see the mail. A letter from Kincaid Academy is on top. Kwame and I decided Ashleigh Lee should finish out the year there. It's her grades. I set them aside for the moment. One more piece of bad news this soon and they might have to take me away, never to be seen or heard from again. I'll be drooling in a corner somewhere. I need a drink.

I pour myself some Turkey, take the bottle and Ashleigh Lee's grades to the sofa, kick off my shoes, sit down and prop my weary feet up. When I'm sufficiently anesthetized, I'll read the bad news. For the moment, I want to chill out, which I can't do just yet. The house is too quiet, too much opportunity to think, which I don't want to do. I turn on the radio and look at Ashleigh Lee's grades. It's perverted, but I can at least comfort myself with the knowledge that someone is worse off than me today. Even if it is my traitor of a daughter. I skip the glass and turn the Wild Turkey bottle up.

Three B's and two C's. Huh? Just goes to show you can't count on counting people out. Three B's and two C's. It sinks in. Ashleigh Lee has a decent report card. I reach for the phone.

"Hi, Kwame. No. Nothing's wrong." I switch the receiver to my other ear and reach for the liquor bottle. "Actually, I was calling to congratulate Ashleigh Lee on her grades. They're damn good considering. Three B's and two C's," I say proudly and swig. "I was starting to tell myself F's stood for 'Fine.' Is she there?"

I hold the phone. She's outside playing with the puppy he

bought her. I twinge with guilt. She always did want a dog. I had my hands full taking care of my two-legged critter. Kwame sounds . . . good. Full-time fatherhood agrees with him. I hate the jealousy I feel. Motherhood had the same effect on me, at least until lately when it turned into a funny nightmare.

I just have one wish. That Ashleigh Lee comes on the phone and says she wants to come home. That she just wanted to see what it would be like living with her dad. My throat constricts from the ache of tears I refuse to spill. I gulp a long drink to relax it. Break into a Kool-Aid smile.

"Hi, baby. Yep, three B's and two C's. One's in math and the other in—phys. ed.? Of course, you can do better. I hear you have a puppy. What's his name? Sorry—her name." I giggle. "Smiles? No, it's a wonderful name. Where are you going? I understand. I just wanted to holler at you." Shame wells up in me. "That was a poor choice of words. Sorry. No, I'm just fine." I pause, another surprise. She asks about Dirk. "He's fine. I love you, baby. Be good."

Kwame catches me before I hang up. He informs me Ashleigh Lee is going to counseling. I can tell the difference. She doesn't sound at all like the angry, resentful child who lived here. I congratulate him.

"Thanks," he says. "Ashleigh Lee and I would like to ask you a favor."

She wants to see me, thank God. We didn't set specific visitation when we changed custody, my decision. I wanted her to see me when she wants to. "Sure."

"We'd like you to come to the sessions. Dr. Wilson thinks it would really help."

I take a deep breath. This could be another set-up. Get me in a room, between Ashleigh Lee, Kwame, and some crackpot counselor, they triple-team me. "Let me think about it."

"Okay." I hear the disappointment in his voice. I bet. Disappointed I won't put my head in an emotional noose while you, Doc, and Ashleigh Lee kick the chair from under me. Ashleigh Lee. I smile. She sounded wonderful. Good for her. Bad for me. I fill my glass to the brim. "So," I observe to myself, ignoring the sour taste in my throat. "The only way she wants to see you is with a referee." I throw back a big gulp to kill the bitterness. "Can't blame her for that."

The liquor starts to numb me as I move around in slow motion. I giggle. When I was in private practice b.w. ("before Willette"), I had a client tell me he smoked dope to slow things down. "Ms. P."—that's what he called me—"they got life speeded up so fast nobody's got time to figure it out anymore." I intend to be in private practice a.w. forever, assuming the grievance committee doesn't pull my ticket. They're trying to make me tell; only if I do, they won't believe me. I set the bottle down, clunking the floor with it. Somebody must've moved the table. I lean over to pick up the bottle. The room starts spinning. "Whoa—"

I lean back. That's better. Close my eyes.

I open my eyes, I hear a strange sound. At least everything's back where it's supposed to be, a little blurry around the edges, though. I focus on the clock. Ten-fifteen. I look around. Ten at night or ten in the morning? I hear the sound again. It's the doorbell. Somebody's ringing it. I wish they'd stop. It hurts. I stumble to my feet, grabbing my head like Charles Laughton in *The Hunchback of Notre Dame,* "Sanctuary, sanctuary—" I spill the Wild Turkey bottle, what's left leaking into the carpet. "Oops." I lift the bottle and sip the last few drops. Smacking my lips, I stagger to the door. "Wait just a goddamn minute."

I open the door. Double Michaels, of all people. "What the hell are you doing here?"

"I took a chance, baby." He steps in and looks around. "I didn't see your old man's car outside for once, so I decided to come in."

My mind is in slo-mo. *For once?* What are you talking about?"

He grins like I'm a sight for sore eyes. "I drive by and check you out all the time, baby. It's a hobby."

"Get out." I try to push him back through the door. He just laughs, closes the door.

"Unh-uh. I've waited too long for the cat to sky." He draws me close. "He doesn't believe in leaving you alone too often. I don't blame him."

I tear out of his arms. "Get out, Michael. I'll call the cops." I stumble to the telephone, stubbing my toe on the console.

He chuckles. "Baby, you're drunk as a skunk."

I shoot him a look, massage my foot as I pick up the phone. I'll show him who's drunk. "911—?"

"You don't want to do that," he says softly, taking the receiver and placing it back in the cradle, forcing me to face him. "What's wrong, baby? I've never seen you like this. He treating you bad?"

"Life," I proclaim, "is treating me bad."

"Tell Daddy all about it." My head suddenly feels like a boulder on my neck. I need to rest it someplace. His shoulder is a good spot. He holds me, strokes me gently. It feels good. I feel him fumbling with his pants. He pulls my hand down to touch him. "You miss it, don't you, baby?"

What is going on here? I try to twist free. "Are you out of your mind? Dirk could come home any moment."

He scoops me up, dumps me on the couch, falls on top of me. "I'll make it short and sweet, baby."

I try to push him off. "No, Michael. No way."

"Don't fight me, baby. You said yourself we don't have a lotta time till your old man gets back."

"No!" I shove him so hard he topples to the floor.

"I'm through playing with you, baby." He bares his teeth like a vicious animal. I sit up, looking around for something to hit him with if I have to. He stands over me. "Where's the bedroom?"

I laugh and stand up. "You're insane." He wrenches my arm behind my back. I cry out. "You're hurting me."

"Good. Now we understand each other." He walks me to the stairs. "Is it up there?" He twists my arm up unnaturally.

"Yes!"

He drags me up the stairs, stumbling and falling, tears running out of me. "Please, Michael, please don't do this—"

"Keep beggin', baby. I like it."

He looks until he finds our room. I kick at him, hitting him with my free arm, doing everything to keep him from getting me inside. He slaps me so hard I stumble to the middle of the floor. I see stars. He yanks me up and throws me on the bed. Sits on my stomach, pinning my arms. Tears drip down my face onto the comforter. "Michael, why can't you just leave me alone? Please, *please*—"

His eyes pierce me as he works my panty hose off, then my panties. "If I could I would, baby. I love you."

He is crazy. "You call this love?"

"You just don't know, baby." He settles on top of me, forces my legs apart.

"No, Michael. Please, don't do this." He feels like a knife entering me. "No!"

"She said no."

Our bodies freeze when we hear Dirk's voice. "Get up."

Michael's eyes drive into me as he lifts up. He adjusts his clothes and stands up. They scowl at each other. "Get out before I kill you."

Michael strolls to the door, turns, and looks at me. "She's mine, man. She always was and she always will be. Ask her." He walks out.

Dirk's eyes swing to me. They're dark with rage. I sit up, hastily straightening my clothes. "He forced me to come up here. I had no idea he even knew where I lived. I passed out. He was at the door—"

He puts his hand up to stop me. "You fucked him."

"No. No, never. He's lying."

His voice booms at me. "You fucked him. Didn't you, Gwen? Didn't you?"

I start to cry. This is so crazy. Everything is so crazy. "No, I swear, Dirk. I never—"

He shakes me so hard, my head rattles around on my shoulders. "Stop lying. You fucked him, didn't you? Didn't you? Tell me, damn you." His hand cracks the side of my face. "Tell me, you black bitch!"

The lights seem to go out for a split second. When the sparks disappear behind my eyes, I come to my senses. This is the second time I've been hit tonight by a man who's supposed to care about me. On top of that, Dirk called me a black bitch. Lord, send me down some more rope. I'm at the end of this one.

"Didn't you?"

I look at him. "Yes," I say slowly. "I did it and it was *good*."

What little color he has drains from his face. His eyes turn to blue steel. "I hate you."

He walks out of the room. I stalk out right behind him as he goes down the steps. "Oh, yeah? I hate you triple. You can go to hell—dog kiss my foot, adios, au revoir, kiss me where the sun don't shine, one monkey don't stop no show!"

We reach the landing. He looks at me like I'm spit. "You nigger." He slams out the door. I didn't realize how much that would hurt coming from him. It takes me a moment to thaw out from the pain. I swing the door open and call after him. "Your dog ass mammy's a nigger!" He gives me the finger and gets in his car. I try to slam the door through the jamb.

"I don't need you," I say. "I don't need anybody."

33

I get the distinct feeling I am the topic of discussion when I walk out onto the Groovey Grill's sun porch this evening. I wouldn't be surprised. Not the way I crashed and burned. Only the boy who flew too close to the sun can top me. My sole consolation for having all my business out in the street is that I have nothing further to hide. And no comment. That's how you take the heat.

My BLFA colleagues greet me like I'm a long-lost friend, though I notice most don't look me in the eye as I shake the rain off my things and set up at one of the tables. A few sneak sidelong glances at me; others snicker when they think I'm not looking. I know the behavior. I used to act the same way whenever the gossipee had the nerve or need to show herself in public. What I didn't know is that as such you feel like the hair's being plucked off your body, follicle by follicle.

"How's everybody tonight?" I say for openers. "The agenda's pretty light and the weather's shaky, so why don't we go get started?"

No one says a word. I turn to Francine Willer, the secretary. "Would you read the minutes from the last meeting? I've got some catching up to do myself."

She hesitates, clears her throat nervously, shuffles some papers and glances at Hillary Tartar, seated across from her. Hillary speaks up. "Gwen, we'd like to go into executive session, if you don't mind."

"Of course not," I say. Whatever's getting ready to jump

off has been pre-arranged. I can tell by their faces. No wonder women don't play poker. I don't have to ask the members to excuse us while we meet. They scurry out like farmers getting out of the way of gunfighters in a cowboy movie. Like Gary Cooper, I make a point of looking at each one as they leave. Three women remain besides me, the executive board minus C.C. and Willette.

"Okay, Hillary," I say with a smile I don't feel. "What's up?"

"We want you to resign. Tonight." I have to hand it to Hillary. She's matter-of-fact, impersonal, the perfect executioner. I should've seen this punch coming. Since I didn't, I need a standing eight-count. Out of reflex, I drum my pen against the tabletop. It's the only sound in the room. "May I ask why?"

"Of course," she says. "We've been advised that our corporate sponsorships and political contributions for the scholarship banquet will be in jeopardy if you remain president. You understand since it's our only fund-raiser."

A nice, clean, mortal wound. I push my chair back and stand. "Far be it for me," I say with my last dying gasp, "to stand in the way of this organization's ability to kiss, lick, and suck out of a white man's ass for a dollar."

I march to the door, my head high. "Which," Hillary observes, "you had no problem doing—until now."

I face them. Hillary looks at me impassively. Rendine Carlisle and Francine Willer are amused and embarrassed in turns.

"You're right, Hillary," I say. "What I said was out of spite. I apologize. But this isn't: any one of you could wake up in my shoes. I just hope you lily-livered, yellow-bellied, spineless bitches can hang. I intend to until somebody cuts me down."

"Who are you calling a bitch?" Hillary starts for me, eyes on fire. Must've struck a nerve. Luckily, Rendine holds her. "Don't get down on her level, Hillary."

I correct her. "You're not on my level. You're beneath

me." I'm ready to fight all three of them. That's how much rage I have stored up.

Francine gets in my face. "Why don't you just leave, Gwen? There's no point in making an even bigger fool out of yourself."

My eyes sweep each one of them. "Takes one to know three." I burst out laughing, which angers them even more. I don't care. "Good night—ladies." I walk out into the dining room, howling in the shocked faces of the membership. Still laughing, I bid Ms. Mert good night. She looks at me like I'm crazy. Tears are streaming down my face by time I reach Black Beauty. I was crying all along, but I wasn't about to let them know it.

Pat smiles sympathetically when I walk in the office. "Any calls?"

She shakes her head. "Geraldo's. They want to know when they can expect a payment."

"Humph," I say, crumpling the phone message. "They're gonna have to get in line. I owe more important people than them."

I take my mail to my office. Junk and bills. I check my checkbook balance. Deduct the two checks I wrote last night for panty hose and food. I'm down to sixty-nine dollars and seven cents.

"Is the eagle flying?" Eddy grins from the doorway. The part of me that doesn't owe him two months' rent is glad to see him. The other part churns with guilt.

I put the checkbook away. "That bad boy's wings are clipped."

He chuckles and takes a seat. "I heard you went off at the BFLA meeting. Told everybody to kiss your behind."

I shrug. I don't want to talk about it. I've been a member of that organization for over ten years. I helped found it. They could've at least let me resign over the phone or in a letter. They didn't have to front me off.

"You and Dirk straighten it out yet?"

Can you straighten out DNA? I shake my head.

"I still don't understand what happened," he says. I look away, shrug some more.

"That's too bad. He was all right."

"He called me a nigger."

"I never did like that white boy. Why'd he do that?"

I look down. "We had a fight."

His eyes laser into me. "This is Eddy you're talking to. My ears aren't pasted on, and my eyes don't glow in the dark." In other words, he's not buying it.

"It's over, that's all."

"Because he called you a nigger."

I look up. "Yes."

He throws his hands up. "I don't get it. Niggers call niggers niggers all day long. Let a white man say it and it's rumble in the jungle time."

"You don't understand." Eddy's "till death and beyond" when it comes to marriage.

"I guess not," he says. "But it's for damn sure his shoes ain't gonna be under my bed in the morning."

I force a smile. "Mine either."

He changes the subject. "I've got some cases I could use some help on. Nothing deep. Coupla juvenile things and a commitment."

Both of which I hate. "Am I that bad off?"

Eddy eases his lanky body out of the chair. "Nah. You just came back into practice at a bad time. Things'll pick up after Labor Day. You want 'em or not?"

"Well, let's see. I'm not even at the bottom of anybody's appointment list, the phone ain't exactly ringing off the wall, my name is mud, and nobody wants to know me. Can beggars be choosy?"

He shrugs. "This is a big city. They can't stop you from making a living as long as you got one of these."

He points at my law license. I can't look at it. It's all I have left, and they're trying to take that too. He reads my mind.

"Whoever's out to get you isn't all-powerful, Gwen.

Otherwise they'd be God. You just got to lower your sights and learn to trudge along like the rest of us. We get there sooner or later."

I smile grimly. "I was taking every shortcut known to man, wasn't I? Why didn't you stop me?"

He shakes his head. "Nobody could've stopped you."

The scaffolding holding me together collapses and my feelings rush out. "I hate private practice, Eddy. You don't have one boss, you've got as many as you have open files. Every judge acts like he's the only one you have to answer to. You never know when money's coming, just that it's steadily going out—for the secretary, the rent, paper, the phone. Clients never want to pay you what you're worth. They don't want to pay you at all. You work like a dog, and yet people think you're on Easy Street because you're a lawyer. You have to look and act the part because nobody wants a broken-down, broke-ass lawyer for a lawyer. The white boys get all the big cases and the big money. I don't know if I can do this again. I hate starting over."

"Don't think of it as starting over," he says. "Think of it as a chance to get it right this time."

I pause. I hadn't thought about it like that. I give my friend a real smile. "How'd you get so wise?"

He throws his head back and laughs. "You see this white hair? Marie didn't put it all there."

"I sure hope you're wrong," I say. "I'll wake up one morning and my hair'll be stark white." We both get a good laugh out of that one. Pat buzzes. "Judge Hendrix for Gwen."

Eddy looks at me questioningly. I have no earthly idea why she's calling. I pick up the phone. "This is Gwen Parrish."

I don't recognize the voice on the other end. "This is Martha, Judge Hendrix's coordinator. Judge just appointed you to a case. I need your bar card number."

I look at Eddy, my adrenaline surging. "An appointment?"

"Yes. Can you be down here before lunch?"

"I'm on my way."

* * *

C.C. and I take the table by the window. It's shrouded with hanging plants. The skylight casting Mediterranean light over everything is very relaxing, which helps. We're both awkward and ill at ease. As soon as we're seated, the waitress takes our drink order. We'll decide on lunch later. We both pretend to study the menu as C.C.'s Jack Black, straight up, and my glass of white zinfandel arrive. She finishes half of hers and signals the waitress for another round before I barely touch my wine. When I protest, she laughingly reminds me lunch was my idea.

"True," I say. "I just wanted to thank you for saving my life, that's all." C.C.'s appointed me to five cases this week alone. I don't ask why and she doesn't say. It's a lagniappe, manna from heaven.

Her dark eyes survey me. "Things are still kinda rough for you."

I try to make a joke of the thin ice I'm on financially. "Builds your character."

"Dog poop." She gulps the rest of her drink. "I see characters all day long."

She's right. I never did like being noble about shit. "You look tired, C.C. You feeling all right?" Actually, she looks sick. Moisture seems to leave her skin as we speak, and her hair looks like chickens have been picking in it.

She smiles wryly. "Ain't gonna catch no pretty young thing looking like this, am I?"

Fortunately, the waitress serves our new drinks, so I don't have to answer. C.C.'s ready to order. "I'll have the twelve-ounce steak, medium, baked potato with sour cream and butter, and the tossed salad with thousand island dressing. You all still have those homemade blueberry muffins?"

The waitress responds enthusiastically. "Aren't they delicious?"

"Bring me a basket of them and plenty of strawberry jam," C.C. says. They look at me expectantly.

"I'll have the chef's salad. Vinegar and oil dressing in separate containers, please. I'll mix it myself."

"Go 'head, girl," C.C. says, impressed by my restraint, running her eyes over me appreciatively, which makes me a little uncomfortable. It makes me remember what she did the last time I saw her. "You've lost a few pounds. You tryin' or cryin'?"

"Both. Dirk and I—we parted company." I laugh like it doesn't matter. "I'm back on the market, girl."

She chomps into an oversized muffin slathered with about a half inch of butter. "Love'll make you either lose ten pounds just like that." She snaps buttery fingers. "Or it'll make you gain fifty."

Her eyes wander around the Strawberry Patch, the most popular white restaurant in town this week with black people, which is crowded with lunch patrons. Widen. "Don't look now. There's your boy." My heart quivers. Dirk? I haven't seen him since the night he called me a nigger. We don't have anything to say. "He's creepin'." Can't be Dirk, he's a free man now. C.C. waves merrily at someone. "Hi!" She tells me to look. I turn casually, surprised—and relieved—to see Bill Carver and Sheryl Jackson, both of whom are married, but not to each other. Bill does a lot of p.i. work. Sheryl works for HISD. Her husband is resident spook at some Fortune 500 company downtown. Talk about being cold-busted.

C.C. returns to shoveling food into her mouth. "Knowing Bill, he's probably telling her about *us*." Her eyes twinkle mischievously. Bill was "Diarrhea of the Mouth" when we were in law school. He knew everybody's business down to dates and times.

"I heard that rumor already," I say, sipping my drink. C.C. and I are supposed to be going together. That's why she's giving me so many appointments. "I can't stand a man who gossips."

"I can't stand men."

There it is, all the way live, up-front and in color for my benefit. The way she said it cracks me up. She laughs with me. The awkwardness is broken. She turns serious. "I owe you an apology, Gwen. For when you were at my place. I don't know what got into me. I know you don't go that way. Do you?" I realize she's teasing. "Bulldaggers get lonely too, you know."

It takes me a moment to respond. The wine's made me draggy. "No, but I hear you. Nobody—no group—has a monopoly on loneliness. Or any other tragedy that can happen to you. Believe me, I know." I lift my glass for a toast. "Here's to downfalls, downturns, and down hearts—no matter who they belong to."

She clicks reluctantly. "Sometimes you can get so down you can't get up, Gwen. You just don't know." That's what Michael said. Judging by what he did to me and the look on her face, I don't want to know. Something's eating her alive. Inside out.

34

"C.C., girl, you are too slow."

I tap my foot impatiently. "Honestly, you're going to be late for your own funeral." She's struggling to get into a jacket two sizes too small. I don't have the heart to say anything. All she has to do is look in the mirror and see for herself she's turning into a porker. I smile. If anyone had told me she and I would be running buddies again, I would've called them a bald-faced liar. We have a lot in common now. My life's messed up, and she's just plain messed up.

"You know what your problem is, Gwen?"

"What?"

"You're always in a hurry. It's going to kill you one day."

I open her condo door. "At least I'll be on time for my funeral."

She gives me the look she reserves for lawyers cutting up in her court. "Knowing you, you'll be early."

I gently push her out the door. We have reservations for eight o'clock at Birraporetti's. We're barely going to make it. She grumbles as soon as I start up the car. "I don't see why we have to go to some fancy-schmancy place anyway. I hate dressing up. It's bad enough I have to sit around in that stupid robe all the time. One day I'm gonna come in with nothing on under it. Nobody'll even know as long as I have on shoes."

"With those titties hanging down like hound dog's ears?" I remind her. "Be serious."

She laughs, her heavy breasts jiggling like Jello beneath the silk dress she's wearing. It's nice to hear a good honest laugh from her again. It's been happening more and more in the weeks since we've gotten tight again.

"What kind of joint is this anyway?" she asks impatiently.

I'm checking out the addresses, looking for the place. "I told you—Irish-Italian."

"I can't stand neither one of them. They hate niggers."

I wrestle her Toyota into a tight parking space in front of the restaurant. "C.C., if we only went places where we're not hated, we'd have to stay home. And I'm sick of pizza."

"What's wrong with pizza? I love pizza."

"We know," I say sarcastically. "That's why we're going to have some real food for a change."

A few minutes later, I'm placing our order. "We'll start with the *insulata di spinaci* and some *pane*. Main course, *frittata di spaghetti al forno,* and we'll have the *torta di frutta fresca* for dessert," I tell the waiter, a short, wiry white man with a pencil-thin mustache.

C.C. makes a face at me. "Show-off."

I laugh. I minored in Italian in college. I even went to Rome one summer. C.C.'s right about the Italians hating us. Probably because they're the niggers of Europe.

"*I'll* have the large cheese and anchovy pizza," C.C. says. "Extra sauce, extra cheese." C.C. dares me to say something. I just shake my head.

"You are hopeless, Your Honoress." She winces. "Sorry," I say, "I forgot." She hates any reference to the fact that she's a judge when she's in public, which I still don't get and tell her so. "I'd let the world know they have to treat me with kid gloves. That's one of the perks."

She waits for our waiter to pour our wine and leave. "They treat you with kid gloves because they're afraid of you."

"That's what's so cool," I say. "Striking fear in the hearts of people, terrorizing them without saying a word. I'd be wearing my robe twenty-four hours a day."

"You'd be a great judge." Her mood darkens. "Too bad it's never going to happen."

"Yeah," I say bitterly. "Thanks to your boy Larry."

"Larry's just following orders."

I look at her real close to see what she means and if she means it. I've been wanting to clear up this thing about Larry for a long time. I just didn't want to have to be the one to bring it up. It's a touchy subject for both of us.

"Michael talks in his sleep," she says, smiling diabolically. "Willette always knows what he's doing."

It's funny how a simple statement of fact can set off seismic shocks in your life. The ground wants to give way under me. I'm holding on by my toes.

"How—how long has she known?" I whisper, unable to raise my voice. I just hope I haven't peed on myself.

"How long have you two been doin' the do?"

I can't answer. My insides are on fire. All the time I thought she knew, she knew. She was playing with me, like a kitten with a yarn ball. I let him blackmail me for nothing.

"I tried to tell you," C.C. says. There's that devilish smile again. "Cheer up. I thought this was supposed to be a celebration."

I did too. I settled my first personal-injury case today, thanks to Eddy. He thought it was booty-butt when he gave it to me. Turned out to be fairly lucrative, as can happen often enough in private practice to keep the suckers in the game. I offered to split the fee with him fifty-fifty instead of the usual referral, but he wouldn't hear of it. "Just pay your rent and I'll be satisfied."

The first person I called after hanging up with the insurance adjuster was the mortgage company. The first thing Dirk did when he moved out was to immediately stop paying the house note, the utilities and the cable, closed the checking and savings and canceled my charge accounts, including Jamail's, so I couldn't buy groceries. He even canceled the Sunday paper. Good thing we weren't together long enough for me to get too used to living in the lap of luxury. If he had his way now, I'd be a homeless person. The first month he was gone, the bills hit me like a tsunami.

So does this. Here I am thinking I'm back in the saddle again, and C.C. smacks me between the eyes with reality. I don't know whether to thank her or knock the pure "d" shit out of her. I take a deep breath. Let it out. I feel light-headed. Probably feeling the truth setting me free of Michael.

"So," I say brightly, "don't you want to know how I got mixed up with him in the first place?"

She rolls her eyes. "People who want to find each other, find each other. I've got my own problems." She stares at her wineglass. "I'm under investigation by the Judicial Qualifications Committee."

"C.C., no." Another seismic shock. I don't get this. Houston has hurricanes, not earthquakes. "What happened?"

She shakes her head. "I don't know. It's all star chamber shit. The only thing they tell you is a complaint's been lodged against you. You don't know anything until the final get-down. If you're unqualified, they probably tear your robe off you."

"When is that?"

"I don't know that either. They keep it all very hush-hush, they *say* to protect the subject of the inquiry and spare the public possible loss of faith in the event there's no basis for the allegations."

"Sounds like the grievance committee."

She remembers I'm under the hammer too. "Have you heard anything?"

I shake my head. "Same dance, different partner. I'd like to know what a white boy from Fulbright and Jaworski or Baker and Botts knows about what we have to do to practice law." I taste bitterness in my wine all of a sudden. "They run all these goddamn 'committees.' They're the only ones with the time to. The rest of us are busy trying to survive."

C.C.'s unmoved. "The people who run shit always have the time. Isn't that what money buys you, really?"

"Yeah," I say, depressed. "You're right."

She sighs like she's shifting the world to another spot on her shoulders. "Besides, what are you going to do? White folks run the world."

It's times like these I wish I could be more like Kwame. He runs his own world. He's "crazy." I wish we were crazy. Certifiably insane. Unfortunately, it takes courage to be crazy.

We both stare at our drinks. So much for celebrating.

"This is a surprise."

C.C. and I look up at the same time.

It's Willette.

"My two best friends together again." Her eyes meet mine, shining like emeralds. She does indeed know about me and Michael. She despises me. I look away. "So, is this a case of birds of a feather flocking together? Or of lying down with dogs?"

C.C. hangs her head like a chastised child. "Hello, Willette."

I look at Willette; she's smiling like an evil genie. She addresses C.C. "You look awful. You should take better care of yourself."

"Yes, Willette," C.C. quavers. "I will."

Willette smiles like C.C.'s been naughty. "We've been telling secrets, haven't we?"

Panic-stricken, C.C. starts stuttering. "I, uh, I-I'm sorry, Willette—"

"It doesn't matter." Willette turns to me, so much hatred jumping off her I can feel it. "Payback is a dog, isn't it, Gwen?"

I swallow and nod. Willette's really getting her nubs in, as we used to say on the block. I want to tell her to go play with herself, but my tongue, thick and unwieldy, is stuck.

"By the way, Gwen," she says. "How's private practice? I hear you're back with Eddy. Good move."

My tongue rips free. "Thanks."

"Oh, yes, Dirk dropped by to see me." Freon dribbles down my spine. I imagine Hitler dropping in on Mussolini.

"I understand you two aren't together. Something about catching you in bed with—my husband. He's very bitter, Gwen. Not just toward you. I tried to reason with him. He hates all black people now."

Smiling like Miss America, she waves at a group of white businessmen entering the restaurant. "My party's arrived. Sorry I can't spend more time with my two *best* friends in the whole, wide world. Oh, yeah—C.C., I'd take that judicial inquiry thing very seriously if I were you. I hear there are allegations of—bribery? Try to take better care of yourself, dear." She squeezes C.C.'s hand and walks off. C.C. looks like she's been bitten by a vampire.

"She sicced the dogs on you too?" I say, amazed. Poor C.C.'s head bobs up and down. She looks ready to cry. Willette stops to chat up two old white men at a nearby table. I feel like doing something crazy. For C.C., if not myself. "Willette," I call. She looks up, smiles sweetly. "It's nine o'clock. Do you know whose bed your husband's in?" Her smile freezes on her face.

I'm still laughing when we get into C.C.'s car. The look on Willette's face—like she could've ripped out my vital organs—was priceless. C.C. didn't like my joke.

"You shouldn't have done that. Don't you know how she is by now? She doesn't forget or forgive a thing."

I deliberately race the engine. "I've got a pretty long memory too," I say, grunting and groaning, trying to steer the car out of our tight spot. I manage to clip the car next to me. "Godammit."

"You shouldn't take the Lord's name in vain like that, Gwen." Hunched over like the grim reaper just told her to meet him in fifteen minutes, C.C. looks around as if she's expecting a thunderbolt.

"Huh," I say. "You have a lot of nerve with your gutter gums." I head out of the parking lot. "Forget Willette. She's not God. There's only so much she can do to either one of us, and I'd say she's done it." When you've lost everything,

what else is there? I feel totally liberated. I glance at C.
She shivers abnormally, teeth clattering. "Are you all right

"I'm cold."

"Cold?" It's still over eighty degrees outside. At her r
quest, I turn on the heat. We ride back to her condo in
lence except for the radio, which I purposely jam alo
with. I refuse to let Willette get me down. I'm through wo
rying about what other people think.

C.C. bows her head, like she's praying. With tonight's e
ception, to my knowledge she's never had a religious bo
in her body. After I park the car in her garage, I ask her if s
wants me to come up. She mumbles something about n
wanting to be alone. She's giving me the creeps. I do
think she even knows I'm behind her as I follow her upsta
to her place. She leaves the door open when she goes insic
I enter, but I don't see her.

"C.C.?"

I don't know how she could've disappeared that fa
"C.C., where are you?"

She slowly walks out of the bathroom, this wild look
her face. Like she wants to laugh and cry at the same tim
She takes her stash out of her rolltop desk.

"C'mon, C.C.," I say, hoping to dissuade her. "You'
been doing pretty good." It's true. Since we've been han
ing out these past few weeks, she hasn't touched any ma
juana. "You know how it makes you subdivide."

She fires up, drags like her life depends on it, holds t
joint out to me. "Want a charge or not?"

"No, thanks. Any wine?"

"In the box."

I'm shocked when I open the refrigerator. There's win
all right—and dozens of boxes of Sara Lee cheese cak
nothing else. I fill two glasses, take one to her. "Nobo
doesn't like Sara Lee," I say lightly. "Especially you."

She shrugs, takes the wine, hands me the joint. At lea
she looks halfway normal. I take a hit. I never could let an
body drink alone. Or smoke alone.

"Want a little something on that?" she asks, really relaxed. I don't know what she means. She shows me a cellophane baggy filled with white powder. She's back into coke now?

"I'm cool," I say. "I'll pass." The smoke loosens me up. My head feels like it's inside a glass bubble all of a sudden. I decide it's not a bad experience.

She sprinkles cocaine on the joint she's rolling.

"Since when did you start lacing your dope?" I ask.

She chuckles. "I like to spice it up every now and then. Sure you don't want some?"

"Hell, no."

She chuckles, turns off all the lights, turns on the music. I think it's jazz, I can't be sure. Whatever it is, it's very soothing. I close my eyes, groovin'.

"Gwen."

I hear her call my name, but I don't know where she is.

"Out here."

She's standing on the balcony, staring at the sky, puffing away. She says she wants to look at the stars. She's going to see stars for sure if she pulls anything like she did the last time I was here. I'm not that blasted. Anyone can see us. "Don't you think this is a little, uh, out in the open, C.C.?"

"What the hell difference does it make?"

My turn to look out for a bolt of lightning from her god. "You're a judge, C.C. If you don't know, I don't know anybody who does."

She stares at me. "I'm in trouble, Gwen."

I start singing. " 'Nobody knows the trouble I've seen—' "

"I'm serious. Big trouble."

"Big trouble, little trouble," I say, toking on the joint she gave me originally. "Trouble is trouble. That's why it's called trouble instead of problems, difficulties, obstacles, dilemmas, et cetera. Ask Willette. She's great at causing trouble." I'm feeling sorry for myself. Better watch it.

"I—killed somebody."

I nod like a wise sage. "Now, that's guaranteed to get you investigated by the Judicial Qualification Committee."

"I killed Willie Shalandar."

I giggle, taking a big puff on her joint. I can just see it: the train comes, she bets Willie he can beat it, she knows he can't. Bam! His head's sitting in the middle of the track, promising a box of fried chicken to everybody who votes for him. I snicker hysterically.

"Someone's in the house," she cautions, pushing me away from what little light there is. "Shut up, fool."

"That's right," I say defiantly. "I am a fool. A big, utter, stupid, weak-minded, blind, blundering, gullible, pitiful ass fool—" I realize I'm talking to myself. When I go back inside, C.C.'s disappeared again. The bedroom door's closed. I'm not going in there on a bet. I'm not a complete fool.

35

Somebody get the phone. Or the door, I don't care which one. I'm good, but I'm not that good. C.C.'s the one who subdivides when she's high. If anything, I solidify.

The banging on the door echoes in my head like the Liberty Bell. The jangling of the phone unnerves me. I cover up with a pillow. They can forget it. I'm not getting up. I can't. I think I'm still high.

Something screeches. Screeches? Nothing's supposed to be screeching. My God, what if someone's breaking in? I sit up, surprised to see I'm in my bed, my heart pounding so hard I can't hear. My ears strain to listen.

I do hear something. Oh, shit. Somebody's coming upstairs.

I scoot out of the bed, consider hiding in the closet until I remember this movie where somebody's coming after this chick and she hides under the bed. Good idea. They always get you in the closet. I stoop down to hurl myself under the bed. Until I remember it's a waterbed. I try to jump up; my foot's standing on my judge's robe. "What the—?" I didn't even realize I had it on. I don't remember putting it on. Only I can't think about that right now. The footsteps are getting louder. Whoever it is is almost to the top of the stairs.

My gun.

I dash for the closet. The phone stops ringing, the footsteps pause. I'm so scared, I'm almost on the ceiling, like the cat in the cartoon clinging by his claws. I run to the bedroom door just to see. Glimpse a brown jacket. Run back to the closet, tear shoe boxes apart looking for my gun. I forget which box I put it in, dammit. I grab the handle at last. The barrel shakes nervously. I hope I don't shoot my foot off.

I ease out the bedroom and listen. Somebody's talking on the phone downstairs. They got a lot of nerve breaking into my house and using my telephone. Slowly, I advance down the stairs. When I reach the bottom step, I lean over the banister to see into the kitchen. The footsteps come toward me. I dash back upstairs, two, three steps at a time. Whoever it is starts up the stairs again too. Out of breath, I just make it back into my bedroom, flatten myself against the wall. When I see the top of the man's head, I take aim.

"Don't shoot, Gwen."

Kwame? "What the hell are you doing in my house?"

"Eddy called me." He looks at the robe. I can imagine what's running through his head. When I take this thing off, I'm burning it. "C.C.'s dead. The police want to talk to you."

The police have C.C.'s building and the surrounding area cordoned off. We pass several checkpoints, identify ourselves without incident until we reach the actual entry to her unit. A self-important white uniformed officer informs us, "This is a crime scene. Authorized personnel only."

"I'm State Representative Kwame El'kasid," Kwame says patiently. "This is Gwen Parrish. We're here to see Detective Garcia."

"I'll need to see some identification."

The cop very cautiously inspects Kwame's legislative ID and bar card. Can't be too careful when it comes to us. Everybody knows we have a monopoly on lying, cheating, and stealing. Kwame and I look at each other. I'm surprised—and disappointed—he hasn't put this cowboy in his place. The old Kwame would have.

"You can go on up," the cop finally says. Kwame attempts to take my arm like I'm a little old lady. I let him know not to touch me. "Why didn't you tell him off? You know he was just giving us a hard time. Since when did you get so tolerant?"

"Since I realized you can fight every battle—or just the important ones."

He takes my arm again.

"You've changed," I tell him in a tone to let him know I don't think for the good.

"Yes," he says. "Why don't you?"

I pull my arm away. "Who the hell are you to tell me to change? There's nothing wrong with me. I'll change when I get good and ready."

He stops me. "You're upset about C.C. I understand. Don't take it out on me. I'm on your side."

His words hit me like cold water. He's right. It's not like he's my husband. "I'm sorry." Which I hate having to say. He still owes me apologies. Wait till I get my hands on Eddy. If I didn't know better, I'd say he planned for Marsha to get food poisoning tonight and have to go to emergency just so he wouldn't be available when I needed him. Never mind he's been calling me all night from the hospital—he said—ever since the police contacted him. They found my purse at C.C.'s. When I didn't come in and Pat couldn't get me on the phone, Eddy panicked and called Kwame. I must've really been blasted on C.C.'s "fixed-up" dope whether I wanted it or not.

A black cop is posted at her door. He recognizes Kwame, lets us pass immediately. They exchange a solidarity dap.

I have to make myself walk in. It's crawling with forensic people and more cops. "I don't believe she jumped, Kwame."

"Don't say any more," he reminds me, interrupting a tall, hawk-faced Latino with glasses. "Detective Garcia, this is Attorney Parrish. I'm—"

"I know who you are, Representative El'Kasid. Pleasure." They shake hands. Garcia looks at me with beady black eyes. "I appreciate your coming, Ms. Parrish. I'll try to make this as brief as possible. First of all, does this belong to you?"

I take my purse. I feel like I have my right arm back. "Yes."

"Can you tell me how it came to be left here?"

I glance at Kwame. He nods. I hate the way he has to know my business like this. "Judge Hendrix and I had gone to dinner to celebrate a case I settled. We, uh, didn't get a chance to eat. We came back here about nine-thirty." I look down, my face warming. "We—smoked some grass on her balcony and talked. I don't even remember how long or about what. I got pissed off—I mean, angry—with her for some reason and left in a huff, which must be how I forgot my purse." I make a joke. "A woman has to be really annoyed to do that."

Garcia smiles. "My wife won't even let me go in hers. You must've really been partying."

I look down. Cops, lawyers, and judges get high like everyone else: you're just supposed to keep it to yourself. "Like I said—we were celebrating." I sound so lame. Kwame probably thinks I'm totally irresponsible.

"Thank you, Ms. Parrish." He gives Kwame a friendly smile. "Seeing how she was the last person to see Judge Hendrix alive, we naturally wanted to talk to her."

"I understand," says Kwame. "So do you have a preliminary cause of death?"

One of the lab boys whispers to Garcia. He excuses himself momentarily, reminding us not to touch anything. I walk around the apartment. Funny how different everything looks in sunlight. I never noticed how cheap the furniture was or how grungy the carpet looked. The rolltop desk looks like its gizzards are hanging out with all its drawers pulled out and secret compartments open, even the one where C.C. kept her dope. I assume the police have her stash by now.

I wander out to the balcony. I didn't notice last night how small it is. There's barely room for the folding chairs we were sitting on. The concrete is spotted with ash droppings. My eyes are drawn to the three floors down below and the hideously contorted chalk outline in the grass. It looks like a rag doll somebody got mad at and threw down. Poor C.C.

"You all right?" Kwame looks down with me, concerned. I cut my eyes. Do I look all right? We walk back inside. Garcia questions me for a few minutes, more details in C.C.'s death.

"I appreciate your cooperation, Ms. Parrish," he says politely when it's clear I can't remember what happened. It's like a black fog I keep chasing without success. "If we have any more questions, we'll get back with you, Representative El'Kasid."

I automatically bristle until I remember Kwame's my lawyer as far as Garcia is concerned. I nod good-bye, waste no time getting out into the fresh air. I've got a headache over my entire head. Kwame stays behind to talk to Garcia. Catches up with me on the stairs, firmly takes my arm, and walks me to his Chrysler New Yorker, which I finally notice. It's black and brand-new. I take a good look at him too as he opens the door to help me in. He's G.Q. live. Immaculate in his custom Italian suit, monogrammed French cuffs, gold cuff links, designer tie, three-hundred-dollar shoes. What lucky woman kissed him and turned him into a prince? I'd never admit it in a thousand years, I'm totally jealous.

"They're calling it an accident," he says as we drive off.

"She *accidentally* hurled herself three stories to the ground?"

"You have reason to believe otherwise?"

"Yes."

"Why?"

"I don't know."

"Figures."

"What's that supposed to mean?"

He shrugs. "It's your m.o. Come to the most outrageous, extreme, irrational conclusion possible first, then work backward to what's reasonable, logical, and rational." He says this all very matter-of-factly, like he's doing a clinical analysis of me. Am I really that crazy? Not the good crazy like he is, the bad one, where people look at you funny, comment behind your back, make fun of you, distance themselves.

"You were the last person to see her alive, and you were angry with her—why, we still don't know—when you left. That makes you the prime suspect if her death's anything but an accident. Have you thought about that?"

No. "It crossed my mind."

"You would've told the police that if I hadn't been standing there, wouldn't you?"

"She was my friend, Kwame. I know you never liked her. I didn't like her either sometimes. Most of the time. But we really got to know each other these last few weeks. I would've starved without her feeding me appointments."

He's unsympathetic. "The hole wouldn't be so deep if you didn't insist on giving me child support."

I'm not even dealing with that. I don't say anything. He did it when he was up at bat, without complaint and come hell or high water. When that's all you can do for your child you can at least do that. Fresh pain from Ashleigh Lee's rejection wells up. She doesn't want or need anything else from me.

Instead of turning left at the Southwest Freeway, Kwame turns right. "Where are you going?"

"To my office. I don't interview clients on the run."

I chuckle caustically. "Look, Kwame, we can stop this charade right now. Eddy got scared and called you. I didn't."

"You wouldn't have."

"Not in a million years." Too much has happened between us. Too much has happened, period. I sorta smile though. "It's nice of you to play Sir Galahad. But it's too late. I'm not a damsel in distress. I'm just damned."

Tears appear from nowhere, choking me. He reaches across me, snatches a tissue from the glove box, and hands it to me. "What makes you think I'm playing, Gwen?" He pulls the car over and parks. "You could be in a lot of trouble, you could be in none. You need a lawyer."

"Fine. Eddy'll represent me."

"You need a big gun. Eddy's a good guy, but you need me and you know it."

"I can't afford you."

"No," he says angrily, driving off. Apparently that wasn't the answer he was expecting. "You don't deserve me either."

"What's that supposed to mean?" Thankfully, the tears have subsided, freeing me to do battle again.

"This." He slams on the brakes. Thankfully, my seat belt locks against my chest. I might've gone through the windshield. A driver pounds his horn behind us to move. Kwame jerks the car out of traffic, stops, gripping the wheel as he glares at me. "I am your lawyer whether you want me or not. I've waited a long time for the right time, chance, opportunity—call it whatever you want—to get back in your life. This is it."

He heads the car to his office again. "You're going to prove that old saying wrong about lawyers making the worst clients. You're going to be the model client." He parks in the space reserved for him next to his building, an attractive two-story conversion in the Heights, with all its fancy houses. He smiles politely at me. "You're going to do what you're told when you're told. Above all, you're going to tell me the truth. Starting now."

I look at him closely. He has changed. He's a grown-up. I feel like I'm in my terrible twos by comparison. How'd I get like this? I bow my head. "I can't tell you the truth, Kwame."

"Why not?"

I have a hard time swallowing. "You wouldn't want to have anything to do with me."

He lifts my chin up. "You remember a lo-ong time ago when we promised for richer or poorer, for better or worse?" I try to lower my head, but he won't let me. "I never broke my promise. You did."

I had no idea his love was so deep. I was too blind. Knowing now only makes it harder. "I don't deserve you."

"I know that."

"Really, Kwame. I'm a fool. I've screwed up everything. I threw away everything that mattered trying to be something that's not about shit."

"You don't know how many years I've waited to hear you say just that. I thought you were ready the night you showed up on my doorstep." I see the pain in his eyes.

"Ready for what, Kwame?" I've got no right to hope he even remotely means anything related to me. I've got to deal with hard-core reality from now on.

"For me and Ashleigh Lee. To be together again."

Tears gnaw at my eyes. "Ashleigh Lee—wants that?"

"It's all she's ever wanted. It was her idea for me to drive this boat, wear these monkey clothes. She thinks if I shine you'll see me. She loves you. I love you."

"How can you?" I break down. Everything—the pain, the hope, the love, the fear—everything rushes out. "I don't love me."

"You just picked wrong, Gwen. Your ideas, your friends, the things you wanted—they were all wrong for you."

"I picked you."

"The one right thing you did." He crushes me to him. "I wish I knew why I love you so. I've asked myself a thousand times. When you married that white boy, I wanted to die. It went right to my core. I just knew it would kill my love. It didn't. It made it stronger." He kisses me. For a moment I actually disappear inside his love. It's magic, heaven, peace—bliss.

I pull away. "I can't just take what you're offering me, Kwame. Nobody appreciates anything he didn't earn. I have to earn it. Otherwise, I'll always feel like you saved me. I have to save myself. I won't be any good to you or my child if I don't. Do you understand?"

He stares straight ahead for a moment. Lets out a deep breath, looks at me. "I have to. I just put my whole heart on the line." He smiles the sweetest smile I've ever seen. "A man doesn't do that unless he's willing to risk getting it kicked to the curb."

I bow my head again, this time to pray. Thank you, Lord, for this man. Kwame starts to get out. I have a flash. Grab his arm. It comes back to me. "C.C. thought somebody was in the apartment. She told me to be quiet. They could've been hiding, waiting for me to leave. They could've pushed her. Garcia said the fall didn't kill her. She hit her head. What if somebody conked her first, then pushed her over?"

Kwame's skeptical. "That's a lot of somebodies. Do you realize how many people it would've taken to get C.C. in dead weight off the floor and over the balcony?"

I ignore his reasoning. "Somebody killed her, I know it."

That exasperates him. "Gwen, why can't you just leave well enough alone? She's dead. From what you said, she's out of her misery."

"You make it sound like she was a dog who lived too long. I know she didn't jump. Or fall. Somebody pushed her."

"Who?"

"I don't know."

That's it. He guides me inside the building. I've never been here before. It's very nice, up-to-date, professional. Like the white firms. He has five attorneys working for him, three paralegals, two secretaries, and several law clerks, all of whom he introduces me to, saying simply, "This is Gwen." The secretaries look me over thoroughly. They're obviously very protective of him, like miniature Schnauzers. Even though he makes it clear to everyone I'm someone special, I hope I pass.

His office is spacious, lots of African accents and pictures of Ashleigh Lee, none of which I've seen before. I go around the room, soaking up each image, one in particular, a recent shot of her leaning against a tree, smiling candidly.

"It's my favorite," he says, standing behind me. "She looks like ьer mother."

I pick it up, peering closely, absorbing every detail. She does. Why couldn't I see that before? He sets it back on the desk. "We need to get to work."

He interviews me thoroughly. I tell him everything— except about Michael. I'm too ashamed. I'll have to take it to my grave. It's past lunch by the time we finish. He offers to take me somewhere to eat, but I ask him to take me home. Before we leave, I check in at my office. A reporter from the *Chronicle* called for an obligatory quote, that's all, according to Pat.

I give Kwame a quick kiss and hop out when he pulls into my drive, making it clear I intend to go in alone. He looks disappointed. I tell him I'm exhausted. I need time to process everything.

"Everything?"

"Humpty-Dumpty's not going to fit back together overnight, Kwame."

"That's why we want you to come to counseling with us. Gwen, I'd love to be able to go home tonight and tell Ashleigh Lee you'll be at the next session." He looks at me so hopefully.

"I'll be there."

I watch him drive off, a big smile on his face as he waves good-bye. I wave back. I think I understand how this thing called life works now. Whatever you plant in it blossoms. The good, the bad, and the ugly. It's about giving, not taking, sharing, not trying to hog everything. It's also about trying to put things right. If not your own wrongs, then someone else's, if you can.

For someone who wanted so bad to be a judge, I only now see that justice isn't man-made. We're simply its servants, agents, and assigns. Justice doesn't have anything to do with the law or lawyers or judges either. Sometimes justice and the legal outcome coincide, sometimes they don't. But justice will be done.

I won't be entitled to live happily ever after with Kwame

and Ashleigh Lee until I put things right. At least as right as they're ever going to be. I'm one reason why they got so out of whack. Going over everything with Kwame helps me to see that. I go into the house to call Michael.

36

"What's this for?"

Michael hands me a bottle of expensive champagne, smirking like he knew it was just a matter of time before I called him. He got here in record time. "For later."

I give him a warning look. "I told you, Michael—"

He kisses me briefly, steps inside. "Yeah, I know. You're serious." He looks around, grinning. "Your boy ain't lurking in the shadows again, is he? He almost caught me in my downstroke last time."

He is such a dog. "He's not here."

And won't be ever again. I spoke with Dirk's attorney yesterday, offering to accept service. He refused. Dirk insists I be served with the divorce papers. He thinks it'll embarrass me. Unfortunately for him, in a no-fault state like Texas when there are no kids and no property, he has nothing else to beat me over the head with. I don't even have to show up at the final hearing.

I take the champagne into the kitchen and set it on the counter. "That's supposed to be chilled, baby," Michael says.

"We won't be drinking it anytime soon," I emphasize.

He shrugs, smiles confidently, leans back, entirely relaxed, appraising me. "Funny. You don't look like you missed me, baby." He reaches for me. Stepping sideways, I just manage to evade him. He grins like this is a game. I have to keep him in the kitchen no matter what, so we can talk instead of have sex, which he assumes will happen. This is not going to be easy. He's checking out the counter as a possibility. I cut to the chase.

"Michael, I don't believe C.C.'s death was an accident." That was the coroner's official ruling, so I didn't need a lawyer after all. That and the fact we haven't automatically gotten back together really disappointed Kwame. He thought his big chance was going to be C.C.'s funeral. He called me at home to find out the date and used the opportunity to offer to drive. I hurt his feelings when I refused. I knew Michael would be there with Willette, my only chance to entice him to my place.

C.C.'s funeral was a sad little memorial service attended by her staff, Willette and Michael, most of the black attorneys in town, and a few white people. C.C. never spoke of her family all the time I knew her, and none showed. I more or less took charge, which made it easy to pass my message to Michael when he offered condolences. Kwame was standing right next to him and saw the look of absolute triumph on his face. I played it off when he looked to me for what it meant.

I can't have Kwame on my conscience when I'm dealing with Michael. I sincerely hope not, but I may have to go to bed with him to make this work. Thank the stars Ashleigh Lee's therapist—my *soror,* as it turns out—agrees Kwame and I should take things slowly. For Ashleigh Lee's sake.

Michael focuses on me intently. "Just what do you think her death was, then?"

"Murder."

He drops his head back and laughs throatily. He looks at me, his eyes amused slits. "You need it real bad, don't you, baby? Your imagination's on overload. Come here."

I take a step back. "I was with C.C. the night she died."

"You're too much woman for one man, baby." He gives me a look that winds up below my waist. "I know you weren't wasting it on another woman."

He's exasperating. "Michael, why do you have such a one-track mind? Everything boils down to sex with you."

"That's because everything boils down to sex, baby. Those that want it. Those that get it. The needy and the greedy." He looks at me with raw desire. "Would you come here, please?"

I take another step back. He smiles coldly. "I have to make you do everything, don't I, baby?" Quicker than a snake he grabs me up in his arms, his hand crawling over me hungrily while he holds me, as if he's re-establishing his territory. I try to stop him. He grabs my ass with both hands and squeezes me playfully. I push him back. He laughs.

"Listen to me, Michael—"

"Let's make love and get that out of the way first." His arms wrap around me. "I'll be all ears after that."

I have to be quick. He's all hands. "C.C. and I were sitting around talking—getting high. She was all the way live scared. Acting really weird."

He scoffs. "How could you tell?"

"She said she'd killed somebody."

His eyes flicker with interest. "Who was the lucky person?" he says just a little too casually.

"Willie Shalandar."

I steel myself for his reaction. To my surprise, he lets me go, just looks at me. I've miscalculated. "Did you hear me, Michael? She said she killed Willie Shalandar."

He glares at me. "Okay, that's it, baby." He grabs the champagne and stalks to the door. "I came over here to cheer you up. You were moping around the funeral like you lost your best friend. Nobody could be that tight with that crazy bitch. All you want to do is talk shit."

I block the door. "Michael, listen to me. I swear to God, that's what she told me. I wouldn't lie about something like that. You *know* me."

"Hey, baby, we're lawyers. We lie for a living. Now move your pretty ass from the door before I have to move it for you."

He means it. I turn the lock reluctantly, opening the

door—Kwame stands on the doorstep. Surprised, shocked, stunned, each of us is speechless, a real feat for three lawyers.

Kwame recovers first, a hundred questions behind half-mast eyes. "Michael, what's happening, man?"

Michael looks from me to him, adds two and two. "You got it, man," he says angrily, so jealous he can't hide it. To me, "I'm gone." He takes off in a roar. Kwame watches him disappear, looks at me coolly. "What was that all about?"

"What are you doing here?" I just hope his showing up hasn't ruined everything. Pain flashes across his face like a shooting star. "Next time I'll be sure to call first."

"You do that."

I have no choice but to keep him out of my life until this is all over. Men are so strange. There are men they don't mind you being with and men they do. Kwame didn't like me being with a white man; Michael didn't mind one bit.

"Is there something between you and Michael?"

I almost laugh. Just blackmail, murder, revenge, betrayal for starters. "No, Kwame."

"What was he doing here?"

"I can't answer that."

"On the grounds that it might incriminate you?"

I can't take the look in his eyes. Why do I always hurt him? I love him. I honestly do.

"Yes."

He lets out a deep breath. "I can't take much more, Gwen. I'm only a man."

He walks out. I want to run after him, fall on my knees, beg for his forgiveness and understanding, but I can't. If I've done what I think, events are in motion that will be beyond anyone's power to control but mine.

37

"He-e-ere's Gwen!"

Eddy merely nods as he finishes instructions to Pat on preparing a brief when I bounce into the office, pretending to be totally upbeat. I collect my messages, breeze into my office.

"Mind if I come in?" Eddy looks at me curiously, probing to see if I'm okay.

"Has that ever stopped you?"

He chuckles as he settles his long frame across from me. "How are you?"

"Mahvelous. I feel mahvelous, darlink," I say in my best Billy Crystal imitation imitating some famous person. I don't know who.

"How's Kwame?"

My mask slips. "I haven't heard from him in a while." Two weeks, three days, and fifteen hours to be exact. It's hell. Fortunately, I'm intimately familiar with the place.

"And Ashleigh Lee?"

My whole face smiles. "She's great. I really think we're going to have a cool relationship one day." The first session with Dr. Watts, her, and Kwame, I felt like a Nazi war criminal the way Ashleigh Lee catalogued in minute detail every wrong I'd ever done her, real and imagined. I walked out at one point.

Kwame stopped me before I could get in the car and drive off. We actually fought over the keys. Of course he won. I had to follow him back in session to get them. He told me when I finished hearing Ashleigh Lee out, I could have them. She got upset because she didn't feel he should threaten me like that. They blew up at each other. I could see then she didn't love him over me. I tried to stop them from arguing, which set off a big argument between the three of us. All the while Dr. Watts sat watching us like Tweety Bird, taking notes. After everybody said what was on their mind for forever and a day, she put it all in perspective while we listened, exhausted.

"Then you're not mad at me for calling Kwame?"

I smile. "No, Eddy. It helped bring me and my daughter back together."

"And you and Kwame?"

I tease him. "Gettin' in my business now."

He smiles. "Just let me know when the wedding is. I'll be happy to come this time."

"I suppose someone held a gun on you to come to me and the white boy's?" That's what I call Dirk now because that's how he's acting. It's amazing how quickly he reverted to type.

"Man," says Eddy. "Speaking of the white boy, I hear he's leaving Legal Services."

That surprises me. "I'm really sorry to hear that."

"Don't be. He's going on the bench."

I jump like my seat's electrified. "What?"

"Your girl recommended him." Willette? The enemy of her enemy is her friend.

"That's too bad," I say and mean it. That can't be good.

"I know one thing," Eddy said. "If he cared about you and called you out of your name, what he's going to do to the rest of us brothers and sisters?"

That's exactly what Dirk wants me to do—think about what he's going to do. It's part of his revenge. The other part is taking the judgeship I wanted.

"I'll say one thing for your ass," Eddy says. "At least you leave your men better off than when you found them.

Kwame's a state legislator, Dirk's gonna be a judge. Marsha'll take the gold out my mouth if she ever leaves me."

I laugh. Something better happen real quick, or I'm going to disbelieve all that stuff I said about how real justice operates. It is manifestly unjust for Dirk to go on the bench. They've got too many judges who hate us already.

"Gwen," Pat buzzes. "Line two."

"Who is it?" I ask. I don't need any more surprises.

"Judge Haynes."

I look to Eddy for guidance. "He's one of the new ones. Why's he calling you?"

I have no earthly idea. "This is Gwen Parrish." I listen as the court coordinator explains why she's calling. My mouth drops open. Eddy tries to understand my change of expression. I thank her politely and hang up. The wheel is finally turning.

"What's up?"

"That was Myra Davenport," I say. "Haynes' coordinator. They're trying something new in his court to move the docket and hopefully save the county—and the taxpayers— some money."

"They all say that shit," says Eddy. "It's just an excuse to dig deeper."

I shrug. "Be that as it may. They're instituting their own public defender program and recommended two attorneys to handle it."

"You?"

"Moi."

"You won't have to worry about money again." He shakes his head admiringly. "You lucky dog."

"Bitch," I correct him. I don't feel lucky. I feel like a spider spinning a web out of my ass.

38

It's almost eleven-thirty. I'm watching Willie Shalandar's house from across the street, hiding in trees dripping with Spanish moss. The bayou's spooky at night. I keep checking over my shoulder, half expecting to see a mugger or worse. The lights go out in the house. Willette comes out, gets into her black Mercedes, and drives around the corner to her house. I run across South Mac Gregor like I'm on fire, even though traffic's almost nonexistent. Houston is a working class city, people go to bed.

I ring the doorbell. The drapes part. Marvella looks at me, I look back. Recognition finally sparks in her eyes.

"Hello, Marvella," I say when she opens the door. She covers her face with her hands. Bursts into tears. I check the street, close the door, and walk her to the family room. "There's not a lot of time, Marvella. You've got to tell me the truth."

I see them.

The two lovebirds, their cage sitting on a table where a picture of Willie and Willette used to be prominently displayed. I look around. All the pictures are gone. I gently guide Marvella to a seat on the sofa and wait. She stops crying. Looks at me with tear-rimmed, blazing red eyes.

"She's trying put me away."

"Willette?"

"She says I'm crazy."

"Are you?"

"It's the drugs." That accounts for her eyes looking like

stoplights. "She puts them in my food. She dopes me up at night too, before she leaves. Fooled her tonight."

"How?"

She reaches in her pocket and shows me three giant candy-colored pills. "I pretended to swallow them."

I thought her voice sounded strange when I called her this evening to ask if I could come by. "I don't take company anymore. I'm sorry." She was about to hang up. I went for broke. "I have a message from C.C., Marvella." Her end was silent for so long, I thought she'd simply laid the phone down and forgot about me. "She comes by between ten and eleven every night." Her voice was deadly calm. "Don't let her see you." Which was why I was hiding across the street. There's nowhere to park Black Beauty on South Mac Gregor at night and not be seen.

"She killed my baby, you know."

"I know."

She hugs herself, smiling, caught up in a rapturous recollection known only to her. "My sweet, sweet baby—"

I wait for the memory to pass, which it does in a moment or two. Her eyes narrow at me. "I know what you're thinking. I'm old. No one would want me but Willie and he's dead."

I speak softly, for I don't want to upset her. "Marvella, anybody can see where Willette got her good looks."

She makes an ugly mouth. "That heifer. She killed my baby. Now she's trying to get rid of me. You've got to stop her. Stop her, you hear me?" She draws a gun from under the seat cushion, points it at me. My life flashes in vignettes before my eyes.

"Marvella, please. Put the gun down. I'm here to help you."

She looks at the gun, amused. "She'd never leave me a loaded gun. She knows what I'd do with it."

To prove it she pulls out the empty clip. I snatch the gun, make like I'm going to slap the taste out of her mouth. She huddles like she thinks I really am going to hit her. Just as I suspected, Willette's been beating on her. One more reason why I'm going to get her if it's the last thing I do.

"All right, Marvella. No more games. I want the truth."

She looks down at her hands, helpless in her lap. "Willette found out about us." She shakes her head sadly. "She wouldn't let her see me. It got harder on her, poor thing. I'm a tough old hoot. But C.C." She looks at the ceiling to keep the tears from spilling. "She was like a frail little bird. That was my pet name for her—'Bird.'"

She drops her head, stares at her hands again. "I didn't have to get married. I didn't ever have to get married. But I wanted children. With the house, the daddy, the picket fence—everything." She looks at me, eyes spilling tears. "I knew Willie was going places as soon we clapped eyes on each other. We had the biggest wedding Houston Negroes have ever seen, until Willette got married." She smiles proudly. "We were the perfect couple. I was the envy of all the ladies." Her smile disappears. "I knew I'd made a mistake as soon as the ink dried on the license."

She lays her head back, falls silent. For a minute I think she's fallen asleep.

"Marvella?"

She opens her eyes. "Dear God in heaven, I made a mistake. My only consolation was my child. My beautiful, beautiful child. He took her from me." She glares at me bitterly. "When I got old and ugly, he made her his high yellow prize to show off to the world." She bursts out crying again. "I didn't know what he was doing. I swear to God."

I let her cry until she calms down. "The first time Willette brought C.C. to the house, I knew we were meant to be. She was so lonely, just like me. I'd make her smile. I was the only one who could make her laugh at first." I flash on C.C. laughing the night she died. "It was so easy after that. So right. I loved her so much."

She lays her head down, weeps uncontrollably. I leave to retrieve a box of tissues from the guest bath. When I return, she's gone.

"Marvella?"

I check all the rooms downstairs, take the upstairs two at a time. "Marvella, where are you?"

She's slumped in a rocking chair in the master bedroom, rocking quietly.

"Marvella."

Stares at me with glazed eyes filled with drug madness. "Is that you, Bird?"

Something tells me to reach into her pocket. The pills are gone. She smiles weakly. "I want to sleep."

I shake her. "Marvella, please. You've got to tell me the truth. I've got to know." I struggle getting her to her feet. She's limp as boiled spaghetti. We nearly topple over.

"Get me . . . bed," she whispers.

I half drag, half carry her to the bed, lift her feet, get her situated, kneel by her side. "Marvella, please. Did C.C. kill Willie?" I'm not sure she heard me. "She told me she killed your husband. Did she, Marvella? Did she?"

She smiles dreamily. "Sure did, honey child." She giggles and mimics the little girl on the Shake 'n' Bake commercial. " 'Unh-huhn. An' I hel-yelped.' "

39

Pat sounds anxious when she hears my voice. "You've got a letter from the grievance committee."

My heart trips. "Read it."

The world stands still while I listen to her rattling paper, murmuring to herself. Her voice rises excitedly. ". . . 'We're happy to inform you that the committee has found no factual basis for the charge and is forthwith dropping its investigation and closing its file in the above-referenced matter. Sincerely yours, blah, blah, blah. Isn't that wonderful?"

"Yeah." I hang up and head for the clerk's office.

Gregory, the gay black clerk who helped me before, smiles when he recognizes me. "Well, hello, stranger. Back again?"

"I can't stay away from you."

He laughs and tells me to "go on." I tell him what I want, and he goes directly to the volume I need, sets it on the counter, digs in halfway, turning a big chunk of pages. Licks his finger and flips a few more sheets.

"Voilà, honey chil'."

I run my finger down the neat cursive entries. When I find what I'm looking for, it jumps off the page at me. "You're a doll, Greg." I give him a big kiss, and he actually blushes. "I need a certified copy."

I pace in front of Kwame's desk. He doesn't believe me. "Kwame, you know me. You know I wouldn't make this whole thing up."

He sits back, frowns. "I thought I knew you. I knew you at one time. I don't know you anymore."

I took a chance coming here. He kept me waiting so long, I began to think he wasn't going to see me at all. His secretary was most annoyed when I barged in after she finally said he was free.

I take a deep breath. "Kwame, I agree I've been off on a tangent these past few years—"

"Try the planet Xeron."

"Take any and all shots at me you want and need to, Kwame. Only believe me when I say I can prove C.C. was killed. Here's the motive."

I lay the certified copy on the desk in front of him. He barely glances at it. "You're a criminal lawyer, Gwen. Talk motive to people who watch *Perry Mason*."

"Just read it, Kwame, please. I found it at the clerk's office. Marvella told me about it." I point at one line in particular. "Could I make this up?"

He casts the document aside. "So Willie Shalandar owned Matoomba House. What does that prove?"

"By itself, nothing. But with Marvella's testimony and mine, we could make out a helluva circumstantial case."

"For?"

I look at him like he's crazy. "Murder, what else?"

He returns my look in spades. "Nobody's going to believe Willette murdered C.C." He walks to his door. "I don't have time for games, Gwen." We've done a lot of things to each other. This one hurts the most, getting invited out. His brown eyes zero in on my heart. "Do you want Michael that bad you'd set his wife up for murder?"

My lungs freeze. He might as well have shot me with a cannon. All of my emotions, all my feelings, hemorrhage out. I walk to the door like I'm doing it for the first time in my life.

"Kwame, I'm going to leave now," I say. "Before you say something else you'll regret for the rest of your life."

* * *

His words ring in my ears as I drive to Marvella's. I promised I'd look in on her this morning, let her know what I found. I park in the circular drive. Willette's not going to be here this time of day. She has a day nurse come in and do the dirty work of doping Marvella during the day. I ring the bell. I promised last night I'd help her. My lawyer-like mind tells me a legal battle to establish her ability to handle her own affairs will be a booty kicker.

I ring the bell again, the hot sun makes me impatient. No one answers. I ring again.

"Yes?"

The black woman who opens the door is massively built and looks mean.

"I'm here to see Mrs. Shalandar."

"She ain't here."

I didn't make myself clear. "I mean Mrs. Marvella Shalandar."

"I know. She ain't here."

"My name's Gwen Parrish. I'm a lawyer." I give her my business card. "I represent Marvella Shalandar." Which isn't exactly untrue, since I will in the near future.

She hands the card back, unimpressed. "You better get in line."

"What do you mean?"

"A whole mess of 'em just rode outta here with her going downtown."

"Downtown? For what?"

She looks at me suspiciously. "For her lawyer you sure don't know much."

"She just retained me last evening. Where did they take her?"

She shrugs. "Somebody named Brenner's court."

"Judge Brenner?" My heart sinks to my feet.

"That's the one. Somethin' 'bout having her committed."

I drive like a demon to the Family Law Center. This is really bad news. One of my clients—an orderly—hipped me to the deal on Brenner and the new psychiatric facility

they conveniently located on the fringe of Third Ward. He
has a direct feed into the hospital for anybody he wants quietly put away. My client said Brenner had his wife checked
in last Christmas.

"Was she sick?"

"Just sickenin', wantin' stuff all the time."

I get lucky. Somebody's pulling away from a meter. I
park and jump out even though I'm three feet from the curb.

The elevators in the Family Law Center are notoriously
slow. When one finally arrives, it's packed like pickles. I
can't wait. I force my way on, getting several dirty looks
from passengers squeezed past endurance to make room for
me. When the elevator stops on the seventh floor, I literally
pop off from the pressure.

The sign and arrow overhead indicate Brenner's court is
to the right. The hall outside is empty, which means he's on
the bench. I peek through one of the glass panes. There's a
full house, but I don't see Willette or Marvella. I enter and
go directly to the clerk, seated to Brenner's right.

"I'm here on the Shalandar matter," I whisper. Brenner
is occupied raking some poor attorney over the coals. "Has
it been heard yet?"

She checks her docket sheet, whispering back. "I don't
see it. Are you sure it's set for today?"

I run down the list with her. Nothing. She looks puzzled.
"I wonder if that's the case the judge heard in chambers."

I have no choice now. I picked this fight. That's what
people pay lawyers to do. Every time we sue somebody
we're asking for it.

I ease through the crack the black security guard makes
when he holds the door open, motioning me to take the lone
empty seat in the back. I ignore him and walk straight up the
aisle to the front. Commissioners court is in full session. A
black citizen has the floor, complaining at the podium about
his taxes. The commissioners look disinterested, except for
Willette. Head cocked to the side, she pays close attention.

He must be one of her constituents. I stand just to his right, a step or two behind. The security guard tugs at me to be seated. I tell him I have an urgent message for Commissioner Shalandar. He orders me to follow him. I look back. Mission accomplished. She sees me.

He takes me to the side of the room. She's watching me, curious. "What's the message?" he whispers.

"I have to give it to her myself. It's confidential. Believe me, she wants it. See how she's looking at us?"

He looks at Willette. She motions to him to join her; he whispers and points at me. Our eyes connect for a hot second. He waves me forward.

"What do you want, Gwen?" she asks, her voice formal, dry.

"Meet me at my office tonight. Nine o'clock."

"Get her out of here," she tells the guard.

"Don't make any trouble," he warns me as he yanks me by the arm. I slide her the envelope. He grabs for it too. Her instincts tell her to stop him. "I'll take it."

When he escorts me out, I look back at her. She's reading. Lifts her eyes, her face unintentionally pale as the paper she's holding. Our eyes meet again. She nods.

"Talkin' to myself, talkin' to myself."

I tap my desktop in time twice with my pencil. "Talkin' to myself, talkin' to myself."

The door opens, my heart skips a beat. "Talkin' to myself, talkin' to myself."

Even on industrial carpet I can tell the distinct footsteps. They head straight to my office.

"Talkin' to myself, talkin' to myself." Tap, tap. I smile magnanimously. "Welcome. Have a seat."

Willette looks around like I invited her to play in mud.

"Talkin' to myself, talkin' to myself."

She perches on a side chair. "Do you have to keep repeating that silly song or whatever it is?"

" 'Talkin' to myself'?" I tap automatically. "Why not?

Someone far wiser than you and I said a long time ago when you talk to yourself, you know you're not talking to a fool."

"That's debatable in your case."

I smile easily. "I'm going to let you have that one, Willette. By the way, speaking of talking to people, I had a nice chat with your mother before you had her shipped off."

"You're lying."

"She told me about her and C.C."

Her green eyes fade to milky jade. "What about them?"

"They were lovers."

Her eyes turn green-black. "I'll sue you for defamation of character if you ever repeat that lie."

"Come on, Willette. First-year torts. We both aced it. Truth is an absolute defense to defamation."

She glares at me. "What do you want?"

"Justice."

"How much will it cost?"

"Your seat on the county commission, for starters. You resign, naming Kwame as your replacement."

She doesn't blink an eye. "What else?"

"You cut the drug trafficking out of Matoomba House. Charles Garrett told me all about it before he died."

A wild shot, but it hits the bull's-eye. Her mouth draws into that thin white line I thought only white people could make. "What else?"

"You get Brenner to let Marvella out."

"My mother . . . is a very sick woman."

I smile. "Now, if that's not the pot calling the kettle black."

"What's that supposed to mean?"

"It means, how can you criticize your mother for going with another woman when you were going with your father?"

Lightning flashes in her eyes. She's using every ounce of self-control to keep from strangling me. I admire her. She's really taking the heat. "I don't have to listen to this filth." She starts for the door.

"You killed C.C."

She pauses and smiles. "Did my mother tell you that? Or did you find a way to con an old, confused woman into baring her soul? What'd you do, offer to eat her pussy?"

She thinks she got another shot off.

"I like dicks, Willette. Always have, always will. Not that I have anything against the carpetmunchers. I say live and let live." I smile at her. "You, on the other hand, have a problem with that particular concept. You might as well have a seat. We're not through putting our heads together. You remember how we used to strategize back in the not-too-old days when I was your all-around patsy, fool, and factotum?"

"Meaning?"

"You set me up and I fell for it, hook, line, and sinker. I wanted to be somebody bad and yesterday. I would've sold my soul and you knew it."

Her mouth twists in satisfaction. "Come now, Gwen— did you really expect me to reward you for sleeping with my husband?"

"Your husband was blackmailing me."

She laughs in my face. "You can do better than that."

My face warms. "Not the first time. That was a mistake. But every time after that."

Her eyes turn to green ice. "If you think that in any way excuses what you did, you've managed to top even yourself in being stupid."

I want this over with. "You killed C.C. to avenge your father's death. Your father found out about Marvella and C.C., and you helped him pressure them into breaking up. After he died, you really turned up the steam. You've been keeping Marvella so drugged she can't even think straight, and somehow, some way you got Charles Garrett to kill himself."

She shakes her head, not fazed in the least. "Wrong, wrong, wrong. Anything else?"

I come to the admittedly thin part of my argument. "You planned on being Daddy's little girl forever, didn't you? All that changed when C.C. and Marvella killed him. You were on your own for the first time in your life. You wanted revenge. Which you got when you drove poor C.C. out of her mind harassing her. When that didn't work fast enough, you pushed her over her balcony. Now you think you're going to get your mother out of the way by having her locked up in a mental institution."

I'm ready for the finale now. "Charles Garrett was the only fly in the ointment. He wouldn't help you put that lethal injection in him. How inconsiderate. He threatened to bust you and Larry Scott and the rest of your big-time drug cronies. Somehow you bumped him off and made it look like suicide."

"I didn't kill anyone. I told you that."

She says it so confidently I believe her. I've sat across from too many guilty people not to. "If you didn't, who did?"

"Me."

I jump. Michael steps around the corner, pointing Marvella's gun. Something tells me it's loaded this time.

"I didn't tell her a thing, baby," Willette says, suddenly simpering before him. The transformation's amazing.

"Shut up," he tells her. He shakes his head at me, his handsome face calm and emotionally blank. "All you had to do was be cool, baby. When I realized how she was the one messing you over instead of her boy Larry, I made her clear that shit up. I even had her get you one of the biggest sugar tits downtown."

"Haynes' court?" I'd recognized Willette's hand wiping my slate clean. I had no idea it was Michael's eraser making her. Michael the hound masterminding everything? "I don't believe it."

He laughs harshly. "Nobody does. I saw how they yanked on my daddy's nuts and old man Shalandar. I figured out a long time ago it's better to be the yanker than the yankee." He laughs again. "Yankee—get it?"

I don't get it. "Why do all this for me?"

His eyes soften, no longer laughing. "You know why, baby."

I have to stand up on this one. It's too incredible. "You really do love me?"

Willette has been taking turns watching us. Stares at him, her mouth an O. "You love—her?"

"Hey, baby," he growls at her, "it's no big deal. You were doing it with your old man, remember?"

"That was different and you know it, Michael." She looks like she wants to cry. "I had to. I always had to."

Michael shrugs. "It's all water under the bridge."

Whatever bridge he's talking about, knowing these two I'm headed off it. I go for broke. "She didn't just sleep with him, Michael. She got pregnant for him."

Willette makes this strange whistling sound, doubles over, like I socked her in the stomach. Michael looks at her. Freezes.

"She had an abortion." I know when to go in for the kill, I'm a lawyer. "They messed her up. I took her to the hospital. She almost bled to death. She had to have a hysterectomy."

He walks up and looks at her, truly shocked. The way she clings to the chair, barely standing, tears running down her face, he knows it's true. "A hysterectomy?" he says.

"He wouldn't let me keep it," she cries. "I begged him. He made me."

"You told me you couldn't have children."

"I begged him, Michael."

"You knew how much I wanted a son." It sinks into him. He aims the gun at her. She closes her eyes, ready to meet her Maker.

I scream, "Michael, no!"

To our complete surprise, Kwame flies through the door, rams him headfirst, wrestles him to the floor. Willette collapses. The gun spins from Michael's hand, and I grab it. I make sure it's loaded since it's Marvella's gun. Kwame plops on Michael's chest, drives his fist into his face, knocking his head to the floor, yanks his neck up by his tie, piles his fist into him again and again.

"That's enough, Kwame."

"I'm not done with him."

"I said that's enough."

Kwame whips around at me like I'm going to be next if I don't shut up. I point the gun. He lets Michael's head drop. It thumps the floor like a melon.

"Get off him." I keep the gun trained.

Kwame shifts to the side, puts his hands up. "Hey, I'm with you, remember?"

"You weren't this afternoon."

"I was a creep this afternoon. That's what I stopped by to tell you. I've been looking for you everywhere. I even tracked Eddy down at his house. He called Pat. She said you might be here. I saw Black Beauty." He lowers his hands. "I'm sorry."

I consider everything he's said. "I accept your apology."

Michael struggles to sit up, coughing and sputtering blood. Willette's crying softly to herself.

"So," Kwame says, looking them over, "now what?"

I pull open the bottom drawer of the credenza and show him my tape recorder, still playing. He's impressed. "You got everything?"

"From the moment she walked in." I pop out the tape from my voice-activated recorder. "As we say in bid whist"—I look at Willette and Michael pointedly—"church is out."

40

Kwame's been on the County Commission for almost a year. Everyone says he's doing an excellent job. Even his fellow white commissioners, whom he jacks up on a regular basis when they don't do the right thing by the people, concede he's effective. Not just on behalf of black people either. That's the most amazing transformation Kwame's made. When he was in the legislature, he represented an all-black district. He had the luxury of seeing things in just black and white. While his county district is predominantly black, he has a hefty chunk of white constituents too. Neither he nor they were happy about this new fact of life at first. Willette was safe, Kwame a dangerous militant radical. Now they "understand" each other.

I'm still in private practice. I inherited Kwame's office. I've made a few changes. For one thing, Eddy's our partner. He had a case in front of Dirk last week. Dirk acted as if he didn't even know him. Gave our client, a young brother who would've gotten probation from anybody else, five years in the penitentiary. They don't call him "Dirty Dirk" for nothing. He gives all the brothers jail time. Eddy was heartsick. This was our client's first scrape with the law, he's thoroughly repentant, works and goes to school full-time, all of which Eddy pointed out. Dirk just banged his gavel and called for the next case. I told Eddy to cheer up. If I'd gone in front of Dirk with our client, both of us would've gotten the twenty-year maximum.

Another change I made is to make Pat my secretary. The

matched set that came with the office are just too loyal to Kwame. They watch me like a hawk. I don't blame them and I don't mind. It keeps me on my toes.

Pat buzzes me. I have a call from Marvella. My stomach tightens. "Marvella, how's the weather in Mississippi?" Our code for Willette and Michael. I was wrong about why Marvella killed Willie. It wasn't over C.C., but because she finally found out what he was doing to Willette.

"They hate living hand to mouth."

She shares a one-room shack with Michael and Willette in the Mississippi Delta in an area so remote they don't even have running water. She walked three miles of dusty road just to call. They spend their days eking out an existence like their impoverished neighbors—and their evenings like snakes in a bag, looking in each other's face, knowing what each one has done.

"They're lucky. So are you."

"Are you ever going to let them come back?"

"You know the answer, Marvella. Please don't ask me again."

I hang up and take out the tape—the key to their "prison." Good thing neither Willette nor Michael ever practiced law. They'd know it's inadmissible in a criminal case.

"Hi, Mommy."

Ashleigh Lee bounds into the family room with Smiles, her black Lab. She plops down next to me on the sofa. "Whatcha doing?"

"Playing solitaire." Actually, I was thinking about Marvella's phone call and the big fat wolf ticket I sold her daughter and son-in-law.

Ashleigh Lee attends public school now, and she's thriving. It's been easier than I ever imagined with us all living under Kwame's roof. Except for Smiles, who chewed up one of my Ferragamo's last week. I liked to wore her ass out with the other one.

"When are you going to teach me to play bid whist?"

I smile inside and out. And they say the younger generation doesn't care about "black bridge." "You really want to learn?"

"Sure," she says. "It's cool."

"Okay," I say, shuffling the cards out of habit. "The first thing you need to understand is that no one knows what's in your hand until you have to put your cards on the table." I spread out the jokers. "These are the two baddest cards in the deck—unless you're playing no-trump. In which case, they're counterfeit."

"What's 'no-trump'?"

Before I can answer, Smiles snatches them. "Give me those, you mutt." She's too quick for me. Ashleigh Lee and I chase her around the house, which she thinks is a game. We bump into each other and literally fall out laughing. Smiles drops the mangled cards at my feet.

"They're not so 'bad' now." Ashleigh Lee picks them up gingerly. "Ick."

I think about Willette and Michael. "Thank God."